LEANNE SCHWARTZ

A PRAYER FOR
VENGEANCE

PAGE STREET YA

First published in 2023 by
Page Street Publishing Co.
27 Congress Street, Suite 1511
Salem, MA 01970
www.pagestreetpublishing.com

Distributed by Macmillan, sales in Canada by The Canadian Manda Group.

27   26   25   24   23   1   2   3   4   5

ISBN-13: 978-1-64567-888-5
ISBN-10: 1-64567-888-1

Library of Congress Control Number: 2022949434

Cover illustration, cover and book design by Emma Hardy for
Page Street Publishing Co.

Printed and bound in the United States

CONTENT WARNING

Violence, blood, and minor gore; abuse of power by a religious authority figure; one interrupted instance of sexual pressure by an authority figure against another adult; minor ableist bullying, pressuring of an autistic to mask, some internalized ableism; brief mentions of fatphobia

To Sophia and Nate,
my favorite miracles

✦

BREAKING AND BOUND

When the gods had driven the worst of the great old monsters from the favored reaches of the earth and divided up the world, the Three Sisters came to a wide stretch of Orabellia and settled here. Little sister Magna, who had struck her chisel to the ground and made beasts spring up to fight the terrible monsters stalking humans, now used it to carve the three hills of what would become the city of Trestatto. The next eldest, Alta, guided the river Argus to pass between them. And as for Stregna, eldest and least tethered to the earth—who can say what workings the Unseen Goddess wrought?

—The Book of Invocations

Gia

Gia pounded her fists against the stone doors until her flesh went numb and her bones ached. "Ennio!" He didn't answer, and the doors didn't yield. There was no other way into the invoking room, clutched in the deep heart of the temple. All she could do was keep throwing herself against the marble. "It's me."

Outside the temple, chaos was erupting. Shouts of the militia and monstrous footsteps like thunder reached even here, resounding through the thick walls that seemed to be closing in on Gia. Ennio would set it right. They could fix it, together. Ennio was nearly as old as her sister Lena—who'd acted old as the gods since she and Gia were children—but he understood Gia. He listened to her.

Ennio's captain scratched his collarbone, eyelids heavy with displeasure, as he stood watch outside the door. The rest of Ennio's personal guard shot her pinched looks, annoyed her presence meant they had to stand at attention rather than lean against the corridor's polished walls while Ennio, his clear, strong voice muffled through the stone, called upon the goddess.

"What is he invoking now?" Gia asked for the tenth time, voice like a whip. But they all stood as useless and silent as statues.

Outranked and ignored.

Not that she had an official rank. Not yet. That was supposed to change today.

The anxiety sparking within Gia threatened to catch and blaze into the anger Lena was always telling her to control. She scuffed her leather boot over the flagstone floor, then smoothed her tunic down over her wide hips. One hand came to rest upon the hilt of the knife Ennio had gifted her, carved of chimera bone. Reassuringly solid. Ennio trusted her. Once he knew she was here, he would explain. She knocked again, and again, calling out.

After an eternity, the door rumbled and swung back. The guards straightened even taller for their head templar. Ennio emerged, the crescent-shaped icon of this temple sheathed and strapped across his broad chest. His jaw clenched hard enough to pulse, his muscular shoulders tense under the fall of his wine-colored robe. His eyes were distracted, but when they took in Gia, his mouth spread into that knowing smile he saved only for her. "I'm glad you're here."

Even this greeting couldn't loosen the knot pulled tight in her chest. "You've called up your stone beasts?" She'd been climbing the hill to Magna's temple when the marble creatures he normally invoked out in fields or the old quarry beyond the city walls, to defend against living monsters or encroaching neighbors, had lumbered past. Gryphons and chimeras and two-headed wolves, each heavy tread of their hooves and paws stamping dread deeper into her bones as she dodged them.

Ennio nodded but made as if to move past her. "It is the last time they will be necessary."

She shot a questioning hand out. Her gaze slid behind him, to where his templar Vassilis stood among the stone prayer tablets, holding the sacred chisel. Avoiding meeting her eyes. "Why send them to the other temples? The council building?" They'd never required their protection within Trestatto's walls before. "What threat has been made against the city?"

Ennio dipped his head, running a hand over his short, dark hair. "We've spoken of this. You said you wanted to protect our home." He took her hand, wrapping it in both of his. "I'm counting on you to stand with me to make Trestatto strong."

His thumb sweeping over her wrist set her pulse flicking

faster. "Of course." Wasn't she here rather than sitting through more endless council talks with Lena and her royal advisors? None of the beloved principessa's district governors ever listened to her little sister. Lena, leader of both Trestatto and its second temple, seemed only to want Gia to stay in her shadow, trailing after her. Practically invisible.

Except to Ennio.

He's seen how Gia ached for her own way to serve the city. She squeezed his hand back. "You know I will."

The hope in his hazel eyes flashed into something more zealous. "Vassilis has worked an invocation unlike any existing that will protect Trestatto better than ever before. It will unify our city and drive all its strength to my purpose of maintaining our greatness."

She frowned. "I thought we'd already unified Trestatto. Lena came to your ceremony this morning as you wanted. Surely she'll invite you back to the council talks now." Gia was the one who had convinced Lena to attend the annual rite with her templars who served the goddess Alta, that taking the mark of Magna's dust upon their brows could be the first step in healing the schism between the temples.

Except now stone beasts were marching through its streets, and when she'd arrived at the temple, the militia had been preparing as if for an invasion, too.

Ennio's voice was a low rumble. "You know why I must stand against Adalena's plans to open the city to foreigners and their gods. The Sisters will be crowded from their own people's prayers, and without their full protection, who knows how many monsters may plague our streets?"

Gia nodded along. This was why she'd hounded Lena until

she'd agreed to attend the ceremony.

"Adalena's never had to fight for what she has—influence, beauty, a goddess's ear—and is too ready make concessions to the visiting emissaries." Gia's chest burned. Everything seemed to come easily to her sister. Lena couldn't understand—not when Gia quieted mocking whispers from other girls about her size with her fists or left a feast early rather than endure the upcurled lip of some emissary's son made to dance with her, only to be scolded by Lena for losing her temper or shirking official duties. Ennio's grip tightened. "The city needs a principessa to be strong. Like you."

Wrongness wound about Gia's insides like a serpent.

"The people will see the royal line continue with you in power, and with me to guide you—"

"I thought—" Gia let out a strangled sound. Not quite a laugh. Ennio couldn't be saying this. "I thought you'd appoint me to the militia."

His face remained serious. Disbelief hit her stomach like a punch.

He didn't notice her distress. "This is everything we both want." He spoke with all the assurance of a man whose desires, once carved on prayer tablets or into the very walls of Magna's temple, could be spoken into existence. He jerked his head at his guards, and they all bowed theirs to her. Ennio's words seeped into her like the oppressive smoke of the censors at Stregna's temple. Sweet and potent. "You are everything Magna loves best. The city needs its strongest champions to stand forth now. Be remembered forever as the city's great protector."

Gia's mouth went dry. She'd wanted to prove herself—but most of all to Lena. No matter how she might resent her sometimes, Gia didn't want her hurt. She couldn't stand the thought of Lena under attack at the council building. "You said today would fix everything. If I convinced Lena to attend your ceremony, to demonstrate good faith between the temples again—" Gia would save the city, he'd said.

"Yes," he said, running a hand up her arm. "The new invocation requires my enemies be marked with Magna's sacred dust." His hand wrapped about her shoulder. "You are the one who made this possible."

Whenever Ennio's tan fingers had gripped her arm, guiding her during the extra training he'd personally given her, seeming to find excuses to linger, all that attention had felt like Magna etching stars in the firmament, sharp constellations lighting up along her skin. She'd often wondered if, once she had a position at his temple, it might lead to something more. Now his touch felt cold, carving only a dark emptiness that hollowed her dead to her center.

Ennio had seen Gia when no one else had. And what he'd seen was someone who would betray her sister.

She drew a long slow breath. Steeled herself. Focused on the press of her boots against the floor. Imagined drawing steadiness up into herself with her next breath. *Magna, make me strong.*

"The invocation?" she managed.

Ennio nodded back to Vassilis. "All that remains is to enact it upon them." Blessings had to be wrestled from Magna, with invocations first carved in rock or bone or metal, the exact right wording building up the strength required to compel the goddess—but then Ennio could direct her power at will, with his icon. There was no telling what he had planned for Lena and the city.

Gia kept her voice flat and careful as a blade. "Show me."

Ennio's smile spread again as he exhaled and squeezed her

arm. "You make this triumph complete."

She unfurled her own smile, a false white flag. Ennio spoke of her strength, yet he thought her weak. Thought he could bend her to his betrayal and exploit her to usurp her sister. Manipulate her. He presumed she was as treacherous as he—well, she'd show him treachery. She kept her face still and placid as Ennio led them all down the corridor, and Vassilis shut himself back up with his prayers. Underneath, molten anger churned within her.

Ennio had never believed in her. He'd only encouraged her because he thought he could use her. Not because of her abilities. Because Lena was her sister. And all his just-for-her smiles and unchecked touches during the militia trainings he'd invited her to? All so Gia would validate his rule.

The guards' footfalls echoed through the halls and misery shivered over Gia's skin. They crossed through the open, empty great sanctuary, out the main doors to the steps spreading before the temple, where lines of soldiers stood, red militia uniforms like stains against the granite. One ran up to Ennio and shouted a report. The council building had fallen, and the principessa was on her way here to stop Ennio.

At the front of the temple's plaza where colonnades curved along the road, stone gryphons with lynx bodies and ibex horns arcing from their golden eagle heads waited for Lena and her people. More men ranged before Ennio.

Two temples facing off. Two halves of Gia's world cracking apart.

She had to stop this. Fix this.

"Ennio." Gia turned to him. His eyes held a bright and fervent gleam. She traced her hand over his chest. "You should know, about Lena—"

She made to pluck the icon from its sheath.

His hand snapped up and caught her wrist. She scrabbled still for the curved blade. It would slice her hand open, but she didn't care. He couldn't invoke Magna without it.

He shoved her back and his captain's arms ensnared her. "Hold her." Ennio shook his head, and the spark in his eyes contracted. His nostrils flared. "You'll see this is best with time."

He couldn't do this. The Three Sisters forbade harming their fellow Trestattans. She struggled half-free from the captain's grip. "Stop this."

Ennio's stare sharpened to a glint of defiant resolve. "I intend to." He turned away. Gia followed his gaze to see Lena's templars, fighting past militia soldiers, reach the plaza. The captain dragged her out of the way, far to one side. She writhed for freedom as the rest of Ennio's men charged down the temple steps and the plaza erupted in violence.

The gryphons swept their mighty paws, sending Lena's templars crashing against the cobblestones. Templars' swords clanged against each other with deadly intensity. And Lena—skirts tucked into her belt, templar's sword drawn—broke through the militia blocking her, slipped past the looming earthen monsters, and entered the plaza.

Yet Ennio did not dive into the fight like Gia had always seen him do out on the fields against monsters. He hadn't even taken the chisel back from Vassilis to create more of his stone beasts to squash those coming for him. He strode atop the steps, watching the fray. Hand to his chest. Lips moving.

His new, remarkable invocation.

Gia had to warn Lena before it fractured the city permanently. Whatever it might do, it would be Gia's fault.

The captain had both arms wrapped about her—nearly

crushing her windpipe. She ducked her chin and sank her teeth into the flesh exposed between the straps of his arm guard.

He cried out, loosening his grip and grabbing for her again, but she broke free. Spitting salt and blood, she started across the plaza and drew her sword to prevent people of either temple from killing each other, unable to fathom cutting down someone she'd trained with—prayed with. She knocked a sword away from where it arced down toward one of Lena's people and kicked the attacking templar with a boot to his belly. But when she turned to see if Lena's templar was all right, the woman looked back with a face of stone. Blank, pale eyes. Dark skin turned cold white. Long braid gone motionless where it swung.

Gia spun. All around her, Lena's templars were becoming statues. One braced a hand to his side and splayed the other against a gryphon's reddened stone teeth—then blanched as pale as the marble creature itself. Another of Lena's fighters, lifting her sword and calling to a fellow, stilled mid-shout.

Ennio's invocation was turning Alta's templars to stone.

This was her fault. The knowledge reverberated through Gia like the tolling of the great bell at Stregna's temple.

A militia soldier pitched toward her. Between blows fending him off, between the whip and flash of blades, Gia tracked Lena fighting across the plaza. With Lena left alone to face Ennio and his forces, the militia she'd already passed turned from their frozen opponents and trained their weapons on her back.

Lena's eyes met Gia's, as dark and sharp as obsidian. As dark as the night Lena had come to tell her their father had fallen fighting the monsters surrounding the city. As sharp as her tone admonishing Gia, who'd raged and smashed a vase and pulled down her bedchamber curtains, to pull herself together for the good of the city. Lena had to know Gia hadn't meant for any of this to happen. That Gia was fighting for her, never against. Not when it truly mattered.

An arrow *thwacked* into Lena's shoulder. The shoulder Gia had cried on when small—before they'd grown apart—was streaked with red. *No.* Gia gaped as the militia fighter's sword shuddered down against hers. Lena tore her gaze away and crashed her sword against another templar, and another. More arrows followed, and spears rained down around her, striking her in the back.

Gia screamed and hurled her sword at her opponent. *"Lena!"*

Even as Lena's shoulders spasmed, her face remained as stoic as if she were running through training exercises outside Alta's temple. And still, she came, cutting her way, step by step, closer to Ennio.

Gia turned her shoulder to the staggering soldier before her and rammed him to the ground. She sprinted forward, as the wave of templars chasing down Lena planted more and more weapons in her sister's body. Swords slashed long furrows; arrows rooted deep. And—as Lena disarmed the final templar standing between herself and Ennio, throwing him to the ground—another templar drove a spear down through her torso.

Her sister's spine rippled with agony. Blood poured down the front of her perfect white gown.

Gia's chest felt as if it were crushed in the maw of a colossal monster. She couldn't even scream. Guilt gnashed her heart to pieces and swallowed it down.

All the stone gryphons had gone eerily motionless. It had grown so still on the plaza, Gia heard Ennio as he continued his invocation. "With Magna, I call and bind you, Adalena."

Stone washed white over Lena's skin, erasing the scarlet

blooming from her wounds, arresting her before she could fall, in a final moment of unending horror. Gia knew she would forever be altered, too. As if Ennio had conjured up a beast from the temple's stone—had changed Gia into something monstrous that truly would turn against its own people. A scream broke from her churning insides, scorching her throat like a chimera's fiery breath. Her fist clenched her nails into her palm, sharper than a gryphon's claws.

Her feet propelled her up the steps past her sister, toward Ennio, racing the words tumbling from his mouth.

"With Magna, I call and bind you—"

Racing any part of herself that might halt what could now be only revenge, what could not mend what had been broken.

All that was left was to break the world a little more.

She hefted her sword and swung with all her might at Ennio.

Remorse fractured the victory shining in his eyes, or maybe it was only the reflection of her sword as it sped toward him. His jaw clenched with determination. Through his teeth, he sealed her fate. "Gia."

CHAPTER ONE

PAPER BEASTS

"Some things you cannot destroy."
—From Magna's Hymn, The Book of Invocations

Milo

The air grew clear and green where she waited.

Milo's breath was heavy as he hiked the last stretch to the top of her hill. Stone pine grew thickly there, and ash, boughs written across the sky like lines of verse. He huffed words of a poem to soothe himself, something he'd been working on while performing mindless tasks at the temple, sweeping out cells and delivering breakfast to sleepy templars. His sandals crunched needles and leaves as brittle as his nerves.

He wasn't supposed to be here.

But he'd needed to escape the temple bustling with preparations for the start of the festival month—all reminders of what he had to do later that day, and how much his fate would be determined by his success. Trestatto's lonely second hill, topped only with ruins, was always where he went when he felt unsettled like this.

And he wanted to see her.

He pushed through low branches, and a figure swung a blade toward his face.

"Good afternoon," he told the statue. She was frozen in mid-strike so that her stone sword seemed about to cut him down where he stood. Everything about her was bold—her strong limbs, her full figure, the scowl of concentration upon her face. All the intensity of her bearing down on him always struck him as if her swing had at last driven home, sending quivers up his limbs and burrowing under his ribs.

He stepped inside the reach of her weapon to brush away the leaves that had fallen upon her shoulders. This wasn't one of his responsibilities—when he'd offered to tend to the out-of-the-way sanct, the temple had only asked he bring the sacred boughs on Grove Day once a year. But it didn't seem fair that she should be left to the elements' whims because of her placement here on the second hill, with only the ruins of one of the fallen temples for company.

He pulled a cloth from his belt and wiped clean the dust accumulated in the serpentine lines of her hair, the crosshatch of her thick braid flung off her back, the folds of her dress gathered at her shoulders and belt, beside the sheathed knife. He turned a fresh corner of the rag to carefully remove any trace of dust from the creases of her lovely eyes and the curve of her cheeks.

It hadn't been that long since his last visit, and soon, after a final swipe over the crescent upon her brow, she was shining. Milo crouched and pulled back the vines encroaching up her low pedestal and tangling about her ankles, where a length of iron wrought like ivy secured her to the block of marble. When he'd first found her, the vines had overcrept high enough to strangle around her neck, and moss fuzzed over her calves and the whirl of her skirts. She'd been lost under blown leaves and sap and seeds, by grime half washed away by rain, running down her face like dark tears. Like Magna Mater's earth had tried to reclaim what the goddess had fashioned in the image of a girl—one who had died that day, centuries ago, when invaders and monsters overran the city.

She'd looked like a monster herself, her fierceness unobscured by the forest's detritus. But of course, no monsters ever came within Trestatto's walls—the temple taught that her sacrifice, and that of all the sancts, kept the city safe. She'd laid down her life, given up everything for what she believed in. Maybe that was why, after completing his survey of all the sancts in the city, Milo had returned to her again and again. Maybe that was why he found a sort of haven in the disquiet she stirred in him.

He stood and gazed at her eternal glower, wondering what exactly it had once been aimed at, which sort of monster she'd died fighting. "I wish I knew your story." He'd imagined so many for her—facing down a chimera or standing between an invader and a family of Trestattans.

If only he could discover it, add it to the store of knowledge the storicas kept for the temple. Weave it into the omelia he'd been working on—a new insight into the life of a sanct would make for a powerful, important speech. One he could be proud of showing the templars. One they might actually want to present at rites. One to truly inspire faith in the people of the city.

While the lives and deaths of most of the sancts were recorded in the temple's archives, she was one of the few forgotten by history. The centuries since her death had devoured the details of how she'd become a sanct.

He had to guess. He swung off the pack slung over his shoulder and pulled from it the pieces of paper and wood he would assemble into a monster. This was the first tradition of Sancts' Month, honoring the bravery of the sancts and reminding Trestatto of the dangers they continued to shield its people from every day. "Glory be to their living brother, Primo Sanct, Pontefice Ennio, hand of Magna Mater on her blessed earth," Milo whispered under his breath, as Trestattans did when presenting an offering to a stone sanct.

He'd inked the gryphon with all the care he put into pages he illuminated for the temple's new manuscripts and waxed the paper with candle stubs collected from the templars' cells. He muttered his poem as he assembled it, slotting the wood scrap frame together.

A paper beast, only what he could conjure himself, out of practically nothing. And like the gryphon, the poem was no great art. It wasn't about any sanct's glory or Magna Mater, just the hush in the early mornings when he walked along the river on an errand, the sloshing of the Argus against its bank, the shuffling of sandals as farmers went to market, the particular wash of light soaked into the Old Bridge's stone arches at that hour.

But perhaps the sanct liked to hear something of the city she'd died for, some of his favorite parts she protected. "What do you think?" he asked her. She was already frowning, so at least he wasn't ruining her day with his trivial verse.

He only wished he could have carried one of his friend Val's sculptures—true works of art, with metal muscles twining and fiery breath wrought in copper—to honor the sanct. The paper monster wouldn't last long up here, unlike the sanct herself. The statues were indestructible, able to withstand any strike and endure any weather.

As he finished, a gray cat slinked out of the ruins at the top of the hill and wound about his ankles. The cat batted an experimental paw at the paper gryphon. "Not your fight, Acci," Milo scolded the cat and scooped him up before settling on a fallen column at the edge of the ruins.

He had his own fight before him still today. His last chance to try for the apprenticeship among the temple's scholars. As Acci bounded away to explore the temple ruins, Milo thrummed a finger against the silver icon he always wore hanging from his neck. But his nerves persisted.

Inside the bag resting against the pedestal was the other packet of papers he'd been working on, which he needed to show the templars if he wanted to be considered for a role working with their storicas. If he wanted to join them in keeping the temple's archives and illuminating its doctrine through their study. If he wanted to turn his fascination with the history of the sancts into more than a distraction from his actual duties.

He knew all there was to know about the sancts by now—had read entire books about the history of Magna Mater and her temple. Yet every time he'd tried to write an omelia, he faltered over what lesson to draw from all that knowledge, what he could possibly say worth sharing with the entire assembly in the great sanctuary—where, above the wide stone altar, hung the sacred chisel templars used to carve up marble and call upon the goddess. What were his frail scratchings upon paper to that? How could someone so unsure of his own faith inspire anything in others?

Without an omelia, he'd never be apprenticed to the storicas. And apprenticeships were assigned during Sancts' Month. He was out of time. The pages waiting in his pack—his best attempt at an omelia—were his final hope of securing a permanent place at the temple that had taken him in as a child.

Acci leaped atop a half-buried block of marble and balanced his way along it, drawing Milo's eye and making him suddenly aware of how late it had grown. The sun angled from well past its summit, lighting up the underside of tumbled columns and the faded carvings on pediments.

Its rays flashed off something small at the foot of the marble. Something Acci had dragged from deeper among the ruins? Milo crouched to retrieve whatever sparked there.

An icon. Like the darkly tarnished one he wore—a crescent, the same shape as Primo Sanct's curved blade, as the mark of dust on every sanct's forehead, strung end to end on a chain. But this was copper, overgrown by a deep green stain. Lost by some-one tending to this sanct, perhaps, long ago.

He stood. He had to get back. He'd promised Val he'd watch her race this afternoon, at the event that marked the festival's start. With a toss, he let the icon's chain wrap about his wrist, and touched his fingers to the statue's free hand, tan upon white.

She'd taken a stand against some long-dead monster, fighting to serve the city. She hadn't yielded, even to the point of death.

He wondered what it would be like to possess that sort of bravery. Something far beyond the dust of books and shadow of temple walls. He thought it might shine like the sun on a sword. If only that bravery, that boldness could come alive for him.

Please make your blessing known, goddess.

He recited his poem again as he slipped the icon into his belt bag, lingering a while despite himself. It was always hard to leave. Finally, he said goodbye to Acci, slinging his pack on and pushing through the branches. As they snapped back into place behind him, Milo almost imagined he saw the sanct's sword drop with them.

He ran from the second hill through the southern neighborhoods of the city. He passed several statues, with families gathered about them, presenting beasts made of painted wood and clay. The most important families paid artisans to craft ceramic monsters studded with jewels for their frozen sancts to fight. Milo sped past them all, wishing he could outrun the day's anxieties as easily as the immobile chimeras and serpents. His sandals slapped the ground in scolding iambs, *too late, too late, too late*, though whether he worried more about missing Val's race or having left his attempt at the apprenticeship until the last moment, only Magna Mater could say.

Still, he was glad of the excuse to run. Racing let his body and mind lift from a world they often felt out of sync with. As he jogged down the wide Via Sanctus, the crowds thickened, pressing toward the colonnades lining the city's main road, out of the way of the impending race. Too many people, too much sun. He threaded through the waiting spectators and turned off the road to cut across the fields between magisterial and guild buildings, where the scent of sunbaked grass rose off the earth.

Val was easy to spot among the crowds at the head of the race, her dark head rising a foot above most as she laughed and shouted with the others checking their chariots' poles and traces.

"About time!" Val clapped Milo in a bone-crushing hug but refrained from the cheek kiss she knew he hated. "You nearly missed my glorious victory."

Suddenly, Milo felt too still, too at the mercy of the noise and movement and smell of the crowd around them. He tapped the pad of a finger against his icon. "I couldn't bear that."

Val flashed a wide grin, brown skin glowing. "And you must witness it to write an epic ode when I win! And when I win the attention of fair Flavia." Her strident voice melted into something softer as she rested on the side of the chariot.

"So now I'm writing you odes?" He didn't wait for an answer, leaning beside Val. "And now it's Flavia?" Milo could recite the stories of all seven hundred twenty-six sancts in Trestatto, but even he couldn't keep up with Val's weekly romantic obsessions.

Val bit her bottom lip and nodded. "Flavia." The name carried itself on a sigh as she sank against Milo.

"Win today's race first, and ask—sorry, who was it again?"

Val ignored his teasing. She pulled a rose from behind one ear and gazed into its petals. "Flavia, the only girl who can save my heart from breaking, if she'd only favor me with one smile, one kind glance—"

"Ask *Flavia* to the carnival," Milo said. "Then we'll see if you need an ode or an elegy." He flicked Val's thick braid off his shoulder and into her face.

Val answered that with a tap of the flower to his nose. "I think I have a better chance than the boy in love with a statue."

"I study the sancts—" A flush burnt up his neck.

She cocked an eyebrow. "You study one in particular." She returned the flower to her hair. "Have faith." She stood, drawing a deep breath, scarred hands braced on the chariot. "When Flavia sees me win, her heart will be moved. It's the perfect chance." She turned her face up to catch the sunshine on her cheeks. "I can feel it. Today's going to be a lucky day. Magna Mater will bless me as she always does our city."

"I doubt Magna Mater's interested in your love life." Still, he hoped Val was right, that today would provide a lucky chance. If he only had faith. He stood and shifted the pack where it slung across his chest. His omelia would purchase him a chance at the life he wanted. Where he wasn't simply a ward but had won a deserved place.

If he did deserve it. He scratched his finger over the pack's strap, trying to chase away his doubt.

The racers were called forward and a templar addressed the crowd pressed closely on a low slope of hill, elbowing themselves room to lift bottles of wine or make last-minute bets. He shouted over the unruly assembly, "We race today to commemorate the bravery of the sancts, who chased invaders and beasts from Trestatto's streets—"

Milo had heard this every year since he was a child, and he'd just spotted his mentor, Storica Lucca, standing near a dais with other important people from the temple. Once Val was on her way around the three hills of the city, he promised himself, he'd take the storica his omelia to read.

Across the road from the templars, a group of children squeezed into the front of the audience. One with straight brown hair and tawny skin caught sight of Milo and waved. Milo gave an affectionate wave back, but once she saw she had his attention, she stuck out her tongue. Senna had asked him to accompany the youngest temple wards to the race, but he'd needed to slip away for a while. The templar was talking about the monsters and demonic spirits that had breached the city walls that day long ago, driven on by the invading empires, so Milo made a hideous face and arched his fingers like claws at the girl until she broke into grudging laughter.

The templar finished his speech. The head templar, Primo Sanct, stepped forward, and the crowd stilled like a field of grain when the wind died. Primo Sanct, average-sized, drew attention like a much bigger man. His robe was pure white, near shining in the sun like a freshly scrubbed statue, his dark hair closely cropped under his iron crown made of a curved blade. It was sharp, but never cut the man blessed by Magna Mater to forever protect her favored city. He had led them since the day of the Great Miracle, and he still looked like the same young man Milo had first seen when he'd come to the temple ten years prior. Whose perfect faith Milo had aspired to ever since. Not that anyone could match the living brother of the sancts, transmuted by the goddess's blessing. As pontefice, Primo Sanct served as a bridge between the godpower of Magna Mater and the statues that spread her protection across the city.

Primo Sanct uttered his prayers for the charioteers and for Sancts' Month in a forceful voice that carried easily across the crowd. Around Milo, people raised hands toward the templar as if to better snatch his blessing out of the air for themselves.

A captain pivoted to the racers and shouted instructions. Val raised the tiny icon hanging about her neck and kissed it before adjusting her hands on her reins. Milo muttered a prayer that she would win. He would even write her that poem. The captain's next shout was swallowed up by the cracking of whips and creaking of wheels. A cloud of dust erupted behind the racers as they sped down the Via Sanctus.

Once Val was lost behind the wave of people rushing out into the road to cheer on the racers, Milo ran for the dais.

Someone grabbed his arm. Renz—with his toothy smile that always made Milo feel pinned in place. "Where you off to?

There's no footrace for Sancts' Month."

Milo rolled his shoulder until Renz let him go. "Need to speak with Storica Lucca."

Renz strode beside him, his jeweled dagger glinting at his belt. "What about?"

"My omelia." Milo and Renz worked together with the other young scribes in the storicas' workroom. Storica Lucca had pulled Milo from among the orphan wards the temple housed to help, and Renz's parents sent their second son to study at the temple in preparation for a role there. Renz knew Milo's wish to remain at the temple. "He said if I brought it today, he'd have a chance to talk it over with the templars during dinner, before the midnight rites."

Renz stopped short and held out a pale hand. "Let's see."

Milo's grip tightened on his bag's strap. He wished he were back on the second hill, sharing his words only with the lonely sanct.

He forced his hands to relax. Renz had not only already submitted an omelia, but it had been presented by Templar Adrian at weekly rites several weeks ago. A sure sign he would be welcomed among the temple's scholars when all seventeen-year-olds were confirmed to their apprenticeships during Sancts' Month. Perhaps he could reassure Milo before he showed the omelia to Storica Lucca.

Milo pulled the omelia from his pack, unrolled the papers, and passed them to Renz.

The boy's eyes scanned the first page of writing, but then he frowned and shuffled the pages to glance at the others for a moment before returning to the first.

Unease twisted in Milo's belly like a nest of snakes.

Renz asked, without lifting his eyes from the page, "What sanct is the basis for this omelia?"

Milo tapped his icon. "Thirty-two of them. All the sancts for which we lack names, or how they died, or what they did to earn Magna Mater's blessing—"

"Milo." Renz looked up and made that little smile he used when he had to explain something to him, something everyone else grasped without trying, leaving Milo feeling as if the ground was falling out from under his feet. "This is Sancts' Month. The templars want to speak of the great sacrifice of the sancts. Hector, Adalena—that's the sort of omelia that will inspire the people to make generous offerings. To take on their apprenticeships, whatever they may be."

"If you read to the end, you'll see—" Milo leaned in and jabbed at his words. "I wrote how not knowing can inspire all of us—that perhaps we can all do acts of importance to Magna Mater, even if they're less striking than dying in battle."

"I see a lot of speculation about these sancts." He wrinkled his nose at Milo. "It's a storica's job to curate proper research for the templars, not use their imaginations." Renz pressed the pages back into Milo's hands. "You can't present this to the templars. This is their busiest month. They already have a pile of omelias to sort through, and this doesn't abide by their standards."

Milo stared at the omelia in his hands, that he'd been so sure would write his way into a position of security, that would prove his faith to Magna Mater. The paper was crumpled, the ink smudged, by his hurried scribbling and his clutching fingers.

Renz said reassuringly, "I'm telling you this for your own good. You'd only embarrass yourself with this, and then they'd never give you any decent apprenticeship at all."

Milo swallowed. "I can fix this." He had to. Temple wards who weren't plucked up for particular talents were always assigned to either the city militia, where everyone already served part-time for ten years, or the farms outside the city walls. His fingers tensed, making the pages rustle like the feathered wings of the gryphons that battered down the door of the cottage where he'd lived before becoming a temple ward.

Renz's drawl cut through his thoughts. "You must accept reality. You were never going to be a storica, especially with your peculiarities." He looked pointedly at the tapping Milo had again taken up. "A ward might serve to copy out crumbling books, but you lack the mind for the serious work of storicas."

"And I suppose you don't." Renz had been hanging around the temple more the last year, making himself useful to the storicas—studying a little, and bringing meat and wine from his family's generous stores. Renz was his friend, but sometimes the way things came so easily for him made Milo feel as if he had a thousand paper cuts at once.

Renz's light eyes sharpened like the flash of the jewels on his dagger. "My family's shown its devotion to the temple for generations. Didn't yours die among the faithless?"

Milo's fingers froze. The icon's curved edge cut into their pads.

He didn't get a chance to say anything—if he would have said anything—before Renz disappeared into the crush of people. He hadn't told him anything untrue. So why did his words grate Milo's insides?

Shouting streamed down the hill as watchers there spotted the racers returning. The crowd swelled closer to the road. Milo needled forward along the Via Sanctus and jumped atop the base of a column for a better view, just in time to see the leaders.

No sign of Val.

His palm slipped over the curved marble as he leaned farther, hoping to see her behind the first charioteers. There she was— too far back to have a chance at retaking the lead. The shouting rose to vision-blanking levels as the first racers flashed by. Val managed to pull ahead of her neighbors' horses. Instead of surging forward, she veered to the right. Sancts, she was driving one-handed—

Val stretched her other hand, clutching the rose torn from her hair, toward the crowd lining the Via Sanctus. The moment she tossed the flower to a dark-haired girl perched on the wall of the colonnade, a chariot coming up behind her—too fast, too close—knocked into her wheel. It sent her chariot crashing into the marble as the spectators threw themselves backward.

"Val!" Shouts accompanying his turned into hoots and cheers as Milo launched himself through the crowd. He was forced to wait while the last chariots traveled by toward the race's finish and the crowd spilled into the road. One of the captains beat him to Val's side and helped her up from where she'd spilled out the back of her chariot. Milo could make out the stern tone he took with Val, but he also caught the wry twist of his lips as he admonished her.

The captain joined another who was checking on the horses and unhooking them from Val's chariot, which only seemed to have suffered a broken wheel. Val gingerly rubbed her hip. A reddish bruise was already blossoming down her thick thigh. Milo had seen her in worse scrapes during their training with the militia, but her broad shoulders slumped as she greeted Milo with a despondent look.

"Bad as that?"

"Two weeks sentry duty."

Milo's stomach clenched. The wild beasts that roamed the countryside needed killing or chasing off when they trespassed onto Trestatto's farmland, he knew too well. Sentry duty meant hours standing outside the sancts' divine protection, waiting for a monster to appear on the plains' far horizon, to find a breach in the faith that ought to shield the city— Milo shuddered. He had to be apprenticed somewhere other than the militia.

Val drew a ragged breath. "It's nothing to Flavia's cruel eye piercing my heart. Shattering it worse than this poor wheel, trampling it like—" Her voice broke, and she gestured at the ripped petals of the dropped rose, smashed into the dirt and paving stones.

Milo couldn't understand Val's passion, but she'd protected him like his own personal sanct since he'd joined her among the temple wards. She'd kept the bigger kids from picking on him for his peculiarities—as Renz called them—and always made a point of including him in the group. He had only his words to try to help her, even if they hadn't been doing him much good lately. "You could hardly have made a greater gesture."

Val's mouth quirked, her brows lifting. "Figured if I couldn't win, might as well throw it all in for love."

"I could still write an ode to your great big stupid heart."

Val shoved his face away, then her hand flew to her temple. "Oh, Adalena's toes! I forgot!"

"What?"

"I promised Dario I'd attend to our sanct duties this month, but now I have to report to the east gate immediately."

The blacksmith who'd apprenticed Val two Sancts' Months ago—winning out over the militia's attempt to recruit her full-time—now had a new baby.

"Need me to cover for you?"

She glanced over her shoulder, where the captains were leading her horses away. "Would you? They'll have all the offerings you need to bring their sanct, and it's not far from the forge—"

"I know where it is." He huffed a laugh. He'd visited each sanct when he'd started learning about them, compelled to know everything about them. The statue Dario's family had tended for generations stood in an alcove in a market square. The worn claw marks of a gryphon that had once ravaged the city raked across the ancient stone edifice just beside his head. "I've got it," he told Val. "Go have fun with the real beasts."

Val made several small nods. "Hacking apart a couple of chimeras might be just what I need."

"Be safe." The words were a cork to hold in the wide, howling worry that he often felt for the few people he loved.

Like Storica Lucca, who shuffled toward Milo now in his green scholar's robe. Milo hustled to the elderly man's side.

"That was quite a spectacle Valentina gave us," Storica Lucca said in his soft, reedy voice. "I hope you have something just as good to show me?" He nodded toward the paper still clutched in Milo's hand.

Val's dashed hopes and Renz's warning forced Milo's arm back. "No, this is—nothing."

Storica Lucca frowned in concentration, a little V like a bird forming between his bushy gray brows. "Your confirmation is fast approaching. This was your opportunity to show the templars how much you've learned. What you can offer them as a storica."

Frustration itched over Milo's skin. Maybe Renz was trying to help, as much as it stung. Maybe Milo's entire plan for his future had been only a dream, as insubstantial as that paper gryphon or the poems and stories inside his head.

Deeper inside him, like a beast curled in its nest, hid a darker worry. Maybe he truly lacked the faith necessary for writing a good omelia, one that templars could use to fill the people with holy feeling. When he stood in the temple, surrounded by worshipers with serene faces, listening to a templar, even Primo Sanct, delivering an omelia, Milo knew he didn't feel quite what he should. A bolt of faith straight from his heart to Magna Mater.

But he tried. He'd devoted himself to the temple's work, and he loved it—far more than militia drills or sentry duty. He loved inking fresh copies of texts, preserving the records of sancts, illuminating them with red and gold. He loved their stories. He'd made a home in them, in the temple, when it took him in. Primo Sanct was his savior.

Renz was right. The problem was Milo had been distracted by his imagination, by what he'd dreamed up about the unnamed sancts. His mind was always drifting off into its own reveries, making up stories about blacksmiths and poems about farmers, drawing him to spend hours with the statue of a girl who'd died a millennium ago. He had to try again. He needed to dig into the temple's records—those were real. Then he could find a way to make an omelia worthy of the great mother goddess.

Milo forced his eyes to meet Storica Lucca's, just as his mentor had taught him to. "Give me until weekly rites before the confirmation ceremony. Nothing will be set in stone so soon. Please."

Storica Lucca stared at him a moment, mouth open, as if "no" were about to slip out any second. Then his lips pressed closed, and his face broke into the indulgent look he'd often given Milo since he'd plucked him from the orphan wards to help copy out messages and records. "One more week. Until *next* week's rites. Then that's it." He patted Milo's shoulder. "There's plenty of dignity in apprenticeships other than under me, my boy." He left with a chuckle.

He was wrong. Milo had managed his stints of sentry duty, but trying to work outside the city, fighting the instinct that still rose in him, all these years later, to run back to the city gate, would break him. It would prove true every cruel thing said by the other wards, the militia commanders, even some templars baffled by the ways Milo was different, annoyed that he had his own way of doing some things, angered that no amount of taunting or training would change that.

The observances and rites of the festival month would follow quickly upon one another, from the late vigil tonight, to Milo's confirmation, and finally the Ceremony of Dust. What his life would look like by that time depended entirely upon his success or failure in writing a new omelia from scratch.

He had one week.

CHAPTER TWO

CITY OF ENEMIES

A great frost crept over Orabellia. As the people of Trestatto starved and shivered, Alta shed a tear. The tear burrowed deep into the earth, a crystal as secret as any buried jewel. The frost relented, and a myrtle tree's roots captured the droplet and washed it up into its leaves, infusing it with sweetness. A wildfire swept over the hillside and released the droplet in a haze of scented smoke, and it rose beyond the younger gods to Stregna's domain. And who can say that at any point the tear was destroyed, or only changed, and what wisdom it bore with it on its journey?

—The Book of Invocations

Gia

Ennio was before her, his invocation choking off her vengeance.

And then he wasn't.

Another boy—younger, slighter build, longer hair—held her hand. He gazed up at her, warm brown eyes lit with sunlight reflecting off her.

She was stone. She couldn't move. Couldn't breathe. Couldn't scream. Even as the boy, speaking soft words, let her go and left her staring at nothing but trees. Gia could hear him reciting verse, the poetry washing away her impulse to panic. The invocation still held her in its grip, a cold mantle fist squeezing a burning heart.

As the boy's voice faded, that heart thrummed to life, speeding with a fury Ennio had engendered and arrested. It shook off his stone like an earthquake. Her stiff fingers clenched. She took a breath tasting of pine, and her sword dropped.

The swing she'd targeted at Ennio practically dragged her off her feet—something bit at her ankle. She winced and drove her blade down to catch herself, and the tip skittered over a block of stone. She stood upon a pedestal beside a paper model of a gryphon. Strange. Worse was the metal vine around her ankle, trapping her in place.

Her breath dug heavily through her chest now. She twisted about, but the boy was gone. Only trees surrounded her, instead of Magna's temple and Ennio's militia and Alta's templars turned to stone.

Or Lena, still and splintered through by spears and arrows.

Because Gia had brought her to Magna's temple. Because Gia had believed Ennio. Guilt pierced through her.

Her one solacing thought was that Ennio's invocation must have failed. Gia was alive, the scent of pine warmed in sunlight running through her lungs, her blood, like the blazing of light on bronze.

It didn't matter. Lena was still doomed, probably bleeding to death on the cobblestones outside Magna's temple right now. And

Gia, wherever she was, wasn't with her.

A slice of hope pricked painfully at her heart. Some of her sister's people might have survived, and Lena often used her icon to call upon Alta to heal illnesses and injuries. Magna responded to forceful invocations, but Alta answered communal prayers. Lena only used her icon at the temple where Alta's followers gathered, so it wouldn't be frozen as stone with her. If there were enough faithful Trestattans left, or awakening, to save her sister as she awoke—

Gia had to get back to her.

She sheathed her sword at her back, pulled free the knife from her belt, and crouched. Sliding the blade between her boot and the iron, she took her deepest breath yet and angled the bone handle down.

Her strangled cry sent something darting away across the forest floor. She shuddered in another breath and rocked the knife forward again. Again.

The edge of the blade bit through the boot's leather. She grimaced and wrenched again. No pain could compare to knowing she had destroyed her sister. She deserved every sting.

The top wisp of iron ivy yielded enough for her to slip the thick curve of her leg free. The blade she'd once treasured was ruined, dulled with scratches and bent. Good. She flung the knife aside, knocking over the ridiculous paper beast, and climbed down.

A creature leaped from the shadows. Gia grabbed for her sword—freezing with her arm bent back as a cat wound through the underbrush and tucked itself against her shredded boot.

Lena loved cats. She was more affectionate toward the three cats she kept in her chambers at her temple than she ever was toward Gia.

Gia squatted and ran a hand over the little beast's gray fur.

She took in her surroundings again. Among the trees were moss-covered blocks of stone and columns tumbled against one another. She didn't recognize this place. With a hiss of pain, Gia stood and shuffled nearer to the fallen stone. A pine's roots and thick trunk pushed aside one column. A long block of marble was half-buried in the hillside. It was carved with a faint relief of repeating swoops like water billowing in the wind.

A frieze of the same waves cut across the entryway to Alta's temple.

Confusion coiled through Gia's mind. She turned her back to the broken stone and started through the forest, the cat skittering away from her first shambling steps. Gia set her teeth, straightened her spine, and headed downhill. She couldn't be far from Magna's temple; it felt like only moments since she'd attacked Ennio. She'd find a sign of where she was soon enough.

But when she spilled into the city at the base of the hill, the cat in her wake, nothing looked familiar. She'd never been to any other city-state of Orabellia, but Ennio couldn't have banished her this fast. She drew her sword, shoulders tensing with the knowledge that she was at war, not with the monsters that beset the city but with the temple that should have protected it.

Signs of ordinary life came from the buildings close by. Smoke rose from open windows, carrying the scent of cooking food. People in short tunics strolled together, unafraid of war or unrest. No one paid her any attention—a feeling as familiar and biting as the gravel under her boots. Unnoticed, she turned a corner and broke into an open space.

And found another statue.

Above a well sunk in the middle of the square, a stone man with one contorted arm raised his other in a warning. The shadow he cast toward Gia as she advanced drew a prickle of dread down her spine like an icy finger. She couldn't be the only one awakened. Couldn't be alone.

A jeweled beast, a serpent, positioned its teeth around the man's wrenched arm. The mockery of it—Gia's rage swelled like the Argus in late spring. She stared up at the man's face, agony cast in the fire and shadow of the late afternoon sun. Hector. One of Lena's closest advisers.

She knew him, and she knew these walls—the buildings boxing in the square, the pattern of the windows cut in them. This was a neighborhood nestled between the city's hills, on the south side of the city. Everything had changed. New stone edged the windows and cobblestones lined what had been a gravel yard. If that had been one of the temple hills she'd hiked down—if that had been Alta's temple, with a weathered frieze and trees grown up supplanting its columns . . . . Bile rose in her constricting throat.

Just how long had Ennio's invocation held her?

She swallowed painfully and pushed on, hunting her way through a maze of the familiar and unfamiliar. The city was a great stone heart calcified. Some ways were filled in with new buildings, small streets and alleys, but she found the main arteries—the old squares, the great buildings of worn stone.

By the time she crossed the river and found the great road, the streets had emptied and the slight moon had cut across the sky like a sickle. The path was now lined with so many statues. Their stone faces watched her. Jeweled monster eyes winked with silvery light. Carved teeth and claws filled the dark.

She drew a slow, deep breath through her nose but felt unable to call upon Magna's strength. Ennio had bent her godpower to trap Gia and all of Lena's people. For how long? Magna's invocations were hardy, some lasting decades, some unbreakable, even by the templar whose prayer worked them. Among Vassilis's tablets, there was an old prayer that turned beasts to stone when marked by the invoker's blood drawn from his sharp icon. Her tutors had told her stories of forgotten monsters waking after a full hundred years.

Ennio would be dead, beyond the reach of her retribution. Escaped from her sword again.

The thought drove her up the road with more urgency. She had to find Lena. She had to know why she alone was alive—if it was only to know that she had truly lost everything, everyone.

After limping through streets abandoned to the night, she was surprised to find the great plaza before the temple thronged with people. The cat that had persisted at her side disappeared, and where Gia had just recently, it felt, seen militia bearing weapons, the people held lit candles. Where massive stone beasts had stood at the edge of the road, a pyre of branches loomed. Instead of draped or wrapped dresses or robes, the people wore simple tunics, and most wore sandals. They must have loved having their toes bitten by serpents in whatever time Magna had thrust her into. A mother paced at the back of the crowd, arms cradling a babe at her breast. Didn't she know a strix was likely to carry off the child this time of night?

The people churned through the space, bringing their candles to the heap of sticks and setting it ablaze. The light grew, and the sense of not belonging drove Gia back into the shadows of the colonnade to one side of the plaza, feeling awkward in her dress, sheathing her sword. The war she'd barely begun to fight had been over for years.

From the hum of the crowd, a name rose, catching on Gia's hearing like a thorn on a sleeve.

Principessa Adalena.

Gia's slice of hope waned, growing smaller and sharper. She wanted the impossible. She wanted someone—Magna, Alta, anyone—to fix things. She wanted her sister, whole and here again.

She snatched up the words on these strange people's lips. They were praising Lena. Speaking of her sacrifice. Calling her blessed. A sanct.

Wryness broke through Gia's chest like a green shoot through hard soil. Some things never changed. Everyone adored Lena, no matter the year.

Ennio must have at least been defeated. Who had been left to fight him? To commemorate Lena in this peculiar ceremony?

Gia's gaze clawed through the plaza. The people pushed past the bonfire toward the temple where a line of guards armed in purple and gold, wearing swords and bearing spears, stood across the lower steps. Several robed figures stood above them, and a white-haired one spoke as the last of the crowd had their turn adding to the fire. Only wisps of what he said reached Gia's ears, but those few words fell like blows. He spoke of Magna, no younger sister but the great mother. Of Lena dying for Magna's blessed templar, who saved the city through the strength of his prayer during a great miracle performed one thousand years ago.

Gia staggered back, resting her sore ankle as she leaned on the balustrade, dropping her head to her hands. The unfamiliar boy's eyes and voice flashed through her memory. Had she been awakened only to see how Ennio had destroyed her sister—stolen not only Lena's life but her true history? Gia hadn't even gotten to fight, and he'd won. He'd built this city into what he'd wanted—exulted his god, his temple, and himself over all. Rewritten himself as a hero whose glory had endured for a millennium.

Cries of "Primo Sanct!" rose from the crowd, only settling as another man began to speak. Gia's head snapped up at his strong, familiar voice, the rest of her as rigid as if she were still made of stone. It carried across the crowd like wildfire.

She'd wanted the impossible. But not this. She rushed forward, back to the mass of people watching one young robed man now come forward before the others.

There was the reason she was alive.

Ennio stood atop the temple steps, right where she'd faced him only hours ago. In his long white robe, he was nearly a silhouette before the torches set in sconces along the temple walls. They licked his form with red and black as their fire snarled and snaked about him. He turned to address the crowd on the far side of the plaza, hanging on his every word.

His profile jolted through Gia, roiling her blood. His image burned into her—that handsome, sculpted face she'd once been so drawn to, that she'd looked to with trust, even longing. The thought curdled her stomach now. She rubbed her hands down her arms, wiping away the memory of his touch.

He was still here. Not just what he had built, but the man himself. Calling himself a sanct. This entire time while she and the others were bound, their very bodies turned into prisons, he was somehow still breathing, living, walking about the city.

Her hand was on her hilt. Her arm was ready to draw it up, to swing her sword, to cut off the life that somehow flowed on and on while everyone else was swallowed up by the earth of Trestatto, long before they ought to have laid their bodies to rest in it.

He'd turned them to stone, and now she would return the favor. She'd steal his breath and blood and leave nothing but a corpse that would crumble to dust—as still as the statues he'd made.

But with one step, the pang in her ankle halted her. She growled in frustration.

She couldn't win like this, not against the man who'd trained her. If she was too slow, he'd mark her with his blood and invoke Magna to shatter her bones or blade. And she'd have to get past his guards first. Ennio would only call up a stone gryphon to crush her for good before she even reached him.

Ennio was talking about the fire now, as another templar made his way through the parting crowd with a tall metal torch, unlit. "The sacred flame is the devotion of Principessa Adalena," Ennio pronounced with practiced solemnity. "It will continue burning in the great sanctuary throughout the holy month as a sign of how we must all aspire to continue that devotion, to the temple and goddess our beloved sanct gave her life for."

"Little Lena," the nearby mother cooed to her baby. "That's your sanct name. You'll grow up beautiful and strong like the principessa, and love Magna Mater and Primo Sanct as much as she did."

Gia forgot the pain of her ankle as her entire body flooded with horror and anger.

The templar tipped the ornate torch toward the bonfire and caught the flame. As he bore it back up to the temple, Ennio held a palm out above the flame as if he were enacting some prayer, though nothing happened. He declared, "May this serve as a holy reminder until the Ceremony of Dust."

Still observing the rite he'd twisted into a trap for Lena. Still spouting lies. And the city believed them. Loved him. Loved his lies about Lena protecting him.

The fire continued to intensify beside her, little conflagrations scurrying along the deeper branches like trapped animals. She was surrounded by adversaries now. As if Ennio had struck the earth with Magna's chisel for aid and called up not a single beast but an entire world at once, a world corrupted by his betrayal.

Or as if he'd transformed Gia not into stone, but a monster, alone in a city of enemies.

Maybe it was only fair she was alone. It was all her fault. She had broken the world and delivered Ennio's vision into reality. He had reigned as victor for centuries.

But she was here now with him in his dream, and her determination to deliver revenge for Lena grew like the bonfire. Ennio didn't seem to know she'd stirred from the hill he must have exiled her to. She would be strategic. Take him by surprise. And then she would strike.

The branches snapped and glowed red. The flames ripped across the dark sky.

The war wasn't over.

CHAPTER THREE

WRITTEN BY THE VICTORS

Stregna teaches: Breath given to sharing wisdom may outlast the strongest stone. Therefore, her temple furthers Trestatto's understanding of the world and educates its children.

—The Book of Invocations

Milo

Chaos was breaking out in the temple. Elderly Templar Daniela, who normally supervised the apprentice templars, was out on the piazza with all the others for midnight rites, leaving the older apprentices free to stop scrubbing the dining hall tables and stand around talking, while the younger ones started throwing sopping, soapy rags at each other.

Milo finished wiping clean one long wooden table, wishing everyone would complete their work. He had more waiting for him, reading through the possible sources for a new omelia he'd dug out of the archives that evening, between taking Val's monster to its statue and helping serve dinner. And first, he still wanted to make it outside for at least the conclusion of the vigil.

He recited the poem he'd been working on to calm his impatience—and a rag landed on the next table he hunched over, scattering dirty droplets onto his hands and face.

"Daydreaming again?" Paolo, apprenticed only last year, grabbed the cloth and flung it back at Olivia, who shrieked.

Milo winced, locking down hard on the impulse to let a shudder tear through him and set his hands shaking. He could never say anything to the others. He'd lived in the temple years longer than any of them, but the apprentices were the ones who truly belonged. As a ward, he was expected to help, but they'd all earned their places here. And not by getting lost in another meaningless poem.

He could only scrub his frustration into the next table, and hurry to toss his rag in the wash bin when they'd finally prepared the hall for tomorrow's busy day. Olivia and Paolo were rushing too, and Milo thought they'd be heading to rites until Paolo arched a brow. "Let's go clean up in the kitchen, then."

"Coming?" Olivia invited Milo.

Milo frowned. "Kitchen's clean."

They looked at one another, and both let out a laugh. Like he'd made a joke.

"Oh, never mind," Paolo sighed to Olivia. "Come on, think I saw some leftover bread that needs cleaning up."

"Straight into your stomach," she said, jabbing Paolo below his ribs, and they turned away—to sneak extra food while everyone was at rites. Why hadn't they simply said that, then?

Milo told himself it was better this way, as he left in the other direction. He preferred the clear inked lines of text, the familiar set prayers of rites, to the unreadable messages everyone always seemed to be lobbing back and forth with ease.

And he had no time. Torchlight licked up the plaster walls of the residency wing as he strode down the hall, hoping the vigil hadn't already concluded. Even after this late night, he'd need to get up early to write before his regular duties took over his day—weekly rites in the morning and helping the apprentices serve meals. It was tiring enough already, tamping down his fidgeting, his reactions to all the bustle. When he passed the nido, however, down the hall from his own cell, telltale thumps and arguing carried through the wooden door.

He pushed into the room full of little beds and noise, trying to wipe the exhaustion from his face before addressing the younger wards. "Is it Carnival night already? Who is being loud enough to wake the sancts?"

Several small bodies froze in the middle of their battle, outlined by the lone clay lamp on a high windowsill. Gregorio, standing on his bed, unabashedly asked, "Did you see Val crash?"

Milo leaned against the door frame. "I did. Was it you who stuck out your toe and tripped her up?"

Laughter erupted, and two children smacked into each other in a reenactment. Senna broke through it to ask, "Why can't we go to the midnight rites?"

"Because you're supposed to be asleep. You'll have your chance at excitement with your festival pageant in a few weeks."

Senna frowned. "At least tell us a story."

Rites. Research. Duties. One week to write an omelia to prove himself.

He sucked his teeth. "If you lay down."

There was a great shuffling about, and Julia, clutching her bronze hands to her blanket like she held a horse's reins, asked, "Will you tell a story about a temple ward who drives a chariot across Orabellia—"

Gregorio hopped on his bed, tucking his knees, and bounced under his blanket. "Over the mountains! To Scavina."

"To kill nochen!"

Milo paced between the beds. No more fantasies, he reminded himself. He should be teaching the wards the truths of their faith. "I will tell a story of someone right here in Trestatto." The room had stilled, anticipation brewing in the dim. "Principessa Adalena." Senna popped back up in her bed, large dark eyes alight with interest, then scrunched her face back into a frown. Adalena was her favorite sanct, but she was still upset with him about skipping out on the wards today.

Guilt prodded at his insides. He remembered how easy it was, growing up in the nido, to feel that no one cared about you. He hadn't meant to make her feel that way. Struck by an idea, he pulled the copper icon he'd found earlier from his belt. He shook out the chain and dropped it about Senna's head, hoping that would be penance enough for his omission. She was always admiring his, old and simple as it was, with no image of a sanct worked in iron or gold like most. Temple wards had to make do. She beamed her crooked smile and examined the icon as Milo settled himself on the flagstones, back propped against the wall beside the door.

"A thousand years ago, the principessa led Trestatto with fairness and grace. Of all cities in Orabellia, it was the finest and most faithful. When other city-states and empires north of the mountains and across the Hagean Sea tried to take Trestatto's wealth and power for themselves, to tear down its temples, she led the battle against them. They drove their terrible beasts into Trestatto—two-headed wolves and great serpents and chimeras—to tear it apart." He swelled his voice with danger describing the monsters. Someone in the darkness, under their blanket, growled in return. Across the room, Senna held up her new icon like she would defend herself with the curved blade, blunt as it was.

Milo told at length how the principessa's militia fought the invasion off, but also suffered great losses. Adalena fought outside Magna Mater's temple—where Primo Sanct prayed to the great mother—protecting it, fighting on even as she was pierced with the arrows and spears of the invaders. "The battle was so fearsome, the sister goddesses fled, never to be seen again. Magna Mater, ever stalwart, protected us. With so many of the city's warriors fallen, she drew upon the earth through which she sustains us, and in the Great Miracle, gave the city the indestructible statues of the sancts in the moment of their sacrifice, to ever protect us. And she touched Primo Sanct with her immortality, so he could forever keep Trestatto safe from monsters and invaders as the principessa sought."

The dark bundles had gone still, the children either dropping off to sleep or lost in imagining beasts and battles and divine gifts. Milo pushed himself to his feet. He could keep the children's attention with the familiar story, so long as he described clashes between sancts and monsters in enough detail, but he'd need something more for an omelia that would capture the templars' recognition. He slipped out the nido's door and made for the temple's nearby side entrance, to see if the vigil on the piazza was still being held.

He was tempted to go outside and keep going, all the way back up the second hill, to see his sanct's face cast in moonlight. The idea of her soothed away the tumult of the day, the jumble of shouts and laughter echoing still in his ears. His hand rested on the door's security bar; he paused before venturing out into another crowd and retreated into thoughts of his sanct as if he could visit the solace of her hill in his mind. Or conjure her here.

Hers was the story he wanted to be told. Hers the name he wished he knew. Not for any omelia but because he felt the fierceness of her might break him open to the full rush of faith he yearned for. He thought it might taste like never having to shelter away from monsters, never hiding away parts of himself. What story might he choose for himself, then, in such a world?

The gust from another door opening around a corner set the torches' flames guttering, chased by the echoing voices of returning templars. They jolted Milo from his reverie. The temple was closing for the night. He'd missed the vigil. Shame burned up his cheeks. He always made a point of attending rites, to show the temple he wasn't like his parents, who never had. He always had to work harder, even for everyday tasks. He had to be careful to avoid mistakes, to check his instincts against the guidance of his mentor and the dictates of the templars.

Milo let go of the door and went to his chamber. Grabbing a candle, he let its slight flame cast itself over the piles of books and half-written omelias upon the little desk in the corner, across from his narrow bed. He would work until it burned out. He would focus. He would fix himself and his words to the rules of the temple. He put away thoughts of nameless sancts and locked himself away in his small stone cell.

CHAPTER FOUR

BLOOD AND FURY

Stregna's moon cuts a wild path known to the Unseen Goddess but divined by those who dedicate themselves to her. Invocations matched to the proper phases and locations of the manifestation of her icon will find the godpower they draw amplified abundantly, like the swelling of its sweet silver light. Poorly harmonized prayers will find their blessings cut off as if by a scythe.

—The Book of Invocations

Gia

Gia persisted in the shadows while the bonfire burned itself to the ground and the plaza emptied. The cat found her again and curled up in her lap as she rested her ankle and tried to plan. She didn't know how to wage a war. She'd never even accompanied the militia to fend off attacks from other cities, only put down monsters. She didn't know anything about the city Ennio had shaped for himself, or how she might catch him alone and off guard. She didn't even know where she'd sleep. Her chamber at her sister's temple was a crumbled ruin.

When the golden guards swept up the steps to usher Ennio and the other templars inside, they revealed a lone statue, the only one left standing right where it had frozen at the end of the battle here.

Her figure shattered the staid lines of the temple's steps and columns, silhouetted by the torches along the wall—a long curve twisting in pain and endurance, spiked with a dozen weapons. Arrows and broken spears feathered the statue's back and shoulders like a nightmare of wings. The final spear shafted down through her front, rending stone fabric and flesh. Gia didn't feel herself stand, or her feet move her from the shelter of the colonnade, but she found herself closer, rounding on the statue, looking up into Lena's face—beautiful and stoic and marked with a crescent drawn upon her high brow.

The slice of hope she'd carried splintered all the way into Gia's heart.

Her rage came alive, like a serpent threading through her veins, through her limbs, like battle cries and clanging swords in her head. Her breath escaped her again. There were no more bright flames or fine speeches now, just her vision narrowing to one black thought. Somehow, she would make Ennio pay for this.

The temple broke open, light spilling from around a door. Gia crouched behind the pedestal. Two men stumbled out.

Templars in white robes like Ennio.

One began down the steps, but the other hung on the door

frame. "You're too drunk to make it."

"The pleasures of Helena's bed call even through three bottles of wine!"

The first templar dismissed this with a wave and a laugh. "You'll wake tomorrow in an alley halfway there and late for rites."

"Better make an offering now, then." He leaned one hand upon the statue's breast, just above where the stone spear pierced her, and with his other jerked up his robes.

The other man snorted and swung himself back inside, fumbling the door closed. The clank of the lock and thud of the security bar followed.

Piss hit stone. Gia rose like lava coursing upward. Why did *he* get to be alive, to drink and bed his way through days and nights never stolen and frozen in stone? Maybe she could make him answer. Make some sense out of this world she'd found herself in. He was only one drunk man. What kind of a templar was he, anyway, who carried no sword, only a dagger at his belt? Ennio always spoke of Magna's strength, but he'd let her temple grow soft.

She drew her sword.

The templar spun, barely steadying himself by the jutting spear. He spied the cat, ambling across the square, and slumped. Chuckled at himself.

He didn't notice Gia until she stepped from behind the statue, one girl shifting into two. One still and stone. One blood and fury.

They sang together as Gia struck. Her sword slashed—the man fell. Blood flew. A proper offering at the statue's feet.

He struggled away, painting the stones a slicker black, toward the steps. Gia stomped her boot to his diaphragm, and he could only gape for air.

"How did Ennio do it?" she growled. Why had everyone else vanished from her life in an instant, to time or stone, yet he remained?

The templar gasped thinly. "The pontefice?"

How many titles had Ennio given himself? "Your Primo Sanct," she spat. "Does he still go to the countryside to kill monsters?" That could be a chance to sneak up on him.

"Why would he do that?" the templar croaked. "The sancts keep the monsters away."

His words shivered over her skin. A way to protect the city, Ennio had said. There was more to Vassilis's great invocation than she'd realized. The statues were tied up in all of it.

She had to explain. Tell this world how Ennio had lied. "They're not sancts, they're people."

"Maybe once," he wheezed, "but they've been dead for a very long time."

No. They'd been just here, beside her. Betrayed by her.

"Join them," the templar rasped. He yanked on her leg. She caught herself with her sore one, then toppled over. The templar was upon her, slamming her shoulder against the ground. Wrestling her sword away.

Her head knocked into the cobblestones and stars blazed through her vision, burning away all thoughts of converting or convincing this man. He was Ennio's creature, as much as any beast of stone. She would not let him steal her chance to avenge her sister.

She bashed her elbow to his face and pulled her sword from his clutching hands.

She'd been right. This city was Ennio's, and Lena and her people deserved Gia's help, not those who carelessly basked in the protection of the lives he had stolen, who believed his lies, who aided him—who were every bit as evil.

She scrambled to her knees. Dragged herself up over the templar and thrust, trapping his body to the stone. The moon had lost itself behind the city walls, but there was just enough light to see the fear in his eyes. Gia drank it in to the last dreg.

Anyone who'd helped Ennio deserved nothing better.

When he was dead, she staggered to her feet and yanked her sword back, hissing as her weight shifted to her sore ankle. She kept moving. There was more to do. This would put Ennio on guard. She had to get to him first. Her vengeance waited in the temple.

Her chest tightened. Gia frowned. She was not afraid. She was the monster stalking this night. She had to be strong. Her next breath came thickly.

Something was wrong.

She retreated to the far edge of the plaza, catching herself against the corner of a building. She fought down another breath. Her palm scraped over the rough blocks. She shoved her way farther from where the temple might discover her, around another corner, down a narrow alley. The cat chased after her and mewled as Gia sank to the ground.

Her mind raced through all that had happened—falling on the reverent face of that boy who had woken her. Whose invocation, whatever it had been, was letting her slip back under Magna and Ennio's power now.

No. She couldn't go back to the prison of stone, couldn't allow the unbearable weight of betrayal and impotence to close over her again. Her fist clenched the hilt of her bloody but unsated sword.

She swallowed a shallow breath and curled into herself as if she could hold on to it. But with a gasp, she became again stone and still.

CHAPTER FIVE

CARVINGS

Alta teaches that a river may bend the earth, as wine may influence a mind, and blood may change the world.

—The Book of Invocations

Milo

The screams rose through the morning like frightened birds.

Milo was buried deep in the archives, but the commotion reached even his ears and distracted mind. He'd been up well before dawn, determined to find a new text to use for an omelia. He'd managed to accumulate a pile of books and scrolls on Storica Lucca's desk, and a layer of dust on his head, after digging around the more neglected corners of the archives.

When the outcry started, he bolted up from the work to see what was wrong. In the hall, a templar apprentice ran past, shouting for the holy guard. Milo sped up, running to where lower templars stood clustered outside the main temple doors. Speaking in low, shocked tones. Cupping hands to faces. Crying.

Milo shifted around them, seeking the answer to what could cause this reaction.

Laid out on the steps, blood darkening the pedestal of the nearest statue like spilled wine, a body twisted away from some unknown attacker. The waking sun sliced beams between the high rooftops that framed the piazza, lighting up the yellow pallor of the still limbs sprawled over the granite and the white templar's robes. Shadow shrouded the grimacing face, cast by the outstretched arm and sword of Adalena's statue looming over the corpse. It was almost as if she were shielding the man—or had struck him down.

Templar Horace. Milo swallowed, choking down the rising bile in his throat. People coming early to rites or drawn from neighboring streets by the commotion added to the growing uproar. They clung to each other, clutched their icons, wailed—or stared, still as the sancts. Milo stood dazed as higher templars arrived, brought by the shouting apprentice, and some of the holy guard, and soon the watch captain from the militia.

How could this happen, here? Right under the watchful eye of the principessa? The sancts ought to protect one of the city's holiest men. Blood spatters wrote themselves across the body and ground like some bright-inked language Milo couldn't decipher.

He snapped out of it when he saw Storica Lucca, brought by the outcry, raise a trembling hand to his mouth. Milo rushed to his side. "Storica." The old man immediately grasped Milo's forearm, unsteady with shock. Milo bore his mentor up. "Let me help you back inside."

"Templar Horace," Storica Lucca rasped as he let Milo guide him away toward a side door into a hall leading to the residency wing. They were interrupted by Senna and Julia racing outside.

Senna wore her new icon. "What's going on?"

Milo's voice stayed even. It often unsettled people but seemed a blessing in a crisis. "Go back to the nido. Julia, tell everyone to stay in for now."

The girl frowned. "But rites——"

"Please." He fought to keep his fingers from clenching too hard on the storica's papery skin. No child needed to witness this kind of violence. Not if they'd come to be wards only by abandonment or illness like most. Julia nodded and ushered the younger girl in.

Storica Lucca ran a hand over his beard and muttered, "I shall have to meet with the templars. The funeral——"

"Let's get you to your cell," Milo told him as they followed the girls. "Rest for now while the guard deals with things."

Milo saw him settled and brought him some watered-down wine, but he found he didn't know what to say or do after that. He and Storica Lucca could spend hours in quiet study side by side or in avid discussion of a single text or playing round after round of tiles, but as his mentor muttered softly to himself, pressing fingers to his brow in prayer, Milo was at a loss. He felt the pull of the archive and his research, and the release from thinking about Templar Horace's murder they offered.

Guilt prickled at the back of his neck. Sometimes, growing up, other wards or templars would look at him strangely for not reacting with the same ready feeling they did. That old sense of being not quite right rose in him now, like there was a room inside himself where he sat apart.

He swept it aside. He might not weep when presented with sudden death or want to throw over his daily routine—might not express his emotions the same as most others. That didn't mean he didn't have them.

So, he left Storica Lucca to his prayers and returned to the workroom just off the archive, to the scrolls half unfurled and books lying open. He sat in Storica Lucca's chair and flipped through the folio abandoned on top of the pile, looking for something that might serve to inspire an omelia, to inspire the people of the city—who'd just seen one of their templars laid out, violently dead.

Milo closed his eyes as if to shut out the vision of Templar Horace, but the dark met him with older images of people struck down—their spilled blood—fear frozen in their eyes. He inhaled deeply through his nose and forced his eyes over the page again, letting its even black lines bar out the memories. He had to focus. He had only days left to secure his apprenticeship.

Milo shook his head and watched dust motes drift through the shaft of light cutting through the room. The important thing was to offer people an insight that would guide them through this morning's horror. And if he couldn't do that, perhaps he didn't merit serving them as storica. They were all small pieces of dust, fragments of something far greater—the bounty and strength of Magna Mater. She and her sancts gave protection.

Which was why such an evil act inside her favored city, at the foot of her temple, disturbed Milo so deeply.

He pushed himself to work but kept getting up to pace before realizing what he'd done. He checked on the storica and the wards before admitting he wanted to keep walking all the way across the city and up the second hill. That he wanted to sit under his sanct's protective sword.

He told himself he was only being responsible. More offerings were to be made to sancts this week, and he had promised Val to take them for Dario. He'd do that on the way.

The afternoon streets felt subdued. News had spread of Templar Horace's death. People went about their business, but there was less shouting, no singing. Another village's refugees were led through the Via Sanctus by militia guards to the district that could house them. The weary people carried large packs of wrapped fabric, everything they'd carried away from whatever little pocket out in the countryside had been overrun by monsters. Milo scratched his thumb along the edge of his icon, letting its bite chase away the memory of arriving like that with nothing in his hands at all, chase away the fact that Val was out there where the monsters were at this very moment. The only beasts he saw were the omnipresent, languid cats considering their tails where they dotted granite steps or stretched out under statues. It was said Adalena loved the creatures, and therefore no one in Trestatto drove them away or drowned their kittens.

Dario used to live above their forge but moved to a larger house a short walk away when they'd married and taken on Val as an apprentice. Dario looked tired, bags under their eyes and ruddy cheeks wan, as they gave Milo the offerings for the sanct their family tended. But they also handed him a second pouch of dates and a little pot of honey sealed with wax around its lid. "In case any other sancts need it," they said knowingly.

Val. He was going to write an ode to her great big mouth. As soon as she returned safely. His fingers clenched the offerings tightly.

He stopped at the market square and placed the first offering of dates and honey at the feet of the sanct Dario's family was responsible for, which stood in a niche just outside the indoor market hall.

It was important to keep up routines, even through dark days. Not just because they were what steadied him. They were what sheltered the city from danger. It was easy to take for granted, but the massive claw marks scraping over the edge of the limestone wall showed how much the sancts provided for each person within Trestatto's walls every day. How important it was to observe every rite, to earn their protection. Milo reached his empty hand to rest against the lines. He could almost feel the power of a giant gryphon's foreleg reverberate up his arm.

Today showed failure could fissure Magna Mater's shield. But what omission could it have been?

As he hiked up the second hill, he reflected on how he'd been rescued from such a slip of faith, when a community of farmers out in the western fields was attacked by wild beasts. They never attended rites and didn't bring offerings to the temple or sancts. Their break of faith allowed the monsters to breach the extended protection of the sancts and overpower the sentries. Every day Milo strove to prove he was worthy of the temple's shelter, and Magna Mater's. His parents had abandoned him to the free run of the beasts, but here he could be part of the temple that protected everyone.

If only he managed the omelia. And yet here he was, leaving the archives for the unnamed sanct again. His stomach hollowed. He'd only stay a short time and then get back to his work.

But when he neared the top of the second hill, an empty block of marble knocked all thoughts of omelias and apprenticeships and festivals from his mind. Milo's hands slackened and the sack of offerings landed beside his feet.

A vine of iron curled up from the stone, like the smoke from a blown candle, grasping at the empty space where the sanct should be. Milo's mind was doing the same. Impossible.

He crunched across the dropped needles, as if coming closer would suddenly make him able to see the statue that clearly—*impossibly*—was not there.

Gone.

Stolen? Who would do such a thing? Who even knew she'd stood here but Milo and the storicas and scribes who'd copied out old records and assigned her annual offering?

His mind answered itself only with another question—who would strike a templar down? The sickening thought sunk through his body. Something evil was working within the city. Who could say what it would do to the precious, missing sanct? The sanct he'd promised to take care of.

He walked about the empty pedestal. The only visible disturbance—there were no paths dragged through the fallen leaves, no wheels of a cart that might haul away all that stone—was the poor paper beast, smashed into the ground. And something metal, half-covered by the gryphon's snapped frame and shredded haunches. He thought of finding the icon here days ago, but this was no holy charm.

This was a knife.

A knife he recognized—he'd seen the carved handle during years of visits. But the last time, it had been made of perfectly white marble. Now it lay on the ground, handle carved of yellowed striated bone, capped with dark iron. A metal blade bent and battered.

He looked up to see scratches along the iron ivy stemming from the pedestal and noticed it was wrenched in one place, a break in its sinuous line.

Break. The shock and questions pressed in too hard, and a terrible idea broke open inside him. What if no one had stolen the sanct, but changed it?

As well as Milo knew every known sanct's name, every recorded detail of their life and death, he knew monsters. He'd read every account of those in Orabellia and abroad. There was a type of chimera that could hypnotize with its song, take possession of its victims' minds, and call them away from their friends and the protection of the sancts. There were monsters with no form, that moved freely through other parts of Orabellia as spirits. Could a creature such as that have transformed this sanct? Taken it over? Even within Trestatto's holy walls?

Kneeling there, he felt the absence of Acci, who would always emerge from the ruins to rub his head against Milo's shins by now. He thought of his prayer the last time he was on this hill. The broken feeling he had during rites. His failures at making omelias. His parents, turning their backs on the temple and inviting beasts to tear apart that cluster of cottages, leaving Milo to escape out the back window with only the clothes on his back and an old icon around his neck. He'd run as hard as he could toward the sancts.

All these thoughts rained through him, settling heavily in the pit of his stomach. What if some evil had gotten into the city because of his imperfect faith?

The birches and pines and ash stood around him, like looming watchers, and Milo pictured going down the hill and telling the templars that he had lost the sanct they'd entrusted to him. The sanct that had stood watch over the city for hundreds of years. Either to some evil—or taken up by it, infused with some demonic animus.

Would they even believe him? They'd laugh at him, at his peculiar mind making up yet another story. And if they didn't— what would they do? Maybe he'd be given no apprenticeship at all. Maybe he'd be turned out of the temple—out of Trestatto—

No. He clenched his fingers around the dirt and leaves and knife hilt. He'd carved out a home in the temple. Found a way to serve. Tried to make it need him as much as he needed it. He had to fix this.

Milo stood, limbs buzzing like the apiary the templars kept near Magna Mater's grove. He retrieved the forgotten offerings and scattered them to the ground, using the emptied bag to wrap the knife blade, and hid it away in his belt pouch. He needed to return to the archive to find more information. He needed to know if it was possible for an evil spirit to possess a sanct's statue. And if it was possible to stop it.

He turned for home, feeling at his back the menace of something in the ruins and trees and growing dark, pursuing him.

CHAPTER SIX

READY TO BITE

Before the great monsters were driven from the earth, leaving only their smaller children to plague humans, Alta steered a river about a forest to defend the fleeing people. When the monsters still chased on, little sister Magna froze the river, trapping many within it. But Stregna cast her influence over the water, drawing it up closer to her domain, and it flowed again—only while her moon was in ascendance, and only until that moon died, catching pursuing beasts each time Magna's ice again took hold.

—The Book of Invocations

Gia

Waking this time was harder. When the invocation began to lift, sometime after the shadows had crawled to one side of the narrow alley, Gia fought as if she might tear herself from the stone and become a spirit—to haunt this city and all her enemies.

So when the stone softened fully, her flesh tensed, her mouth snarling for breath. Her fist shoved against the cobblestones—launching herself off the ground. Her sword's tip clattered over the stones. The cat, who'd been asleep against her feet, sped away into the sunshine. Gia let the breath sink deeper, running her thumb over her sword's etched hilt.

When the stone had taken her again, she'd despaired over delivering the vengeance she'd kindled in her heart. To think that one fallen templar of Magna would be her revenge.

A failure and a disappointment on her part. Again.

Her shoulders tightened. She squared them and stalked back toward the square, prepared to examine the temple, to look for any chance to cut her way to where Ennio might be vulnerable. Her ankle was even feeling better. She was ready.

There were a few dozen people congregated under Lena where the templar had died, somber-faced or worried. Gia stiffened, but they didn't notice her before she ducked halfway back behind the building and sheathed her sword. Growing up, as her body thickened and swelled into a figure with no resemblance to Lena's lithe form, Gia seemed to turn almost invisible. It would be an advantage now.

She didn't seem to have lost too much time in the stone—someone must have scrubbed the blood on the steps away, but a scattering of charred twigs showed where the bonfire had been.

Lena's sword pointed at Gia, accusing.

She wanted to rush into the temple where Ennio lurked, to throw herself into the battle, into wood and guards and swords, destroy them and herself upon their shattered pieces. But one or two was not enough. All she was good for now was vengeance; she needed to make sure it was worthy of those who were betrayed, of this chance she had been given.

She needed to stay alive, awake, to cause as much pain as the city had given, far beyond one mere templar. How could she be sure the stone wouldn't steal her back again? How could she keep this life, this chance? How was she awake at all when Magna's invocation still held everyone else?

The boy. The boy with his sweet words. His prayer.

And with that icon.

Gooseflesh danced up her limbs. She tilted her face up, to where the crescent moon sliced between the buildings on the far side of the plaza and the colonnades of the great road. She remembered an old story her tutors at Stregna's temple had told her, about an invocation of Magna's being broken only while the moon lived in the sky. Only for half a day.

And only for one month.

That wasn't very long at all if the invocation that had awoken her was the same. Even if this moon was young, it wasn't much time to work out a strategy for trapping Ennio and executing it. What if the boy told Ennio what he'd done, or Ennio already knew someone was running around with another temple icon? Was the boy waking other statues?

He couldn't wake them all. Not the ones that would wake only to die of injuries inflicted a thousand years ago. It was up to Gia to act on their behalf. And her time was already spinning away from her.

Maybe there was a way to pry free more time for herself. She had felt the power of the icon, felt that boy wish her to life with it and his prayer. She needed to get her hands on it and its ability to invoke—to make herself stay human for good.

She was getting strange looks, at her clothes, her face. She tried to smooth her expression, turning away from the temple.

Where would the boy be?

And why had he been looking at her like that? Not merely curious—almost entranced. She cast her mind back to those moments of first waking for details of him. He'd been reciting verse. Giving his breath not only to his prayer but then weaving it into words as if garlanding it about the grove where she stood. She remembered his poetry and the hush it conjured in her as she struggled not to panic. Calming the hurt inside her like a frantic animal fighting to get out.

Now the animal was free and ready to bite.

Suddenly it struck her. The river. He'd spoken of it in his poem as he'd slipped away.

She pivoted and strode from the square, down the statue-haunted road. The river cut through Trestatto east to west, but the bank was steep on this side of the city. Nowhere the boy might walk along composing verses in his head. She followed the road to where she knew bridges once stitched the two sides together, back before she broke the world. It grew more crowded, with people strolling or heading home with arms full of baskets of bread and tomatoes and greens. Here and there armed soldiers wearing sashes of militia red patrolled. Gia dove into the masses, down a wide side street that cut south, and a square opened up before her, full of market stands and shoppers.

And statues.

Gia's heart clenched and she hurried through, thinking this way must lead back down to the river. She passed tables laden with boxes of melons, stacks of lemons, and piles of golden squash flowers, then shops facing out from the tan and ocher buildings, selling baskets and bags and jewelry. An old man perching on a stool just outside a shop selling leather goods was conversing loudly with a woman, and his words caught on Gia's hearing like a burr—something about murder. Her feet slowed. The woman shook her head. "That poor templar."

Gia fought the grin off her face. Any part of her that should have felt remorse had been killed by Ennio. Squinting looks followed her, so she pressed on.

The street sloped sharply upward. The shops here—jewelers, perfumeries, places selling the finest goods—were built over a bridge. She cut through one and out the open door in the back overlooking the river. Her hands crashed into the low balustrade edging a narrow walkway behind the shops and above the flowing Argus.

The city spread from its banks, the imposing temple in the distance. Where was she to find the boy in all Trestatto? Could she even locate him before turning back to stone for good? Her slick palms slipped over the wall. She balled her hands and huffed. There was nothing else for her in this city or the wider world, Orabellia and beyond, but to search out the best way to pour pain and retribution upon that temple. Upon that man. The boy on the hill had also mentioned a market in that poem of his. She would search every one for him. Her nails cut determination into her skin.

She would hunt him down.

Gia spun back to resume her pursuit, to be met face to face with an elderly woman who clutched her by both shoulders.

"You look nearly prepared for Carnival already!" The woman ran her papery hands down Gia's dress with an appraising eye. Her thin lips smiled broadly with a hint of a question to them.

Gia stiffened. She shoved down her instinct to draw her sword, where it clattered about in her speeding heart. Finally, she pulled the corners of her mouth up in what she hoped was a smile.

The woman's lips pursed. "You must have a mask, though. You don't need—" She gestured at Gia's face. By Alta, what was so wrong with her face? People had never remarked on it like they did Lena's beauty, but had people grown so rude that they'd stare and comment like this? Her old nurse used to do that sort of thing, pointing out how the drape of Gia's dresses fell all wrong over Gia's stomach and wide hips.

The woman turned away to pluck masks from where they hung above a table laid with fabric and ribbon, and Gia caught her reflection in a small, mirrored glass hung on the wall beside it.

A crescent of pale dust smudged her forehead. She'd forgotten. She rubbed at it, quick and harsh, with the back of her hand. Wiping away the memory of Ennio's fingertips on her brow. The way she'd gazed into his eyes, so sure, so proud. So trusting.

She almost missed what the woman said as she rambled on. "We were almost sold out, and I've been sewing nonstop to replenish our stock." She paused, one hand still free and briefly touching her brow, a quick gesture of prayer. "Even with the sadness this morning, everyone will be at the carnival this week."

Gia dropped her hand from her own brow. Everyone? Reborn hope prickled over her skin. What young man could resist a night of revelries? She'd need a new dress as well as a mask. She couldn't wear her own and risk being recognized when she found him. She had to be stealthy. And then pounce.

The woman turned back and held two masks out to her, white and red. "If you wanted to play sanct," she said, holding up the white, with a crescent stitched in silver over its curved brow. "Although we have many beautiful choices."

Gia looked to the red.

A large mask, oval with a curve scooped out for the mouth, and two eye holes. It was covered in red silk, with black cut-lace netted over it and stitched down with gold thread. The woman nodded encouragingly, so Gia took the mask, held it up to her face, and turned again to the mirror.

She was hidden behind the stiff fabric, yet something about her was revealed. She'd wanted to become a spirit, and now she looked the part—molten danger lurking behind gauzy darkness, sparking like flint as if about to blaze out, to consume.

Perfect.

CHAPTER SEVEN

WORDS AND WALLS

The Three Sisters may be found in the one image of a lamp. The vessel of clay. The oil that fills it. And the light that illuminates.
—The Book of Invocations

Milo

The archive was Milo's favorite place in the city. Cool and quiet and at the heart of the temple, its chamber was stuffed with records—bound pages and scrolls and ancient tablets, even wall carvings from the temple's earliest days. Yet, they opened expansively into the ideas held within. It felt far airier than outside often did, blaring with noise and blazing with the sun.

Today, its walls were closing in on him.

He'd rushed back to the temple from the empty hill and searched by candlelight for anything about sancts or monsters that might explain how a sanct could vanish—how her knife could turn from stone to bone and metal. He'd searched for hours again today, every free moment he had, completely abandoning any effort to write an omelia. And still he'd found nothing.

Milo finished flipping through a volume resting upon his thighs and shoved it back at its low shelf. Nothing again. He stood and leaned back against the wall, letting his head thunk against the stone. Maybe it would knock some inspiration into him.

He paced farther into the archives, searching for another text while running his hand over the relief covering the southern wall with images of hills and fields scattered with scythes. The pads of his fingers grew numb.

In the farthest shadowy corner, he slowed and skipped his hand over to the next wall and stopped. He'd never examined the carvings here, but right there, in ancient, small, block-ish lettering—STATUE. That was odd. The invocations on the prayer tablets and walls of the temple dated from before the Great Miracle, back when Magna Mater answered prayers with regular abundance. They focused on success in battle, good crops, and safety from monsters. He peered closer. This carving had probably been transcribed into a scroll or folio long ago, something Milo himself may have copied out to preserve.

His breath stilled.

Milo had taught himself to read from an old book of the sancts' lives left in the nido, back when he and Val slept there. He'd read portions of hundreds of scrolls and journals while making clean copies of omelias for templars and helping older storicas with their scribing work. He'd spent a year copying out a crumbling book onto fresh vellum independently. He'd struggled through an ancient medical treatise where he found the word *autism* like a door opening to reveal himself standing under its archway. He'd studied text after text while preparing his never-read omelia. He'd hidden away, rereading accounts of battles the temple blessed, offerings brought by merchants who wanted to trade from Trestatto, the lives of old templars, and signs marked in the earth and sky of Magna Mater's will and bounty.

He'd never read this.

The writing, in an alphabet like the prints of bird claws in the muddy banks of the Argus, was archaic. Likely indecipherable to anyone who didn't study old texts, but Milo could make out phrases. Enough to understand the gist. Something about the statues being tied to great strength. Could it be an account from the time of the sancts? It couldn't be the prayer Primo Sanct used to invoke the Great Miracle. That had been lost to history, like many works were in the battle that day, their tempting titles— *Prayers and Days, The Oralliad, The Book of Invocations*— referenced in surviving works, but their knowledge forever lost.

Milo pressed his fingers to the stone. This was exactly what he needed, information from those who were present when the sancts were created. He only needed to unlock the rest of its meaning and it might offer the answer he'd been seeking.

Days later, Milo ran his finger over three small crescents. The charcoal smudged across the parchment, blurring the three forms into one. It was odd, how the curved blade of Magna Mater repeated three times above the passage. Maybe it was typical of the carving's inscriptor, Vassilis, whose name Milo had found edging down the side of the text. He'd made a rubbing of the carving to study every spare minute he could. For days he'd been working his way through the archaic language, but as he stopped to rub his eyes, he considered the ornamentation at the top of the writing. Had he seen this before? Somewhere in the city? Mostly, only a single crescent was carved into walls and wells and hung about people's necks, like his.

He shifted an account of Principessa Adalena's life, bound in leather, from atop a stack of books and dragged it closer to his notes. He'd sneaked back into the workroom while the rest of the temple took their riposo. At this hour, everyone in the city would be resting so they could attend the carnival that night. Even the templars, still feeling the loss of their brother, would put on a brave face, with their masks, and attend. It was a shame Val would miss it this year; she was always at the heart of the dancing. Even though he'd been holed up in the temple all week, Milo could imagine how, like every year, swathes of colored silk would festoon across archways along the Via Sanctus, and boughs of olive and laurel and birch would wind about columns and balustrades, tied with golden cords that would shine in the torchlight that evening.

He would miss it all, too. He couldn't spare any time on his translation, on his search for answers. Couldn't face having to confess the lost sanct to the templars without any explanation. He'd used the history of Adalena to pry out a shaky understanding of the opaquer passages of the carving, each line revealing more about the statues and power. Orabellian spoken language hadn't changed much over the centuries, according to the storicas, but the written word, even the characters used to form the words, had shifted gradually, eroding until their significance was almost buried like the ruins of the forsaken temples.

The history he'd found wasn't a famous one. There were so many of Adalena, and this was only an account from a storica living some years after the Great Miracle. It had been recopied over the centuries, and along with the author's words were quoted pieces of a journal from the time of the principessa—the last principessa before Magna Mater had blessed Primo Sanct so he could take up the role of leader of the city. The journal was from an unknown writer, and the book transcribed what it said were descriptions of Adalena's birthday celebrations and ceremonial meetings with leaders from other city-states.

Milo had been working out the meaning, correlating similar words from the journal and the carving and using clues from the explanations in the history. He wasn't confident his translation would hold up. The last journal passage he'd been mining for clues seemed, to him, to say Adalena was templar of another temple, while the summary in the book spoke of her simply being at the second temple when some emissaries arrived from the south.

It was like a snag in linen that his mind kept trying to smooth down, to make it take its proper place in the whole. As he hunched over his work at his borrowed desk, he twisted his lips. He was bound to make mistakes. He wasn't even an apprentice. And probably never would be, now. The thought harried him like the sound of a strix's wings before it fell upon sentries.

He had better luck early that morning with a paragraph giving an account of a festival. The journal keeper described Adalena as shining like a torch, blazing with a beauty that lit people up and drew them toward her, even as it threatened to burn them with her zeal or throw them into shadow. Amid his frantic searching, Milo was taken with that line. He'd have to remember it for Val, who held the principessa in her heart as her personal role model and inspiration, wearing an image of her as an icon and leaving little offerings at her feet even outside Sancts' Month.

He'd tell her when she got back safely. The passage cut off before it could relate much about the festival, but still gave Milo a few more words for his dictionary. Slowly, he was conjuring meaning, rubbing two sticks together, drawing heat, then unfurling smoke—hoping they would catch and blossom into a flame of understanding.

He became so caught up in the work, he hardly noticed when other scribes and storicas returned to the workroom, their quiet shuffling of pages at the edge of his perception. Before he knew it, they were gone again, the windows dark, when another piece of the translation delivered its meaning to Milo.

He ran his finger over the charcoal once more, rechecking what he'd read. His other hand drifted up to his icon. The shadowy word he'd been puzzling over translated as "break." Rendering the line to read something like, *Only who made this can break the statues.*

Milo sat back in his chair and pulled his hand away from his notes. The words seemed to threaten to escape the golden dome of candlelight he sat within.

He pinched the fabric of his tunic and worried his thumb over the rough weave. Could this mean it was actually possible to harm a sanct? Did this explain how a sanct might disappear, or might—what? Break from stone into something unknowable and walk away?

Did it mean this could only be done by he who had carved this text? Vassilis, whatever storica or templar he had been, was long dead. Or could it mean Primo Sanct, who might have been the one to enact whatever prayer this was? Was he the one who'd "made this?" He would never hurt a statue or Horace.

Whatever the specific meaning, that the sancts could be destroyed was a horrifying possibility, potentially devastating to Trestatto. He had to find Storica Lucca. He had to get him to translate the rest of this carving, at least quicker than Milo could manage. He needed to know if what it was saying to him was true.

He ran from the workroom, from the temple. It was dark out, but shortly down the Via Sanctus torches burned away the starlight. After days of quiet in the archives and workroom, the throngs of people and music crashed into Milo like a wall. The carnival was kicked up dust and sudden smells and people turning to shout to friends too close to his ears. Already on edge, he struggled not to push them away. The drumbeats rattled his heart and stirred nausea through him, accompanying his worry for the sancts. He wished he knew his was standing yet upon her hill, protecting. He wished he knew she was safe. He fought his way through toward the temple's pavilion, neck bristling. All along ahead of him, the moon peered over the carnival like a watchful eye.

CHAPTER EIGHT

MASKS

Alta loves offerings of summer fruit and wine, and the communal chants of many voices. But some workings call for blood.
—The Book of Invocations

Gia

Gia struck the woman across the back of her head. She went down soft as a sigh. Gia might have felt guilty if everyone in this city wasn't already guilty as sin itself.

And none more than Gia.

She caught the woman and dragged her back into the shadows of the quiet street a few turns away from the raucous Via Sanctus. The woman's head lolled against Gia's shoulder, but she was breathing. Gia had used the flat of her sword this time, and only targeted the woman because she shared a similar build to Gia—average height but bigger all over. Gia stripped her fancy carnival dress from her limp body. The wine-dark gown wrapped about Gia's curves perfectly and the ripple of pleats across her shoulder blades hid the sword slung low on her back, especially with Gia's long hair pulled loose from her braid. The woman's sandals were another matter—the strappy things were too big and their braided cords that wound between Gia's toes and about her ankles would be no help if she needed to kick anyone tonight.

Good thing she still had her sword.

She left the woman her feathered mask. Gia had bought the one from the shop over the river. She'd traded the few silver coins she always kept in her breast band to a jeweler a few doors along the bridge and purchased the mask as well as a plain tunic and leggings from a simpler shop off the bridge, to better blend in on the streets these last few days. She'd considered stealing what she needed—after what the city's temple had taken from her, it would only be just. But she was happy to get rid of the strange new coins with Ennio's face on them.

Gia didn't want to risk drawing more attention to her presence in the city. The dead templar made it likely Ennio would be on alert; the temple had been locked and guarded whenever she'd been awake. The gray cat had found Gia when she circled back there during her wanderings, after searching several markets for the boy, and they had haunted the building for hours that night. Lena would chastise her for letting her anger get the better of her, for striking at the templar instead of waiting to solve the real problem of Ennio with calmness and calculation.

But Lena would never admonish her again.

Gia's lips pursed tightly and she blinked. She pulled the red and black mask from where she'd left it, stowed away her tunic, leggings, and boots, and fit it to her face. She was determined to find this boy tonight. The stone had overtaken her again each night as the moon set, closer to morning with each passing day, and Gia had to assume it meant she had mere weeks before it trapped her again forever. She needed that icon, needed to finish what the boy had started, so she could cut a path to Ennio without interruption or restraint.

She stalked nearer the great road, and the noises of carousing grew stronger. Torchlight reached and receded over the colonnades, glinting off the decorations. Somewhere, musicians struck drums and plucked strings. Feet stomped.

Gia could almost imagine she was back at a festival thrown in Lena's honor, except for the crescents on the brows of so many revelers' masks reminding her how she had led her sister to the Ceremony of Dust, and to her downfall.

The carnival extended along the road farther than Gia could see in both directions, another set of musicians coming within earshot as soon as the previous faded, tables laid out with fruit and seed cakes and cheeses and wine every few streets. A man reached out to her, and she jolted back before seeing he was offering a pastry topped with walnuts and drizzled with honey.

Gia took it with a tentative hand. As she continued through the carnival, doubt mixed with the food in her stomach. How could the people of the city give so freely and yet allow Lena's people to remain prisoners in plain sight?

The road opened into a square on one side where a pavilion had been built. It was ringed with bough-laden fences and filled with long tables and benches—and full of templars in their robes, with Ennio at their center. He was outside the temple at last, but again swaddled in protection; guards in purple and gold staked about the pavilion, along with more of those red-sashed militia soldiers she'd seen on patrols through the city and especially near its gates to the east and west. Gia veered away from them, even as her fingers itched for her sword. She steeled herself, forced her legs to keep walking, her face to turn away. She didn't want to see Ennio in person, even less than on his money. Not when she couldn't do anything to him. As much as her blood sung to spill that of Ennio, one smear of it to her skin and he'd be able to channel his power to break every bone in her body. A direct attack with all those guards around would never work.

Only as she was nearly past the square did something arrest her steps.

"I need your help."

That voice. She recognized it—the first voice that reached her as she woke, that sank through her stony sleep. That freed her.

She pivoted. Behind two guards, a boy leaned against the pavilion, speaking urgently to an old man in a green robe.

"If you could check the translation—" Gia could only see his tensed back. His hands were braced against the structure—and a thin chain hung about his neck.

A boy in a jewel-encrusted mask crowded next to the old man, goblet in hand, voice drawling with drink and derision. "Milo, it's Carnival, stop bothering the storica."

He beat a hand against the wall. "I think I made a mistake."

"Like lecturing as if we're at rites and not a party?" The other boy laughed. "Or flapping like a strix?"

The man looked at the boy with kind eyes peering from out his mask. "Let's talk tomorrow."

"But—"

"First thing, I promise. Find me at breakfast."

Gia's blood pounded through her head like the vibrations of the nearby drums. The boy worked for the temple—that's where he'd been hiding from her. She should rip the icon from his neck, let the chain choke and bleed him. Leave him here in the pulsing crowd, let these dancers trample him in the dust of Trestatto. See if he liked it so much then.

The old man—storica—turned away with his friend. The boy stayed at the fence, frozen. Behind him, the moon caught in the branches overarching the stone columns and rooftops.

Gia stalked closer.

The boy turned, the distraught look on his face unhidden behind any mask. His bare face looked vulnerable, honest— which made it all the worse that he was working for Ennio.

Gia glanced at the guards again. As easy as it would be to take the icon from this boy here, she was better off being discreet. If she could manage to get him away from these others.

The boy launched himself away from the pavilion, moving quickly through the crush of people but stopping with a jerk every time dancers passed too closely in front of him. Gia gave him room as she followed. Finally, he darted to the side, and Gia thought he was going to leave the road and break away. She rushed forward, but he stopped at one of the feast tables, slamming his palms against it and dropping his head.

She halted just before crashing into him. Growing the distance between them, she circled the table, never taking her eyes off her prey. His shoulders rose and fell with controlled breath. He lifted his face, and it was painted with such self-doubt and guilt, so familiar to Gia, she felt he must see through her mask to where it burned like acid over her skin.

She was so startled by the emotion that she forgot to look away, and now he had caught her staring. A crease formed between his brows.

There was no way he could actually recognize her. Right? Though she didn't know anything about him or how he came to be standing before her on that hill. What was he even doing with a temple icon? She needed control of this situation. She wouldn't let another of Ennio's people get the advantage over her again.

Nothing to do but plunge into battle. She stepped forward— but a couple danced between her and the boy, and she let them, glad to see he listed his head to see past their bodies, to keep looking at her. The guilt and frustration drained away from his face. When the pair moved out of her way, Gia walked nearer to him—to Milo, they called him.

She reached him, crafted a smile, and said, "You have to save me."

He blinked, long lashes glinting in torchlight. "Excuse me?"

"I've lost my family." She waved vaguely at the masses of bodies around them. "And now I have no one to speak to or dance with. And since you appear just as in need of company, I figured we could save each other."

His gaze shifted off her face. "True. I was just wishing my friend was here." Something of that strain again pulled along his sharp cheekbones, his wide mouth, but he smoothed it away. "It's not fair she couldn't come to Carnival this year." His eyes flicked back to her and away again. "Maybe you know her? Valentina?"

"No."

"Everyone seems to," he explained with a shrug and pointed to the people celebrating. "She would be leading the dancing." His lips quirked in a rueful smile. "And making sure I didn't stand over by the food all night. No one can sit out when she's around."

Ah, one of those. Like Lena. And Milo, was he as drawn to this girl as everyone was to Lena?

Once, even Ennio seemed to want to be something more to Lena than only fellow leaders of their temples. Just another trick to grasp more power, Gia realized now. He'd become head templar to Magna very young—though nowhere near as young as Lena had stepped into her place as principessa and templar. When Magna's former head templar was killed in battle, Ennio took up his icon and managed to invoke Magna powerfully to save the rest of the Trestattan forces. After that, he remained at Lena's side for every feast and assembly. That was, before understanding Lena's indifference to his attentions and moving on to Gia, who fell for them, and worse tricks.

Something twisted inside Gia. If Milo felt for the girl he'd mentioned, it would pose a greater challenge for tempting him away somewhere she could strike in secret. So, she let the feeling inside her coil tighter, sharpening her resolve to get that icon off his neck. Whatever it took to capture his attention.

Yet Milo was already peering at her quizzically. "Your accent— forgive me—you must be visiting Trestatto for the festival?"

Why not? "Yes. Although my family lived here long ago."

He gave a mild huff of a laugh. "Why would anyone leave?"

She kept her voice as balanced as a blade and let her mouth twitch into a slight smile. "Yes, how could they?" The world Ennio had built was a paradise as long as you weren't a statue.

"You like what you've seen of the city so far?" He was being polite, as if speaking lines from a festival play. He picked up an anise seed from a clay bowl and popped it in his mouth.

Maybe she could get him to take her for a little tour. "I haven't had much of a chance to see anything yet." And then, because she was always one to poke at a bruise, she added, "I'm looking forward to seeing Adalena."

His eyes sparked with interest, a signal fire lighting. "You can see her from here right now."

"What?" The word startled out of her like a bird escaping.

He pointed over her shoulder. "That's her there."

Lena? Had she awoken? Gia spun, seeing nothing but musicians and dancing. Her heart thumped faster than their beat.

"It's still low," Milo said, "but others are up well past the trees and roofs. There's Hector and Cassa—"

Constellations. He was talking about stars. Who was this boy?

She turned back to see him gazing up at the river of sky visible between the colonnades. "And the beasts—that's the gryphon, and the serpent, and the nyk, or in Scavina they call them nochen—" He broke off, eyes darting to Gia and then down. "Sorry," he told the plate of figs on the table.

"Why?"

"It's not—I mean, it's a party." He shrugged. "I tend to get carried away."

He'd handed her the power in their conversation. Good. "I haven't learned about these constellations. My tutors emphasized keeping my head out of the clouds." At least Ennio did, even if her neglected tutors at Stregna's temple had more open minds. She just hadn't been very good about listening to them.

Milo cracked a half smile. "Mine too. Once I started learning about the sancts, though, I wanted to know absolutely everything about them." The crease over his nose appeared again, and he lifted a hand to tap distractedly at his breastbone—no, something under his tunic there. The icon—her freedom.

She leaned closer, like a magnet in her was drawn to that

metal. "Will you tell me more?"

He squinted back up at the sky. "You really can't see well with all the torches. And I should get back—"

"Then let's go where it's darker." She let her hand pass lightly over his arm as she stepped into the road, heading again toward the pavilion. Across the square a short street led down to the riverbank. She didn't look back. Wouldn't give him a chance to beg off. This was clearly a boy who was good at following orders.

The crush of people in the road was tight, and Gia's body substantial. She shuffled forward and back like a fighter who couldn't find an opening for a strike. If she gave up, Milo was going to leave, as he was clearly about to do before she pounced on him. Turning around, she shrugged at him and curved one arm up before her like the other dancers. "Like you said. It *is* a party."

He stared a moment, then lifted his opposite arm to twine about hers, carefully keeping empty space between them. They followed the dance—easy enough, at first, to step nearer and then apart, switch arms, and back again. Then the musicians' fingers flew faster over their strings, notes slid quicker and quicker through their pipes, and soon the dance pitched each couple into a whirl. The boy hooked his elbow in Gia's to keep them from crashing into the other couples, pulling her into an orbit that was just his brown eyes and soft, surprised smile and endless air pumping through her, through her lungs and blood and heart.

The dizzying music broke at last, and several couples fell away from the crush of dancing, gasping for breath. "Stars!" Gia shouted. As the musicians shifted into a new song, she cut through the thinned crowd like a knife, trusting the boy would follow faithfully. She stepped off the road, heading across the open space behind the pavilion as he caught up.

Just as they reached the far edge of the square, he whirled about. "Oh!" he said, chest still heaving for breath. "I forgot."

By Alta, what was it now? What was it going to take to get this boy to herself for five minutes? If he insisted on going back to the temple to learn more about his sancts, she might scream. She squeezed her fists tight to prevent them from dragging him into the shadows by those glossy, dark curls of his.

He stuck out an open hand. "I'm Milo."

Who *was* this boy who talked with enthusiasm about sancts and stars but had to remind himself to make the proper small talk and introductions? Before she could stop or strategize, she let slip, "Gia," and lifted her own hand, crescents from her nails bitten into her palms across her godlines, to shake his.

At her name, his mouth spread into a full, delighted smile.

Might as well use the opportunity. She kept her hand clasped to his and towed him on, to the Argus flowing under that river of stars flooding its banks, spilling wide across the open sky.

With the flaring of the torches and the hardest edge of music behind them, Milo gave a little sigh. His shoulders seemed to ease.

Good. He'd be totally off his guard. She looked up, feeling the cool press of her sword at her arching back. "Where do you even start to pick constellations out of all this?"

His voice pitched low, fitting the quiet space above the steep bank. Below them, boats stored upside down rested like slumbering beasts. "Searching out patterns. Finding connections. Stringing meaning one star at a time. Look—there's the Principessa." He lifted a finger to trace the stars. "That band there is her crown, and her sword, and those lines are the spears—"

Gia tried to follow his finger but shook her head. She could only make out the constellations Stregna's templars taught her—meaningless jumbles to everyone in this city now. "I think whoever named these made up whatever they wanted to see."

Milo tore his eyes from the sky long enough for her to see how they flared earnestly. "No, see—" He leaned nearer, bringing his cheek close to hers, lining up their gazes. He guided her with a gentle crook of his hand, breath brushing her mask. "There."

Once, she'd ached for this kind of closeness. Ennio had ruined all that, doused her in shame. She was a traitor, and now a murderer. She swallowed painfully. For a moment, as brief as her sleep in stone was long, she let herself imagine what it would be like if she was just a girl talking with a boy she'd danced with at a carnival. A boy who smelled of anise and vanilla and leather instead of sweat and ambition. She stared out at that tall, stern Lena made of stars, and wondered if there could still be any way to find light in something so unendingly black.

The only way for her to do that was with her sword. Or a quick headlock to choke the breath out of the boy at her side.

"They're beautiful," she said as her muscles tensed in readiness. "They look as if they've been carved out of the sky."

He laughed again in that gentle way. "You'd need a terribly big chisel to—"

He broke off, just as the shouting from the road halted and another voice rose in its place, carried from across the square.

Another voice she would know anywhere.

Her own was a hollow rasp. "Ennio."

Milo wasn't paying any attention to the voice. The crease was back, and he stared, hands splayed, as if caught in an epiphany. "The carving's talking about *a chisel*."

She couldn't help herself, couldn't keep from looking at Ennio now across the square. He stood on a raised platform among the tables, speaking to the crowd pressing near, before sweeping off it and out of the pavilion, waving away the guards who moved to join him. He dove into the adulation of the people as they reached out for his blessing.

This was her moment. Who cared if she turned to stone forever next time, if she could reach Ennio while hidden among the others and kill him now he'd shed his guards? They could both end tonight.

Gia was already moving after him. Lena wasn't here to stop her from following her anger, a bright molten path down an inevitable hill. She left all thoughts of the icon and Milo muttering to himself.

His words lapped at her heels like the rilling of the river. *"Only what made this can break them."*

A greater tide pulled her back from the shadows to the crowd swelling around Ennio.

Gia could see him more clearly here than before the temple's torches. He was wearing a crown—he was in charge now, like he always wanted. She'd realized that too late. Oddly, the curved blade of his icon was fitted to a circlet resting upon his short hair. The smallest satisfaction flared in Gia that he couldn't steal Lena's actual copper crown, frozen on her marble head.

But he had the love of the people he walked among, who strained to touch his robes and accepted his blessing upon their brows with eyes falling shut as if in ecstasy. Ennio drank it all up, a hunger Gia had seen on his face many times pulling his kind smile apart at its edges.

He wanted to bask in all that power and glory badly enough to venture free of his guards. Why wasn't he more wary, after she'd left a dead man on his doorstep? She'd show him the danger of ignoring her. Grabbing a knife from a table of cheeses and fruits, she joined the throng. Ennio wouldn't even know she was near before she'd threaded the blade through his ribs, right into his liver. But the crowd was thicker than ever and streaming after him, and though Gia fought to get nearer, without actually pulling hair or throwing elbows she fell further behind her target. All that devotion massed around him was protecting him still.

As the crush finally began to subside, the other robed men, escorted by all those gaudy guards and militia, caught up with Ennio. The revelry in the street didn't show signs of winding down, but the guests of honor looked to be heading home. The brace of guards pushed a path clear along the road, and more circled the templars. She'd missed her opportunity.

A tingle danced over Gia's shoulders as she recalled the boy she left by the river. She should have grabbed the icon when she had the chance. She berated herself as she trailed after the exalted group making their way back to the temple, keeping herself hidden among the many Trestattans who broke off dancing to cheer as their templars passed. At the edge of the carnival, people let their children race around where the crowd thinned, and some lifted their babes for the templars' blessing before the guards ushered them along the last unpopulated stretch of road to the temple. The men shoved their masks up to their hairlines, revealing faces glistening with sweat.

Gia eased off, backing into the shadows of the colonnades, but the templars began arguing, something about being out on the street, and she risked keeping pace to hear better. Their voices would cover the occasional slap of her ridiculous sandals.

A templar walking beside their leader declared in a dark but dismissive tone, "Horace went too far with his women and drink, and it caught up with him."

Another said, "We need to show the people that there's nothing to fear. Or else that threatens the offerings and the attendance at the Ceremony of Dust!"

As they reached the square before the temple, their back-and-forth died when Ennio opened his mouth. Even though he looked younger than most of them, everyone halted to listen as he spoke in a low voice. "We demonstrated our confidence this evening. And we have posted guards nightly, but we must make plans for safely carrying out all this month's ceremonies. We know how important it is not to let Horace's death disrupt them. We all rely upon the strength they grant."

He swung his gaze to a dark-skinned young man in a red sash. "We need to ensure people still come from our territories to make their offerings. Your men can encourage them."

The man gave an attentive but confused look. The man's fellow—or commander, judging by his age and how his red sash was covered in shiny pins—snapped a reprimand. Ennio held up a hand, and waved the young man over, guiding him apart from the others. Closer to where Gia lurked.

Could she close the distance between herself and Ennio before the others reached him? Before the one beside him drew his sword? Her toes flexed against the leather soles of her sandals, elbows crooked as if she might run.

"Franco," Ennio said with a bland smile. "I know you love protecting the city. People like your family rely on the important work you do."

Franco drew himself tall, hand on his sword's pommel. "My brother is nearly to apprenticing age."

Ennio beamed, his smile drawing wide. "You want to save lives. Find a nest of ventroni or gryphons—they're easiest to shepherd—and use them to guide a nearby town to the sancts' protection."

Franco looked confused, his thick brows darting together. Ennio reached forward and gripped him by the forearm, just above his wrist. "Lives will be saved if people are inside the sancts' protection and make offerings to sustain it. I know you want to save lives."

The remembered taste of training yard dust nearly choked Gia as Ennio's gesture recalled the many times he'd spoken to her like this. The final time he'd talked her into betraying her sister. She shook her head, trying to clear away the memory, trying to make Franco say no. To stand up to Ennio like she had failed to do.

Franco nodded.

Ennio patted his arm where he'd gripped it. "Take your most trusted soldiers. Get it done." The militia headed farther along the road as Ennio turned to the others. "Inside the city, though, we show no fear. This is Magna Mater's haven."

They gave solemn nods, and walked up the steps to the temple. The building was about to swallow them up, and here she was in a clingy dress and what couldn't justifiably be called shoes.

Left in an impotent rage again by this man who ruined everything.

She watched him enter his temple. It didn't escape her that all his templars were now men, all the special guards he'd wrapped about himself like armor.

The thud of the doors echoed in her head as she stood watch outside. The statue Lena pointed her sword in condemnation, and Gia knew she'd let her sister down once more. She knew she should retrieve her clothes and return to the narrow alley she'd found to hide in when she turned to stone, behind some of the smaller warehouses south of the river, with the cat for company. But she could not face the stone without something to show for this night. Others returned from the carnival over the next few hours in a slow trickle, let in by the guards, but she never spotted Milo. Her thoughts returned to the boy again and again. The next time she tracked him down, she wouldn't hesitate. She needed that icon. Then maybe she could make a real plan to work her way through this place straight to its rotten heart.

Then, when everything was quiet, one of the templars came back out. The one who spoke of offerings and the Ceremony of Dust. Of showing that they weren't afraid.

He strode through the square, humming a tune played earlier at the carnival. Maybe Horace wasn't the only templar with excesses.

Gia cast her gaze to the sky. Its black was softening. The stars had grown murky. Moonset and stone would come for her all too soon.

There was still time.

She tore off her sandals and followed the templar. One man wasn't too great a challenge, even barefoot. She would not hesitate this time. Ennio had made her into something hard, something broken. Now she'd drive every last shard of what she had been back toward him and his men in vengeance. They weren't afraid? That was one thing she could fix. Hunt anyone who stepped outside their precious temple's walls. She thought of Ennio's high-held head, that bizarre icon crown. She thought of filling that head with fear. She wanted him to know she was destroying everything he had made this city.

That she was coming for him.

CHAPTER NINE

STORIES TOLD

*The original carvings in bones invoking Magna have not survived
but crumbled, as all things do.*

—The Book of Invocations

Milo

"Please stop killing them."

Gregorio pulled a face at Milo, but Milo crossed his arms
and watched him patiently until the boy put down the wooden
sword he'd been swatting at the smaller children. Then he
got back to assigning the rest of the children their parts. He'd
nearly forgotten about helping the younger wards prepare for
the pageant they always performed before the Ceremony of
Dust, and even with them all gathered, he was distracted by
weightier thoughts. Was it really a chisel that might be able to

break Trestatto's statues? And what had killed another templar the night of Carnival?

The morning after, Templar Adrian was found slaughtered under a birch tree in a grove, blocks from the temple. Everyone in Trestatto must have felt weighed down with worry.

The children's shrieks, echoing off the walls of the temple's enclosed courtyard, slashed through Milo's thoughts like a sharper sword than Gregorio's, and he turned to the last waiting wards. "All right, Julia, you're Magna Mater this year. And Senna can be Adalena."

Gregorio snorted. "She's too short, and too Hagean. Adalena was Trestattan."

"Senna is Trestattan." Sometimes using his matter-of-fact voice, which could otherwise get him in trouble, helped with these kinds of arguments, and Milo had no time or will to argue today.

Gregorio shot Julia a dubious look, but she was busy practicing her goddess posture, so he let it go and went chasing after the wards who were playing monsters again. Milo raked a hand through his hair. He had to get this organized and get back to his research.

Normally he'd enlist Val to help, and she'd complain but then spend the entire time sword-playing with the rowdier children and swinging them upside down or letting them climb on her back, and Milo could focus on getting everyone sure of where to stand and what to say. If there was one thing Milo was practiced at, it was scripts and saying lines. He studied how other people greeted one another, asked about their days, and learned it all by heart as well as any prayer for rites. But now, when he was facing something that traveled off any written record's page, when he wondered if it was indeed his fault, he was at a loss.

He wished again that Val was here, that he could ask her advice and share everything on his mind. He'd been thinking just that when Gia had come up to him at the carnival.

Gia. The girl who spilled over with vitality, who'd never stopped moving, it seemed—except for some reason to stare at him as he agonized over the missing sanct and to stand by his side seeking stars. When he'd realized she was walking toward him, her waves of hair dancing about her mask like dark flames, every practiced script had flown out of his head. Sancts, what must she have thought—she'd been so eager to hear Primo Sanct speak—and he'd just run off, sprinted back to the temple, without saying goodbye.

But she, and everyone else visiting or living in Trestatto, could be in danger. Whispers of what happened to Adrian passed through the city like a chilling wind, all the way into the temple's halls. Milo looked at the wards, who deserved to feel safe, to be safe—and saw Gregorio sitting on top of one of the now-wailing monsters. "Gregorio, *please*."

"This is what happened! Isn't the point of the festival play that Magna Mater rewarded us for killing all our enemies?" he asked, grudgingly shifting onto the gravel.

Milo came over and helped the little monster to her feet. "No. The point isn't the killing." He crouched down at the boy's level. "Do you think it's stronger to kill something or love something?"

Gregorio shrugged.

"Say you love something. You'd want to protect it, right?"

The boy nodded, his lips pursed in solemn thought.

Milo nodded back. "And it's easy to sacrifice others to protect what you love. Kill them to keep a kind of peace. But the point of the Great Miracle is being willing to lay down your own life to protect it. Loving something that fiercely."

Milo could hardly imagine. His parents hadn't even bothered to attend rites or keep faith enough to ensure the sancts might shield their own son. And he'd never felt glad to step outside that haven once he'd achieved it. He hadn't even told anyone yet what he'd discovered atop the second hill or in the archives the day of Carnival for fear of losing his place here.

He told Gregorio, "Magna Mater rewarded the city because so many loved her enough to make that self-sacrifice. And she saw how great the cost was, how many had been lost, so she gave us the sancts and Primo Sanct to protect us while we were weakened from it. Like how her great earth can take a fallen leaf or crumbling trunk or even the bones of an animal and make new life from it. And now we're strong again—"

Milo saw that the other children had quieted and drawn near, listening as if they were at rites, though he was glad he didn't have to give omelias like Primo Sanct. The wards were one thing, but he'd be a wreck speaking before even the sparsest temple gathering on a dark winter morning. "And you get to help teach all Trestatto's children—and some of the more forgetful adults, too"—Gregorio flashed a sly smile, and others giggled—"why we do the Ceremony of Dust each year. We take the mark of Magna Mater, the dust of her holy stone, to show that we lay our lives down in service to her as the sancts did."

The rest of their practice wasn't without chaos, but the children seemed more focused. When they'd gone through the

familiar pageant a few times, Milo told them they were free
to kill each other as much as they wanted until it was time for
their chores.

He sank to the ground, leaning against a raised bed of fennel.
"Next year, this will have to be your job," he told Julia, who
balanced on the edge of the garden box. "Unless they decide to
apprentice me as a nursemaid to you all." Which seemed about
as likely as anything at this point. He had no omelia to show
Storica Lucca before weekly rites. Milo couldn't even get the
attention of the storica, who'd been locked in meetings with the
templars and taking Renz to accompany him on his afternoon
passeggiatas, turning Milo away when he'd tried to summon the
words to share all his theories and worries. Milo had spent all
his time since the carnival brooding over the second murder, and
whether he knew what had allowed it to happen—what might
cause even more harm to the city and its sancts.

Julia grinned down at him. "I hope when I'm confirmed it's
to the militia."

"You may feel differently after you begin training next year."

Senna dropped to Milo's side and slumped against his shoulder. Looking out at the children's battle, she said, "I want to be
a templar."

Milo rested his chin atop her glossy head. "You can be a templar, just as you can be Adalena."

Something pinched in his gut as he said this. He knew how
uncertain apprenticeships could be, and there were hardly any
women templars, none at the most elevated levels, and none who
had been wards. He knew from the archives that there had once
been more, but maybe telling Senna it was as easy as playacting
a sanct was unfair.

Maybe Renz was right. Maybe wards weren't suited to the greater work of the temple. Look at what Milo had done with the sliver of responsibility they'd allowed him. Something had happened to that statue. Something was killing templars. His mind kept going around and around. Just like his dance with Gia the other night—though that had been far giddier, had made him forget for a few minutes his guilt over what might be happening. Amid the noise and crowd, he found sanctuary in her full lips parting to shriek as they spun, her soft curves pressing against him for the barest moment.

And thanks to Gia's poetic turn of phrase, Milo now understood that the text could be speaking of a chisel, that the one that carved it could have been used to hurt the sanct—or still might be. The thought of the sanct in danger, of his care and faith failing her, stirred an icy finger through his chest. Only one such item might have been kept safe through the centuries—the sacred chisel. The symbol of the strength of templars' prayers had hung in the great sanctuary above the altar for longer than any record told. Except during preparations for Sancts' Month, when it was used to grind the dust for the ceremony. When anyone might have taken it from the sacristy.

Maybe he was spinning stories again. There was no evidence that the carving had anything to do with what was happening now, which he remembered every time he considered revealing everything to the templars. If he told, he faced either being believed and guilty or laughed at and scorned. Either way, he'd lose the one safe home he'd known.

Gregorio had amassed the other children into a Scavinian raiding crew, ranged about another garden box as their ship. Senna and Julia ran off to be shieldmaidens, leaving Milo sitting alone, fidgeting with his icon. No, first, he needed to determine if he was right. If he had proof that the words about breaking statues could help explain or halt the danger stalking the city, he could protect the temple. But to get that proof, he'd need to take the sacred chisel to compare to the lines of the carving itself.

And to steal this artifact out of the sacristy—that went against every impulse Milo had trained into himself. For years, he'd worked to understand, or at least memorize, the edicts of the temple to fit himself to its expectations. Theft was a clear sin. Even if he intended to put it back, taking what belonged to Primo Sanct felt like a fearsome transgression.

As he twisted the icon, its chain cutting against his skin, a shadow swept over the children, throwing their game into gloom for a heartbeat.

A few glanced up. Milo dragged himself to his feet and peered up between the courtyard walls, squinting at the bright spring morning sky.

Another shadow cut through the yard. A gryphon's long, stretched underside passed over them, razored wings splayed wide.

Milo spun back to the children. "Gregorio!" The boy's pale face looked up at him. "Lead your crew to the feasting hall." Thank the sancts, the boy bellowed and charged for the doors, followed by the others. Julia scooped up the smallest and bore him inside.

The suddenly quiet afternoon broke into the ringing of alarm bells. Milo's pulse flicked in time with their peals. For several rapid heartbeats, all he could think of was Val—on sentry duty while a pack of gryphons stormed the city. His imagination exploded with a stampede of monsters.

He rushed out the side entrance of the temple. The bells clanged in his head from the militia station nearest the western gate. People were pulling windows shut, racing for doors, silently staring upwards. He joined the others heading to the station, hurrying as fast as they could with their eyes half on the sky, watching for the impossible sight of monsters over Trestatto. Some looked like small insects, vaulting high, but every time one swooped lower over the streets, people cried out and Milo's stomach dropped, wondering if it would trespass on Magna Mater's blessed ground.

At the station, the captain was shouting to people to arm themselves and get to the wall. Others in orange training sashes were handing bows, spears, and slingshots to those rushing in. Milo grabbed a bow and quiver and slung them over his shoulder. Before he knew it, he was nearing the western stairs. People already lined the top of the wall that blocked out the wild expanse of Orabellia and shouts carried down the steps, carrying word of farmers chased by the beasts.

As Milo climbed, the reeling, agile forms of several more gryphons came into view. He sprinted along the pathway and pushed forward to the outer wall where he could see the fields draped about the city, the clumps of people scurrying for protection.

"Can you imagine?" someone nearby asked one of the people crushing shoulder to shoulder with them.

Milo didn't have to. He could remember. He could taste the fear, borne on the kicked-up dust, snagging on the broken stalks of grain.

Vaguely he was aware of the neighbor replying that they'd heard the fortified town to the west had been heavily attacked, making the people flee for the sacred protection of Trestatto.

This kind of thing happened to smaller villages, certainly—Milo took note of such reports, and cared for some of the children who ended up in the temple's nido when it did. Worryingly, these were farmers whose fields lay too far from Trestatto for them to journey there daily but were successful enough to have the resources to protect themselves—usually. And yet these gryphons had harried them, broken through their defenses, driven them here. Gryphons normally weren't even seen much during daylight. And they never flew over the city.

A few sentries escorted the townspeople, fending off the low-arcing attacks of the pursuing beasts. But none looked to be Val. She was likely guarding the other side of the city. This calmed Milo until a gryphon flapped its sharp wings and drove its lynx body ahead of the others. Its shadow cut over the sentries. With a scream from its eagle beak, it rounded on the unprotected town folk nearest the wall. Its muscles coiled, then it sprang down through the air.

The shouts from the wall were thunderous. Maybe even enough to spook the gryphon from its course. Instead of snatching up a victim, it lurched to the ground before its cowering prey, dirt erupting from under its paws, then darted back across the sky.

Milo notched an arrow and readied the bow at the gryphon gliding back toward the wall. His movements were practiced, automatic, but his mind raced with questions. Why were the beasts pressing so near the city? Serpents hid in the old quarry, but Magna Mater's blessing had always dampened any such vigorous attacks this close. The sancts' protection was like lamplight—burning truest within the walls but spreading outward beyond with gradually receding power. Was it fading now?

The bowstring cut against his finger. Could one missing sanct diminish the city's protection?

His arrow loosed and struck the haunch of the beast. A few others stuck in the monster's thick hide, and one rock glanced off its golden beak with a crack that was swallowed up in the cheering of the crowd. The gryphon screeched and flapped its razor-sharp wings, abandoning the group of farmers clutching each other and cringing from the sky. Wheeling high, the gryphon stretched its claws toward the wall as if to shatter the sancts' holy shield. Several atop the wall ducked from its sweat-matted fur. Drops of blood fell like perverse rain over the spears raised against the beast. But the sancts' protection must have held well enough because the monster cried out again, its wings dragging it back out over the fields in an erratic flight.

It wasn't until hours later, when the farmers had been taken in through the city gate, and the gryphons dispersed, that Milo descended. The sancts upon the nearest stretch of wall stared at him. They were vulnerable, one of their number already lost. The thought that there would be no safety without the sancts sank through his mind, heavier with each step he took down the stone stairs. Like there wasn't for farmers who fled to the city, from towns or villages. Or their children who ended up in the temple's nido.

He paused halfway down the stairs, jostled by others heading off the wall. He turned his face back toward its height. From here, any lingering beasts were out of view. He stared at the blank blue sky—no stars, no scripts—as if he might still read answers there.

+ ✦ +

Back inside the temple, Milo strode past the sanctuary and stopped several paces down the hall from the open door of the sacristy. Using the sacred chisel, three templars worked to prepare for the ceremony at the end of the month. One lugged broken hunks of marble brought from the quarry to the worktable and helped hold them in place. One ground powder from each block. The third made sure not a crumb of the dust was lost to the floor like so much dross, even wiping up the table with a damp cloth that would be later burned, the ashes returned to Magna Mater's earth with respect.

They would lock the prepared dust away in the tabernacle and repeat their work every day—except on the mornings of weekly rites when Milo might sneak away the chisel they were using.

The templar with the chisel lifted a rag-wrapped mallet and struck. A chunk of white marble broke off, falling to the table. Suddenly, all Milo could see was his missing sanct. Her fierce, forlorn face. A crack of worry shot through his heart.

It didn't matter if the templars expelled him. Everyone in the city could be expelled from Magna Mater's benevolence if the sancts' protection failed. He needed to listen to his own words to the wards and take the risk upon himself. Like how he'd gone along with the beautiful girl instead of shutting himself away to research, and actually made a breakthrough. She'd dropped the idea of the chisel in his lap as if she'd pried one of those stars from the darkness and gifted it to him.

And now the idea was burning him up as much as any star would.

It burned away the final scrap of his hesitation. He needed to check the chisel against the archive wall to see if the carving offered knowledge worth sharing, knowledge to help hold back the tide of violence that seemed to be creeping up the Argus's shores into the city and threatening to rain down from its skies.

CHAPTER TEN

MONSTERS

Some blessings follow even imperfect prayers. Some things must break to become what they might be.

—The Book of Invocations

Gia

Gia waited still and silent in shadow, ready to slice another thread holding this city together. The swelling moon behind her cast silver light over the city wall where she crouched, the gate's pediment and columns below her, and the pale quarry out beyond the walls.

Mined far more than when she'd last seen it, the quarry cut into the base of the hill, pooling marble below the temple of dust and lies. A place for monsters.

She'd heard people on their way to the market saying that

serpents might make it as close to the city as the quarry and hide among the crevices until unwary prey crossed their path. One man hauling a cart of fish to his market stall told his companion that when they found the killer of the templars, they'd be left in the quarry for the beasts while the city watched from its walls. A fitting end for such a monster, he'd said. And when she'd woken again, the streets were full of talk of gryphons marauding Trestatto's sky, of a fear almost palpable at the thought of monsters violating its ground. Franco had done his job well for Ennio.

Gia smiled at the statue beside her. A monster was inside the city. And tonight, her prey was right here at the gatehouse.

She'd followed a group of high-rank militia here from the temple and hid herself before she froze among the statues cluttering the balustrade above the gatehouse, waiting until she might catch one on his own. Ennio must have made the force separate from the templars—who mostly seemed to enjoy the adulation of the city and do nothing but hide inside their temple.

Until she could breach it, Gia would make do with the target she'd woken to find awaiting her—Franco's commander, the one with gold pins decorating the red sash over his tunic and marking some important status.

The gate was quiet, the outer doors shut for the night. One small cart hitched to a donkey waited inside the courtyard set between Trestatto's walls. The pale-skinned, peppery-haired commander gestured for its owner, a small Hagean woman, to stand near the inner wall.

"Orders," the man said. "Have to keep the city safe. We need to search you."

He said "we" but there was no one else with him. He must

have sent away any others posted there. Even in the growing dim it was crystal clear why. His hands slid over the woman's torso, cupping curves where no knife could hide. The woman went rigid, staring nowhere, reminding Gia of the blank eyes of the statues beside her.

"You brought an offering for the temple?"

It took a moment for the woman to find her voice. "I—I was supposed to?"

"Of course, since you'll be under Magna Mater's protection."

"I have—" Her voice broke off, as the man's hand passed lower. She seemed to force herself to continue. "Toys I've carved and painted. To sell during the festival. I could maybe—"

The guard stepped back suddenly. The woman, unbalanced, was left wavering like a sapling in a harsh wind. "You should have brought a proper offering. They're being very strict right now. I can't let you in without one."

"Please, we came with a caravan with armed guards through the countryside. Our village was overwhelmed with monsters." Her arms began to reach out in supplication, but she seemed to catch herself from getting in any way closer to the guard and clasped them together. "If you don't let us in, we'll have no protection from the beasts, especially at night."

"You should have come earlier. You might have had time to trade for an offering from someone else."

She slid her hands over her arms, hugging herself. "Your eastern gate was shut when we arrived and we had to cross the river and travel to this one."

"You must have something you could trade." He closed the distance between them and pinched the fabric of the woman's dress at her shoulder as if inspecting the weave.

Gia took the moment of his distraction to swing herself over the balustrade where the statues stood, catching her toes on the niche carved into the wall below her, mostly filled with a statue. He did not want to make room for Gia or the space her body took up. She braced her hands to either side of the niche while judging the rest of the distance to the ground.

The guard ran a hand down the woman's arm and began to pull it out of his way.

The woman shoved him away, hard.

He laughed. "Go back the way you came, then."

Her face crumpled. "Please, my children—"

Gia's fingers clenched against the stone.

"They can stay." The man drew himself up into his stiff official posture. "The templars are benevolent like that. They want all innocents to have the chance to earn Magna Mater's blessing. To serve her."

Gia glanced to the cart and saw two little faces peering out from under a blanket. One staring at their mother.

One staring up at her.

Gia checked her balance and risked a finger to her lips.

She readied to leap down, but her foot knocked into something tucked between the statue's legs—a carved serpent, tipping over the side of the niche. Cursed toy beasts. She grabbed for it and righted herself, shoving her forearm against the wall to keep from dashing her brains on the paving stones below.

Luckily, the guard was still focused on the woman, waiting for her to consider her choice. He didn't turn until Gia's boots hit the ground. His hand was on his hilt, but she swung first—the stone serpent bashed against his jaw. She dropped it and drew her sword while the man's eyes fought for focus.

She drove the blade straight through his center like lancing an infected boil, letting the corruption spill, then wrenched it free.

His guts slithered over the dusty road beside the bloody serpent. Like the fishmonger's wares spilling across a table.

Gia turned away as he fell, hearing his body join his innards on the stone. She shoved the doors of the inner gate open and turned back only to tell the woman, voice digging low, "Go."

The mother stared at the blood spilling on the ground. Gia dragged her back before it got on her sandals and pushed her toward her cart. "Get out of here. I'll make sure no one follows you."

The woman's instincts seemed to kick in as she faced her children. She hiked herself onto the cart. The children's little hands gripped the board fencing it, eyes on Gia as it rolled by.

Gia shouldered the doors closed and stalked into the city in the cart's wake, but only a block or so. Other guards were bound to come to the scene sooner rather than later. She was determined to make sure they didn't get a chance to find or blame that family, to turn that mother into yet another innocent victim of Gia's recklessness and violence.

She tucked herself into a doorway and waited with this idea in the dark for too long. How many mothers had never returned home to their children after Ennio turned them to stone? How many more families had his men pried apart because Gia had handed her sister's throne to him? She could never forgive herself for that. She shouldn't.

She stayed there, pressed in on by memories like that statue crowded into the niche with her, far past when the family must have been safe.

Gia had blamed Ennio for everything that had happened,

everything she'd become. Betrayer. Murderer. Destroyer. But the truth was, Gia had come into this world with an instinct for tearing things apart. Knocking over game boards, getting in fights. The only attention she ever earned was scoldings. Maybe she'd always been this. Maybe Ennio had simply seen that and used it.

His mistake, then, because someone that poisonous was dangerous to deceive and not destroy completely.

She thought of how the most devoted of Stregna's templars would undergo transcendence to commune with their goddess after careful mental and spiritual preparation. Through invocation, they would rise to Stregna's realm in a holy blaze, returning after moments or years with profound wisdom. Or, long ago, if a battle against one of the last great monsters was all but lost, a Trestattan soldier might volunteer for transcendence. They would give in to the worst of their bloodlust and battle-fury before the invocation was laid upon them. So as their bodies melted into pure energy, they would use it not to reach the goddess but to sweep incredible destructive power against the enemy. It was almost always fatal.

She'd been turned to stone rather than fiery air, but she still felt now like a transcendent spirit. Visiting devastation upon Ennio and all his closest followers.

At last, a cry went up inside the gatehouse. No one chased from the gate, but she heard footsteps speeding away atop the wall.

Gia shoved out of the shadows and headed farther into the city, a smile clawing itself into her stoic face. Thinking of how those cries and those feet would carry this murder straight to Ennio. She wanted news to reach the temple that even the men meant to protect him there could not escape her blade.

She was the monster she always knew she was.

Hours passed as she stalked the city, hoping to hunt down any-one else she saw the night of the carnival daring to step out into the streets. The stars wheeled across the sky, reminding her of Milo—believing so fervently in all the wrong things. Too soon, morning threatened. Light brimming to the east had chased the moon nearly to the horizon. A few people were already on the streets, like ghosts in the mist from the Argus. Gia's fingers tensed into fists, as if to strangle the worry that shivered down her arms. She'd been glad of the distraction the previous day, as she'd sneaked into position among the other statues. Every time it grew harder to wait for the change to take her over. It was like knowing she was about to drown.

When Magna's godpower had first closed over her, it had come quickly, but now that another invocation dragged her out from under its influence, the change was slow and horrible, and her awareness lingered even after she could no longer move. It was the same when waking—until she finally broke free, she was caught immobile, powerless, clutched in the control of Ennio's ancient prayer.

Enough. She turned for the temple, losing her battle against the impulse to break down its door and fight through its guards to avoid marble lungs stealing her breath even one more time—but when she arrived at the edge of the square, she was rewarded with the sight of the great front doors opening wide for early worshipers.

No more waiting. At last she could get inside that place while awake, hidden among the rush of people. At last she could find that boy and get that icon. At last she could ensure she'd never have to turn to stone again.

CHAPTER ELEVEN

KEY TO LOCK

Stregna may take the breath of prayer and increase it to a cyclone.
—The Book of Invocations

Milo

Milo's fingers wrapped around the chisel. It was long, its metal darkened with age, and only a remnant of the etching on its handle was visible near its cap. He lifted it from its nest of wool batting in the polished box where it was kept while in the sacristy. Cool to the touch, the length of metal seemed to shiver in the dim light of the single candle stub he'd brought. He went to slide it into the narrow sleeve of his tunic, but when he removed his fingers from the box, its lid slammed down like a beast's maw snapping at him.

He jerked back—surely someone would hear, would come—then slipped the chisel up his sleeve, tucking it into the tight lacing at his wrist. He nudged the box back where the templars had left it yesterday, on a high shelf, and snuffed the candle, then left it among the basket of sanctuary candles ready for weekly rites. He hurried from the room, trying not to look like he was hurrying.

Fear prickled at his shoulders until he was several corridors away. He was sure everyone he passed—not many this early, thank the sancts—could see it trailing off him like sparks until he was finally alone in the archive.

Get it done, get it back.

He tugged the chisel from his sleeve. Careful not to scratch the ancient carving, he lifted it to the text.

It fit into the letters like a key to a lock.

He checked words from different parts of the text. The three crescents. The smaller etching of the name along the side, even—it could have been made by angling the point. Standing there, bringing the instrument to the writing, an impression of immense time washed over Milo—as if it might pull him back like a wave returning to its source. Someone had stood here, carving this.

With this tool.

He let the chisel drop, let its weight hang in his hand. He rested his forehead against the wall, as if the answers he'd hoped it would offer when he'd begun his research could sink into his mind and guide him. Had someone taken this before? Sneaked it away as he had, and returned it in time for the templars not to miss it? Used it on his sanct? Even if not, this meant the sancts were vulnerable. Trestatto was vulnerable.

He had to tell Storica Lucca and the templars everything. He had to make them listen.

He tucked the chisel away again. He would return it first. His admission might go over better if he wasn't in possession of a stolen artifact. Though, letting it out of his sight, even for a short time, was worrisome, knowing now what it likely could do.

Still, he thought, as he strode down the hall approaching the residency wing, at least he'd managed to match the chisel against the carving, and nothing terrible had happened. He hadn't been caught and sent to the catacomb cells for a month's penance. Magna Mater herself hadn't walked the earth again to smite him. And he should be able to get it back as easily—it was still early, the halls were mostly empty, though rites were likely to be full again today. Lauds had been busy with people looking for comfort, pressing offerings to the temple that gave it. They spoke of merchants choosing to remain in the city until after Grove Day and the Ceremony of Dust, hoping Magna Mater would bless the city's offerings and restrain the monsters. They spoke of the gates flooded with people hurrying away from the riled beasts in the countryside, into the safe hands of the city—even as gryphons and strix were spied above.

Milo was so caught up in his thoughts, he didn't register the noise. Then he turned a corner to see the girl from the carnival killing Renz.

They were clutched together in struggle. A basket of eggs was smashed to the floor near their feet. She'd caught his wrist above his head and squeezed until Renz, teeth bared, dropped his jeweled dagger. It clattered beside the broken shells.

She withdrew her sword from where she'd braced it against Renz's collarbone—his fine tunic was slashed and darkening— and shifted her weight back to gain room to strike. It was an awkward swing as she struggled to hold Renz's arm where she'd caught it. Renz struck out with his free fist—but when her blade met his side, his grunts broke into a long, terrible wail.

The sound pierced Milo's shock and he found his voice. "Stop!"

She turned toward Milo, dragging a slumping Renz along. In a perverse echo of when she'd approached him at the carnival, her eyes lit up at the sight of him. "Milo. Just who I needed to find." She shoved Renz away, letting him drop.

It was Gia. And seeing her there, maskless, he knew her face as well as he knew his own. He'd recited his poems and stories to that face, cleared ivy from that body, made offerings to that girl.

His sanct had come alive. And she was the one reaping lives through the city.

He could be next.

Her chest heaved, and her breath gave her words a throaty intensity. "Give it to me." Tendrils of her braided hair snaked loose about her round face. Specks of blood dotted her tan cheek.

Fallen to his knees, Renz braced one forearm on the floor, gasping. Good. He was still breathing. "Renz. Get inside my cell. Just there. Bar the door." Fear thrummed up through Milo, catching in his throat, but he pushed out the words.

Renz struggled to get to his feet—his boot slipped on the egg whites and he crawled. Milo couldn't see if he managed to shut himself away safely because Gia was walking toward him.

One side of her mouth curled up in something like a smile. "Don't make me take it." Her tone carried a threat on its sharp edge, and that smirk reminded him of Magna Mater's curved blade.

Coming for him.

His pulse spiked past any recognizable measure. He took a step back, farther down the hall. "Take what? What do you want?"

She matched his step. "The icon you woke me with, of course."

The one he'd found at the ruins? He'd held it as he wished for something of the sanct's bravery—wished it to come alive for him. Horror struck his gut. "I—I don't have it." He'd carried it home and given it to Senna—his eyes flashed to the door to the nido before he could stop himself. The children would still be in bed this early.

Gia rushed forward.

Every thought crashing through him evaporated. Everything Milo had ever studied and read burned away, leaving him with just one, vital piece of knowledge.

He could not let her reach that door.

She was three paces away—two—he flung himself between her and the wards, palms out. She shoved him sideways, against the plaster wall. Lifted her sword, ready to dispatch him.

He threw up his arm, by instinct, as her sword swung down. It shuddered off, with a dull crack, dragging a surprised Gia back a step.

The chisel. Still in his sleeve, thank the sancts. But he needed a weapon, something to stop her from getting to the children, anything, even just to slow her down—to buy the holy guard time to hear and come. He had no fancy dagger like Renz—

His hand fumbled at his waist, and he lifted the ruined knife he'd taken from the hill. Only to hold her off. It was bent and scratched, but still sharp enough to threaten.

Except Gia didn't hesitate and threw herself back upon him as soon as she recovered from the jolt of striking metal instead of flesh. When he jabbed the blade out, it caught her across the neck.

Knife to throat, like chisel to carving—again, it was as if he fit a key to a lock. One he'd never wanted to open.

Blood sprayed across his arm, his chest, his face.

Gia's eyes flared with horrible surprise. She grabbed at him, at his own neck, but then she twisted and fell. Her sword rang against the floor.

He dropped the knife and knelt beside her. Instinct again took over, and he pressed his hands against her slick red throat. Her hands came up to clutch at the back of his. The blood didn't stop.

"I'm sorry." He shouldn't be. She'd killed templars. Terrorized the city. She was an abomination to Magna Mater. Her mouth gaped for air, and panic ringed her eyes.

She was just a girl, and she was afraid.

His face mere inches from hers, he pressed tighter, as if he could hold the life slipping away from her inside there. His fingers slipped over her skin. She sucked in a gasp. And with a little hiccup, went still.

Milo didn't realize what was happening. It was all so wrong—so terribly, horribly, monstrously wrong. The way her flesh immediately cooled nearly didn't matter. Her fingers went stiff over his, and he saw her lips—that full, berry mouth that had talked and laughed and mesmerized him at the carnival—going paler. Her eyes, brown and blank, began fading to white.

He pulled his red hands free, peeling them from her neck like some appalling flower unfolding, like one of Val's games, plucking petals and guessing if Flavia loved her back until she got the answer she wanted. Leaving a dead bare thing.

And then there was only stone.

She was a statue again, supine, hands resting open upon her chest, hair and blood pooling about her shoulders. All of her still and white and cold.

Milo's mind burned with questions, racing around what had

happened like a chariot on the circuit, circling again and again. He only broke from it when someone else gasped. Renz?

No. A slice of Senna peered at him through a crack in the nido door. "Milo?"

She couldn't see this. He pushed himself to his feet, blocked the hall from her view, braced one hand on the door so it couldn't open more and the other on its frame so it wouldn't tremble.

Her little face was ashen, her dark eyes rounded with worry. "What's wrong?"

"It's all right." He thought of Gia stalking forward, asking for the icon, saying it was what stirred her to life. Whatever she was—had been—he'd given that thing to Senna, had drawn this danger to the wards' very door. "Can I have your icon back?" She frowned at him. He wanted to pull the chain from where it hung about her neck, but his hands— "I'm sorry, I'll get you a new one," he promised wildly.

Julia appeared, bleary-eyed, behind Senna. "What's happened?"

"It's all right now," he said, relieved as Senna pulled the chain over her head. He plucked it from where it dangled from her fingers, careful not to get blood on her. "Keep the door shut."

Julia shoved her dark hair back. "Why—"

"Please. Wait. Keep them inside, all right?"

She opened her mouth to argue but glanced down at what was visible of him and pressed her lips in a line. She nodded.

He didn't wait to watch them shut the door and turned back to the hall, praying that they'd be patient until someone came, that they wouldn't see this—or more of this. He felt sick, realizing that his sandals and leggings were as covered with blood as his hands.

Renz lay halfway into Milo's cell. Milo rushed over and crouched awkwardly over the other boy.

"Don't—" Renz shivered out. But his eyes, red-rimmed, pleaded.

His bleeding seemed to have slowed. "I'm going to get help." Milo gripped the doorway, careful as he stood not to slip in the mess of blood and egg over the tiles. He didn't let himself look back down the hall at the other figure on the floor.

They needed a doctor. To send for Renz' family. And he needed to make a very different report than he'd been planning just minutes ago.

Just minutes ago, she'd been standing before him. Because he'd woken her, she'd said.

He didn't stop to knock at Storica Lucca's cell or any other templar's. He ran through four more corridors until he arrived at the offices of the holy guard, outside Primo Sanct's chambers.

The guard seemed convened for some meeting, and a crowd of bright uniforms and stern faces stood before Milo as he thrust out the bloody chain and informed them Renz had been injured. "And there's—a body."

A guard ran a hand down his face. "Another one?"

"Two in one night," another said, shaking his head and shifting his hand to his sword's pommel. "First the general, and now?"

Milo didn't know how to explain, not while Renz needed help. He hurriedly led them to the hall outside the nido to tend to Renz, and to show them Gia. Two guards carried Renz away. Another fetched Primo Sanct, who came down the hall, white robe churning above his hurried steps like a wave rushing in. The head templar stopped and raised a fist to his lips. He stared at Gia's form laid out as if looking from a great distance to the bottom of a deep well.

Milo attempted to explain. "She was a statue. Before. She—it—" Primo Sanct knelt beside Gia. Stray blood still shining on the tiles marred his robe. Milo began to tap at his own icon, tucked into his tunic, but his finger was sticky upon the fabric. The guards turned to Milo, while Primo Sanct didn't lift his eyes from the girl. "She's the one who's been killing the templars, but I—" Pressure built up within him so much, he felt as if he were the one turned to stone. So many pairs of eyes were trained on him, serious and incredulous. He swallowed. "I killed her."

He'd killed a *sanct*. He'd been thinking of the trouble he'd be in for not reporting the missing statue, but what kind of consequences might there be for *that*? Not only from the templars but from Magna Mater herself?

Primo Sanct stood. "Remove yourself, boy."

Milo didn't argue.

A guard told him to stay in his chamber and shut the door on the blood and mess and the body. Statue. Gia.

Milo sank to the floor just inside, the stone beneath already a mess of Renz's blood, and listened to their low voices. Even Primo Sanct's dropped to a hush. Eventually, their talk was joined by scrapes and grunts. They were taking her away.

He had to get the blood off himself. He tugged loose the laces of one sleeve, and then the other—

The chisel slid down and caught against his hand. He'd forgotten all about it. Did it even matter now? He laid it on his little table and stripped off his ruined tunic. Using the clean part and the bit of stale water left in his pitcher, he wiped away as much blood as he could, scrubbed at his sandals and the smears on the floor, then changed into his other tunic and leggings.

He sat on the edge of his narrow bed, rubbing his thumb back and forth over the wool blanket until it went numb. What would happen now? To him? To the city?

His door swung open, scattering his thoughts. Milo shot to his feet and slid in front of his desk and the chisel. He didn't need to give the templars another reason to throw him out on top of the sanct he'd just murdered.

One of the holy guards filled the doorway.

"I'm sorry," Milo blurted, but the man didn't want to hear it, only to interrogate him about what he'd seen, when the statue had disappeared from the hill, what it had done.

Primo Sanct came up beside the guard, fixing his eyes on Milo with a piercing curiosity. "Did she say anything?"

Milo fought the urge to drop his gaze. Primo Sanct had spoken to him personally maybe once or twice in his life, but Milo didn't need to make himself look any guiltier. "Only that she wanted the icon I found. I think it must have some power—"

"All power flows from Magna Mater through her humble pontefice." Primo Sanct pressed his hands to his chest. His lip curled. "Not trinkets. These are lies from an evil spirit trying to lead you astray."

"Then why did the sanct awaken?" And why on Magna Mater's good earth was Milo questioning his head templar?

Primo Sanct sounded truly pained when he said, "That was no sanct."

No, she couldn't have been, not attacking templars. And the general, they'd said—the head of Trestatto's militia. Milo should listen to Primo Sanct, it must have been the spirit of some monster trapped inside the statue or possessing it.

A flash of Gia's eyes staring out from her dark mask passed through his mind. Her mouth shouting about stars. Her warm hand taking his and not letting go. She hadn't seemed like an evil spirit that night.

And what did that say about him, then? That he'd liked her? That he'd been glad to dance with her and might have liked to do more? That while he should have been worrying about the missing statue, he hadn't seen whatever had been hurting the city was right before him?

Primo Sanct broke him from this reverie, bracing him by the shoulders. "Your faith must be stronger." His fingers dug into Milo's biceps with a punishing grip. "Do not spread whatever lies this evil thing told you, it would only threaten others' trust in Magna Mater."

"I promise." Milo nodded. "To do better."

Primo Sanct's tone softened, and he gave Milo an encouraging shake. "You did well. You protected the temple." He dropped his hands and turned away, muttering to the guard, "He doesn't know anything worthwhile."

The guard loomed over Milo. "Don't leave the temple." He firmly shut the door.

Milo sank back onto the bed and dropped his head into his hands as if they could make a crown to hold in all his worry. Some protector he was. He wanted to keep the truth of the temple close to his heart, but he knew Gia had been after the icon, and somehow Milo had used its power to free whatever she was. The weight of four lives settled on his shoulders like a heavy black cloak. If he hadn't run off that night, if she'd seen he didn't have that copper icon on him—she would have killed him, too.

Instead, he had ended her. He'd wished so many times to learn her history, and, like a miracle, his sanct had lived and breathed. Her eyes had glittered as she'd told him her name. Her body had softened from stone for him to hold in his arms a fleeting moment. And he'd destroyed her.

For one reason or another he deserved to be expelled from the temple. He'd made no omelia. He hadn't even spoken out about what he knew. Too afraid for himself. Too sure he could find the answer, that he had anything worthwhile to offer. The carving he'd found must simply have been a warning, telling how to use the chisel—perhaps any iron, even—to stop a statue that came to life like Gia had.

Primo Sanct was right. He knew nothing. He'd misunderstood everything.

It was dark, and he was disoriented, waking from a dream of the carnival. He was back at the river, and Gia was prying stars from the sky with her sword. She was leaving the sky rent and bleeding, and Milo sensed with a brewing dread that as she pulled them down one by one, the whole thing would crash upon them.

It took him a moment to register the crying coming from down the hall. He lit one of the leftover stubs he'd collected from storicas' and templars' rooms and went to check on the nido. Someone had cleaned the hall floor, though in the rippling firelight Milo couldn't tell if a stain would shadow the tiles in the morning. He'd stayed in his room all day worrying and falling into a fitful sleep, but heard the wards as they went to dinner, chattering happily. Now, as he swung the nido's door open, the crying turned into a shriek. Senna.

Gregorio leaped from his cot to stand before the door, shoulders tensed until he took in Milo.

Milo looked about the chamber, dark and full of arguments and sniffling. "What is it?"

"The lamp went out," Gregorio said quickly. "And Senna's scared because it's dark, but Julia says we must keep the door closed. In case whatever it was comes back."

The paleness under the boy's freckles told Milo perhaps someone other than only Senna was worried. Milo gave his shoulder a squeeze. "It's all right. Let me see to the light."

He carried the candle, cupping its flame, to the lamp at the window. There was still oil, the twist of wick had just broken off. He tugged the cloth out and held his candle close until it caught. The light crawled dimly over the walls and beds. "There now. I'm sorry that you were scared today. Everything is all right. Nothing bad can get you here."

Julia, sitting up in bed, frowned. "But you were hurt."

"No, I'm all right, see?" For now, at least.

"I'm still scared," Senna shuddered out through her tears. "What if the monsters get in? Please stay. Tell us a story."

Milo found he couldn't begin to grasp the threads of any story just then. What tale could he tell them more than that he was fine and everything would be fine? His head ached. His arm was sore. His stomach was beginning to claw at him. "I can't tonight. But I can stay. I'll sleep in front of the door, so you'll know nothing bad can reach you. Now try to sleep. We've taken care of it. The danger is gone."

What had stalked through the city right to their door was dead. The only killer here now was him. He lifted the candle close and blew out the flame.

CHAPTER TWELVE

SANCTUM

Magna chased one of the great old monsters into a cave, though her sisters called her back. She was lost for three days inside its dark reaches. She carved her own way out to the top of a hillside at last and told her elder sisters of her struggles against the beast she left buried under the immeasurable weight of the mountain.

—The Book of Invocations

Gia

She was surprised not to be dead.

Gia wasn't sure, at first. How was she to know what death felt like? As she fell into the stone for what she thought was the last time, her foggy senses perceived men's voices, their words halfway stuck in the sludge of stone that trapped her. Men standing over her—lifting her—touching her like a thing.

And *him*.

Before the invocation claimed her mind completely, she knew she was inside that same sanctum of his, under that carved grid ceiling. She strained to listen for more voices, plans, but her mind sank down too far within itself. And she didn't like remembering. She'd been a fool rushing into this place, sure she would find the icon—if not a chance to strike the man she truly wanted dead. Slipping from the great sanctuary had been easy; she still knew the temple, and she'd stuck to the unguarded corridors. That's where she'd found that snobbish boy, dealt with easily enough, and Milo—who was not. She'd been so focused on the chain she could see peeking from his tunic, she hadn't even seen him going for a blade. And to be honest, she hadn't expected him to have a weapon on him or use one against her. Certainly not her own cursed, cast-off dagger.

But decisions were like taking a knife to the world. Cutting away what you didn't choose. She'd decided to enter the temple, so there was no use grasping at other possibilities like so much spilled blood.

Like Milo, even when he'd bested her. As if he could undo his own action. As if anyone could heal what this corrupt world broke.

She was remembering again. The look in his eyes. The slick feel of his fingers over her skin, in her blood. His whispered apology like a sincere prayer.

Falling fully into the stone, she thought that when she woke it would not be for long.

Going by moonrise the past few nights, it must have been near midnight when her consciousness lifted to the sight of Ennio sitting over her.

The stone was all that stopped her trembling. And soon it softened. For once, she wished it would keep her, that she could hide within its strength, even as it consumed her. Her terror of being in Ennio's power sparked into anger, driving her to find the strength to rise, to strike at him. To do anything but provide a show of her gasping once more for breath, for a life he'd stolen, a life that would only escape his control now as she died.

When the stone receded fully, she was charged and ready to defy him in any small way. Ready to deny the pain she knew would come, ready to wear a warrior's face to mask her fear. Her limbs obeyed her—she wouldn't think of when her air would fail her—she rose.

She stood over Ennio.

He gazed at her, his pensive look breaking into one of mild surprise, wide jaw slackening, thick brows arcing, lifting that blade set upon the circlet on his head. The lamplight cast a sheen over his silk nightrobe and broad shoulders. His large carved chair was drawn away from the massive desk along one side of the room, so he could view her there on the plush red rug. Enjoy seeing her in her defeat. Her eyes darted about. The room was full of lamps, a candle near at hand on the desk, and papers, a wax seal—a dagger.

She was about to lunge for it when it occurred to her the pain hadn't yet struck. She was breathing quickly, but easily. Her fingers brushed tentatively across her throat. She could feel sticky flakes of blood, but her skin was whole.

She was surprised, once again, to not be dead.

For now.

"Gia," Ennio breathed in surprise. There were no guards. Her limbs tingled with knowing she was finally near enough to strike.

She knew his power if she made a move and was too slow.

He cocked an eyebrow. "I should have known you were too strong to be ended so easily."

A part of herself remained focused on the dagger. "Will you use your invocations against me now? Break my bones? Make the earth swallow me?"

"A lot has changed." His wry, wistful look dissolved into that wide smile of his. His voice dropped to a gravelly rumble. "But some things never do." He gestured between them, and left his hand outstretched, as if to pull her to him.

No, she had always been angry and destructive. And he'd always been horrible. She had only been too starved for affection to know. A hungry wolf drawn to food offered by a human, not realizing he was a dangerous hunter. Everything in her recoiled.

"Some things should," she told him. "Like you." She was careful not to move too fast, and set him acting against her, but her hands clenched. "Dead instead of alive."

He folded his hands in his lap. "I never wanted you to become this. I wanted you by my side."

Still lying, centuries on. And still sitting there, unworried about her threats, as if he hadn't made her into a killer. As if he were the one hardened into stone.

Too calm, too assured. Her nails bit into her palms. She wanted to make that facade crumble. Years of needling her sister had taught her how to verbally provoke. "You wanted Lena's crown. And you didn't get it."

Ennio sighed through his nose. He shook his head, brow drawing in almost a wince. "When you turned on me, I couldn't bear to look upon you. You were released on Alta's hill?"

She only glared. He wouldn't get anything from her again.

A pulse ticked in his jaw, and he went on, his voice spread thickly over his words. "If you wouldn't stand with me, I wanted you to stand out there alone. Forgotten. I wanted the rains to pelt you and the earth to swallow you up. I wanted it to erase your betrayal."

Her stomach flipped, like a griddle cake. Spitting hot oil. "*My* betrayal? You turned me into a statue."

Ennio was all coolness. He sat back in his chair, draping an elbow over one arm. "I sent you home."

"Because I reminded you of how you usurped my sister. Do you actually feel some shame for that?"

"No. It was necessary." He jutted his jaw up at her. "See how Trestatto is still strong, all this time later? Adalena would have destroyed us."

"You destroyed us! Or what do you call my sister outside like that? What do you call the hundreds trapped in stone? Or the people your guards harass at your gates—"

"They're not true Trestattans. I keep Trestatto safe. You know nothing of what challenges we've weathered while I've guided this city. The sacrifices I have made." His hand gripped the arm of his chair. "I gave all my capacity as templar to the invocation that protects us. Vassilis discovered how Magna tied her god-power so closely to the gifts she gave humans, to the icon she forged for us to call upon her, to the chisel that we used to carve the prayer, that we could wrest an invocation from her to bind all her power in one great working. So, no," he said, with a tone of condescension he'd never used with her before, "no more beasts or earthquakes, only year after year of standing stalwart for every child of Trestatto." She gaped at him, but he went on, nostrils flared. "Your sister was weak and letting our power crumble.

I had to take it. The strongest deserve to rule. They need to rule."

She'd lost everything to him, and he spoke of his sacrifice? He thought himself noble for giving up his power when he was trapping others so he could play the immortal protector?

But what he was saying meant he couldn't call on Magna to smite Gia where she stood. Couldn't use his blood to drive god-power against her and fracture her bones. She could fight him on equal footing.

She drew herself tall, triumph puffing out her chest. "You've grown forgetful in your old age." The taunt tasted good on her tongue, bright and acid. "For me, your betrayal is fresh. You couldn't even take this city by proper force. You sneaked around with the ceremony and the invocation."

His mouth fell open and his eyes flashed dangerously.

She swallowed painfully. "With me." He may have stuck her on that block of stone up the hill, but he'd placed himself upon a much higher pedestal, and she was going to kick it over. Take him down to his true height. "You have everyone believing you're nearly a god, but I know what you really are. What kind of man you are."

He shook his head, one fist balled inside the other hand, gaze cast away. Denying her words. "I was the only one strong enough to save Trestatto," he said. "You were my only weakness." He brought his gaze back to her—hunting for something, his thumb brushing along his wrist. "My one regret."

Under his probing look, her body churned up a confusion of her old attraction and growing revulsion.

"And now," he said, "what you've managed, to come back as far as this—" He inclined his head as if to acknowledge some accomplishment of hers. His lips crooked in a smile. "You must be meant to return to me. You will always have a place here at the temple. At my side."

A nest of serpents writhed in her belly. The brush of a chimera's bat wings prickled the back of her neck. She had seen a home for herself here once. He had made her feel that. He had used that. How dare he speak to her now like he hadn't ruined everything? Ruined her?

She grabbed the dagger.

It took only a moment, a hand braced on the arm of his chair, a thrust of the ornate, slender thing. "I'm not yours anymore," she told him through her teeth.

So long—for days, for centuries—she'd seethed for revenge. Knowing it could not fix things but wanting to break everything left standing around her as much as she'd broken.

He didn't flinch. She looked to where blade had slashed through his robe—but left his skin unmarked.

He wasn't merely immortal. He was invulnerable. Unbreakable as any sanct.

Ennio glanced down at the dagger tangled in fabric, and back to Gia, his face near. "Little Gia. So prickly." His cheek twitched faintly—the hint of irritation, or another smile? "As you've shown us this week. I understand you. I've always understood." He laid his hand upon hers. His voice was all honey and mica, rich with enticement. His thumb stroked her wrist. "To want something so badly. Sometimes people get hurt in the pursuit. Everything I've done was to secure protection for my city. And if you pledge to me, a few dead are nothing." He reached with his other hand to cup her jaw.

She trembled. They were alike. She had never hated herself more.

And he was right—things had changed. He was different. His gold eyes watched her, keen as always, but like a bird's. Somehow apart from her in a way he'd never been before, even when he lied to her, manipulated her. What had he done to himself?

A spike of fear traveled from his unharmed chest, through her arm, to her racing heart.

Decisions were like strikes of a blade, and she cut quickly. "There are going to be a lot more dead, I can promise you that." Finally, doubt seeded in his eyes. He grabbed her face hard now, his other hand leaving hers to reach for the knife.

Gia wrenched herself free, from the something too ancient to be fully human, and stumbled back as he rose, fuming. She made to run past him, and he caught her by the hair. It was all she could do to kick the chair over, knocking Ennio to the floor.

There was no point in tackling him. She couldn't kill him.

But she could still punish him.

His power lay now with the people he'd fooled into thinking him a savior. If her vengeance would only rebound off him, then let them see where her blades landed—she could still tear his life apart. Smash all his toys and playthings. Find out how he liked being prince of a ruined world.

One that saw him for what he truly was. "When your people keep dying, how long before their faith in you breaks?" she spat, charging out the door.

She kept the knife.

No one stood watch in the hall. Only when she rounded the corner did his voice rise, with a strangle, calling for the guards. Her threat struck true. He was afraid of her pulling down his mask to show everyone—even himself—the man underneath.

She slipped away ahead of the guards, through the darkened

temple. She traveled away from Ennio's sanctum, turning back when boots sounded too near, until she found a quiet hall of closed doors.

Her lips pressed together hard. This wasn't vengeance anymore. She had to become a beast to prevent the real monster from playing god. Kill Ennio's followers and the city's belief in him would die.

She chose a door and kicked it open.

The templar had been asleep in bed. She gave him just enough time to cry out before using Ennio's dagger to silence him forever.

As she retreated from his chamber the next door opened. A dark face looked out.

Gia let the hall's lone lit torch set the blood on the dagger glistening. "See how Ennio failed to protect him." The man's eyes widened. "And you." She whipped her fist around and knocked him out.

She left the witness and launched herself down the next hall. Her boot planted against the wood of another door. Another templar anointed the dagger with his blood because it could not taste Ennio's. Another man, hearing the noise, swung open his chamber door and took two rapid steps her way. She threw her forearm up into his neck and rammed him back against the door, lifted the dagger, and traced it down the side of his face. It bristled against the gasping templar's stubble as she whispered, "Ask Ennio why he let this happen if he's so holy." When the man's face went slack and he fell against her, she let him drop.

Shadows and slashes. More cries in the night, more warnings. She wrote her message in the blood of Ennio's followers, leaving a living witness to each death to bear her message to the rest in the morning. Ennio could not protect them. His doctrine was blasphemy. He was a fraud.

A guard caught sight of her and gave chase. She fled and hid until he'd lost her scent. Then she sprinted away to her next victim, setting the torchlight dancing in her wake.

She'd dispatched half a dozen and was barreling toward another door when her surroundings brought her up short. This was where she'd been struck down the previous morning.

This was the hall where the children slept.

She rocked back on her heels. There was no message for her to leave at this door.

Yet the urge to keep running prodded, not from any guard but from the realization of what she'd done. Worse—she had carried out her rampage nearly to morning, and moonset. She was out of time. She could not be caught out as a statue again and brought back to Ennio.

She turned to the other side of the hall, where another door waited.

This was also where Milo slept.

She thought of him offering sanctuary to the boy who'd bullied him at the carnival, even as she turned her blade toward him. She thought of the regret in his eyes when he thought she'd died.

After he'd cut her throat.

Gia squeezed the handle of her knife and made a choice.

CHAPTER THIRTEEN

ILLUMINATED

Stregna welcomes offerings of bells and honey and incense and song. Any breath bearing true faith will stir Lady Epiphany to extend her grace.

—The Book of Invocations

Milo

Milo woke up on the cold hard tiles of the nido when it was still dark. He couldn't stay, couldn't face anyone when they woke. Besides, his stomach was begging him to break his fast. He slipped the cold stub of candle rolling about beside him into his pocket and shoved off the floor, wincing as his limbs let him know what they thought of him sleeping on the ground.

He went to the kitchens and scoured his hands of the lingering rust color around his nails. By the time he was finishing some leftover bread and sausage, a few apprentice templars arrived to make the day's bread and water down wine to set out in the dining hall. They went about their work silently, instead of with their normal chatter, and Olivia jerked sharply when Milo caught the pitcher she'd almost knocked over, splashing red wine upon the scrubbed table. She sopped it up with a cloth, the pinch of her face more like fear than frustration. Milo's shoulders tightened. Had they already heard what he'd done? That he was the one who had ignited the evil in the city, and killed what had once been a sanct?

It was only worse at the funeral for Horace and Adrian that morning. Holy guards made rounds through the temple's halls, startling everyone as they walked to the great sanctuary. The guard had never kept active watch like this inside the building—not until Milo had drawn a murderer to it. An air of panic choked the halls like the thick smoke of censers, and, for once, everyone was avoiding Milo's gaze instead of the other way around. He slipped behind the rose granite columns, hoping to take his place unnoticed, but Storica Lucca waved him over to where he sat among the other temple officials and well-dressed merchants and landowners near the altar.

The storica reached out and gripped Milo's hand. "Glad to see you're safe."

"You heard?" He ducked his head. "Is Renz—" His voice strangled.

Storica Lucca tugged at him to sit. "Renz is all right. His parents fetched him home."

Relief drenched Milo like cool water. His actions hadn't taken a fourth life. "Storica, I still don't understand what she was—"

The funeral rites began, and the storica hushed him. "The

less said about what happened the better."

Milo nodded but slouched down on the bench. Everyone already seemed to know he was responsible for the deaths they were mourning today.

Templar Tadeo finished reading the opening prayers and walked away from the stone altar with a slight limp.

Milo whispered to Storica Lucca, "What happened to Templar Tadeo?" He frowned. Another templar, sitting in his stone seat at the front of the chamber, bore a plaster bandage upon his brow. Several seats beside him were empty. Milo's spine stiffened. Had Gia attacked others in the temple before Renz? "Did—whatever the evil was—did she—"

The storica only shushed him. "Let's leave such matters to the templars."

But where *were* the templars?

Primo Sanct rose from his stone chair to grasp Tadeo's hand, before addressing the gathering. He waited for a moment, blanch-white hands clasped together tightly, letting the silence in the chamber brew. "It is a sad time when we must say good-bye. I have lived through many sad times, said many goodbyes. What sustains me is the knowledge that everyone I've seen pass back to Magna Mater's earth was given the opportunity to live upon the rock of our faith, to know the great mother's love, to be bound to her power."

Primo Sanct paced to one side of the altar. "In that power we can never doubt. When the specter of doubt stands before us, with all its taunts—" He broke off, voice twisting with regret. "When we encounter evil trespassing in our midst, it is our duty to the goddess to strengthen our faith." He paced back and pressed his palms to the altar, leaning forward. His gaze fell on Milo, his expression turning more severe. "Only the weak surrender to such a test. Magna Mater will never falter, never flee like lesser gods. My children, these evil acts serve to remind us how she holds off such harm from us, that others with lesser faith face."

Templar Tadeo nodded emphatically, as did other templars, and many in the assembly. The templar with the bandage, however, was gazing steadfastly away from the altar.

Unease prickled at the back of Milo's neck. Primo Sanct's words were strident but didn't make sense. Evil had penetrated the inviolate city. This very temple. Even more had been injured—or worse—than the two these funeral rites were for. Why wasn't anyone acknowledging what had happened?

He couldn't help asking his mentor, "Isn't it the duty of the storicas to study how this might—"

Storica Lucca cleared his throat, interrupting. He murmured, "We serve the templars." The V appeared between his brows and his jaw trembled. "I cannot determine apprenticeships, but for a short time more I can still protect you." He dropped his gaze and shifted in his seat.

Milo pushed his hair back. Perhaps entertaining these questions only proved his own failings. Perhaps he'd been right— by escaping from among the faithless, he'd brought evil inside the city.

Or maybe the problem wasn't him at all. Maybe something was wrong with the temple. With its teachings.

Dread kneaded through his chest as he looked back to Primo Sanct expounding at the altar.

The head templar's voice rang out, echoing off the arched ceiling and the walls covered with frescoes of the sancts and mosaics of Orabellia's pastures and mountains. "Trestatto is strong. Ever strong. Each of us serves it in the militia. Each of us guards it with our iron faith. We must draw on the strength of Magna Mater to fight, as Templar Horace fought." He raised one hand toward the back of the sanctuary, toward the doors and the steps beyond. "Laying down his life right there as Adalena did." He let his hand drift over the crowd, as if he could gather the hundreds up in one sweep of his robed arm. People leaned forward, ready to be reaped by his words.

Milo gripped the edge of the bench, fighting the mild dizziness sweeping through him. The temple was everything. He needed it to be his rock. But his questions wouldn't stop. How could everyone act like nothing was wrong? Why was Primo Sanct telling them to?

"My children. We must be as unchanging as our mother's strength. The solemnities of this month will not be interrupted. We must ensure all visitors to our city learn the glory of Magna Mater as we acknowledge her greatest miracle on behalf of our city. We will say goodbye today to our friends, and, as they would wish, continue to prepare for the Ceremony of Dust, when we commit ourselves to our great mother."

As soon as the funeral ended, Storica Lucca set a long list of tasks for Milo to complete, pulling books and copying out pages upon pages. Milo buried himself in the distraction, in the clean parchment and neat black lines of text. In what would likely be one of his last days with the archives.

If Renz was apprenticed to the storicas and Milo to the militia or farm work, it was only fair. Today, he was grateful for whatever duties kept him busy, whatever staved off questions of faith and memories of blood rising between clutching fingers, and left him spent. He only returned to his residency hall long after dark, when the younger wards were all asleep. He dug out the candle stub from his pouch and held it to a wall torch so he'd have some light in his cell to prepare for bed. He felt as worn down as that nub of candle. He hoped he'd be too tired to dream this night.

The wick caught and flared. He cupped a hand before it as he walked to his cell door. When he opened it, the air sent the flame into a frantic dance, and he curled a hand around it again as soon as he'd pulled the door shut. He turned for his table, for his lamp, letting the candle carve out a circle of yellow light from the darkness. The arc of gold caught on an unexpected object. Gia's face loomed before Milo.

He knocked back against the door. The candle spilled its wax over his hand, and he only just caught himself from dropping it completely. His heart was clattering inside him faster than a chariot horse's racing hooves. Gia stayed motionless—her face carved of stone. He set the candle upon the table, and its light glinted on the shivering metal of the chisel he'd forgotten about.

He snatched it up and raised it between him and the statue.

His heartbeat thrummed a rhythm through him. *Not dead, not dead, not dead.* She'd died right before him. Yet here she stood, defiant, no longer laid out, arms at her sides, knife in one hand. He dared a closer look. Her throat curved smoothly under her soft jaw, her jutting chin.

She could come back. Somehow, even when slain. She was statue, then alive, statue again—

And here before him.

The simmering panic in the temple, the extra watch of the holy guard, the nervousness of the apprentices, the missing and injured templars—it all made sense now. The threat wasn't gone. It was here, immobilized in stone but ready to strike out again.

Had she come here still looking for the icon he'd taken from her hill? For revenge against him?

Only what made this can break them. His fingers tightened on the cool metal of the chisel. He raised it high. He would strike first. His work had uncovered the one thing that could end this nightmare for Trestatto, return the templars and citizens to safety. He'd awoken a monster but he would fix it. He would stand up to protect them. He would finally make a worthy offering.

He wouldn't even have to witness the fear in her face this time. See the light in her eyes die. Feel her warm blood go cold on his hands.

The candlelight wasn't much, but the dim still showed him his lie. Pulling along her cheeks, shaping her eyes—there was a tension born between bravery and fear. Subtler than most artists could catch in a statue carved by mortal hands. He'd studied people's expressions too carefully for too long to miss it.

It didn't matter. He needed to deal with her. Primo Sanct and his guard must be on watch for her—why not raise the alarm through the temple? All the unsettling questions from the funeral rushed back. Could Primo Sanct have his own reasons for hiding the truth of the threat?

Keeping the chisel ready, Milo held up the candle, illuminating Gia's face like a gilt manuscript. He stared longer than he'd studied any parchment. Why turn to stone? Why wait at his mercy?

Unless she couldn't control it—suddenly, her expression made sense to Milo. She knew she'd be trapped here before him. She'd known, and she'd stood in acceptance of it. Refusing to cower. Was there an appeal in that mix of boldness and surrender?

Too many questions. He'd thought he'd killed her, the act

done before he'd even realized what was happening. He could not knowingly choose to take her life now. He lowered his arm, let the chisel drop to his side. He knew he should report what he could not kill himself. He didn't. He stood there, soft, warm wax in one hand, ready to transform into fire and light and smoke, and the chisel in the other. Meant for breaking, the same tool could also write, could create words, work them from hard stone. Milo felt they needed less breaking and more words right now.

He used the candle to light the lamp, set down both candle and chisel, and sat on the bed to think. Rocking in place, he imagined what Val might say to him in this moment. "You have the monster that's been killing our people, and you decide not to destroy it? Not to call for help?" Before he could take any action, something began to happen. Gia began to change.

Color blushed across her deeply tanned olive skin. It seeped into her dark hair, mussed in her braid and in thick waves about her face. Her lips returned to that berry shade, her eyes that warm brown. Her tunic turned a red-orange along its drapes, like the sky at sunset when farmers set burns in their fields. Everything about her became softer, and present, and quick.

Milo jumped to his feet, feeling he was allowed a nameless grace to see the reversal of the loss he'd witnessed in the hallway the day before, stone breathing to vibrant life.

Her eyes sparked and her fingers twitched. Those wrapped around the hilt of her dagger held tight as she lifted it. Her gaze slid to the chisel laid on the table, and one side of her mouth rose in a pleased smile.

Milo wondered if he had misunderstood again and made a very grave mistake. "Maybe we should talk," he said, voice low.

Her elegant eyebrow arched. She spoke, but her words were

all challenge. "You killed me."

"You killed those men," he blurted in his defense. "And struck down Renz. And what did you do with my cat?" This was not going how Milo imagined. He was finding it hard to keep his thoughts straight.

Gia let the dagger drop and shrugged. "The cat followed me. It's around somewhere. Keeps me company when I—" She waved her hands and the knife vaguely. "Change."

"And you're not dead." He took a step nearer.

"No thanks to you. And now I—"

He cocked his head. "Do your injuries always heal when you return to your form as a statue?"

She frowned. "I hurt my ankle getting off the pedestal, but the next day it was fine." Bristling, she told him, "I've been a little busy running for my life, I haven't had a chance to think about—" She went slack and stared somewhere beyond Milo, mouth open, the dagger nearly dropping from her hand. "But that means—" She swallowed. A shiver of something like pain flashed across her face. "Lena."

He was trying to understand and leaned forward with interest. "Who?"

Gia lifted her arm straight out, meeting his chest with the dagger. She was all hardness once more. "I need that icon."

So that was what she was after. He eased back, afraid to move too quickly, afraid to set her off. "I don't have it."

Her voice had a sharp edge. "Stop lying to me."

He just needed to explain, to learn from her what was actually happening. Either she was an evil spirit taking over the form of a sanct, or something else entirely was going on. "I'm not. I want to talk. I promise, I'm a terrible liar." Val had always told him so.

"Yes, you are. So why are you still denying it to me?" Her words were alight with anger, like they were written on a page set to flame.

"Why do you want it, anyway? To wake other evil spirits?"

She broke into a laugh, and the dagger's point drifted farther from his chest. A pitying realization dawned in her eyes. "You think you know so much. You don't know anything." She said this last word through clenched teeth.

He wanted to understand. "I know a sanct would never kill—" She lifted the blade again, this time to his neck. She angled it, using its flat to tilt his chin up. Her eyes cut down from his, and Milo could only think she was considering doing to his throat what he'd done to hers.

He fought down a swallow. "I handed in the icon. Gave it to the holy guard. Primo Sanct will have it by now." If he hadn't tossed what he'd called a useless trinket out.

"Still lying." She drew the flat of the dagger down along his jaw, his neck, to his collarbone. She shifted one step nearer, almost as near as when they'd crashed together and erupted in blood. His heart thrummed, and he couldn't be sure if the thrill that coursed through him was fear or something else. She gave a little flick with the blade, and he thought she'd done it—but instead of blood, she drew the chain he wore from out of his tunic.

Her eyes flashed with satisfaction, locked on his old silver crescent. "This is the icon that woke me. This is what I need to save my sister."

He gulped a breath, still astonished to be alive. Did she mean another spirit? No, she'd said— "You can't mean—Adalena?"

CHAPTER FOURTEEN

BROKEN HISTORY

Fruitful invocations to Magna are pried and hoarded like jewels from the earth. From Alta, they flow like a stream that may be drawn from again and again. From Stregna, a trail of smoke, a scent of incense, a breeze we cannot see or know.

—The Book of Invocations

Gia

"I told you," she said, sliding the knife from the loop of chain with a *shink*, "you don't know anything. How could you, listening to all the lies of that templar of yours?" Lies she needed to cut through if she had any hope of gaining his help. She'd been forced to trust he wouldn't report her to Ennio when she'd found his room empty and changed back to stone. And now—she could rescue Lena. She could show everyone what Ennio had stolen and what he truly was. If she could convince this boy.

Milo's brows pressed together. "Primo Sanct? He lives to protect the city."

It wasn't going to be easy.

"That's what he's calling himself now." She rolled her eyes, took half a step back. "Alta's tits. He's just a man. Not a good one. And that knife of his" —she waved the dagger and held it up across her forehead— "that he's wearing like a crown. That's just his temple's icon. And that" —she pointed to his chest— "is the icon of Stregna's temple." Tarnished by the years, but no mistake. She'd skipped out on lessons with Stregna's templars often, but they'd taught her enough to recognize the power coming off it when Milo had woken her. "I knew it at once, hanging from your neck, even before I was fully free."

His hand drifted up to the silver crescent. "No, everyone wears these, or images of sancts—they're just reminders of faith."

She scoffed darkly. Ennio had created quite the little dominion for himself. "You gave some other icon to Ennio?"

Still looking a little lost, Milo nodded. "When I—" Guilt washed over his face, sitting so comfortably on his features she felt a tug of affinity for a moment. "When you changed."

She twisted her lips. "He's aware you know the truth, then. He'll take your life without a second thought." Milo needed to escape this temple as much as she did.

He barely seemed to notice her warning. Squinting, he murmured, "I thought it was the copper icon I found. On the hill. I thought that was what caused this." His fingers tapped the icon he wore, the one he'd actually used to channel Stregna's godpower and awaken Gia with his prayer. "I'd given it to one of the children. That's why I tried to stop you."

She'd been murdered over nothing. "You think I would attack a child?" If that's what he thought of her, she was never going to convince him. He probably thought she ate his cat.

He threw his palms up. "You attacked Renz!"

"Bullies should be ready to take care of themselves," she snapped, even as Lena's voice scolded in her ear, reminding her not to blow up. Gia choked down the urge to shout. She needed to explain and get him on her side. "You probably gave Alta's icon to Ennio if you found it at her temple. You're wearing Stregna's."

He was still two steps behind. "Stregna?" He shook his head. "What are you talking about?"

She clenched her teeth. Ennio had distorted Lena's history, but he'd destroyed that of her goddess, Alta, and Stregna. Wiped them from people's memories and prayers. "Who do you think the other two temples were built in honor of?"

"The other goddesses fled during the battle before the Great Miracle. They were unworthy." Milo spoke as if reciting, gaze drifting to the side. She wanted to take whatever scroll he had read that in and rip it to shreds.

She got in his face so he couldn't evade her. "That's the story of a blasphemer. I'm trying to tell you the truth."

His eyes fixed on her. There was such intensity in them, she began to understand why he let their gaze fall away more often than not. "So tell me your story." His voice was low and grave. "Maybe start with how those templars ended up dead."

She struck back fast. "Because we are at war!"

The crease appeared between his brows. "There hasn't been war in Trestatto for centuries. Our strength grants us peace."

"This isn't peace." He needed to listen, not quote from books Ennio had dictated. She gave his chest a shove, and his eyes widened again. "Maybe it seems that way to you because your templar says you won. To me, the war he started only just began. His temple stood against the city, and we lost, we all lost, so much. Ennio betrayed——" Her voice wavered dangerously. Milo reached out toward her elbow—she took a quick step back before realizing he was only offering a steadying hand. She frowned and rushed on. "The principessa."

Milo drew his hand away quickly, to rub it behind his neck. "The records state she was protecting the temple."

Gia shook her head. "She was trying to stop Ennio. The curse caught her before she reached his doors." Her fingers tightened on the dagger as she remembered watching helplessly.

He dropped his hand. "Why would they fight? Why would Primo Sanct go against the principessa? And what curse?"

"Because he desires power. Control over the city—over everything. He doesn't care who he hurts to get it. He justified it with the rising beast attacks and threatening empires, but he thought Lena weak, so he turned her and everyone who fought for her to stone."

Milo kept looking at her, or rather just to the side of her, like she was speaking another language. "The statues were created by Magna Mater. A miracle." His voice made it sound like something precious, something he was just realizing was fragile.

Gia wanted to smash it.

She thumped her free hand to her breastbone. "Not a statue. A person. Trapped. Just like every other statue out there. Your exalted principessa."

He blinked and dipped his head toward her questioningly. "Your sister?"

"Turned to stone." It was as if a block of it sat on her chest.

"I thought she was good as dead." She cleared her throat, and growled, "On display out there like a pincushion. I was fighting for her sake! But if she can recover, like I did—" If there was any chance, she had to bring Lena back. The idea of facing her sent a shiver through Gia she hoped this boy didn't see. He'd think even worse of her if he knew she'd betrayed the adored principessa.

But Milo was tapping away at the icon, thinking. "You'd have to time it just right. All those wounds and weapons. She wouldn't last long."

He was right. With a strangle, she said, "I'll need help." Milo stilled and shifted nearer, though he did not reach out a hand this time. "With the timing and getting her to safety—I don't know where." She didn't know this city anymore, didn't have a place in it at all. She had to figure it out for Lena. She looked to the boy before her. She needed to win Milo as her ally. "You have to believe me. Or at least in something more than Ennio. You prayed to Stregna. You must have faith—"

Doubt shadowed his eyes and his lips gently pursed. "I don't know—"

"There's so much Ennio erased." Her voice rose, almost to breaking, and the candle and lamp on Milo's table flickered. She felt as if she were sheltering a small candle within herself, all that remained of everything she'd lost—temples and hymns and people. She was the only one who remembered. And she was likely to smother it, as with her dark actions the previous night. But if she shared it again, Milo could help her grow the flame. "Three goddesses," she said in a rush. "Three icons—"

His brows flicked up. "Three crescents?"

She nodded. "To channel power granted from their patron gods. To invocations either carved or said or sung. Blade of iron, which Ennio's made into a mockery of a crown. Wave of copper, Lena's icon, which could be the one you found in Alta's temple's ruins. Moon of silver—" She grabbed the crescent where it hung against his chest. He leaned nearer again, and she appealed directly into his open gaze. "You have her icon! If you don't believe, where did you even get it?"

The curiosity brewing in his eyes died. His face went blank. "My mother." He didn't pull away, but his throat bobbed, and he cast his gaze aside. "You think one of these gods who forsook Trestatto can wake Adalena?"

"Forsook?" Her fingers pinched white upon the tarnished silver. "They didn't go anywhere. The goddesses can always be called upon. Even without an icon, you can always look to them for strength or assurance." Magna had helped her find her footing when she couldn't anywhere else. This temple had been a place that meant something to Gia—until Ennio twisted it all into something ugly. She had to get back what had been lost. "You must have prayed to Stregna, and she answered your prayer."

"I wouldn't say a rash of murders was exactly the answer to my prayers," Milo said darkly.

She dropped the icon. Ennio had twisted her into something ugly, too. She'd visited death through Magna's temple.

She was no one's answered prayer. She was a nightmare.

"What did you pray for?" she rasped. What she'd done through the halls of the temple the night before had been necessary. Righteous. It threatened to set her trembling. She'd lost so much; she feared she could be losing herself as well.

"Bravery." Milo gave a half smile that didn't curl at the edges or reach his eyes, which still avoided hers. "The strength to stand forth and do the right thing."

She thought of how he'd stepped before her, weaponless, because he thought she was going after a child. How she'd betrayed Lena, worse than anything Ennio had done. "Then no," she said, voice thick. "You certainly didn't get that." He practically flinched away from her, and she stepped back and tried to shrug off the moment. "Stregna wasn't said to be a trickster god, but she's the most mysterious of the Three Sisters. Stregna the Unseen, Lady Epiphany, goddess of inspiration. All transcendence and smoke."

She dropped her eyes to the knife still in her hands, balancing its hilt between her index finger and thumb. "But if we can wake Lena, she'll fix things. She can always get people to listen, to pay attention."

He perked up at this. "I've read something about that." Still clinging to his books. "About her last birthday celebration when she turned twenty. Shining like a torch."

The blade stilled in her hand. "What?"

His voice shifted, like he was reciting again. "Drawing people in or casting them in shadow."

"You read this?" She looked up at him. "Where did you read this?"

"A firsthand account, someone who was there—" His gaze came up to catch on hers, and his words broke off as he realized. For a moment they stared at each other, both horrified.

Her voice dropped low, just as deadly as when she'd accused this boy of murdering her. "You read my diary."

His eyes flared. "It was only recopied in another history?"

She slammed the knife into the table at her side. "That doesn't make it any better." This was hopeless. No one would help her. She was alone. "You still don't see."

"This is what storicas do! And I want to understand, but this is—everything I believe." He shoved both hands through his hair. "There are questions I can't answer, but Primo Sanct is our savior. My savior. This temple took me in when I had nothing."

She clenched her teeth and muttered, "Yes, he's your savior. If I hadn't let him distract me at the carnival, I would have taken that icon and killed you then and there like I'd planned."

Milo threw his hands in the air, eyes wide. "And I should believe you! Who admits she would gladly murder me, who tells me none of it is true, that it's all some curse the holiest man I know somehow managed to place on half the city? That it's all lies? The sancts, the historical records—"

She snapped then. "It's not history, it's my life, and I'm telling you what happened. What that man did to me. What he's still doing to us." Her voice vibrated with the emotion she couldn't hold back. It shivered through her words like light along a blade in early morning.

He dropped his hands. Made himself meet her gaze. Something looked broken in his eyes, and she felt a pinch in her chest, almost sorry to be the one who had caused that.

But she hadn't. Ennio did.

Milo blinked away the fissure in his eyes, frowned seriously, then nodded. "All right."

Her eyebrows drew together. "All right?"

He nodded again, although he looked a bit queasy. "If anyone in this temple is going to break faith, I suppose it was meant to be me." He blew out a breath. "I can take you someplace safe. Somewhere to bring your sister. First, we must get you past the guards as quietly as possible. If I can do it without the temple knowing, I'm coming back."

She shook her head. "You can't trust Ennio. I've made that mistake."

"I can't just abandon my place here."

He still didn't trust her fully. Not as much as his records and histories. He was only helping her because Lena, beloved in this era as much as her own, was in need. Never mind that Gia was probably saving his life by warning him before Ennio could silence him.

Milo looked about the room, distracted, but with more intention than when his gaze would flit away from hers. "Much of the holy guard has been moved to posts inside the temple, but there will be at least one stationed at every door." He came away from the wall and scooped up some papers from his table.

She snorted. "I can get us past one."

He paused, squeezing by her in his tiny room. "You didn't get past me." As the back of her calves bumped against the bed, she was uncomfortably aware of how much space she was taking up, how close his face was to hers. Most infuriating, there was no boast written there, he was simply reminding her of this fact. Almost as if he was worried for her. Like he would protect her.

She'd give him facts. "Because I was already half-drowning in marble. The change is tied to the moon, and I didn't realize how late it'd gotten."

His brows rose as he added a pile of candle stubs to his laden arms. "The moon?"

"Which rises and sets later and later every day."

"Yes," he said flatly, "I know how the moon works."

"If you think some scholar, who probably spills more ink than blood, could best me under fair circumstances—"

He pressed his lips in a line, crouched, and began stuffing

everything he'd gathered into a worn sack plucked from a hook on the wall. "I'm trained with the militia."

She snorted again. "You've been hiding in this temple almost the entire time I was looking for you." She pushed the loose strands of her hair back, but they fell about her face again immediately.

Milo frowned, his face still downcast. "They know——" He glanced up at her, and his sharp gaze softened. His mouth was open a little, as if he'd forgotten what he was going to say. Gia was struck by the memory of him staring up at her when she first awoke, eyes full of reverence and longing. Milo swallowed and stood. "The temple can't spare its workers during Sancts' Month." He pulled a key from a small wooden box on the table and slipped it into his belt bag.

She brushed aside the memory. Milo's veneration was for a fiction of a goddess he'd been taught. He'd nearly destroyed her, and could barely tolerate her, only for Lena's sake. "What are you going to use to fight? That stick you almost tickled me with?"

A shadow of that guilt rippled over his face, and he grabbed the chisel from the table. "I'll take it. Just in case." He looked askance at the pile of rust-stained clothes under the table and tied shut his bag, then slung its strap over one shoulder.

Gia took the dagger. "I'll handle the one guard at the door."

She led the way out of the hall where she'd nearly bled to death and made for the nearest exit path she knew. Before she could turn down the next corridor, Milo gripped her shoulder and nudged her in the other direction. "Templars' cells," he whispered. "Sure to have guards posted." He guided her deeper into the temple. Past the entrance down to the catacombs, past the invoking room, now stuffed full of books. They backtracked and wound their way out the other side. It was like some intricate dance, the only music the occasional beat of the unseen guards' boots, as she and Milo shuffled away through dark, empty passageways.

Finally, they cut through the kitchen, barely lit in the cold blue of the moonlight through high windows, and Milo pointed to a small door.

She smiled, though it was nearly too dim for him to see—a smile between her and the dark. She was leaving the temple with what she came for, and more. Ennio couldn't control her. Neither his invocation nor this place could hold her. No more disquieting revelations from him or sneaking about. She and the truth would escape now with a swift, clean strike of her blade.

Milo let her go forward—thinking he could keep out of this if he stayed out of sight. He still didn't grasp it. This was war. If you didn't choose a side, a side would choose you.

And a choice was like a knife.

CHAPTER FIFTEEN

FALSE SKIES

Mortals possess only one life, and therefore invocations binding or breaking them to any state of being, which are but the expressions one life may take, hold their potential only once.

—The Book of Invocations

Milo

The opening door sliced a shard of moonlight into the kitchen. It rippled over Gia, and she seemed to come alive from the silent presence in the dark he'd led here. Before he knew it, she was upon the guard, who spun and knocked into her with his spear. Gia gripped the staff and shoved him back. She swung her feet out from under herself, kicking the guard and sending the spear clattering away as they stumbled into the garden.

They were two shadows grappling, punching, outlined in

blue. When the guard slammed Gia against the wall beside the door, Milo found himself stepping forward. He halted. If he intervened, if he revealed himself to be helping the temple's enemy, he could never return. Gia was already throwing herself back against the guard, landing a punch before he could draw his sword. He jabbed at her, and she took it across the cheek, then lunged at him. He dodged and grabbed her from behind—yanking her off her feet, choking her. A flash of teeth in moonlight, a grunt, and he dropped her. She hauled him over her shoulder, and he sprawled on the gravel, fighting for air. Gia bent over him. Her knife flashed as she drew it from her belt.

Milo ran for her. He pushed her back from the guard and danced away from her blade. He still wasn't entirely sure she wouldn't use it on him. "Stop, stop."

She stomped a boot into the guard's torso, keeping the dagger ready. "I need his sword."

He was breathing as hard as she was. "No more killing. Or I won't help you."

She huffed. "He's seen you now. If I leave him, you leave for good."

No time for that. He gripped her shoulder. "I know you've been hurt, but I promise not everyone in Trestatto is your enemy." Though the city would now see Milo as one for aiding Gia's escape. "Come on, I'll take you where you can have your pick of swords."

Recovering his breath, the guard scrabbled at Gia's calf. She growled and escaped his clutching, swung one powerful leg, and connected with his side. His gasp cut off ominously as he rolled to one side. Milo only waited to see he was still moving before tugging Gia away.

+ ✦ +

"Trestattans have gone soft. In my day, you had to be ready to fight for your life at any time. Now, with no beasts to worry about inside the city ever?" Gia made that cute little snort as Milo led her up the shadowy stairs to Val's rooms over the blacksmith's.

He wasn't sure about Gia's last comment, considering how she'd bitten that guard. It was true her training appeared as good as, if not better than, anyone's in the militia. He was a serviceable fighter, able to keep up in sparring matches after years of Val cajoling him into extra practice, but Gia fought with an intensity like unwatered wine, vivid and consuming. He pushed open the door and let her pass inside before shutting and barring it.

Val would still be at one of the sentry cabins out in the fields for another week, so they'd have her two little rooms to hide away in.

Because he could not go home. His stomach dropped. Either Gia was lying, and he'd just betrayed everything that ever sheltered him, or she was telling the truth, and things were much worse, and his home still lost to him.

His lack of sleep crashed over him like a wave, threatening to drag him into oblivion. He dug out a candle and fire starter from his bag and lit a lamp so Gia wouldn't trip over Val's minimal furniture. "We'll be safe here. The bed is through there." He pointed beyond a pretty curtain and considered the little space before him—a cupboard and small fireplace in addition to the chair, bench, and table. "The floor will do for me." He was tired enough.

Gia tugged the curtain an inch but didn't go into the small room. "Your friend won't mind?"

He rubbed a hand over his face and told the truth. "Val never minds the idea of a beautiful girl in her bed."

She stood there a moment, still, before pivoting and stalking toward him. "I'm not tired."

"How? Did Trestattans not sleep in your day either?"

She shrugged. "Maybe it's to do with the healing." She was close enough and the lamp was burning warmly enough for him to see a bruise clawing its way along her cheekbone where the guard had struck her, purple over flushed pink.

He clenched his hands to stop from reaching to cup that cheek. His instinct to care for the girl he'd tended so long only grew now that her boldness had come alive and Gia was her own living, breathing, passionate person. One who could clearly take care of herself. Who'd declared his lack of bravery obvious back in his cell, who'd called him too soft, who'd only accepted his help because he had the icon she needed and she was desperate. He flexed his hands and asked, "Think it works that way?"

"Don't really care. I don't intend to become a statue again." She held out her hand. "Give me Stregna's icon."

"I—" He never took it off. Still, he'd said he would help. It got stuck on one ear and pulled his hair, but he handed it to her. "Here."

She took it with both hands, holding the crescent balanced like a ship. The glint in her eyes softened into something more hopeful. She pressed them closed and turned away. After a few moments, she sighed and lowered the icon from where she'd held it before her heart. "Hopefully that did it. I'm least familiar with what invocations move Stregna best, all those hymns used to call her godpower through the icon, but if you managed, it can't be that hard." She set her jaw. "I have to know I'm really free, so I can focus on getting Lena out."

Milo's fingernails scratched over his collarbone. "Can I have it back?" Or would she want to keep it?

She wrinkled her nose. "I suppose." She returned it. "And you can take the bed. I won't sleep." She hugged her arms around herself.

"Go ahead." He grabbed a small pillow from the chair. "I promised you a choice of swords."

She narrowed her eyes at him but returned to the doorway and shoved aside the curtain. *"Oh."*

Milo knew he was past tired, that he needed to carve out a new word to describe the level of exhaustion claiming him, because he smiled as he folded himself down to the floor and fell asleep to the sounds of Gia drawing swords from Val's collection hung across her chamber wall.

He woke to Gia with her hands at his throat.

He bolted up, pressing shoulder to shoulder with her where she knelt. Her eyes were frantic. He looked to the door—still barred—and around the room, lit by sunlight sneaking around the shutters of the one window. "What is it?"

She said nothing, just clutched at him. At the icon about his neck once more. He grabbed at her hand, before she could choke him with the chain. Finally, one word slipped out on the breath she'd held. "Pray."

"I will. I am." Her eyes pleaded, her brows swooping in exquisite agony. He let her tug him nearer. "I am." He did, asking whatever goddess might listen to please stop what was happening to the girl before him.

Yet she paled, and her face stilled in an expression of pain and resignation, edged with fury. Milo hadn't realized how violent the change still was when her life wasn't bleeding away. He slipped his hand from hers and leaned back, careful not to let the icon's chain catch on her rigid fingers.

He wrapped his arms around his knees. "Well, I did say I didn't believe a goddess would have answered my prayers." He imagined invocations ringing with perfect faith resounding to a goddess's ears. Nothing like his fragile wishes. How could he and Gia rescue Adalena if it relied on them? Maybe Gia had been wrong about the icon, about him.

Maybe nothing she told him was true. He swallowed his worry and gazed at her face, that face he'd found so comforting and inspiring for years when he'd pilgrimage to her hill.

It was impossible to doubt her belief. She'd been desperate for him to use the icon. She didn't like being left powerless as a statue, even believing they were indestructible. That wasn't good enough for her. Simply to be safe.

He noticed a sword on the floor beside her stone form and thought of the chisel in his bag. She was vulnerable, and he determined to tell her about it when she . . . woke? It would be sort of like sleeping, being a statue? Then he realized she'd spoken of seeing him wear the icon, before her first waking, and it must not be like sleeping entirely; she was probably aware of what was going on around her even as a statue, and—oh, sancts—*he was still staring at her face.*

He ducked his head, casting his gaze to his intertwined fingers. "I'll wait for you to wake," he murmured, feeling nearly as foolish as when he tried to pray during rites. He pushed off the floor and went to see what Val had in her cupboard.

He spent the meager remainder of the morning questioning every decision he'd made in the last day. As the afternoon passed, he dug out the papers he'd brought from his cell—rough translations of the carving. He found a charcoal pencil among Val's things and began making notes of everything Gia had told him, goddesses' names, and the plot of the man he kept thinking of as the benevolent guardian of the city.

He'd agreed to bring Gia to safety, but he wanted answers, too. The part of him that had searched out every record of the sancts, that cataloged every detail of monsters, that tried again and again to write an omelia, that wanted to understand the world so he might find his place in it—that part needed answers. Everything he thought he knew was abandoning him, leaving his mind grasping. He desperately wanted to talk with Storica Lucca.

Gryphons had flown over the city with only one sanct partially broken from the invocation. As much as the idea of the sancts' imprisonment set Milo's skin burning at the injustice, he didn't want to see Trestattans running for their lives like those imperiled farmers every day. He couldn't fathom the younger wards made to stay inside, behind locked doors, rather than just the city's stone walls. What would his choice to help Gia actually mean? If they succeeded, what would they have wrought upon the city?

He left the table to clear the bed of swords and take a riposo. But even sleep couldn't calm his mind for long. As day turned to night, back at the table, his neat scratchings shifted from orderly notes to fragments and images and full lines of poetry. The first lines he'd written since trying to remake his omelia. A poem not about goddesses but the trees on the second hill, still standing where the statue had fled.

He was reading over the pages by candlelight when her voice interrupted.

"You must have done it wrong."

He flipped over the verse and turned to see Gia awake, kneeling, palms on thighs, a frown on her unbruised face. Irritation twisted in his chest. "Probably." His dream from the other night came to mind. All the stars were unpinned from the sky, and the black was falling over him. He'd lost all points of reference for doing right. "Or you were wrong about the icon. Or me."

"I'm not wrong." She stood, and paced back and forth across the small room. "Maybe it doesn't work on myself, but I *felt* you free me the first time." She stopped in front of him, wiping her hands on the sides of her tunic as if preparing to spar. "Do it properly, exactly like you did on the hill."

He wanted to be certain of something. One answer to start. "You can see and hear when you're a statue?"

She scrunched her nose. Thinking. "For a while, as it traps me, and before it lets me go. It can be murky. Like dreaming."

To be imprisoned like that for centuries—his stomach knotted. It was one thing when he thought a monster might have been frozen in stone, but a person? *This* person, so vital, so proud. When that had become clear the night before, he'd known he had to help her. He stood, ready to pray as many times as she asked until they figured out how to free her and her sister.

She faced him directly. "How did you do it?"

"I just—" He held out a hand and waited for her to give him hers. She stared at it a moment, and he realized it was smudged with charcoal. He rubbed it on his side, face flushing. "Sorry. I just held your hand." Even after he offered a cleaner hand, she hesitated. She lifted hers at last, and he pressed the tips of her fingers between his. "And—" He stared at their hands and tried to conjure the same feeling as on the hill. Her fingers were flecked with blood and calloused, but not like his from writing. Rough skin lined the outside of her index finger and thumb. He realized he was concentrating hard on not sweeping his thumb over hers. He redoubled his efforts to pray. He thought of Stregna, of what Gia had said she was like. No goddess of earth and stability but smoke and transcendence. Somehow that seemed easier to call upon, as confused as he was feeling, in the lamplight and shadows. Finally, he looked up at Gia. His breath hitched when he saw her eyes this close, brilliant and brown, watching him intently. "I wish I knew how to tell if that worked."

She yanked back her hand, blinking. "If you did it right, it will."

Milo swallowed the impulse to debate the fairness of that. Trapped in stone for hundreds of years, he reminded himself.

He said, "There's food if you're hungry?" Thankfully, Val always was and had a nice store of food that kept.

"Not very." She picked up the sword left on the floor, laid it on the table, and settled onto the bench. "I think it's like sleep and healing. But you look exhausted." She cocked her head. "What's the matter? Wary of sleeping with me around? Only one of us has cut the other's throat."

This he could argue. "That was an accident."

"Well, I was trying to kill you." She leaned forward with her elbows jutting out like knives. "Now, how are we going to free my sister?"

Everything. He'd given up everything for this. "I need to understand better before I interfere with any more sancts." He'd already done enough. He was *not* going to be responsible for killing the city's beloved Adalena. Even Val would toss him in the quarry then.

Gia blew out a breath. "Let's make a plan and finish this war. I only have a few weeks."

He frowned. "What do you mean?"

Her shoulders made a tight shrug, almost a shudder. "Stregna's godpower is connected to the moon. This has happened before, that she impeded one of Magna's invocations for one month. If I'm only waking with the moon, it's likely that when it dies—"

No. His throat went dry, and he felt the urge to take hold of her, as if that might prevent her returning to that silent state she'd stood in so long. He'd figure out the prayers, he'd make the icon work, whatever was needed. "I'll simply wake you again—"

"It won't work!" she snapped. She shook her head, staring at where she dug a fingernail into her palm. "I'd hoped, but look at how your efforts today are going. Some invocations can only be laid once upon a living creature. Stregna must not be able to break Magna's invocation any further." She heaved a breath. "This is my only chance. Even if I can't stop changing when the moon's down, I can't waste it. I can't let Lena down. We must free her so she can fix things. If we can just bring her back—"

Helplessness washed over him. She was in dire need and his prayers were failing her. "You might still stay," he said. "This last time might have worked."

Her gaze lifted to him, molten. "You should have woken a different sanct."

His curiosity evaporated in irritation. There was no other sanct he would have wished awake, and none other he'd despair over more not being able to help stay. "You're welcome for breaking your thousand years of captivity."

"For a month." She turned away dismissively. "You didn't even know what you were doing." She peeled up the top page he'd left on the table and wrinkled her nose at the script.

"Stop." He lunged forward and snatched the papers from her. The candle's flame danced like it was trying to escape the wick where it burned.

She glared, her mouth open in disbelief. "*You* read my diary."

"*You* stole my cat."

She threw up her hands. "It's not your cat!"

He didn't know why he was arguing with her about Acci of all things, didn't know *what* he wanted to be doing with her, only that he felt a compulsion rising in him to grab her hands and pull her to her feet, show her he could be as bold as she.

He stared a moment at her full lips as their corner rose in an uncertain quirk. He straightened the pages crumpling in his tightening grip. "Aren't you practically a principessa? Didn't anyone teach you any manners?" He should be glad she was showing off her bad manners and not her skills with that sword. Why did he keep trying to provoke the murderer he'd brought home?

She was speechless—for a moment. "There's only one principessa, and all that means is a lot of people bothering you all the time. Meanwhile, I was tutored and trained at the three temples. What no one taught me was how to read this writing." She waved a hand at his sheaf.

Of course. He'd been so panicked at the idea of someone reading his verse—he'd only ever shared a few pieces with Val—he'd forgotten. And now he was fighting with Gia instead of showing her he could help her, in some way, if not with the icon. He understood how lost she must feel, ripped away from everything familiar. He could at least help her find answers. "The writing system has changed a lot. In the time of the miracle, inscriptive symbols were used to represent—"

Gia huffed, fidgeting with the hilt of the sword. "Is this going to help us free my sister?"

His mouth twisted. For a girl who had been a statue for a thousand years, Gia was all action. But to rescue Adalena safely, they'd need knowledge too. "I found a carving in the temple, made by someone named Vassilis—"

"Vassilis?" She sat up straight. "That was Ennio's closest adviser. He made the invocation that trapped us." She frowned. "He seemed so unhappy in the days before what happened, I was surprised when Ennio said they'd crafted a successful prayer. He must have based it on the older one that trapped beasts in unbreakable stone for a hundred years." Her chin dipped, a look of guilt he didn't understand the reason for. "If only he had failed."

"The carving I found talks about the statues. And about this." He ducked down for his bag, stuffed his papers away, and drew out the chisel. He sat and laid it on the table between him and Gia. His gaze darted to her and away. "Vassilis used it to make the carving and built it into whatever invocation it was. I'm pretty sure it's the one thing that can destroy a statue."

Now he would see how far he could push things before this dangerous girl picked up that sword.

Gia peered at the gleaming metal like she hadn't really looked at it before. One eyebrow sliced up as she gave him a reassessing look, longer than she had the chisel. "Not as harmless as you seem, are you?" The nerves buzzing chaotically inside Milo swooped like a murmuration. She was actually impressed. "I mean, I knew that already because of how you cut my throat."

He blinked. "I told you—"

She barreled on. "You realize what this is?"

"It's called the sacred chisel. They use it to grind the stone for the Ceremony of Dust."

"That was how Ennio marked his victims." Gia let her fingers hover over it. "And Vassilis used it to carve the invocation that created the curse."

Milo had found the invocation of the Great Miracle. Any wonder he might have felt was stifled by the lies he was discovering. So many things hidden or obscured, even among the storicas who mined for truth. Primo Sanct must have used them to change the historical records and protect his version of events.

He'd dreamed of Gia causing the sky to fall, but the whole time it had been a false sky, nothing but a swag of silk like at Carnival or the children's pageant, blocking out the true stars.

"It channels immense power," she explained. "Ennio used this to create stone beasts back before he bound all his potential to invoke the curse. Magna gifted it to Trestattans after forging the temple icons, when the gods still walked the earth."

Sancts, it was actually a goddess's possession he'd taken. "How do you know this? Even your time would have been ages after that."

"My tutors at Stregna's temple." She shrugged like she hadn't just unlocked a treasure of lost knowledge with an offhand comment. *"The Book of Invocations*—"

His jaw dropped. "You've read it?"

She scrunched her nose. "Not all of it? I'm not a very good student."

"It was lost to history." Again, Milo was struck by the feeling of something reaching across time—no indefinite wave, but this girl, sharp and purposeful as a sword. "What did it say? About this?"

Gia gestured with her chin to the tool. "She fought the great monsters with it—made her own living creatures to fight them. Some said the beasts we have now are her strong invocations lingering. Some said they're the children of the greater monsters that were driven away." Gia shook her head. "Where do you keep coming by all these holy relics?"

"I sort of stole this one." He cleared his throat. "Borrowed. And forgot to put it back." And almost smashed her to pieces with it.

A small grin bloomed on Gia's stern face. "Ennio must be furious you took this. Even if he doesn't know what it can do to statues. If he did—" Her smile died. "He would have used it on me."

Milo leaned nearer across the table. "Why—?"

She interrupted, giving her shoulders a little shake. "Vassilis was the one who designed the details of invocations. Ennio would have only been interested in the power it granted him." Her mouth fell open and she hushed him with one hand splayed, though he was already listening. "The night of the carnival! I heard Ennio speaking with some of his templars and guards with the gold stripes and the red sashes. They sounded worried."

"You murdered one of them that night," Milo reminded her, as if he were chastising a young ward, or Storica Lucca explaining something that had escaped Milo's understanding.

She shook her head, but Milo didn't miss her lips' slight purse, though he couldn't read if it was pleased or rueful. "They spoke of how important the offerings and ceremony are. It sounded like they couldn't afford for people not to observe them."

He frowned. "They were more worried the murder would make people stay away?"

"And when I tried to stab Ennio—"

"You *what*?" A fresh burst of anxiety skittered down his limbs.

She waved away his concern. "It's fine, because—as I learned—Ennio's scrounged up some invincibility for himself along with his immortality."

He stilled. "With the same miracle that brought the sancts. It's all tied together. The one offering the temple made sure I gave to you—your statue—was the sacred boughs, the day of the ceremony. After taking the mark." His fingers drifted to his forehead. "The curse is still being cast every time we perform the ceremony, every time thousands wear the dust and pledge themselves to Magna Mater and the model of the sancts." Milo let out a strangled huff of realization. "And dedicate the offerings in the name of Primo Sanct. He's supposed to be the pontefice—a bridge for the goddess to send her strength through to the sancts—but it's really the other way around. They protect the city, but him most of all. He's drawing on them." And at least some of the templars knew, and holy guard and militia leaders.

"He's stealing our lives." The restraint in Gia's voice was belied by the storm brewing in her eyes, the tremble of her jaw. Milo couldn't be sure if she were about to take up that sword at last and run back to the temple or do something surprising again, like loose the tears he'd seen her fight back for two nights. "All our lives, the statues and the city, using all of us."

He rushed to reassure her. "This is good." She snorted in disbelief, and he amended, "Not good—but this means he can't risk the ceremony, if that's where his immortality comes from. He can't throw the city into a panic. That's why they're acting like things are normal, at the temple, why the holy guard didn't ransack the entire place. He can't be seen as fearful." Milo pressed his lips together. "Maybe that affords us some time to save Adalena before he comes hunting for you." For both of them. Before the waning moon stole away the girl sitting before him forever.

The possible consequences for helping Gia were unspooling too fast for him to catch hold of, like an armful of scrolls dropped over the archive's floor, but he didn't need them, even if she was stomping all over their parchment. He'd wanted to know her story, and it was full of more pain than he'd imagined, worse than facing and dying by a monster. If there was any way for him to take some of that burden from her, he would.

Gia ran a hand through her hair. She'd let it down sometime the morning before, and dark waves swept about her shoulders like spilled ink. "Maybe Ennio wouldn't have tried to silence you after all if you'd stayed. You couldn't still use your position at the temple to help us get Lena away safely, could you? What was your exact role there, anyway? Who are you to the temple?"

"Nobody." He laughed a little to sweep away the threat of regret. "I was supposed to be confirmed to an apprenticeship this month. I'd hoped to join the storicas—study the archives, write omelias."

"What's that?"

"A speech. A prayer. Based on the records of the temple, given at rites. To express devotion."

She huffed. "To teach all of Ennio's lies."

He bit his lip, but he could only nod. He'd wanted to believe so much. His heart twisted like a wrung-out rag. His fingers reached for the icon at his chest, but even that didn't mean what he'd thought. Everything felt strange, uncertain, and he knew if he let this feeling grow—he didn't need Gia learning how he could get without the comfort of routines and rites.

He shoved away from the table and retrieved a small leather bag from a shelf near the window. Sitting, he upended the bag and poured the ivory tiles—a gift from Dario—over the table. "It doesn't matter now anyway. We need to determine how we're going to recover your sister." He busied himself, and the smooth tiles clattered pleasingly as he stirred them about and began flipping and arranging them. "Can you explain more about the invocations?"

Gia's face went pensive as she rotated one tile between fingers and thumb. "Magna and Stregna can be in opposition, but Alta keeps the peace. That's why her head templar is principessa. Lena used to say her job was making sure everyone got along, including the Three Sisters." She leaned forward on her elbows to pluck tiles from the starting arrangement and make the beginning of an array. "Different offerings can strengthen appeals depending on the goddess, but each can be called upon with the help of her icon and the right prayer."

They talked and played, discussing invocations, arguing over the rules of the game, and casting tiles into all the different winning formations over the hours, mountain and river and moon. Milo brought a jar of Val's sugared almonds to the table as light bled in at the shutters. Gia's appetite seemed to grow the longer she was awake. Her hair lit up golden before the daylight, and as more hours passed Milo almost thought his prayer had been enough, until she bolted up from the table.

Hugging herself, shaking her head, she rushed into the shadowy bed chamber. Milo wanted to follow—but wanted to give her space. He tapped one tile against another for a few moments, then went to check on her and found her curled up against the side of the bed, stone head bowed.

His shoulders sank. Mere weeks, then.

Until she was lost to this permanently.

CHAPTER SIXTEEN

THE BROKEN SANCT

The weight of Magna's earth may crush or create a stronger stone.
Stregna's transcendence may cause a thing to perish or purify it.
Through extremes our faith may reveal hidden brilliance.

—The Book of Invocations

Gia

Even in the crowded morning bustle, Gia could practically feel the nervous energy coming off Milo as they sneaked back from spying on the temple. They'd lurked at the edge of the busy plaza and confirmed no guard had been set outside during the day. Ennio was still keeping his fear of her hidden from the city. People had kissed prayers to their fingertips and smudged them on the stone hem of Lena's dress before hurrying on with their days, and the streets were thronged with people, either come for the Sancts' Month festivities or forced to shelter from the monsters rampaging the countryside.

Milo twisted the icon on its chain a little as he walked beside her. "We'll need to be careful."

Gia watched the sky for gryphons, nevertheless relieved for some fresh air after being cooped up in the temple and Val's little rooms for days. "I know, I know, we can't do it too early before moonset or Lena might succumb to her injuries before the stone can heal her."

Suddenly, Milo hooked an arm around her shoulders and spun her about. Her back was against the wall of a shop, and Milo blocked her body from the crowd with his.

"Militia patrol," he muttered. "Give them a minute to move on."

She tilted her head to see for herself, and Milo shifted to keep her shielded from the people streaming past, near enough she could see the racing pulse at his throat. It matched the drum of his heartbeat under her palms braced against his chest.

"It's not only the timing," he said, voice low. "If we bring the statue of Adalena to life on the temple steps in the middle of a crowd like this, it's going to draw attention."

"Good. Let everyone see how Ennio imprisoned their precious principessa." Let everyone hear how it happened, whose fault it was. Fear spiked up her limbs like a thousand tiny knives.

"And then what?" he asked. His grip tightened on her arm. "Let the holy guard drag us all back inside?"

She turned the blades toward Milo. "You're frightened," she accused.

He dropped his gaze to one side. "Yes, that Ennio will kill you both when you wake. What am I supposed to tell the people when you two are statues again?" He raked one hand through his hair and gestured vaguely back in the direction of the temple, at the people on the street around them. "They might listen to a sanct, a principessa, but—" He shook his head, and for once seemed at a loss for words.

More ready to face Ennio's guards than a crowd on the plaza— she shouldn't call him a coward. But she was no sanct, nobody's savior. That was why they needed Lena.

Milo eased back. "I think we're okay."

Gia set off down the street once more. "I don't have time to wait until the moon's setting in the middle of the night again." She was staying awake through a good part of the morning now.

He followed her. "If we wait a couple days, moonset will align with riposo—"

"What is that?"

"People return home to eat and rest. The streets are almost entirely empty. The shops close up." He held out an arm to help her squeeze through a bottleneck around a stopped cart, hurrying them on. "You won't have been awake to see one yet, but it's nice. Like the whole city takes a deep breath in the middle of a busy day."

"That does sound nice," she admitted, matching her voice to his hushed tone. Milo had been explaining lots of details about life in Trestatto now, and it was making the city feel more familiar, more real again. She felt more real, too, more rooted in it, instead of like a vengeful spirit haunting it. "But we'll stick out even more, then."

They turned the corner to the alley, and Milo's shoulders relaxed. "We can rush back here. No crowds to fight. I can help Adalena, carry her, if you can handle any militia we may come across?"

"Of course I can." She answered too quickly, and didn't

realize for a breath—after he was already climbing the stairs—
that she'd agreed to his plan. At least they had one. It was messy
and reckless, but when had she ever held back from smashing her
way through things?

As they went inside, he said, "I'm not sure I could protect you
and Adalena well if we ran into someone I've trained beside." He
replaced the door bar and looked up sharply. "But you have to try
to disarm anyone we encounter. I meant what I said when we left
the temple." He sat at the table and began rearranging the tiles
again, shifting the mountain configuration into the river. "No
killing is a rule."

He really thought she was some wild beast. She sat on the
bench facing him and leaned back, fingers laced behind her head.
"So careful of everyone! Hearing you talk, you'd never know that
you cut open my throat."

He hung his head, dark curls masking his face, before raising
it again, revealing a wry smile. "I'm never going to get you to
stop bringing that up, am I?"

"You could probably stop me," she admitted, kicking her legs
out before her. Let him think her a beast, as long as he didn't figure out what she really was. What kind of sister she was. "Keep
me distracted. Read me some of whatever it was you were writing last night."

Any humor drained from his face. "It's nothing important."

There it was. She'd smashed that smile to pieces.

And she still didn't stop provoking him. "It can't all be notes
about temples and goddesses."

"Some verses," he muttered. "I used to waste too much time
on them, but I figured now that I won't be making any omelias
anyway . . ." He shrugged.

Gia dropped her feet and leaned forward. "I've got bad news for you." She shifted a tile so the mountain began growing again in the middle of his bank, but he was looking at her too intensely to notice. His eyes were like two dark pools—this was a boy who was always ready to hear the worst. "I've already heard your poetry. Now don't fuss." She wagged a tile in his shocked face. "You read my writing, too, and I wasn't even there to object. You recited a poem right in front of me, remember?"

"You said it was like a fog." A tile dropped from his fingers and his face went blank as if too many thoughts were churning below the surface for him to keep up any expression. Oh, gods, she broke him.

"I said," she explained, "some things came through clearer than others. You may as well help us pass the time until the moon cooperates with saving my sister."

His tan skin ruddied, and she thought he was about to argue. It must have been easier to go along than fight with her because he drew the wrinkled papers from his bag and smoothed them out on the table. He took his time turning the pages over until he found what he was looking for. Gathering the papers back into his hands, half-masking his face behind them, Milo began to read.

It was different than when he recited on the hill, where his words seemed to fly out to the many trees like birds alighting. With the shutters closed, the room was a cave of lamplight and shadow, the rustle of Milo's papers, and his breath, his words— kindling like small flames building to something greater. The verse was about the second hill, she thought—he described the different trees, the birches and ash, her companions for so long. And then one young pine that grew near the ruins, winding its trunk against a stone, warping itself to take the broken column into its form as its prickly boughs reached to the sky. Milo's words stirred unease within Gia, a feeling of being a small, hunted thing under the shadow of those trees, until the beauty of the verse overwhelmed the dread, the flames grown to a wildfire sweeping through it all.

When he finished, she sat silent. She felt cleaned out, like there was more room inside her for breath to run, light and awake.

Milo broke the spell. "I told you they're nonsense." He reached for the bag, but she trapped it with her boot.

"You're ridiculous. Read me another! Gods, you left the chance to write like that for the temple?" No wonder he didn't want to leave. She hadn't realized just what she'd done when she'd broken out with him.

"Not like that." He played with the edge of the sheet. "And I wasn't going to earn the apprenticeship anyway. I couldn't write a decent omelia."

Her eyes thinned. "Trestattans must have grown stupid as well as soft." He looked up at her, uncertain. "They're fools if they think you can't write. You're a fool if you believe them."

"I also— I have—" His hand lifted from the page halfway to his icon. He set it upon the table carefully. "I'm a little different. It's understandable if they can't entrust the role of storica to me."

"Alta's tits," she muttered. A thousand years later and Ennio was still making people doubt themselves.

Milo blinked at her crude oath, lashes glinting in the lamplight. "It's nothing that will hinder my freeing Adalena. Just not what the temple needed, I'm realizing. Storica Lucca tried to help me. He saw I loved working in the archives. But it's not only up to him, and there are other responsibilities in such an elevated position."

Milo was so ready to take everyone at their word. It was clear to her, if not to him, that the temple never intended to elevate him to any such position. The way he'd been dismissed the night of the carnival—it was obvious who was allowed into Ennio's inner circle of womanizers and snobs. They'd drawn him in, let him devote himself to them, used him—and cut him loose when he no longer served their purpose.

Just as Ennio had done to her.

Milo pursed his lips and let his gaze fall, wisps of his long curls kissing his cheekbones. If his differences meant it was difficult for him to understand this, she'd slash through the lies until it was clear. "That was never why they wouldn't have apprenticed you. Can you still not see that place is rotten through and through?"

"Not everyone," he said to his fingers splayed over the table. "Some there are trying to do good work." So earnest.

"I'm sure there are very nice people worshiping the goddess clutching hundreds of lives in her benevolent hand."

His index finger tapped. "I was."

"Maybe you're no better than the rest." Now who was casting lies about? As stark as Ennio's corruption was to her now, Milo's sincerity and innocence emanated with his every breath. That temple hadn't broken him like it broke her. She wanted to steal that breath for herself, wanted to feel like she did when he read his verse, wanted to drink it from his lips.

Her own breath came as roughly as when she became stone. She almost prayed the curse might take her now; she could feel a flush advancing over her skin. Anger sneaking up on her again, Lena's voice scolded in her head. How could she and Milo work together to save Lena if Gia's emotions got the better of her? It had been easy to hate Milo when she believed him to be knowingly working for Ennio. She forced her breath to steady. If she wasn't careful, she'd drive Milo away, even from his purpose of saving his blessed principessa.

Gods, he could barely stand to look at her half the time. "But you're all I've got. So, read another poem."

The third time Milo went over the directions to the market square and the value of the meager coins he'd pulled from his belt pouch, Gia snapped. "I've got it. This is my city, too. Long before it was yours." She stuffed the coins into her breast band before he could change his mind and decide it was too great a risk to let her loose on the city. He was too familiar to the people here, and they needed things for getting Lena back safely, and food for after.

He frowned but lifted the bar from the door. He gripped it angled across his chest, as if still worried about shielding every-one. "Just don't—just be careful."

She headed out the door. "I'm not going to murder the fish-monger, gods!" She tromped down the steps and Milo shut it after her.

The streets were mostly empty, washed in cool morning light. Rounding the last corners to the market, the street began to fill, and Gia was struck by the memory of wandering the city on her own this time of day. Slipping out before Lena appeared at breakfast or tutors could get their claws into her. Taking any path through the maze of alleyways and zigzagging lanes until she was as lost as she always felt before finding herself in a small square lined with hanging pots of bright flowers. Or a private stable of horses she could give the seed cake or apple stuffed in her belt pocket. Or an expanse of grass out the back of a line of large homes, room to run and ramble, outside of the shadow of anything or anyone.

She dragged in a breath of cool morning air and let it lift and loosen her chest and shoulders as she turned into the market plaza. She hadn't asked to come from her time to the city as Milo knew it, but maybe she could still find her place here.

Then she saw the statues.

They stood lining the large square, set into niches of the tall buildings, along the roof line, on pedestals edging a portico. Still among the early shoppers. Even the vague air of unease in the market—the tightness in a passerby's mouth, the whispers among neighboring stall owners—barely registered. This was Ennio's city now. She needed to get supplies and get back. She didn't waste any more energy on daydreams and used her coins and stubbornness to bargain for enough food so she wouldn't have to come here again any time soon. Milo's bag, slung over one shoulder, filled quickly. She even managed a handful of anise seeds.

She found a suitable cloak for wrapping Lena in after they got her off that pedestal and free of weapons. She hugged the folded fabric in her arms, not wanting to think of how well its dark color would hide Lena's blood as they tried to get her off the streets. Passing the last few stalls—wagons set to balance on blocks—Gia heard a different note in someone's quiet gossip. She paused, inspecting one cart's wares—woven baskets in spiraling Hagean patterns—and listened.

"The children are saying an avenging demon killed that guard."

"No, it was a sanct. It leaped down from its place on the city wall."

"Whatever it was, may it protect us, from beasts and worse, since the Primo can't."

"Hush," the one woman said to the other, glancing to where some vendors across the way shot them dark looks.

Gia tucked a loose strand of hair behind her ear, hiding her face and smile with her hand, as she strode past the Hagean leather goods and Lomian silks. At least she'd managed to put some cracks in Ennio's world. Ignoring Milo's careful directions, she left the market by the lane leading river-ward. She had one more thing to get before returning. Gia might enjoy being a demon to Ennio's city, but she needed to be something different to the boy who could still decide to run back to the temple and tell them everything— who would soon meet Lena, and the truth of what Gia had done.

First, she was going to bring him an offering.

She'd almost reached the warehouses where she'd hidden away as a statue, when— *"Hey!"* Down the almost-empty street, a militia soldier jerked his gaze her way.

Ennio must have finally acknowledged her threat and given them her description.

Gia took off running.

Footsteps behind her. She ducked into a side street and stopped short, scraping her hands along the stone wall to slow herself as she spun. When the guard raced around the corner, clearly expecting her to have sprinted on, she caught him by the neck and slammed him against the wall.

He was young, golden-haired, and it was easy to trap him in a chokehold. But well-trained—he stomped on her foot and pain screamed up her leg. She didn't yield, clenching harder. His blond hair, dark with sweat, stuck to her cheek. He was frantic now. Fighting for his life. Ennio hid behind his temple walls and immortality and sent youths to protect him and his lies. Gia's fury tensed her muscles tighter, only overtaken by the whisper of Milo's voice in her ear.

No more killing.

For a heartbeat, as the soldier's struggling waned, Gia was terrified she wouldn't stop. She'd told herself those men she'd slaughtered in the temple were close with Ennio, privy to his horrible secrets. This boy could have been Milo, merely trying to protect the people of his city.

He could have been Gia, once.

She let the boy drop to the cobblestones and rushed away.

Tracing her way back down another side street, she managed to spot the offering she was searching for. It had been a few days, but the cat—Acci—was there behind the warehouses, curled against the crumbling bricks warmed by the first touch of bright golden sun.

Gia crouched and he rubbed his head against her hand. "Come on," she told him, burying her fingers into his gray fluff to hide their trembling. She gave him a scratch beneath his chin. "Someone misses you. He deserves softer company than me. Maybe you can help him stick around." The cat nudged her fingers again, and she obliged with more strokes down his bony spine, then set off to the blacksmith's, watchful for patrolling militia. The cat followed at a respectable distance.

In the alley outside Val's, she scooped him up to show him into the chambers at the top of the stairs. She tapped at the door with her boot, and it swung back fast, revealing Milo waiting just behind it. "Where have you been?"

"I went to—"

"You were supposed to be back ages ago. The market is only a few streets away." His brow was furrowed, the crease above his nose a sharp line.

"I went across the river," she tried to explain again.

His eyes flared, the morning sun catching in their brown like honey, but there was nothing sweet in his tone. "Why would you go there?" He lifted his hands as if to shake her but stopped before touching her arms.

He was afraid of her. He must've thought she was out to kill without him watching over her shoulder. Even though she'd stopped, she was still trapped by what she'd become.

They'd kept their voices low, but her body had gone tense, and Acci wriggled from her tightening grip. He bounded back down the steps and into the alley.

She scowled at Milo. "To bring you your cat." She shoved past him, dropped the bag of provisions on the floor, and kept going all the way to the bed chamber, where she stayed until her hunched shoulders and frown froze into stone.

When the invocation released her, well into the night, she was perfectly controlled and cold. She ignored Milo. She ate some of the food he'd laid out in neat lines in the cupboard. She ran through the calming training poses taught to her by someone either dead for a thousand years, or still imprisoned somewhere in this cursed city.

Only the next night, as the hours sped closer to the time they'd planned to go to Lena, did she begin to feel the cracks in her careful demeanor. She'd woken well past midnight. Morning and facing her sister threatened nearer. She fidgeted worse than Milo ever did. She bounced on the balls of her feet and stomped about the chambers, checking the sword she'd chosen and sitting down to the mess of tiles cluttering the table, before springing up again to look for Acci outside.

But Milo was there. She'd been keeping her back to him as much as possible and thought he'd gone into the bedchamber to escape her latest eruption. He sat on the top step, long legs bent before him, a wrapper of food in his lap.

He didn't turn her way now, either, and simply asked, "Are you worried for your sister? About the timing?"

All her bluster died. She sank to the worn stone beside him and dropped her forehead to her knees. "See, that's not even—" She groaned. "I truly am a monster."

"What? Why?"

"I *should* be worried about getting Lena to safety. Like a decent sister. All I can think about is—" Anxiety clawed its way back up her throat as she lifted her head. "I haven't told you the entire truth of what happened."

He was looking at her now. "Is this where you admit you're actually an evil spirit who's tricked me away from the temple?" His voice was wry, and his mouth quirked.

It gave her the strength to whisper, "It's my fault Lena and all her people were trapped."

The starlight illuminated the doubt in his eyes. She wouldn't give him a chance to protest, to waste any of his faith on her. She would show him what she really was. "Lena was always so busy, and I caused her nothing but trouble. I was too impatient to sit through all her rites and meetings and congresses. But Ennio—"

Her throat caught on what felt like a hot coal. She swallowed it, letting it sink and burn in her belly. "I thought he cared about me. He let me train with his temple's militia." She heaved two quick, deep breaths that threatened to reignite the painful ember in her gut. "He let me think I was special to him, too."

The wrapper Milo held rustled sharply—his fingers constricted—but she couldn't look at him. Her hands clenched her thighs, mangling the drape of her tunic. "He told me about how the other city-states, the emerging empires around us, wanted to take our gods away. That the protection they gave Trestattans could fail with worship and offerings divided, and monsters would pass freely through our streets like never before. No place would be safe." Children would be carried off by gryphons or swallowed whole on their way to the neighborhood well, he'd told her. She was so eager to be of use, so ready to believe. "Lena still wanted to consider the plans put forth by the other Orabellian city-states for an alliance. She and Ennio fought about it. When he wouldn't stop disrupting the talks, she barred him from the assemblies."

She was staring down the steps but could only see Lena, tall and slender, brown braided hair touched with bronze. Serene and calculating, except when that look of disappointment with Gia's behavior fell over her features. As if she'd given up on her.

In the shadows left by the memory of her sister, it felt as if black insects were crawling all over Gia's skin. She rushed the rest of her story out—how she'd thoughtlessly done what Ennio asked, how she'd only cared about pleasing him, about sealing her place in the home she'd thought she'd found at his temple.

It was too late for her to take any of it back. There was no escape, not then, and not now. She felt the same dread pressing in on her, making her voice husky. "I've been trying to make up for it. All I've wanted to do is avenge her, avenge them all." She shook her head at the sky, its dark already blanching away. "Striking back at her enemy was easier. What if—" Lena would be right to assume the worst, that Gia had chosen to stand with Ennio against her, and give up on Gia completely. "What if she thinks I'm her enemy, too?"

Milo listened patiently. He took a moment to respond once she quieted and dared a glance toward him. In that moment, Gia felt as if she'd taken a running leap off the city wall and hung suspended, waiting for the ground to spring up and attack. She almost flinched when he spoke. "Then I pity her. Because I would not bet against you in any fight."

She snorted and brushed her hair behind her ears. A flush warmed her cheeks.

He tipped his head at her, eyebrows arching. The gentlest rebuke. "Didn't I switch sides from an immortal sanct so I wouldn't have to fight you?" His expression deflated, and he sighed. "I'm sorry for snapping at you when you got back. I was worried."

"You don't have to apologize." It was understandable that he wouldn't trust her not to cause more problems, to destroy more lives. She'd been too close.

"The militia could have taken you, or—I don't know what." His fingers were curled against his chest, his thumb rubbing the silver icon.

The dark insects transformed to lightning flies, sparking and shivering over her limbs as she realized—he was worried *for* her? She sat still as stone as he cast a look to the sky and went on.

"I get these—I get stuck. When things don't follow what I

expect. Or there are too many sounds or lights or smells." He gave a huff of a laugh and waved the packet of food he'd brought, some of the dried fish she'd haggled. Though the only smell she'd noticed was the anise on his breath. "And I have things that work for me to manage, but everything is so different right now, I—" He dropped his head and scratched beside his ear. "It's no excuse. But I'm sorry."

It occurred to her that this boy she thought was the perfect follower of Magna might not feel so flawless. Perhaps they'd both spent years looking up to sancts and feeling as though they'd never be enough. "It's all right. You know I can take care of myself, right?"

A smile cracked through his solemn expression. "I've seen." His eyes searched over her face. "I always knew, even when I was the one meant to be looking after your statue." The rising light meant she could read the rich warmth in his eyes, the rough stubble emerging above his upper lip. She suddenly became aware of the closeness of their step. How her hip pressed against his. How near he was to her.

And yet as distant as if a thousand years of stone still lay between them.

His gaze fell away and he leaned forward, holding out a salted fish. She was confused, and busy smothering the unexpected anticipation that had flamed within her for half a moment until Acci slunk out of the gloom to nose the offering and rest his paws on Milo's leg. Milo darted a glance to Gia and back to the cat. She wondered if holding eye contact was another thing he had to manage carefully and felt an unbidden ache of gratitude for how often he shared his intense gaze with her. He fed Acci while rubbing his knuckles over the cat's fluff. "I'm glad you're on my side."

A realization struck her like the first finger of dawn touching a new sky. He saw her as what he'd said in his prayer that woke her. Something to be wished for, a strength to be called upon. Maybe she could still be that. It wouldn't be enough to ever make up for what she'd done, not enough to be what she might have been—someone like Milo, who'd been drawn into Ennio's clutches and remained unbroken. Maybe just enough to find the bravery and boldness to face Lena.

"Come on," she said, stretching her legs. "Let's go get this city its principessa back."

CHAPTER SEVENTEEN

THE LAST PRINCIPESSA

Bearing the icon requires fierce responsibility and judgment, in what a templar does, and what a templar passes over. Invoke a goddess with solemnity.

—The Book of Invocations

Gia

"I must have passed her ten thousand times," Milo said.

They waited in the shade of the colonnades, having petted Acci goodbye and left with enough time to reach the temple with the cover of people heading home for their meals and rest. Before that, they'd gone over the plan and prepared as much as possible. Now there was nothing between them and the reality of Lena

A PRAYER FOR VENGEANCE

out in that square, stark in the sunlight, shadow pooled beneath her like a bloodstain.

Gia wiped her hands on the sides of her tunic under her cloak. She could do this. This was why the goddess granted Milo's prayer. Not for Gia. Not as a trick. As cruel as fate had been to Gia, as much as her faith had been shredded, Stregna wouldn't have played such a joke on Milo.

The moon had already fallen behind the buildings on the far side of the square, like a silver coin sent ahead in payment. The square was deserted, the occasional person crossing on their way to or from the temple. Every time they disappeared around a corner or down the road, Gia shot a pointed look at Milo, and every time, he shook his head.

Finally, when an elderly woman emerged from the side door of the temple and made her way down the first little street cutting off the square, Milo nodded. "Templar Daniela supervises the apprentices. She's always last to leave after they clean up the kitchen. Takes leftovers to her unwell sister nearby."

They crept forward. So many arrows and blades pierced Lena's back. So much blood about to spill. Gia's fingernails cut into her palms. They had better get this right. She positioned herself beside her sister so she could keep an eye on the temple while Milo prayed. He considered Lena, one hand holding out her sword, the other flung back high, and rested his hand upon her ropey forearm. Gia's eyes darted from Milo to the temple doors and back. She did not turn her face up to Lena's. She swallowed dryly, not sure if she were more afraid for her sister or of Ennio spotting her here.

Milo closed his eyes. Gods, how long was this going to take? How long before she'd stirred while Milo recited his poem that day on the hill? She paced forward. Ennio might not have wanted to alarm the city with a wall of guards around the temple, but the watch might have changed. Any moment another guard could round a corner.

Whatever blessing Milo thought Gia was, she hadn't been able to protect Lena when the templars battled here. She might still fail her again. She turned to face her sister—just in time to see Lena fall from her pedestal into Milo's arms.

Gia rushed forward to bear up Lena with Milo. She slipped her arms under his, feeling the surprising strength there, as he held Lena and prevented the weapons in her back from knocking against the steps and wrenching her flesh apart.

"We've got you," she breathed, nudging her forehead against her sister's, where her copper crown sat. Her sister's head lolled heavily. What if they were wrong? What if Lena was already gone?

Lena's eyes flared open. Something distant swam in their wide rings.

"What have you done?" Lena rasped.

Her body jerked, and Milo shifted forward, taking her full weight. Gia stepped back. "I'm sorry," she whispered to her sister.

Gia rounded on her and grabbed the first arrow. Her hands shook on the shaft. Lena's words, so fragile, still reverberated through her like a strike of sword to metal armor. She steeled herself. Yanked. But the tug, the squelch, and Lena's weak cry— Gia was trying to take back all the hurt, all she had done, but she was only hurting her sister more.

She pulled the next arrow free more quick than careful. And another. Bloody weapons fell at their feet on cobblestones dark like serpents' scales. Lena hung limp in Milo's arms without even a flinch. Terror shot through Gia. Lena couldn't slip away before the stone healed her. The stone couldn't take her before they got all the weapons out.

Only one spear was left. Gia shoved forward, but the angle—cutting straight through Lena's torso—was awkward. She moved to Lena's front. Milo took one look at her face and shifted Lena to her arms and took hold of the spear. Gia clenched her fingers into her sister's flesh, its reassuring warmth.

They slipped in her sister's dripping blood.

"Ready," Milo murmured, low and grim. Lena's body slumped with his first motion, and Gia tried to hold her tighter. Braced for what was coming.

Milo dragged back the spear. Blood bloomed wider than the stains covering Lena's dress.

Fresh blood meant she was still alive. She had to be alive.

Milo wrenched the spear free, tossed it to the ground, and tucked himself under Lena's shoulder.

"Blood on you," he told Gia. She unhooked her cloak, wiped it over her face and hands, and threw it over Lena's ruined back. She rubbed the crescent of dust on Lena's brow into a less noticeable smudge, lifted the crown from her head, and hooked it on her empty knife sheath.

They dragged Lena from the square, and Gia would have offered the honey from every hive, the dates from every tree, to whichever sister goddess let them escape before the cry was raised inside the temple.

They saw no one but the occasional disinterested cat and two curious Lomian merchants—who did not question their lack of red sashes and their lie that she and Milo were helping a sick sister return from militia duty. Gia stopped worrying she and

Lena would be stranded in the street and began praying the moon would set before Lena died.

She knew no goddess could bring anyone back from that.

When they reached the alley, Milo took the lead, hauling Lena up the narrow stairs. The cloak dragged from Lena's shoulders, revealing shredded skin. Her blood drenched Milo.

She was dying.

"What are you doing?"

Gia spun, trying to hide her panic, restraining herself from pulling her sword. When she saw the tall, muscled girl coming down the other side of the alley, she regretted it.

The girl's eyes widened, taking in Milo and Lena on the stairs, then flicking to Gia. The girl didn't wait to draw her sword from under her red militia sash.

Gia's hilt was in her hand. She drew and swung in one motion, just in time to meet the girl's first strike. Thank Alta she was on the stairs—this girl was a mountain. Gia deflected her blade, but the force knocked her back against the smith's wall. She threw her weight against the girl's next blow. Now it was she who shuffled back, her long brown braid swinging behind her.

In the corner of Gia's eye, Milo strained to see what was happening. He had no room to turn with Lena draped against him, no wall or railing to prevent their toppling if he tried.

Gia braced her sword against the girl's and gritted her teeth. "Get her inside!"

Instead, eyes widening, he barked, "No—stop!" She didn't have time to decide if he was more worried for her or this Trestattan, as they exchanged blow after bone-shattering blow.

Forget Milo's rule. She would protect her sister as long as both of them still drew breath.

She might get herself killed. She might have only moments before turning to stone. She would not leave Lena and Milo at the mercy of the militia.

Gia drove the girl back with her sword, stomped her boot forward to the brink of the open steps, and jumped after her.

Their swords knocked together. Edge sliced down edge. The girl spun away, and Gia crashed to the ground. She rolled, the grit of the alley biting into her shoulder. Her knuckles ripped across the ground as she dragged her sword up fast and regained her footing.

The girl's sword crashed down upon her again. Between flashes of their blades, Gia tried to make sure that Milo had gotten her sister to safety. All she saw was Milo, open-mouthed. Shock and horror in his eyes. And Lena, utterly limp upon the landing.

Gia's heartbeat thrashed louder than their clanging swords. She'd failed Lena again. She howled and slammed her sword against the militia soldier's. She wished she could achieve transcendence like the warriors of old. That she could break open into pure fury and brutality. She would have given her life to release every last part of her power to protect Lena. Now she would loose whatever she could against Ennio's soldier.

She whipped her sword against the girl's. Again. Faster. Nearly pinning her against the stairs. The girl's footwork danced her away, but Gia caught her face with a jerk of her elbow. The girl shouted and landed a kick to Gia's knee.

Gia yelled and struggled to stay on her feet. To keep her sword up. Slash after slash of the girl's sword rained upon her. Gia could barely fend her off. She scuffled back, but her foe's sword followed.

Gia stumbled and fell to one knee.

"Monster," the girl spat through gritted teeth edged with blood. She raised her sword high.

"Stop! Val!" Milo leaped from the third step.

The soldier hesitated. Gia grabbed her chance. She screamed and hauled herself up, staggering forward, driving a killing blow at the girl.

Milo hurled himself between them.

Gia twisted and pitched to one side. Her sword's point veered away from Milo's chest and slid just past his raised palm as she fell.

The girl—Val—grabbed Milo by the shoulder and shoved him behind her. "Did she attack you?" She strode to where Gia lurched to her knees and punched her across the face. Gia fell flat to the ground.

"Val! No!" Above her, where her vision clouded with white flares of pain, Milo gripped Val's arm, holding her back.

Val kept her sword pointed at Gia. "How badly are you hurt?"

"I'm not, she's—"

He tried to push past his friend, but she clung to his arm, her gaze turning to where Lena's blood covered his tunic and arms. Her voice went hoarse. "Milo, you're bleeding." She caught Gia reaching for the hilt of her dropped weapon and stomped on her hand. "And that's my sword."

Gia shrieked and writhed against the ground. Milo wrenched Val back and crouched beside her. He grimaced, eyes bright with concern. "Gia."

Behind him, atop the stairs, Lena stirred. She propped herself on a trembling arm, a wild look possessing her.

Alive. Her sister was still alive.

Lena spasmed. With a gasp, she tumbled off the steps. Gia tried to shout, but her chest went hollow.

A second sword clattered beside her as Val sprang to catch Lena. She turned back to Milo, Lena draped across her arms. "Milo! What is going on?"

"We've got to get them inside." Milo's face swam before Gia again. "Are you all right?" She couldn't answer, couldn't sigh with relief for Lena, couldn't yell at Val, could barely breathe. Her good hand clenched his bloody tunic. He helped her up, but her knee nearly collapsed under her. He caught her by the elbows and slid an arm around her waist. "I've got you." He turned to his friend. "Inside. Now."

Val snapped to action, eyes still incredulous. She strode to the foot of the stairs and ascended, careful not to knock Lena's head against the wall. Milo held out his free hand for Gia to lean on, and helped her limp up the stairs.

Inside, Val shifted Lena in her arms before laying her on the floor beside the stove. "I have bandages and—"

Milo hung on to Gia, steadying her, as she rested against the wall just inside the door. "They don't need them."

"This woman is dying." Val ran into her bed chamber.

Gia let out a strangled sound and slid to the floor, clinging to Milo.

He sank before her, supporting her the whole way down. His eyes never left her face. "She'll be safe in a moment."

"She'll be dead in a moment!" Val rushed back with a bundle of cloth and knelt beside Lena, still and unconscious again. "Look how pale she is."

Gia's chest constricted. Her knee and hand throbbed. Her unhurt fingers tightened on Milo's arm. He lightly cupped her aching cheek. "Hold on," he murmured. "For one more moment. Everyone will be all right in one moment." The tension around his mouth and the distress in his eyes belied his confident words. She strained, wide-eyed, wanting to beg him to save her sister. As if he could work another miracle. As if there was anything to do but see if death or Magna would claim Lena first.

CHAPTER EIGHTEEN

THE TEMPLAR

"All are one."

—From Alta's Hymn, The Book of Invocations

Milo

Tension gripped every part of Milo as tightly as Gia's fingers pressing into his arm. They went bloodless, and glossed over with the sheen of stone, but he would let her hold him as long as she needed. He would wait out the entire day at her side until she woke.

Her eyes, pleading, faded to white. He knew she didn't care about her own transformation or injuries. She thought only of her sister.

Val shouted, and he turned, his arm slipping from Gia's grasp.

"What is *happening*?" Kneeling beside Adalena, Val gaped at where the color leached from her face. "Sancts!"

Milo's chest heaved with relief. Adalena would heal now. And Val was here, returned safely. He twisted back to Gia. "She made it," he told her statue. "She'll be all right."

"All right?" Val demanded. "She's—she turned—" She stared as Adalena paled and hardened, and her pinched, fierce look blossomed with wonder. "Wait. This is—How?" She reached her fingers toward Adalena's shoulder, but didn't press them to the stone, instead pulling them back and touching them to her brow in wide-eyed prayer. "She's—"

Milo moved to her side and put a steadying hand on her shoulder. He nodded. "Principessa Adalena."

Val stared at her own blood-streaked hands and forearms and pressed her lips together. "And her?" She pointed with her chin at Gia. "They told us at the gate to watch for a girl like her. Said she was deadly."

"She's a sanct." He settled on the floor next to Val. Explaining would not be easy. "My sanct."

Val shook her head and leaned nearer. "Did you kill the principessa?" she asked quietly.

"No, she should be fine," he reassured her, and himself. "She'll wake up again. She looks like Gia did, and I nearly killed her."

"You *what*?" Val lifted her hands to her temples.

He sighed, exhausted. He had shifted to sleeping whenever Gia was stone, afternoons through the first half of the night now. "It was an accident. And she's fine, as you saw when you just tried to kill each other. It's the invocation. They'll both be fine." At least he hoped they would be. There was no reason to think it would act differently on Adalena than her sister. He found himself wishing he could consult with his mentor.

Val wiped her split lip with the back of her hand and muttered, "An invocation. A sanct trying to kill me. And Principessa Adalena. In my chambers." Acci slinked from under the curtain of the bedchamber and Val let out a little scream. "And there's a cat," she said, pressing her eyes shut and exhaling. Acci threaded between them to curl up against Gia's statue. Val fell off her heels and sat facing Milo. "I was gone two weeks. What have you gotten yourself into?"

"We needed someplace safe," was all he could say. Everything that had happened, everything he'd learned—it was too much to share all at once. "And we didn't think you'd be back for another day or so."

"They recalled us. Said they needed more militia to patrol inside the city. Which is weird, considering the gryphons. I guess I see why now." She stared at Gia. Seriousness tugged around her mouth. "They gave us her description. I won't be the only one watching for her."

Worry caught the tightness in his chest and squeezed. "I know."

"We're supposed to take her to the general. The new general. Apparently, this girl killed the old one."

His fingers scrabbled against the floor, tensing. "You can't—"

She cocked her head. "You should be back at the temple, and I—"

"Val, please, I just need to tell you—" He pushed himself up on his heels.

"Tell me what? Why you're hiding a murderer?"

He reached a hand to grip her shoulder. "The truth."

Her eyes, searching him over, thinned. She dipped her face nearer his arm. "You *are* cut. Did we hit you when you came between us?"

"No, that's not my—" He remembered the pain as Adalena fell against him. He'd had to push it aside at the time. "It must have been the spear."

Val took his arm in her hands. "Not too deep, but long. Come on," she sighed, and picked up the dropped bandages. "Let me bind it."

He followed her to the bed chamber, where she dug around for a moment in the open trunk in the corner, and then sat beside him on the bed with a box of supplies. Her expression was still serious, but her fingers were light as she wiped ointment from a little bottle across his cut. "I don't think I have enough to treat all of the wounds waiting out there," she told him.

"You won't need to. When they wake, they'll be healed." Watching Val wind the cloth around his arm, he explained the nature of the curse and why it had been cast. It felt like inflicting a wound even as she tended his. She listened with more exclamations and interruptions than he had subjected Gia to, but at least he could present it all in an orderly way to make it easier to digest. He was circumspect as he explained Adalena attending the ceremony that had allowed Ennio to enact the invocation. The details had clearly been difficult for Gia to share. That part of the story wasn't his to tell.

After tying off the bandage and packing away the ointment, Val listened to the last of it, fiddling with her small icon. "It's a lot. An awful lot to take on faith. I trust you. Do you trust her?"

He picked at the tied-off end of the bandage, letting its frayed edge run through his fingers. "I know what they told you, what she's done. She's been through a lot, too." He thought of Gia coming to his cell, subjecting herself to freezing there, demanding he listen to her side of the story. "She's so direct, I never doubt what she means, or where I stand with her. I trust her."

Val's face transformed again, her eyes rounding with comprehension and delight. "I see what's happened. Our Milo has finally fallen for a girl."

Her words were like the full sun in his eyes, too many voices, hooves stamping—he couldn't reach through it all fast enough for the right script to reply. He didn't even know what he would want it to say. All he could manage was to mutter, "Quiet, she'll hear."

Val dropped her head dubiously, eyes still alight with glee. "She's a statue."

"Still. Sometimes she can. And I haven't—" The words of protest dissolved in his chest like an unwaxed paper beast in the rain, trampled underfoot by something stirring to truer life.

"You have," Val sighed.

"Whether or—" His hand balled a fist of the blanket they sat on. "The point is, not everyone is as obsessed with love as you are. Gia needs justice. For her sister. Will you help them?"

Val had taken up her icon again. "Adalena," she murmured, looking to the miniature image of the principessa marked in metal there, and shook her head. "How could I not?"

Milo awoke to shouting. Half-dressed, he pushed through the bed chamber curtain, belatedly thinking he should have grabbed a sword from the wall first.

The door to the stairs was still shut and barred, and Gia was shouting at Val, stretching to her full height, and jutting her jaw.

"If you put my sister at risk ever again—"

Val tucked a foot behind the chair she must have been dozing in, dragged it closer and sat, resting her hands on her thighs. "Welcome, make yourself at home," she said wryly. "Oh, you already have, so shall we discuss how you put the closest thing I have to a brother at risk?"

Milo ran a hand over his face. "Val's going to help," he told Gia, hoping to calm her down before another sword fight broke out.

Gia cut her gaze to him, mouth open and ready to argue. She didn't say anything. Her eyes, aflame with anger, softened as she took him in—then flared. "You're hurt." She glared at Val. "Did she strike you when she attacked us?"

"No," he said. "It was at the temple. It's fine."

Gia was back to staring at him. Then Adalena stirred, where she lay on the floor, and Gia crouched beside her. A taut look passed between the sisters, unreadable.

Stiffening, Adalena asked, "Why are you here?"

Milo, at times, struggled to understand people's emotions, but Adalena's unhappiness dripped from her every word.

Gia stiffened, one hand balancing herself, one reaching out for her sister. "Stregna," she said finally, shifting back. "Are you all right?"

"Am I—" Adalena's wretched face softened to a frown. "*Am* I all right?" She moved to sit up, and Gia took her arm.

Val jumped to her feet, hand at her icon.

"It's part of the invocation," Gia explained. "We'll turn back to stone every time the moon sets, but we heal from any injuries then, too."

"We're still trapped?"

Gia's stoic face rippled with hurt.

Adalena asked, "How old is this moon?"

Gia said thickly, "Days past full." She stepped back as Adalena stood, stretching tall and breathing in a long breath. Gia unhooked the crown from her belt and reached to hand it to Adalena, her neck and shoulders sloping in a tentative shape Milo had never seen her take. Adalena accepted it without a second glance, letting it hang from her hand. "What of the others?"

"Others?" Val asked.

"My people. They were turned before me."

Milo began, "We can—" Adalena fixed her stare on him, and he found his voice caught in his throat. Even knowing what he did, speaking to the most exalted sanct he'd studied and stared at for half his life was daunting. He cleared his throat and said, "We can free them as well. I think. With the icon." He tapped where it lay visible on his bare chest. "Even the others near the temple, if we watch out for Ennio's guards."

"*Ennio?*" Adalena's voice rang out. "Has the stone not trapped us for a hundred years? Isn't that how this invocation works?"

Gia said quietly, "It's a different one. It's been a lot longer. And it keeps him alive. The whole city thinks he's halfway to a god."

Adalena pursed her lips. "Just like you always have."

"Not anymore," Gia said hotly. "Ask the half dozen of his men I've taken out."

Adalena pinched the bridge of her nose. "Of course you did." She inhaled and spoke with restrained command. "Tell me what's happening."

Gia said nothing. Milo knew she'd been nervous about seeing her sister, and he was starting to understand why. He did his best to explain to the intimidating principessa what had happened in the hundreds of years since her last free day. She peppered him with questions like an exam on all his years of studying sancts. When he couldn't tell her for certain which Trestattans of her time had lived or been killed or turned to stone, he thought she was going to make him recite all known names of the seven hundred and twenty-six sancts.

She cut him off when he named a sanct who stood atop a well south of the river. "Hector. He was by my side as the talks with the emissaries were beginning that day. Five other Orabellian city-states wanted an alliance."

"Because of the growing beast population?" Milo asked.

"False reports." She gave a single decisive shake of her head. "Templar Ennio was driving rumors of a surge of monster attacks in the countryside. And then my advisers found evidence he was using his stone creatures to attack farmers, leaving no one alive, letting it be thought of as the monsters' work. Or he'd drive monsters toward villages. He thought he could force the city into closing itself off."

Gryphons awake and hunting over the city in daylight flew through Milo's mind.

"He's still doing that kind of thing," Gia muttered. When he looked to her, she added, "I heard him, after the carnival, directing the militia to rout a town. To bring more worshipers for his ceremony."

"Despite the murders," her sister cut in darkly.

Gia shot back, "If you knew Ennio was working against the city, why didn't you tell me?"

Adalena was dismissive. "Would you have listened?"

Gia's mouth clamped shut. She was more subdued than Milo had ever heard her. "There are several statues at the nearest market square," she said.

"Then that's where we'll start waking more with the icon."
Adalena spoke with authority. She tugged the cloak around her
stained dress, looking strangely diminished, even as she stood
with all the dignity Milo would expect of a principessa.

"It'll be daylight soon," he said. "We can't be seen covered in
blood."

Val leaped forward, scooping up a bundle from the table.
"I went out for a little passeggiata to get myself a proper bath
and all of you some clean clothes." She tossed a folded tunic to
Milo. "There's something for everyone, but my coin purse is
officially empty." Milo's leggings had been salvageable, but his
second tunic—his last tunic—had been beyond saving, thanks
to the blood of another sanct. He'd left it balled up in the kindling bin before falling asleep. Val turned to Adalena, her expression becoming reverent. "Of course, I'm happy to give whatever
I have to a sanct. You can't exactly go out looking like you're
dressed for Carnival."

Adalena smiled blandly. "I'm not sure I know what that
means."

"Right. Of course." Val patted the pile she held. "Well, these
will be cleaner, too. Even though you look lovely."

Adalena's brows flicked up. "Thank you." Val beamed at her.
"Still, I will gladly take those?" She held her hands out.

Val jolted and finally passed the clothes into Adalena's arms.
"I brought fresh water before dark, as well."

"Thank you," Adalena said again, politely. "And for your aid
earlier. I would love to clean up."

Val nodded warmly. "You have provided so much comfort and
inspiration to me, even if the miracle turned out not to be real."
Val's brow creased. "And you weren't actually a sanct. I mean—"

Her eyes and mouth went wide. "I am glad you're not dead."

Milo pulled on his fresh tunic. It was pointless to hope Val could curb her devotion to her favorite sanct. Frustration knit in his chest for Gia's sake, though. He pushed his hair back to see her watching Adalena, worrying her hands. He was grateful to Val as well, but Adalena hadn't even acknowledged that Gia had freed her from Ennio's invocation. If they had some more time together to smooth things out between them—

"Maybe you two should try waking the others," he said to the sisters, "while Val and I keep watch for any militia who might happen past. You being head templar and Gia being trained at the temples, you might be able to invoke Stregna to greater acts. Perhaps wake more at once? Even all the sancts."

Adalena frowned. "I am Alta's templar. It will have to be you." At Milo's blank look, she went on, "The temple icon binds a goddess's power to her devotees, through one intercessor. One templar. If you've invoked Stregna successfully, that's you."

CHAPTER NINETEEN

FISSURES

Magna forged the blade, wave, and crescent to bend godpower into the hands of the Three Sisters' beloved people. Each icon of their power points that force to an intercessor who wields it into the world, to bear their unseen will even as the gods untether from the earth.

—The Book of Invocations

Milo

Gia filled the silence Milo couldn't, voice low as a blade dragged across stone. "Only one person can use the icon? I never knew that."

Val, wide-eyed, breathed, "Milo, you're head templar."

He shook his head. No. That didn't make sense. He almost laughed. "Of a destroyed and forgotten temple." That sounded about right. Fit better.

He was hardly keeping up with what Adalena was saying about icons and the succession of templars. "The icon can only bind godpower to a new intercessor when the current one dies. Stregna's head templar must have lived and died, not become a statue. Or Ennio killed her." She frowned, her head bowing. "She was a friend." She sounded distracted when she continued. "Yes, only one templar can use it."

Gia erupted. "One more thing you never shared with me!"

Adalena went straight and stiff and tall. "I have many responsibilities. If you attended your lessons at Stregna's temple instead of always running off to see that monster—"

"Yes, yes," Gia shouted. There was a pinch in her voice. "I was so in love with Ennio, I cost you your entire city!" Her face crumpled as she shoved past Val and out the door, slamming it behind her.

"I never said that," Adalena huffed under her breath, her fingers slack where they held her crown. It was the first time she seemed at a loss since taking possession of herself.

"Then maybe take it easy on her," Milo finally broke in. "Everything she's done since I woke her, she's done for you."

"Killing indiscriminately so the entire city is on the hunt for us?" Adalena tsked. "Gia has always done whatever she felt like."

"You're wrong."

"Milo!" Val's eyes widened at him. "You can't speak like that to the principessa."

He could only answer, "She shouldn't be out alone." He opened the door, ready to chase Gia down the stairs and into the night.

Yet she stood just outside, looking out over the alley, her figure blocking out the stars peering over the roofs.

She cast back one glance, then turned her face away. Milo closed the door behind him carefully and leaned against it. A question stood between them like a third person. Before he could ask it, or decide not to, she posed one to him.

"What's it like having a sister who actually cares about you?" Her voice was jagged but soft, like the torn edge of his bandage. "Takes real devotion to be willing to fight me."

He dropped his head with a huff of a laugh. "Val would say she was only trying to live by the example of the sancts. When I was brought to the nido, ten years ago now, I—" He folded his arms. "I was a mess. I'd seen beasts tear apart the stand of farm houses where I'd lived. Everyone killed. I couldn't sleep. Bigger children were annoyed, shoved me around, until Val stopped them. She told me all about Adalena protecting those in need. I followed her everywhere after that. She used to call me her shadow." He thought of the other wards and worried what they were being told, if anyone was checking on them, soothing their nightmares.

"How did you get away from the beasts? If they killed—" She softened what she'd almost said. "Everyone."

Another unspoken question blossomed between them. He didn't speak of them, parents too profane to attend rites or teach him about the sancts. Yet they had Stregna's icon. It didn't fit. He shrugged, though she couldn't see—more to shake off their memory. "Leaped out the back window. Ran for the city. I don't even remember, really. Next thing I knew I was being bundled off to the temple." It still felt like a refuge. He thought of Adalena looking familiar and unfamiliar at once—he wasn't used to seeing her without all the arrows and spears about her shoulders. The temple, the feeling of it being his home, hovered about him similarly. So much a part of him, but injuring him as well. Needing to be ripped out. He couldn't think about templars' succession and intercessions to Stregna until he managed that. "And I never really left."

"Until I made you."

She was a shadow too, black against the only light filtering down to this world. Maybe his invocation that delivered her here had been answered to give him a chance to grow brave, to fight her darkness.

All he wanted right now, the only thing he could think to pray for, was to let their shadows wash together without any of the careful restraint he'd practiced and relied upon to survive. His hands dropped to his sides. His fingers pressed against the door's rough wood, ready to push him forward, to launch him toward the bravest act he could imagine.

She should know how much she was cared for—the devotion she inspired. He may have found comfort in her presence when she had stood on that hill, but Gia alive and fully herself was something entirely different. Like speaking a whole new language without study or translation, a full manuscript lit gold with one strike of a fire starter. Every time she stirred from stone, it pulled a tide he was helpless to fight through his blood.

She turned to him then. "I was only infatuated with Ennio, but I'm afraid I love being the killer he made me."

He shoved it all aside—everything he might be, everything he might do. She'd taken a knife to the throat of that third person standing between them, dared Milo to pull away in horror.

He held still.

After a moment, she slumped from her aggressive stance. "Even that's cowardice to say. I made myself this. I chose this."

She stepped forward and leaned against the door beside him. "What Lena doesn't understand is, I loved *Magna*. I loved how Ennio made me feel I could do something important with her temple. I was no good at statecraft or studies, but I was strong and quick. Lena's right, though, I'm not worth trusting with any of her work. I let Ennio use my devotion, and look what I did here, hurting the people I say I want to protect. Not only Ennio's men. The people fleeing the beasts he's stirred up. That boy in the temple—"

Her voice cracked. Never in his life had Milo wanted more to offer something, anything, to his sanct.

"Lena hates me for giving in to my emotions. Says it's a weakness. When our mother died in childbirth, she cried and cried, but stopped the day of her coronation. When our father fell in battle, she never even shed a tear. She was always the perfect student, the perfect principessa." Gia pointed. "Look at her up there, her own constellation. Literally above me."

He could hear the hurt under the scorn Gia slathered upon her words and see some of the stars in the strip of sky cut between buildings. It was only a piece showing, not the whole pattern.

"Sancts—" He growled away the useless oath. "Or whatever you want to swear by. The last thing you are is weak." He wasn't the only one with false stories shaping him like that twisted tree on the hill. If there was one truth he was certain of, it was that Gia was brave and powerful, worthy as anyone else. "And Renz lived."

She sucked in a breath. "He did?"

Milo nodded, and went on, forcefully, "It's not your fault that Ennio deceived you like so many others." She dropped her gaze to his, eyes round and wounded, and his voice softened. "I know how easy it is to believe his lies." His breath sent a wisp of her hair dancing like a silver flame. The starlight stroked through her curls, down her cheek, and along her trembling jaw. "And if your sister hates you for it, she's wrong." He didn't see it, but Adalena seemed reserved, the sort of person he had a hard time reading. He wanted to remove every barb, every lie, from Gia as they had the weapons from her sister's back. Pull them from her like the poisonous thorns they were.

"Principessa Adalena? Wrong?" She snorted. "She looks elegant even in a bloody cloak." Gia's hands clawed over her shoulder, her arm, in something more akin to a strangle as she hugged herself. "How am I supposed to talk to her? I thought it would fix things if I brought her back, but I just made it worse. She's freed an hour and wants to help everyone. You! You write verses and jump between children and someone you think is a monster. I'm only after revenge. I am a monster."

She'd said that before, but there was no wryness to her declaration tonight. And he'd believed it, once. Now, he only saw a girl who cared as fiercely as she fought for what she believed in—cutting away the rest of the world, even cutting away herself.

She huffed and stomped the flat of her boot against the door. "It doesn't matter if Lena blames me or not. I blame me. Ennio chose me because he saw what I really am, and he knew he could use that. And when I try to mend things, I only break them more. I broke whatever sisters are meant to have between them. I broke our entire city. And I keep breaking things, smashing everything, because I'm the one that's broken—too broken to ever put myself back together."

He knew then that he hated Ennio, even if his temple still felt like a sanctuary to Milo. Thanks to Gia smashing apart his world, he was digging himself out, hacking away bits of himself to wrench free. He didn't know if he could be what Adalena said he was, but he could try—wanted to try—because of Gia. For once, he was ready to dive into the uncharted black. Gia had never been given any chance like that—besides what Ennio tried to twist her into, before being ground down by it and his curse. She deserved so much better. She deserved to make her own chance.

"So don't," he told her. "Don't try to remake what you might have been. Become something new."

She inhaled—almost a shudder. After a moment, she let her arms relax. Her shoulder rested against his, warm and soft as their silence together, until she was ready to go back through the door.

Before they ventured to the market, Val sneaked down to the workshop below, where she was due to work later that morning, and returned with a sword for Milo. It was a simple weapon with hilt and pommel etched in an even crosshatch pattern. "Made it to give you after confirmation," she told him as she placed it in his hands. Youths were only allowed to carry swords outside militia duty once confirmed.

He thanked her, even as the thought of missing his confirmation rites this week pressed on him more than the weight of the sword. He also suggested Gia stay home since the militia was on alert for her, but she only snorted and sheathed the blade she'd adopted from Val's collection.

"Won't matter once we begin," Adalena said, looking like any Trestattan with her new tunic and the mark scrubbed from her forehead. "Wake enough sancts, gain enough allies, and the truth will flow through this city and wash it clean of Ennio's lies."

Truth seemed slipperier than ever these days, but all Milo could do was hope his prayers wouldn't fail since so much more was resting on them.

Outside, the morning air was cool and gray between the shadowing buildings. No monsters interrupted the cloud-wisped sky. They walked together in silence toward the market, swept along by others on their way and the restless gossip people greeted each other with—of the gryphons, the murders, and the sanct that vanished from the temple steps. Rumors were already spreading of the temple moving her, of an evil taking her, of her disappearing to perform miracles where she was needed. Adalena's dark, hooded cloak hid her face and its dried bloodstains, but as she strode beside him, Milo caught sight of her haunted eyes.

He tamped down his nerves, but as he turned the corner, they stirred and erupted at the sight of soldiers set at every statue in the market square.

Gia gripped her sister's shoulder, bringing her up short. "Militia," she hissed.

Milo groaned. "Ennio knows I gave him the wrong icon." There was no way to free all the others now—even if Val and Gia held off the guards while he woke one, they'd never reach all the statues in the square, let alone the city, before they were overwhelmed and arrested.

Val shook her head. "No wonder they recalled us. They're going to need every reinforcement to keep all the sancts under guard."

Adalena stared at the stone men and women set about the little piazza. She turned her serious face to Milo. "You must wake them from here."

Any anxiety was trampled by annoyance with himself. He didn't know much about how to use the icon, really, or performing invocations. Except that Stregna had answered his for some reason. He glanced at Gia. "I was holding Gia's—the statue's—hand when I prayed the first time, and we knew we'd have to be at your side to help you because of all your injuries. I'll try." Milo focused on the nearest statue and tried praying, tried again, listened to Adalena's repeated advice on invoking goddesses, to pray aloud, and tried again—but nothing happened, besides Milo growing self-conscious enough to wish Magna Mater's earth might swallow him up. Gia and Val pretended not to be keeping wary eyes on the guards as Gia kept up a running commentary of how she would have beaten Val if Milo hadn't stopped their fight, until Val cheerfully asked if she'd like to go again right there in the crowded market.

Finally, Adalena's calmness slipped and she snapped, "Are you even listening to me?"

He jerked his gaze from where it had drifted to one side.

Adalena's eagle eyes bore into him. "Please try your hardest. Prayers to Stregna require only true faith."

Wasn't that always his problem? He'd thought perhaps his fumbling prayers had finally found some purchase with this Unseen Goddess, but now it felt like grasping at smoke.

"Hey." Val towered over even Adalena. "Milo's physically incapable of not trying his best. We should regroup at home." She turned and led the way down the street.

Adalena's mouth opened indignantly, but she snapped it shut and followed.

Feeling defeated, Milo shouldered past the people coming into the square. As they made the short walk back, Adalena's shoulders tensed. "We don't have the time. We don't have the people—"

Val threw an arm up, blocking Adalena from following her into the alley.

Between the girls' heads, Milo could see the steps up to Val's were full of vivid purple and gold uniforms—the holy guard. A blur of gray streaked between their boots as Acci escaped. Ennio's men had forced open Val's door.

Val shoved Adalena back, almost tripping her over Gia. "Go, walk—" They moved away from the alley, departing quickly but not running. "Ennio's personal guard. They'll search the area next when they see we're not there."

Gia clenched her hands into fists as they turned back for the market. The square was dotted with militia, but there were more people to hide among. They swept back among the stands. "Where do we go now?"

He didn't know. The militia and guard were the protectors of the city, like the sancts. If Gia hadn't come to him, if he hadn't left the temple with her, he could have been watching one of these statues right now. He didn't know how to keep Gia and Adalena safe from them when he didn't know how he wasn't still one of them.

They walked slowly through the square, letting people push past to get to stands selling hand pies and greens. Near the next corner, where Lomian silks hung between carts, Gia rushed forward. Milo worried that the holy guard had entered the piazza, that she was jumping into a fight. Instead, she approached a short Lomian woman at a stand selling carved wooden goods, toys and bowls and cups. Gia reached a tentative hand toward the woman, who looked up from the figure she was carving, set her things down, and grasped Gia by both arms. Her brown face lit up like people in the sanctuary during a powerful omelia.

Words spilled quickly from Gia. "I need help. We need help."

The woman glanced to the rest of them, and then at something beyond them. Milo looked over his shoulder to see the flash of purple and gold. The holy guard was in the market. He turned back to Gia, his hand going to his new sword at his belt. Ennio couldn't take her.

The woman's face fell, but she nodded. "This way." She waved them behind her cart. That would buy them some time, but if the guard searched the square fully—

The woman spoke to her neighbor standing among the silks in Lomian, pulled Gia along, and they all followed. Milo could see through the fabric as the guard came farther into the market stalls. Flashes of silk—pink—more guards at the corner—orange—stalking closer—green—and then Gia was climbing into the silk seller's cart at the stranger's direction. He hauled himself up after her. Val gave Adalena a hand up, and then the swirling silks above the cart fell slack as the two women pulled them down around them.

They all flattened themselves to the bottom of the cart, like sardines in a jar—tension thicker than oil.

Gia's breath was in his ear, and Milo's pulse thrummed in his neck. He thought of the icon and pressed his fingers to it, wishing he knew how to invoke Stregna. His prayers did nothing. Milo wasn't what Adalena had thought. He couldn't be. He'd freed Gia by accident, with a prayer only for himself, and only woken Adalena because of her. He wasn't a templar. He hadn't even been able to get confirmed as a farmer, let alone a storica. He was no one.

Spring zephyrs brushed their fingers along the colorful silks. They glowed with the warming sun, with shadows of people moving across them like dark forms deep in the Argus. Finally, the Lomian woman pulled them aside. Her dark eyes were serious, but her round face seemed calm. "They left a little while ago. It should be safe enough."

"For how long?" Gia asked, sitting up. "Lena, what do we do? We can't wake the others. Soon we'll be trapped like them again."

"The chisel," Milo choked out at the thought of Gia turning back to stone. "I left it at Val's." What might Ennio do with it now that he knew Gia and her sister were awake in the city together? If he discovered its power—if he caught them out while statues—

Val squeezed his forearm. "You didn't know they'd come searching there."

"All my notes, the start of the translation—" He was insistent. "Where can we take them?"

The woman angled her head at Gia and asked, "Do you need someplace to stay?"

Adalena answered, "Yes," at once.

"No," Gia said. "We can't ask them to take any more risk for us." She turned to the woman. "We'll get out of your way."

"Please," the woman said. "After what you did for me at the gate, I would be glad. You're not the only ones the guards frighten."

"What happened at the gate?"

They were secreted away in a set of rooms at the top of a

narrow building crowded against the northern city wall. The woman—Kadri—had asked her cousin the silk seller to watch her wares and guided them here while Milo steered them away from streets with statues and militia. She and her children were staying here with her cousin. When they reached the small square outside, shadowed by ocher buildings, her children ran up from where they played among carts with wool blankets thrown over their frames, and hugged her around her legs. "Many of us would have camped outside the city for the festival, but with the gryphons lately, it's safer here," she said, patting their heads. "Once you get inside."

She made the children fetch water and a plate of figs for them before returning to her cart, saying they could stay as long as they needed. There was no kitchen, just three rooms full of beds with neat little bundles at their feet. One had a loft with a small cot and a skylight in its low roof propped open to the spring air.

Milo felt as if everything were closing in on him. The stone would settle over Gia and her sister in a few hours—and forever, in less than two weeks. He leaned against one wall, lost in the gloom of knowing the holy guard had likely claimed the chisel.

"What about the gate?" Adalena asked again from her perch on the bed, eyes narrowing. Gia backed against the wall, arms crossed against the attention from her sister and Val, who sat on the floor petting a cat that Milo presumed belonged to Kadri's cousin.

Then Gia, stone-faced, explained killing the general at the gatehouse, and why. How he'd abused his position to try to take advantage of Kadri.

Milo's insides burned with shame hearing of the gross betrayal of the general's duty—for not seeing what happened at the city walls he was so glad protected him. What kind of monster was he? Gia flinched from his stare. It was a wonder she'd accepted his help, even in desperation.

As Gia finished her story, Val drew her head up from her propped knee. "He was going to separate the children?"

The implication struck Milo at once. He locked eyes with Val. "Who knows how many wards weren't actually abandoned or orphaned?"

Adalena's nostrils flared delicately as she exhaled. "What did Ennio do to my city?"

"But this means—" Val's hand stilled on the cat, her voice the thinnest Milo had ever heard it. "Maybe my parents—" She blinked back tears.

"I'm sorry," Gia told her, looking stiff and miserable. "Though I'm not sure I'm sorry for killing him."

"No time for that," Adalena said briskly. "We must find a way for Milo to call upon Stregna and free my people. Quickly."

"I'll try," Milo said, doubt closing his throat. "Sometimes it takes me a while to get the hang of something new. To think through it."

"That's not good enough. I'll train you, but I need you to listen—" Milo was losing his fight not to rock in place, letting the knock of his head against plaster soothe his anxiety.

"Lena—" Gia began, shoving off the wall.

Val stood, her voice steeled with displeasure. "If the invocation requires physical contact, pressuring Milo's not going to help."

Adalena matched Val's stance. "I know all about pressure. Everyone is always expecting me to solve everything. I don't have the luxury of finding my way or failing. I have to get it right. I have a duty to my people."

"You have," Val said, hands on hips, "a stick up your ass."

The air sucked out of the room. Adalena gaped, and Milo braced for her to unleash a royal tirade against Val's atrocious manners. Instead, a laugh spilled out the principessa's open mouth.

Lost, Milo looked to Gia, but she only stared wide-eyed at her sister. Adalena clamped her mouth shut, but another laugh broke free, and another, until her shoulders were heaving with laughter. "I'm sorry." She pressed her hands to her chest. "No one's ever spoken to me like that."

"Rudely?" Val's shock softened to a bemused smile. "Thought Gia had that covered."

Adalena drew in and blew out a satisfied breath. "Like I was just another girl." She smoothed back her hair, and told Milo, "Right. I'm sorry. We'll figure out how to help you." Relieved, he nodded. It had to be a lot to take in—to go from principessa to fugitive all in what felt like one day. Adalena settled on the floor beside the low table and the plate of figs, folding her knees to one side. "Could we go to Stregna's temple? The concentration of offerings made over the years there, even long ago, would strengthen invocations."

Milo shook his head. "The temple's buried. There aren't even ruins. The whole thing's lost to the erosion of the hill."

Taking a seat and a fig, Val grinned. "I could get you there. I know a spot where the stone fell to make a little cavern."

He stared at her. "How do you know this?"

"You might know too if you'd sneaked out of the nido more often with the rest of us."

Adalena considered Val. "How dangerous would it be for us to reach it?"

"There's a group of statues near the top of the hill," Milo said. "So, guards will be set there."

"Let me teach you more about invoking so you'll be ready to work fast." She launched into a lecture on the incense and burned herbs offered in small prayer circles at Stregna's temple, rather than the large assemblies at the others. The cycle Milo had learned at Ennio's temple, of stone and bone and returning to the Great Mother, wasn't too different from what Adalena was saying about the connection between all three godpowers. He felt like he could grasp this, and grew more at ease with Adalena, mirroring her across the table, lacing his fingers together as she spoke.

After Kadri and her family returned for riposo, Adalena sighed and said she was concerned it still wouldn't be enough while the statues were all under guard. They huddled in one room, whispering while the children slept, ignoring the adults' curious glances, struggling to think of any other way to take the city back or buy more time past the new moon.

Gia kept throwing Milo worried looks, and he sank deeper into his own bleak thoughts. His stomach clenched at the idea of everything continuing after the sisters returned to stone forever. He had escaped once before when others fell to danger, had found a haven in this city. Now, even if he'd never discovered the lie of that, all of Ennio's corruption, this world without Gia seemed more like a tomb. He'd called her into life bereft and alone, his prayers hadn't protected her, and now he'd let the chisel slip into Ennio's hands. He cast about for anything to give as remedy and dredged up only dread.

As the afternoon pushed forward, Gia told Adalena what to expect when the moon set. With that, Gia scooped up the orange cat from where it had curled against her as she sat on the floor, deposited it onto her sister's lap, and disappeared into the next chamber.

Milo followed her up the narrow steps to the loft to find her sitting on the edge of the cot, knee bouncing rapidly like the heartbeat of a frightened animal.

"I don't want her to see how nervous I am," she muttered. "It'll only make it worse for her." She closed her eyes. "I hate it, every time."

"I can only imagine," he said, voice low. "Acci helped?"

She nodded.

"Can I help?"

He thought this might go unanswered as his invocations that morning. That she might scorn his offer, remind him again how he'd been loyal to the man who'd done this to her. That he'd handed over both her sister's icon and the means of her destruction to Ennio.

She opened her eyes and turned her face to him—full lips slightly pouting, soft cheeks brushed with rose, eyes inky and unguarded. Almost painfully beautiful. She nodded again.

He sat beside her and wrapped one arm around her, the other over to rest on her thigh. It stilled. She eased her head into the cradle of his shoulder.

They didn't know quite when the moon would go, but Milo didn't mind waiting. He'd run from every home he had, run with nothing, was nobody. It seemed beyond belief, beyond the greatest blessing of any goddess, that his arms had anything to offer her.

CHAPTER TWENTY

LIKE A KNIFE

The blazing of fire is a violence of transcendence, just as death can catch a life suddenly in the earth's churning.

—The Book of Invocations

Gia

Milo's voice fissured through the stone, pulling her from the hard grip of the invocation. Seeping through the spell and cracking it apart, like roots, like water, like heat. Everything sped, and bent, and breathed.

She awakened.

Gia followed Milo's voice down the little stairs, to where he sat on the floor talking with Val, looking half-asleep on the bed, and Lena, stretching awake in the corner. "I only wish we knew more about the original invocation," he was saying. "If I had my notes.

Or finished the translation." The crease drew itself between his brows. "Maybe I should go see Storica Lucca. He could help us."

The thought of Milo being swallowed back up by that place made Gia crouch and take ahold of his arm. "Don't go back there," she scolded him. She was always out of sorts when she emerged from the stone, angry that Ennio's influence over her was still so tangible, feeling out of control. She tried to wrap herself up, armoring herself until she felt better. But Milo was the first good thing she'd found in Ennio's world; she was going to keep him safe. He was far too trusting—the way he'd set down that chisel a day after she'd almost killed him proved that. "Honestly, it's a good thing you have me watching out for you."

A smile broke across his face, somehow cutting open the armor she'd put up. She gave his arm a shake before dropping it. "I'm serious."

She had to find a way to protect him, and everyone in the city she'd hurt—maybe not by making prayers but by breaking one. She sat, struck by an idea. Milo was right—the invocation was the root of all this, and what Ennio cared about more than anything. Forget trying to reach the other statues. This was where they had to come at him. "If we stopped the Ceremony of Dust, could that break the invocation? Weaken it to give us more time?"

Milo crossed his arms and tapped a thumb against his bicep, frowning. "Perhaps." His gaze lifted to her. "The ceremony is just before the new moon. If we're wrong, you'd have only a day at most before the invocation took you forever."

The hope and ache in his eyes, a distant signal fire, called to her and left her feeling lost. She wanted so badly to make the right choice this time. She was starting to understand Lena's outburst the previous morning; Gia *had* hoped she would handle everything if she was freed. Vengeance was so much easier. But Milo made her feel like she could stitch her fate into something new, even if the seams showed like godlines tracing her past.

He mused, "How would we even do it?"

She leaned nearer. "Like you said." Milo had shown her the way once before. "If the principessa came to life on the steps of the temple, people would listen to her. She doesn't even need her icon to work her influence on people."

His gaze shuttered. Maybe he didn't think it was a good idea.

"I agree," said Val, sleepily cradling her cheek in her palm. "If we can't reach the sancts, get the principessa in front of the people. Everyone loves her."

Lena had finally shaken off her stiffness, enough to cast Val a vexed look.

Val shrugged. "Put all that adoration to good use, Principessa."

Lena considered this. "Maybe Kadri could find others to join us. We'll need more people to stand against Ennio if waking all the other statues is impossible." Milo turned stone-faced. "But we should confirm disrupting the ceremony would work," Lena added.

He sat up straight. "I can get my mentor's help. Storica Lucca would want to know the truth, and he can finish the translation." He nodded. "At least I can make sure of this."

"I told you it's too risky to return to Magna's temple," Gia said.

"I won't need to. Storica Lucca visits the bookshop once a week during his passeggiata. I'll find him there."

"Good," Lena said as if that decided it. Irritation with her sister stoked in Gia's gut. "And Gia, you ask Kadri about reinforcements. She's grateful to you. That's our best chance for getting more help."

Kadri didn't owe them that much. Each time Gia spoke to her sister, she wondered if this would be when things collapsed into shouting, as every conversation between them seemed to before the stone. Still, she had to try, like testing an injured limb to see if it would hold weight. She took a breath. "Kadri may think of me as more of a protector than the temple, but plenty of other refugees are just as likely to see Ennio as their savior." She threw her hands up at Lena. "And most of them think I'm a demon."

Lena gave a smile, a small one. She was always holding so much inside. "And I'm the sanct that temple had on their steps for centuries. We talk to them. Convince them."

Lena could find solutions even if they had to be rooted out and finessed with the help of others. Nothing like an impatient bite of a blade. Somehow, she believed enough in herself to make them happen. Gia wasn't sure how she did that.

As the sun rose, they both spoke to Kadri, who gathered a few trusted others in her rooms before they left for their work at the market or in the fields. People she said had reason to dislike Primo Sanct, thanks to his militia at the city gates. Gia was prepared for them all to swoon over Lena like Val had. She was surprised when they greeted Gia with as much quiet reverence or glint-eyed excitement, gripping her hand with their fingertips while pressing their others to their brow. Lena listened to their stories of families harassed at the gates or denied entry and left to the fields while waves of monster herds passed through.

After a time, Lena said, "I know it must have been difficult to choose to come here and share these stories. It's not easy for me to admit I'm in a vulnerable position while my city is ruled so poorly by Ennio—and that is the man's name. No one made him a sanct but himself." Lena folded her hands together.

There were nods from the room. Lena pursed her lips before continuing. "From what I'm told, Ennio's done nothing to make things safer for everyone, even as Trestatto's risen in strength and influence. Meanwhile, his temple ensures all children in the city advance only as they decide." Her voice rang with conviction. Her knuckles were white. "It isn't good enough."

It wasn't. Training and spending as much time as she was allowed hunting monsters was the best Gia had ever done to help, listening to Ennio but never her sister. Shame bent her face away from Lena to Milo as he stood listening from halfway into the next room. His gaze was downcast, and she felt a flare of anger that Ennio, with his centuries of opportunity, had let Milo face those monsters alone in the fields, face losing his family.

Yet he'd been the one comforting her yesterday, offering the strength of his arms and the softness of his breath as her own deserted her. As lost as she'd felt when she'd awoken in the world Ennio had wrought, if someone like Milo could exist in it, that made her feel it could still be restored to something better.

Val, standing next to Lena, explained their plan to interrupt the Ceremony of Dust—how they'd need more people if they didn't want to be lost in the crush and grabbed by Ennio's men before they got the chance to speak. If Lena could, she'd draw even more Trestattans to their cause, enough to stop the ceremony completely.

"Now," Lena said, "what about supplies? Is there any way we can arm everyone who agrees to help?"

One of Kadri's children ran in from the other room, from behind Milo, rattling some noisy toy until his mother scooped him up in her arms. "We can help with that. I can carve spears as well as toys. We needed plenty of them out in our village."

"What? No," Gia said to Lena. "These people aren't trained soldiers."

Lena turned to her, voice low. "This is war. We must be prepared to fight."

"But we should plan to do this another way." They couldn't take advantage of people who practically worshipped them. "If we gain the crowd, we can ensure people don't partake in the ceremony, and break Ennio's power over us without any more death."

"One moment." Lena flashed a smile at their little audience and pulled her into the corner, dropping her voice lower. "I swear I'll never understand you. Since when are you afraid to run into battle?"

"Since Ennio stopped meeting us on even ground. He doesn't fight fair. This isn't your city anymore, Lena. Not the one you knew. His violence is hidden in what he does to those without power." She jerked her head at the refugees, the temple wards, who looked on with concern and curiosity. "That's who it'll rebound on if we give him an excuse to attack before you speak."

"If this is because you had feelings for Ennio—"

"No! *Gods.*" Gia raked her hands through her hair. She was trying to find a less violent path forward, but right now, she wanted to strangle her sister.

"We'll discuss this later," Lena hissed coolly. "Not in front of these people. We need—"

"They're not just tools for you to get your templars free. You've been acting like you only care about the other statues, but these Trestattans need our protection, too."

Lena scowled, then blinked and ran her hands down her tunic, brushing away her anger. She always treated her emotions as if they were as tamable as one of her long-dead cats she'd always had more time for than Gia, and not roaring beasts stirring her blood with their claws. "Any ideas then?"

She was actually asking to hear her thoughts? Gia turned back to the others as Kadri's boy wriggled free and raced away. Milo was no longer gazing at the floor, but at her. She fought to concentrate over her thundering pulse. "Maybe not spears, but we could use staffs? To block people from going into the temple." She pointed to the toy the child had left in his mother's hand. "And what about noisemakers, like this, but larger? Louder. The more attention we draw from the crowd, the less Ennio can tell them to ignore us. We want to start a conversation, not a fight." She looked to Lena. "Isn't that what Alta would have us do?"

"You're right." Lena stared at her, then looked to the others. She nodded once. "You're absolutely right." Never in a thousand years had Gia expected to hear that from her sister. "This city doesn't belong to Ennio, but it isn't mine anymore, either. The city belongs to itself." Her gaze softened at those gathered. "The emissaries I met with before the curse shared ideas with us, brought tablets from their leaders—in one city, every person selected their preference for a leader. Whoever took the majority assumed the role. When we've won Trestatto back, I will establish such a system, with representatives from each district. Including this one. And," Lena added, looking to Milo, "schools, with historical archives, to keep the truth strong and safe."

Her sister had managed to surprise Gia even more. "You'd give up your crown?"

Lena almost looked giddy at this before schooling her face back to its usual solemn dignity. "I will do what I must to protect my people. All of them." She turned back to the group. "But we need your help."

"What about the monsters?" a man asked from the back of the room. "The Ceremony of Dust and the statues are what keep them out, so what happens if we do as you say?"

"People will blame us for the city's protection failing," Kadri's cousin said. "They don't need any other excuse to mistreat those they see as outsiders."

Lena nodded seriously. "It will be a challenge, but I have every faith we can find solutions together." She inclined her head toward Val, who was sucking her teeth appreciatively, eyes gleaming. "Starting with ordering the militia to put all their efforts into guarding the fields and city from monsters, not harassing people at the gates." She raised her palms. "With the alliance I was working to establish, coordinating our efforts, we could have spread protection across the continent. We were on the verge of so much, for the people of the city and beyond, before Ennio took hold of everything."

"Let's take it back," said Kadri, with feeling.

The others murmured in agreement. For the next few days, they prepared, meeting early mornings or over risposo with anyone Kadri or the others found to join, whispering to those they had close ties to through their families or villages. They shaped boughs from the groves at the foot of the nearby hill into staffs. Gia looked forward to meeting Ennio once more outside his temple and getting it right this time, even as Milo's worries that it might all be for nothing eddied within her.

All those worries in mind, when the day came for Milo to intercept Lucca at the bookshop, Gia insisted on accompanying him, so Val sat her down and braided her hair into a more current style, gathering her locks little by little into a rope winding over one shoulder. Gia wore her new tunic, which pulled tightly over her chest and around her hips but would blend into the crowds on the streets, along with a straw field worker's hat Kadri had found for her.

Fingers woven through Gia's hair, Val laughed at the scruff Milo had grown, saying it would be disguise enough for him when he went out. He scratched his jaw, pulling his gaze from where he'd been watching Val's work, and said he couldn't exactly visit the barber. His eyes shot to Gia's. "And I'd probably only cut my own throat if I tried myself."

She laughed, making Val's gentle fingers tug her scalp almost painfully.

Milo also borrowed a hat, and, sword tucked through his belt, took the lead through the late-afternoon streets. Gossip stalked their every turn more persistently than a chimera. Of monsters spied flying over the city more frequently. Of towns emptied for refuge in Trestatto. Of the missing sanct, of the faith placed in the remaining ones—of doubt in Primo Sanct's protection, when he couldn't protect his own templars.

Milo guided them away from the guarded statues, but at an intersection with lemon trees edging the buildings, a clutch of miltia were pulling people from the cross streets.

"They're not stopping everyone," Milo murmured as their footsteps slowed, "only—"

Gia glowered at the soldiers examining a few frightened-looking girls and prayed Alta would drown Ennio with a permanent rainstorm over his head. "Only the fat people who could be me," she said darkly.

Before they could turn back, a soldier grabbed her wrist and drew her toward the wall. "Just the sword?"

"She's been confirmed," Milo's voice came from behind him.

"She's allowed to carry it. Hey—"

The soldier swept his palms over Gia's tunic. She huffed through her nose as the search travelled over her curves, as if Ennio still had his hands on her like he did during training, like he was still controlling her body as he did with his curse. But things would be worse if they discovered the dagger in her boot, took a better look at her face under this hat, and dragged her straight to him.

She was about to order Milo to run when he rushed forward, hat falling back. The soldier's eyes lit up with recognition. Heart kicking in her chest like it was trying to leap between Milo and the guard, Gia readied to grab for that dagger. But the soldier's hands fell away and didn't reach for the weapon at his belt. "Val's friend, right? Haven't seen you on any of this extra guard duty."

Milo's mouth opened and shut once. "Temple's been keeping me too busy. Festival preparations."

The soldier barked a laugh. "Val always says how they ran her off her feet. Sneaking away for some of the fun at last?" His gaze slid slyly back to Gia. "With your friend?"

The word was laden with teasing. Gia took the opportunity to lean against Milo, clutching his arm and ducking her head as if demure.

Milo jolted at her touch but quickly clasped his hand over hers. "Hoping to," he said, with a hoarse edge to his words. His vanilla and leather scent filled the breath she held, waiting, heart racing even faster.

The soldier jerked his head toward the next street with a smile. "Better get moving before the captain comes along and puts you on duty."

Gia wasted no time tugging Milo past the citrus trees and around the corner.

He stared at their hands before letting go and clenching his into a fist. "Are you all right?"

"Of course." She gave her shoulders a shake. "Let's get this information and get back to Kadri's." Before Ennio's grip tightened around them like a serpent.

Milo took them the long way down the smallest alleys, avoiding squares, peeking around each corner, and turning back when he spotted another checkpoint. Gia chafed at every suspicious stare from others on the street. Ennio had stripped her of her body's invisibility, using it to turn the city against her. They had to hurry or risk missing Lucca entirely. And the moon would still set before the sun today.

They ended up in a maze of streets not far from the river, crammed with shops. Milo headed for one with wide shutter doors opening an entire side to the street, with racks stuffed full of scrolls and shelves piled with bound volumes. His eyes, sharp and circumspect, lit up.

Gia tucked herself to one side of the door. "I'll watch from here." Among the books she pretended to peruse, hidden from the street, she could keep an eye out for any errant militia. Milo gave a quick nod and slipped between the bookcases, waiting for his mentor.

The narrow street was bustling, and Gia was on edge peering at everyone who passed. Finally, a man with dusty gray hair in a dark green robe shuffled into the shop. She recognized him from the carnival. Skimming the displayed volumes, his gaze caught on Milo. He reached out and grabbed him by the arm. "You're alive," he said, eyes wide and mouth open with relief.

"Of course I am."

Storica Lucca exhaled. "Milo, I thought you might be another victim. You must return to the temple at once—"

"No. I need your help." Milo clapped a hand over the storica's and pulled him into a lonely corner of the shop. Gia grabbed a book and shifted to keep them in sight through a rack of scrolls. "I found the invocation that created the sancts. I must know more about it."

"That knowledge is only for templars and storicas. But we can discuss it back at home," he told Milo urgently.

"You knew of this? Why do the records say it was lost?"

Lucca waved a hand, speaking quickly. "Because it's essential to the safety of the city. It isn't history or scripture but living prayer. The basis of the continuing intercession of the Great Miracle."

"But what I translated means the sancts are vulnerable, to Magna's chisel—"

"Storicas leave the great invocation to the templars," Lucca insisted.

Milo squared his shoulders. "I need to know how to break it."

Lucca stared. "Oh no, my boy." The old man glanced around the shop. "I told him you wouldn't betray the temple."

A warning voice inside Gia's head drew her a step closer, book still in hand.

"If you come home, then they'll understand." Lucca held out pleading hands to Milo. "You know your judgment of people isn't always a strength."

Milo didn't move. Hurt burned across his face. His brows furrowed. "What did you do?"

"These people are taking advantage of you, making you help them."

"No one's making me. It was my choice."

Lucca reached for Milo's arm. "Come. He thought you might reach out to me, but he promised. You have to come back, or else—"

"No." Milo pulled away. "I'm supposed to watch over her."

A holy guard burst from the back of the shop, another raced in from the street, and the warning voice turned into a scream of panic pulsing through Gia's blood, through her tightening chest.

One guard grabbed Milo. One threw an elbow to his gut. Gia flung the book at the first guard's head, dazing him long enough for Milo to wrench free. The other guard shoved him against a wall of books, but Milo caught himself—his hands gripping a low shelf as he kicked the guard's knee. Gia heard the crunch from two paces away, weapon ready. The guard cried out and fell to the floor. Milo drew his sword.

The other guard had recovered and drawn his as well. Milo was cornered.

Gia wrapped her arm about Lucca's frail shoulders from behind. She dragged him back, balancing her blade against his throat. "Let him go."

She ignored Milo's horrified look. Whether it was for the ambush they'd fallen into or how she was threatening his beloved mentor, she didn't know and couldn't care. Not now. Let him hate her, as long as he let her save him.

People were screaming, rushing into and away from the street. She wanted to cut it all away, slice Milo free from the threat of the guard. The militia was probably being called right now, and she only had a trembling old traitor in her grasp.

The guard slashed his sword at Milo. He fended him off, but there was no room for him to maneuver, trapped among the shelves. "Hey!" she shouted, and shoved Lucca into the guard.

Thank all Three Sisters the guard slowed. Lucca stumbled to the tiles. Gia shoved again, planting a foot and a palm against the nearest rack. It fell toward the guard and Lucca. Scrolls slid free, crashing into them and over the floor. Milo slipped around as the guard braced the rack up with his shoulder.

Gia grabbed Milo's hand. "Run!"

They plummeted through the streets, shouts following them around corners as they fled. Milo darted around those too foolish or brash to move from their path. Gia kept pace, shouldering her way through. She knocked the flat of her sword into the faces of men who looked as if they were about to grab her.

The militia watching the statues were less daunted. One saw them coming early enough to stand ready in the middle of the street, sword raised.

Milo sped ahead, running straight for the sword. He met it with his own and didn't slow until he'd rounded on the woman, pulling her into a fight away from Gia. The guard swung her blade after him, and Gia reached them as they were locked in battle, dust kicking up from their sandals.

Gia timed her first swing to follow Milo's. Together they drove the soldier back toward the plaster wall between shop entrances. Wide-eyed shoppers pressed themselves as far away as they could get, shoving each other out of the way to escape. Gia, about to shout to Milo to knock out the guard after she pinned her to the wall, spotted another scarlet sash through the pulsing crowd out on the street.

She dove around Milo. She was barely able to block the newest arrival before he hacked his sword down upon Milo's neck. His blow screamed against Gia's steel, all the way to the hilt. She felt her back press against Milo's—felt him turning to attack this guard before the man could force both swords into Gia's face. The guard raised his blade to meet Milo's. Gia whirled on the first guard, crashing her sword against the woman's as it chased after Milo. Gia threw all her weight at her, knocking her head against the wall, where she slumped.

Every strike of swords behind her was accompanied by grunts and shouts. She turned to see Milo furiously meeting the guard's every blow. This man was big, but Milo was quicker. He seemed to anticipate the guard's moves almost before he made them. People crowded the fight. The fearful had fled, and those left shoved Milo into the drive of the guard's sword. They grabbed at Gia, too—she threw elbows, and was almost upon the guard with three steps, but another man caught at her, wrapping his arms about her.

She slammed her head into his, driving him off her. Roaring through the pain, she bowled forward and knocked against Milo's opponent, shoulder to shoulder. Milo didn't miss his chance—he slapped the flat of his sword against the man's temple. Gia fell to the ground with him as he lost consciousness.

Milo grabbed Gia's forearm and pulled her to her feet before their audience could crush them. She bellowed and waved her sword, anything she could do to clear a path. Some people shoved each other—as if a few were trying to help Gia and Milo slip away. She only had a moment to catch Milo's wild look—nostrils flared, eyes sparking—before they broke through and sped from the street.

They raced around the corner—she knew this place, where the paving stones sloped toward the Argus. They'd shaken any pursuers, but there was nowhere to go in these crowded market streets hemmed by the river, and it wouldn't be long before they were cornered again.

Was that an outcry behind them? She slammed her shoulder into a jeweler come to see the commotion. He ducked back into his shop.

Milo tugged his hand away from her. "You should run, I'll stay and—"

"You're too smart to be that foolish," she told him, trapping his hand in an iron grip.

And too caring for his own good—he couldn't see the corruption behind anyone's smile. He probably wanted to go back and check on that betrayer, Lucca, right now.

Luckily for Milo, she'd never been very smart or caring—but always adept at destroying things.

A glass blower's shop sat at the corner of where the street lifted over the river and split off to a series of workshops lining its bank. Gia risked letting go of Milo's hand and ran forward. The artisan and her apprentice flinched from Gia's sword, even as she sheathed it, and Gia stole a long pipe from the fire basket where they worked.

"What are you doing?" Milo called after her.

Gia dragged the incandescent glass along the walls of the shops up the bridge, hoping its heat would catch on the wood built into the stone, the shutters, the carved signs.

"Gia! You're going to kill someone—"

She was trying to save someone. "Plenty of time to get out," she growled, hefting the burning glass along a window frame. "Water all around." She spotted the perfumery she'd passed those first days wandering the city in search of Milo. She surged forward and smashed the dimming glass into the shop's shelves, igniting the jars and vials and pots of oils. The flames snatched and spread. As the shop owner ran out, Gia threw the rod into the blossoming inferno and grabbed for Milo's hand. He'd stuck by her side. A thrill flashed from their clutched hands straight to her heart. She pulled him beyond the blaze.

He shouted, "There's a militia station just on the far side, this isn't—"

They'd all be blocked and kept busy by the fire. "Come on!" He was caught in her gravity now, and they barreled along together, veering through the entrance of a shop—its keeper on the street, wide-eyed at the fire clawing over the roofs covering the bridge—and straight out the other side. Gia vaulted upon the balustrade—Milo's grip the only thing preventing her from going over the edge. He let Gia pull him onto the stone wall— and they jumped together into the air.

CHAPTER TWENTY-ONE

OMELLA

Invocation is speaking god into the world, power borne on human breath and tongue, communion of sacred and earthly at a templar's lips.

—The Book of Invocations

Milo

They crashed through the surface of the water together, white shards of froth scattering. It wrapped them in its tumult and murk, muting the chaos they left in their wake. The current took them, and the only thing Milo knew for certain was he could not let go of Gia's hand.

They bobbed to the surface, gasping, and Milo located the bank, an uneven stretch between bridges where boats were left on a jutting stone platform or tied to poles lining along its side.

They dove back under, away from anyone's watch. He kicked his legs and dragged Gia toward land, hoping in the press and pull of water she'd understand.

The river nearly pushed them farther than he meant, and they broke their hands apart to reach its edge. They couldn't let themselves be swept to where the Argus passed under the city wall, through a grate, and get trapped there. Milo felt his toes scrape pebbly mud and almost released his breath. He'd lost his sword—he couldn't remember if it was in the water or in the waves of crowds buffeting them—so when he caught the side of a boat hanging upside down halfway off the dock, he had a hand free to grab for Gia and pull her to him.

She tried to get her feet under her on the steep slope of the bank, bobbing into him and clutching at his arm. He shoved his feet against the mud, dragged himself up through the crest of water, and pulled her under the cover of the boat.

Still too exposed. He had to get her somewhere safe, somewhere unseen. Through the strip of air between wood and water, he could see where old boats awaited repair or removal, nestled in the corner of the dock and bank, some falling nearly into the river.

"Come on," he told Gia on a rasp of breath. He ducked his head again underwater, and only emerged once they were both beneath a boat that cupped itself completely to the river.

The current tugged at their legs and hips, rocking them together. Gia's hands splayed against his chest, fingertips pricking his shoulders. His arms went around her, hands over her back, steadying her. Light stole through small holes in the boat's floor. Water clapped against its sides. Both were breathing hard.

"Lucca," he said, voice rough from running and shouting and

swallowing river water. And from the confession of culpability the name carried. He managed to catch his breath, though something pinched painfully within him. "You were right. That place is a nest of serpents." He wouldn't let them tangle themselves around anyone anymore.

Gia met his attempt at apology with her own. "I'm sorry I—I don't think I hurt him too badly."

"I don't care if you did."

She almost winced. "Oh, Milo."

If anything, it was Milo's own doing. He'd put her in danger when he was meant to protect her. Milo couldn't help how he saw the whole and parts of any situation, and all the facts were falling into place in his mind now—and the conclusion they pointed to. "They know we're trying to break the invocation. They have the chisel! They could—" He shoved his hair back from where it was dripping in his face. "We can't be caught here."

"We should go—find good ground to fight." A wave pushed her sideways, and she braced herself against him, her face stern. "Even if it's hopeless. Better than being taken here."

No. They needed a distraction so Gia could get back to Adalena—finish her fight.

He needed to make her one last offering.

Milo fought down a shiver as a truth possessed him, more certain than anything he'd ever known. He would sacrifice everything for her.

"I'll make sure they look elsewhere," he told her. "I can swim to the far side, upriver, and pull them away from you."

She scowled. "I already told you, don't be foolish. We'll find another way to get out of here." He recognized the uncertainty and panic edging her voice even as she strove to keep it even.

His fingers traced little circles on her back, trying to write comfort into her. "Your sister needs you at the ceremony. No one else can fight like you, and no one else will protect her better."

Her brows arched, then drew together. "I'll distract them, and you can go. We'd have a better chance that way. You don't even want to face your own militia. I'm a far better fighter."

She was trying to provoke him into not doing this for her. But he felt this conviction deep in his bones, and no words, no matter how barbed, could pry it from him. "Once I draw them away—"

"Milo." Her bluster melted. "You can't." Her voice quivered, and she blinked back tears. "You should be somewhere safe writing your omelias." She groaned with frustration. "I should have left you in that temple."

She probably would have been better off without him. Just look at how he'd fallen back into trusting the very people she'd told him were treacherous. So much misplaced faith. It had felt safer to turn to what he knew for answers. He'd given into the fear he might not be enough—might not be what he was supposed to be simply because he possessed an icon from his parents. Uncertainty hounded him, like when he'd balanced the sancts' freedom against the city's safety, wondering what a more just world would cost. If he'd be strong enough to pay it.

"Gia." He slid a wet curl from her cheek, tucking it behind her ear. The bowed wood about them, struck through with spears of sunset's gold, was like their own small sacred temple, someplace there could be no lies. "This is my fault, but I'll make it right." He didn't know anything about goddesses or invocations, really, and maybe never would. For too long, he'd locked himself up in the lies Ennio and the others told him. And the worst part was the lie he'd told himself, that he could be safe and content there, reciting their falsehoods, without ever finding what he believed or wanted. Or daring to speak it aloud.

Right now, he wanted to be more like Val. Throw it all in, whatever might happen.

Gia's fingers dug into him. "No, you're not doing this. Why would you do this—?"

"I need you to break the invocation. To be free. I need you—" His voice broke.

She stared at him, eyes wide, but he couldn't read with what. "You destroyed your entire life to help me." The anger in her voice collapsed like a wave, spreading thin into a warning. "Don't break your heart on me."

"It needs breaking," he insisted. "Break it, batter it, burn it in your fire." His faith in the temple, every lie it burnished as truth, needed to be extinguished. And waiting in stone for seemingly forever, she was like an ancient, true star, sending light through time—to him.

She was the only star he needed in his sky.

If she didn't feel the same, he'd leave it and simply help her how he could. He had plenty of practice with unanswered devotion. But he had to let her know before it was too late. Even if he couldn't find the words, he could make her understand she was no monster, or if she was, he welcomed every way she tore him apart. He could show her.

His hand cupped her cheek, fingertips grazing where her escaped curls were drying into looping script. When he leaned forward, never taking his eyes from hers—gilt with light scattered from the river—she didn't pull away, even as the tide buffeted them. He pressed his lips to hers.

His heart thrummed when she slid her hands up to cradle

around his neck, tugging him nearer, deepening the kiss. Gia had always been more action than words. She kissed like she fought, consumingly, and his own hands moved, over her hips, fabric slick and slipping under the water. Here was the bolt of connection he sought. Here was a prayer he could deliver straight to she who held his full faith.

She broke away for air, and he bit his own lip, as if he could keep her kiss there. But there was no time. "You'll be safe here. I'll lead them away."

"No—" She still didn't have enough air. Her fingers clawed at his neck now. "Milo—"

He dropped his forehead to hers and waited out the change, pulling her hands from him before she stilled. "I know you're angry," he murmured. His purpose was clear now, finally. "If I can make it free, I'll meet you at Kadri's. If I don't—" He didn't expect to. He knew this was goodbye. "I trust you to make things right. Remember the wards."

He needed a moment to draw several deep breaths before sweeping a farewell caress over her cheek, plunging under the water, and kicking away.

He was a strong swimmer. He often beat Val in their races down the Argus over the summers. On his own, he could make it a good distance before surfacing, and farther before returning to the bank. By then, no one would know where Gia hid until moonrise, when she could slip under cover of night to safety.

He fought the current and emerged far from the little dock, past the bridge they'd leaped from. He gulped a breath and dove back under. When he broke for air again, he was nearer the next bridge, the one lined with sancts.

Milo tried not to think of his—his, for a moment—as he

hauled himself toward the shore. He would make the soldier guarding the statues here see him. He wiped dripping water from his face and plodded up the bank. Shouts came from behind. He glanced to see a militia soldier across the river calling out to the stationed guard. Pointing to Milo. Racing for the bridge.

Every part of him burned with exhaustion, but he forced his limbs to work a little longer. To try to get away. He sped the rest of the distance over the gravel and mud, veering from the bridge, then careening around the corner and down the first street. The rush of buildings, the smell of dust kicked up—it almost felt like just another evening spent running through the city with Val. Until the guards cornered him at either end of a short lane.

Trapped. He'd lost his sword. He tensed, ready to charge one soldier or the other. That was Jason at the far end of the street— Milo had taught him to read during long militia watches on the wall when Jason had admitted he'd never learned. Milo would scratch simple words over the stone with a piece of charcoal.

Natalia waited at the other side. She and Milo had killed a ventrono together when a wild herd kept stubbornly stamped-ing at the western gate. The determined scowl on her face told Milo she'd chased him from the shops across the river. Footsteps pounded nearer, ringing off the stone walls around them—more hunting guards had been alerted by her shouting, drawn by his emergence from the river.

He barreled toward Jason.

Both soldiers must've recognized him, despite Milo being unshaven and soaking. Jason didn't draw his sword, but braced to meet him. Maybe he felt compelled not to hurt his fellow soldier. Milo had worried about fighting his own people, but he threw himself at Jason without hesitation.

He wasn't sparring now. He fought for Gia.

His fist landed. Jason's head snapped back. Milo tried to get past him, but Jason caught him with a quick jab. Hands gripped Milo's shoulders. Natalia pulled him back. Jason, teeth bared, aimed a punch across his jaw. A blow across his back knocked him to the ground. His head cracked against the paving stones.

Jason pressed his lips together as he hauled him up. "Orders are to arrest anyone helping the girl. Didn't think it'd be you."

"Ennio's hurting the sancts." Milo struggled against his grip. "He's lying—"

Natalia struck him across the mouth. "Blasphemy."

More militia and a holy guard found them then. They took him back toward the river. Blood dripped down Milo's chin, making it impossible to focus on anything else for more than half a thought. They had him hard by the shoulders, and it was all he could do to keep his feet under him. When they returned to Jason's post, Milo saw, up the Argus, the dark smoke of the smothered fire against a bruising sky, and the ruined bridge. It looked like some tremendous monster had taken a bite from it. He laughed a bloody laugh—until the first sanct on the bridge blocked his view and he remembered he still wore Stregna's icon.

His chest seized, strangling his hoarse laughter. He should have left it with Gia. He was so used to it he hadn't even thought to do so. If he could invoke the goddess to help free himself—he didn't know how, and there were others he could focus on freeing before losing his last chance.

He jerked toward the next sanct, surprising the guards holding him enough to make them all take steps toward the edge of the bridge. He stretched his arm as far as the guards' grip would allow, splaying his fingers—

They almost brushed the stone.

Natalia grabbed his wrist and wrenched his arm away. Milo tried to take the chance to slip from her hold on his upper arm, but Jason yanked him back by the shoulder and threw him to the ground. Milo scrambled and crawled. *Let me free one more.*

The only answer to his prayer was oblivion.

+ ✦ +

Later, he realized they must have been directed not to kill him. He woke in an unfamiliar chamber. The walls were plaster, not stone. The bed he lay on, while narrow, had a well-stuffed mattress and fresh blankets. A sconce lamp was lit.

The door was locked.

He didn't bother knocking or calling for anyone. If he was lucky, Gia would make it back to Val and Adalena, and they would succeed in breaking the Ceremony of Dust and the invocation. They would free the rest of the sancts, and make a safe place in this city again for them all. He didn't dare hope he'd be lucky enough to find out one day, to have one of them unlock this door and tell him they'd done it. He swallowed, his throat painfully dry. That would be all right. He sat back on the bed and crushed two handfuls of blanket, rough and yielding, in his fists. He'd only traded one small cell for another, and it didn't matter how long he lasted in this one.

It only killed him to think that if everything failed, if these were Gia's precious final days, he was confined here, barred from being at her side.

The door opened after some unknown time. Milo jumped to

his feet, ready to tell whoever was on duty the truth of Ennio. Everyone who heard could possibly pass along the real story, could help Gia and Adalena and the city that didn't know they were trying to save it.

It was a holy guard, and he didn't stay longer than to see that Milo was awake before locking him in again.

Milo couldn't sit, but paced the little room, wondering what was coming next, until he tired and sagged against one of the blank walls. He rubbed his filthy hands over his grimy face—his lip was sore but had stopped bleeding.

When he closed his eyes, all he saw was Gia. Was she still where he'd left her? Or was it morning? Was she safe?

Before long, the door opened again. A holy guard holding the key stood aside, next to two of his fellows, and let Ennio walk inside.

A shudder of anger ground through Milo. He clutched a fist into his other hand. Here was the same templar and sanct who'd taken him in when he'd lost everything. Here was the same man who'd betrayed Gia to the point where she didn't even trust herself any longer.

One of the guards carried in a platter of food and left it on the mussed bed. Another bore two small wooden chairs. They retreated and Ennio sat. The shut door stayed unlocked, with the three guards outside it.

"Milo," Ennio said, a mild look on his face. He gestured to the chair across from him. "Please, sit."

Milo hadn't even noticed he'd stood at attention. He was tempted both to follow Ennio's instruction and slouch back against the wall. He ended up staying still.

"You've been through quite an ordeal." Ennio adjusted his

robe and clapped a hand to one thigh. "I'm sure you're longing for the comfort of home after being away, the familiarity of your own cell, but here we can keep you safe. And once we've dealt with the current disruption to our city, you can be back there. Very soon, I hope."

Milo stared. Was he going to pretend like this? Did he actually hope Milo hadn't learned everything Gia and Adalena had to tell him, everything they both knew were in the notes the holy guard had surely found? It grated through Milo's senses. His fingers reached for his icon out of habit and found it gone.

Ennio went on, soothingly. "You're a victim of this evil that's attacked our temple and our general, but I know you're glad to be able to help stop it. To prevent more deaths."

"Maybe—" Milo's throat was still so dry. But this was his chance to speak directly to the man who had caused pain, stolen lives—who would keep doing so unless prevented. And all Milo had were his words. "Maybe the general needed killing." Maybe that bridge needed burning down—the false peace Ennio hid his sins behind needed tearing down. Maybe Milo's rule about no killing was too simple in the face of that.

Something sparked in the templar's eyes, the flash of an ancient blade wielded by an unknowable hand. Ennio's words remained even. "It pains me to see how your ordeal has affected you. I know you love Trestatto, love our temple." He pressed his palm to his chest. "And without a strong general and his militia keeping faithful watch at our gates, who will protect them? Who will ensure dangerous people—monsters—don't enter our city again? Who will keep the young wards safe?"

Milo's stomach twisted. The dissonance of Ennio's words and the threat they carried made his vision blink. His palms pressed into the wall—wanting to shove him forward, wanting to reach for this man with violence.

He was untouchable.

The templar's eyes were kind again. "We need you to tell us where the lost sancts are. Only that, and you can return home."

Milo said, more a hope than a prayer, "You can't stop them."

Ennio raised his hands, supplicating. "I want to help them! We must restore the sancts, rescue them from the evil that's targeted our blessed city, help them return to their true purpose. It is vital nothing impair the Ceremony of Dust's power to strengthen the faith and protection of our city."

"You mean the city protecting you through the ceremony. That is how it works, right?"

Ennio smiled. "Such a perceptive, inquiring young man. We were sorry you missed the confirmation ceremony. It was hardly your fault this evil prevented your being there. In fact, you will be quite the hero when you help us track it down. I know it must have been a trial, but we're fortunate it attacked you next, and you, being so faithful, were able to survive long enough to be rescued, and lead us to it." He cast his gaze over the food platter, as if considering the cured meats, cheeses, and honeycomb. "A suitable role for such a hero can still be conferred, in a smaller ceremony performed by me, once you are recuperated and the city safe. With so many templars requiring replacements, we have room for another apprentice there. Or Storica Lucca informs me you would be a valuable addition to our scholars."

Milo wondered at the power Ennio flaunted—creating whatever reality he preferred, even without invoking his goddess.

Ennio leaned forward, hands clasped, forearms resting on his lap. "I need your help to support the one true goddess Magna

Mater. She is calling you by name to serve."

Once, these words uttered to him by Primo Sanct would have meant the world to Milo. Only it was a broken, false world, one that would crumble when the truth rang out. "You can't silence the principessa." Milo almost smiled. "And I can't wait to see what trouble Gia makes for you next."

Ennio got a distant look in his eyes, not that cloudy kindness he sometimes wore, almost an ache. "Gia." He swiped his tongue over his teeth. "She could have been a proper principessa and ruled under my guidance."

The shudder of anger was back, and Milo had to clench his teeth to get his words out. "She deserved better than you."

Ennio waved a hand. "This trouble, as you call it, is a mere pebble. When seen from down the stretch of time I've lived, it is imperceptible in the long smooth road of Trestatto's good fortune. It will be dealt with, and forgotten, in a few generations."

No. The truth couldn't be buried. "Gia won't make it easy for you to sweep this aside." Milo wielded his next word as his only weapon. "Ennio." Stripped of all titles. Bearing the long-hidden sins they both knew Gia had revealed.

Ennio leaned back, indifferent. "You think this hasn't happened before? You think other children haven't wandered astray?" He rubbed a finger along the side of his nose, then dropped his hand casually. His next words fell like an axe. "Like the farmers a short time ago, gathering in the fields, telling tales of goddesses who forsook this city. They would not be shepherded by the temple. So they were driven to pieces by beasts."

Milo stilled—heart squeezing to a stop.

Ennio nodded as if remembering. "Storica Lucca told me of how you came to us." The edge of a cruel smile lifted his lip. "Your parents had to die not only because of a lack of faith but because of their lies—their blasphemous devotion to false goddesses endangered this city. I understand you have worked hard to be worthy of your place in my temple. I know you do not wish to become like them."

Milo's fingers clawed at the wall behind him, scraping away plaster dust. "That was you?" Gia had said he'd done this to other villages. It hadn't been his undevout parents damaging the sancts' protection at all. Milo saw flashes of teeth—blood—images he'd squeezed his eyes shut to since he could remember. More memories flooded in with them. Cries rising above the crops. The rough wood of the high window he'd escaped from. Screams and sweat and the smell of sunbaked fields he fled through. The metal chain newly around his neck.

And something he'd nearly forgotten from before the day it all began, or ended—three crescents drawn in the dirt, wiped away after a story beyond Milo's recollection.

Ennio's voice cut through the veil of memory. "I do what I must to protect this city. Its people are my children. Only I have the gift of seeing how best to shelter them; to help them sustain their strength; to guide them to what is right. I care for them, but they cannot understand the responsibility, the sacrifices that must be made."

Milo blurted, "But never your own sacrifice, always someone else's, even Horace and—"

Ennio rose, and his voice rang out louder as if he stood before the assembly at rites. "I gave up the freedom of my power as templar. You are right, I tied it all to the invocation that would allow me to protect Trestatto forever, bound myself to it as much as the statues."

He stepped closer to Milo, trapping him against the wall. "And you can either submit to the same purpose and tell us where to find the girls, or we will take the knowledge from you and cast you out." The man's eyebrow twitched. "It would be tragic to inform the people that these violent acts were perpetrated by a lowly ward, a jealous nothing, against the very templars and city who took him in. But the city would rejoice the evil had been plucked from it like an irritating splinter before it could fester." He peered at Milo and cocked his head. Milo used to think Primo Sanct's unworldly gaze was something of the holy touch of Magna Mater. Now he wondered if simply the centuries and unchecked power had brewed a kind of detached cruelty there. "Tell me," Ennio murmured, "what fate appeals to you more: to be written down in the archives as the beast that made the city bleed one Sancts' Month, or to be forgotten forever?"

This silenced Milo. There was no point speaking up to a man who wove his own truth and outlived even the books that might have tried to tell a different story.

The templar swept back and rapped once on the door. His guard opened it as Ennio told Milo, "Be sure to let the guard know when you reveal where the girls are hiding."

He was gone, but two of his guards stepped into the room at once. No new conscripts, no friends from Milo's training—the holy guard were men who'd risen through the militia for years. A fist found Milo's jaw before he could turn away—his vision cluttered with stars. His shoulder slammed into the wall. He pushed himself off it and swung at the guard, but the other struck him in the stomach. Milo doubled over, trying to catch himself before going down. The platter crashed to the stone floor, food scattering. He was heaved up by the shoulders and shoved into the chair he'd refused.

He got one good kick in—one guard went down, knocking over the empty chair. The other clamped his hands on Milo's shoulders until the first pulled iron chains from his belt and locked Milo's hands behind him.

There was a lot of spitting and swearing. The guards switched off—the one at Milo's back secured him by the shoulders while asking for the girls' location, leaving the other free to deliver his fists to Milo's face. They gave no rhythm to the blows, no set pattern. They'd ask and strike before he had a chance to answer, then ask three times before hitting him again.

Milo's mind reached for anything to hold onto, to brace himself against the temptation to give them what they wanted. It felt like only moments since he'd sheltered at the edge of the river with Gia. It felt like forever.

The guard before Milo paused his assault to swear at him again. "Sancts don't break," he told Milo. "But you will." He drew a dagger from his belt and passed it to the one behind him before repeating Ennio's question again. And again. And again.

Milo had wondered often if he didn't know how to pray to a goddess—if something inside him simply didn't fit the purpose. Perhaps he'd lacked motivation. The keen pain of the dagger prodding under his nails, slicing up his arms, provided a bright, sharp path for his prayer now. But it only rebounded upon him, resounded through him—building in intensity, finding no outlet, until everything in him was white hot agony, driving out all thoughts, names, words. And then he was screaming.

CHAPTER TWENTY-TWO

LOVE LIKE KILLING

Templars must remember their goddesses' power flows together, as sisters share bone and blood and breath.

—The Book of Invocations

Gia

He was kissing her.

The stone rocked her in its drowsy sense of time, and part of Gia could stay in that moment when Milo breathed his sweetest words to her and followed them with kisses. They drew a galaxy of feelings across her skin—surprise and thrill and wanting. Her heart nearly erupted as the warmth she felt for him transformed into something fiercer under the spell of his words. With his burning hands on her, with how he wrote a story for them with each brush of fingers and press of lips. He'd stirred her awake once before, but now his words and touch brought her flesh alive in a wholly new way.

Another part of her howled after him, unable to follow, to fight, until she broke free again, too late to pursue him.

Gia could only stare into the dim of the empty, inverted boat for some time before forcing herself to move. The pain from fighting her way here was gone, but her mind was stiff and slow with aching.

She'd once thought Milo a proud adherent to Magna's temple, but it turned out he was a ruin like her, broken and shaped by abandonment and hurt. And now he'd made a terrible decision just like her—only instead of others' lives, he could be sacrificing his own.

Her blood lashed with the knowledge that she would burn down a thousand bridges, take a knife to a thousand throats, to save him. She couldn't say how it had come over her—her feelings had ambushed her. Overthrown her. This was mad, and dangerous—the last time she'd thought she cared for someone, it broke the world. And look at all the destruction surrounding her again. At Milo. Gone.

This decision felt like a blade wielded by some other hand, threatening to slip through her ribs, or Milo's. She should tell him once she saw him again to stay away from her, for his sake. That she didn't deserve his worship.

If Milo was still alive. It was almost a new day.

Her fingers tensed where they gripped the cold dock, guiding her to where she could quietly climb up the shore. If Milo got himself killed, she would call down the Unseen Goddess herself, templar or not, to restore him, just so she could kill him again.

She would not throw his sacrifice back in his face. The day balanced on the edge of morning, and she had to get back to Lena before the sun helped Ennio hunt her down. She had to finish their fight, with Kadri and everyone she'd promised to help. She did her best to follow the path Milo had guided them through, avoiding statues and their guards—though part of her, the part still rough from screaming through the stone, wanted to find them and take them out. She wanted to show Ennio what he'd get if she was left without the first person who'd made her think she could be more than a monster.

The idea that Ennio might be thinking the same thing, that he could write a warning in the blood of the enemy he could get his hands on—that he could be inspired by her own acts against his men to do so with Milo—Gia almost stumbled into a wall as she checked around a corner.

She took a stuttering breath. She wasn't alone in her fight against Ennio anymore. She had work to do with her sister and their allies. Together, they were going to take back this city, and they'd take Milo back, too.

She clung to this on her way home, sticking to the receding shadows. But when she climbed the stairs to Kadri's, she flooded with fear. She'd lost Val's friend. She'd lost Lena's fellow templar. She knocked with an annoyingly unsteady hand.

"It's me." *Only me.* Lena would give her one of her disappointed looks, tearing through her like a knife through a sail. Gia didn't know Val well, but she imagined throttling was a possibility. Or punching. Maybe dragging her to the temple to trade for Milo. Gia wouldn't even fight her.

The bar scraped and shifted away, and Val pulled open the door. Behind her, Kadri stood, and Lena—hands lifting like birds until she caught and held them to her waist. Gia made herself look Val in the eye, now that she had seen Gia was alone. She couldn't say what she wanted to, only answered Val's questioning look with her own of apology and determination. At least that's what she tried for. Her eyes were hot and stinging.

Val reached her arms about her and crushed her in a hug.

"He could still make it back here." Val worried her hands in her lap beside Lena, sitting on the bed in the room they'd all been crammed into for days.

Gia squeezed the hem of her tunic, stiff with drying river water. She wanted to believe that as much as Val and didn't have the heart to say how unlikely it was. "Or we'll get him out when we go to the temple for the ceremony."

"No," Lena said, scraping one of Kadri's knives down the bough she was shaping into a staff. "That's not the plan. We must put everything into stopping the Ceremony of Dust."

"What?" Gia felt the argument coming, like always—as if one clumsy word would ruin their fragile partnership like a vase smashing to bits upon the floor. She pressed her lips together, determined not to be the first to bungle things. "We can't let Ennio kill him."

"We can't divide our resources—not with everything hanging in the balance."

Gia drew a deep breath but couldn't help growling, "I wish I could just kill Ennio." Fix it all with one strike.

"Making threats is pointless." Lena dragged her blade along the bough.

They made Gia feel better, though. And weren't Stregna's templars always saying something about giving breath to truth? Gia would break Milo's rule about killing to save him. He could be mad at her all he wanted as long as he lived. Maybe it was better for him to see straightaway she didn't deserve his adoration.

"We have to be realistic," Lena said. "Ennio's invulnerable with the invocation. If he has Milo, he has Stregna's icon, and reason to take over its power or give it to someone loyal." Gia didn't like how Lena was skirting around saying Milo might be lost already. "He holds all three icons and the chisel. Our only chance against him now is breaking the invocation by preventing the Ceremony of Dust." She looked grim as she snapped a branch off the bough. "We'll have to take it on faith that it will work." With her tone, Lena set the imaginary vase upon a high ledge, beyond reach of her little sister. As if that settled things.

"You only care about losing Stregna's icon and the templar who can use it. Not about Milo himself." Did her sister have a single real feeling anywhere in her, or had her heart always been made of stone?

"And you're allowing your feelings for a boy to distract you again." Gia gaped, and Lena rolled her eyes. "You think I never wanted to ignore all my work as principessa to run away and spend a quiet day at my temple or with someone I admired?" She stared down at the branch and blade in her hands. "Sometimes we must bow to the greater good."

That was all Gia wanted. Not to get Milo back for her own sake. "You think I'm being ridiculous trying to save him, but when I thought you were as good as dead, I waged a war by myself for you. And as soon as I learned you could be rescued, I did everything to get you out. And so did Milo." She raked her fingers through her escaped curls. She didn't want a thank you. She wanted Lena to shout back—to tell her how angry she was that Gia had betrayed her and cost her everything in the first place. Her body felt as out of control as when the stone took it over, as if acid bubbled up from its depths, as if shards were about to erupt from under her skin. She clenched her teeth to stop from snapping at her sister. "Val. What do you want to do?"

Her dark skin was ashen. She met Gia's gaze with fiery eyes. "I'll go any time to get him out of danger."

Lena set down the knife. "Do you know where they'd keep him?"

"Could be at the temple. Locked in his room, or in the catacomb cells." Val shook her head. "Any of the militia stations."

"Too many unknowns."

Val wiped her palms over her face. "He's my family."

"I understand." Lena gently pulled Val's arm down and gave the stick in her other hand a waggle. "Maybe I still have one of these where you said, but I really am trying to watch out for everyone."

Val heaved a laugh halfway to a sob. "I know you are. I do know that."

Lena slid her hand over Val's and squeezed. "The best way to break him out is to break the ceremony. If we win, we'll find him afterward. If we fail, it's over for all of us."

Val's chest shuddered with a deep drink of air, but she nodded.

"We have to be united in this." Lena looked to Gia for agreement.

Maybe it was her worry for Milo buzzing over every inch of her skin; maybe it was how Lena was able to get along with everyone but Gia that made her huff bitterly. "Sure." At Lena's raised brow, she blurted, "You don't even want me here." Nudge that vase nearer the ledge.

Lena's hand slackened on Val's. "Why would you say that?"

Smash it to the floor. Grind her heel on the shards. "*You* said it. When you woke at Val's." Gia threw up her hands. "Of course you did. I'm the one that got you to the ceremony when Ennio used it against you. You're right not to trust me, to never share anything with me—what you were learning about Ennio, the pressures you felt as principessa—"

Lena was on her feet, face blanched. "I'd hoped you'd escaped the curse! And I—" Her shoulders tightened. "No one ever asked me what I wanted. Maybe that's why I made such a mess—" Lena's hand rose to her brow. "I failed the city. I failed you. I didn't know how to be templar to Alta and principessa to the people and like a mother to you—"

What, by the gods, was she saying? "Are you drunk?" Gia asked. "I don't need you to be anything but my sister." Shame burrowed into her gut for all the ways she'd made that harder. Made everything harder for Lena. "I haven't been a good sister to you. I'm going to fix that." She straightened. "I'm with you. I'll make sure our plan against the ceremony succeeds. I'll see you get your chance to speak."

She needed to trust Lena's instincts. Her own led to so many dead ends—rushing to Ennio first in infatuation and then in anger, causing Lena's downfall and then failing in her vengeance. She had to do better this time. She had to prove her loyalty to Lena. She had to stand beside her sister.

She loved Lena, even if it felt like walking barefoot across those smashed shards sometimes.

Gia smoothed her hair and tucked it behind her ears. Dread

and confusion fumbled together in her stomach. Milo deserved someone better than her to rely upon. It felt wrong to leave him in the temple's hands a moment longer than necessary. If only someone had pried her away from Ennio when she'd been under his sway.

If only she had done it herself.

The door opened. They all looked as it swung in—

Kadri slipped inside. She'd gone out, checking for news. "No word on any arrest." Her face was solemn. "Though the guards have been pulled off the statues."

Lena pressed her lips in a line. "Ennio has the icon."

He had Milo.

The bonfire crackled under the full afternoon sun.

Gia marched toward the temple with Lena, Val, and everyone they'd managed to bring to their cause. It had seemed an impressive group gathered outside Kadri's, but they were nothing to the streams of people they joined in the streets. Trestatto was bursting, and it looked like most of the city was coming to honor Magna and the sancts. The moment Lena stood atop the steps and threw off her cloak to reveal the most beloved sanct returned and alive, it would be like Lena turning the Argus from its path, directing its force against Ennio and his invocation.

They just needed to win her the chance to speak.

Worshipers wound a solemn procession past the bonfire rebuilt with the sacred flame, into the temple to receive the mark of dust, and back out again. Then each took a branch offered by the templars to smolder in the bonfire and present to a sanct. Val had gone over all of this with Gia and Lena as they'd planned how they'd block the way into the temple and spark the message that Principessa Adalena had returned.

Except it wasn't just templars who stood in the plaza. A brace of holy guard stood at either side of the entrance to the temple.

Under her cloak, Lena halted. Beside her, Val put up a hand, letting the stream of people flow around their group, into the plaza. They'd expected that Ennio would set a watch for them. They'd prepared to hold a few back from alerting Ennio to Lena's appearance. But not so many, not all holy guards.

Val looked stunned. "He always has his whole guard at his side during the ceremony. Always."

"It'll take all of us to engage this many." Lena stared at the entrance. "And even then—"

Angling her head nearer to Lena, Val told her in a low voice, "I can keep plenty of them busy for you."

Lena dragged her gaze from the plaza to meet Val's. "There's no point in sacrificing yourself if we'll still be overrun before I can speak."

Val gripped Lena's arm. "Throw everything we have at them."

Lena's brows drew together and her lips pursed. She looked like she wanted to say "yes." Everyone was waiting on her word.

The sun beat down. Gia's ears and arms began to burn. No more long shadows, nowhere to hide. It was time to step forward and let the city see her. "We have to distract them before you and the others take the plaza," she told Lena. "Pull them away."

Lena nodded, biting her lip. "That could work—"

"I'll do it. Draw them inside the temple."

"You can't."

There was no time. "Ennio banished me to Alta's hill because he couldn't stand the sight of me. I can distract him. Once I'm inside, you take the steps."

"No. It's too dangerous."

Gia huffed to the pale blue sky, the moon a mere wisp. She wanted to scream at Lena that in another day she'd be perfectly safe as an indestructible statue. "This city needs to hear from you. And I need to make up for what I did to it. To you." She shouldered past her, letting the oblivious crowds sweep her toward the temple. This was their last chance to save Trestatto, and Milo, and any future Lena and Gia might have where they could figure out how to be better sisters.

Or maybe they would always fight like this, like the goddesses ever at odds, in a tug of war over them still.

The crowd washed her forward like a pebble caught in a rushing river, past the bonfire and across the plaza. She arranged her tunic to make the dagger at her belt visible and pulled her braid to one side so the hilt of her sheathed sword showed—ready to be drawn. As she stomped up the steps, a holy guard with a bruise across his temple caught sight of her. Gia raised her chin. She'd use worse than a book against him this time.

The guard cocked his head at the others, and they fell in behind her as she reached the door.

She should have known. Ennio wouldn't have her killed, not when he still wanted her to absolve him of everything he'd done to her. Not until he could see her destroyed himself, and know she was finally, fully ended.

Gia kept her spine straight. If Ennio thought he could intimidate her with a few of these half-trained soldiers, he really had gotten old. He'd forgotten what a templar used to be. She followed the line of worshipers to the front of the sanctuary.

To Ennio, who stood before the stone altar.

His robes were down, hanging from his leather belt, leaving his chest, anointed with holy oil, shining like a slab of marble. Once, he'd been the mightiest warrior in Trestatto, and his solid build still spoke to this. His head was bare as well. Val had explained that he always presented himself like this for the ceremony, in obeisance to the goddess. Without the crown upon his hair, he looked almost shorn, and younger—more like the boy she remembered. Still hungry for power he hadn't yet seized.

The entire temple focused on him, the carved reliefs curving behind him, the crowds gazing at him. The score of holy guard stood at either side of him. Ennio dipped his finger in a bowl of dust held by a templar and drew a crescent upon the forehead of the supplicant before him. "We all come from dust and—"

His eyes lifted to Gia. He pushed the man out of the way. Gia closed the distance between them, all raised jaw and challenge. Their gazes locked—Ennio's full of lightning. "To dust we shall return," she completed the prayer.

Let him trace his powder upon her. The curse would take her when it would, and nothing Ennio did could hurt her anymore. He had tried to destroy her—banished her to that hill, let the centuries lash at her. Yet here she was, standing in the temple of Magna, who had given her strength no invocation could ever steal.

She was no pebble in a stream. She was a mountain with a belly full of fire.

Her voice didn't waver. "I've returned for what's mine."

He made no move with the dust but gestured at the guards behind her. "I've always sought to give you what you wanted.

Even a vital role in protecting this city." She heard the temple doors thudding shut, and a confused murmuring from the lines of people blocked from going in or out. The light in the sanctuary dimmed, the flush of daylight receding to the glow of the torches along the walls, and all the candles burnishing Ennio in a golden cast.

He thought he was trapping her. But she was the one holding him here. She only needed to buy Lena some time. She'd play along. "Maybe I'm sick of it. Sick of being trapped in stone again and again." He didn't seem to know about the moon's control of her, at least. She could make him think she sought a full release from his invocation. "Maybe I'm ready to taste another kind of power."

His lip curled, pleased yet haughty. "You're already weary of that sister of yours, aren't you? Didn't take long once you had her. Here you are running back to me like all those times you complained of her." He reached out to brush his knuckles down her cheek possessively. "You always were better than her. Why be with someone who makes you feel that way? Why devote yourself to anyone who fails to see your full value?" His hand trailed down farther, over her shoulder and the sweep of her hip.

Gia closed her eyes a moment and swallowed down the saliva rising in her throat.

She couldn't help herself.

Maybe it was the memory of Milo's reverent touch. Maybe it was just her emotions ruling her again, making her impulsive. She came here to distract Ennio as long as possible—to win her freedom from his curse. But if she failed, if she was going to blink out like a candle in another day, she would see Milo free first.

She hoped Ennio would hear the rasp in her voice as attraction and not fear. "I only need to know you're actually still trying to protect people. Show me. Let Milo go."

The lightning in Ennio's eyes dulled. The danger of it leached into the earth all around. He reached for her again—this time to draw her sword from her back. She twisted away, but his guards were close by. He grabbed her and flung the weapon aside. It crashed against a candle stand. Shouts from the people waiting in the aisle rose with its echo.

She went for her knife, but his hand gripped over hers atop the hilt. His arm wrapped around her waist, crushing her to his chest.

"Why would you want a nothing like that scribe"—he dipped his face toward hers—"when I am offering you a place beside me?"

The pungent balsam aroma of holy oil flooded her senses. One arm was trapped to her side, but she pushed away from him with her free hand. "You? All these people are learning who that is now. Aren't you worried about tarnishing yourself in their eyes? Their living sanct?"

"Strange, but I do not care." He drank in a breath. "It must be your influence. Everything's become so tedious—the stasis and stability." His fingers claimed the hilt from hers. "But you spark something in me. You make me reckless." He slid the dagger from her belt and traced it up her side, her arm, marring her skin with no more than gooseflesh. He tapped its length along her jaw. "Enough to show you this." Then he drew it back and flicked its tip against his chest.

It etched a small cut into his skin. The blood wept down to her splayed fingertips.

CHAPTER TWENTY-THREE

DUST TO DUST

Only through all three states, through knowledge of all three god-
desses, can we achieve the wisdom of what we are.

—The Book of Invocations

Gia

She stared at the scarlet rivulets. Her blood thrashed in her ears.
"How—"

She fought against him, going for the knife, but he wrapped
that arm around her too, the blade flat at her back.

No one else in the sanctuary could see the wound, hidden by
their bodies pressed close. He smiled widely at her. "This one
day a year. While the ceremony is completed, and the invocation
renewed. So many years lived, and I never feel more alive than
these rare days. Just like with you. These children with lives that

flicker out so fast, so peacefully, they're all like ghosts. But you—"
He tightened his hold on her. Pressed his face even nearer, gaze
piercing, mouth dangerously close to hers.

She turned away, heart galloping. His breath was in her ear.
"You make me feel real again. Alive again. I hold the entire city,
but I am alone. It has been so long since I spoke to anyone who
was my equal. Someone who truly knows me. Understands me.
You're ruthless and brutal and strong, just like me. All the things
that always made you better than your sister. All the things that
would make you a perfect principessa for this city at last."

Gia squeezed her eyes shut. Ennio wasn't looking to use her
now, no more than any of his playthings. He wanted her for herself, and what did that say about who she truly was?

People behind them were crying out now—his holy titles,
and prayers, and confused exclamations.

Ennio spoke of them like they weren't there. "They will all
love you. They deserve a principessa who loves their Primo Sanct
as she should. You think I can't get my storicas to dig up some
way to release you from stone?" His fingers dug into her side. The
knife pricked at her back. "I would do this for you. I would open
the invocation for you. I bleed for you. You belong at my side."

An ache darkened his voice. His vulnerable flesh pressed
against her, around her, holding her tight.

It would be so easy to surrender to it. So easy to take the offered
place. Never having to work to redeem herself. Live at the center of the world he'd sculpted—at the seat of all the power he'd
accumulated. She could make him bend it to better use. She could
climb back on a pedestal and let the worship wash her clean.

And it would be so easy to fall into the trap of destroying it.
This was no true gesture of vulnerability. He was playing with

her. Taunting her. His guards were within a sword's swing. If she thought they would only reach her after she killed Ennio, she would attack in a heartbeat, but he would never actually place himself at risk, for all his words of tedium and sparks.

She still needed to fight her way out of this.

He'd stripped her of her sword. Taken her dagger.

But she was made of sharp edges.

Opening her eyes, she remembered what he had told her in his sanctum. How she had hurt him. She ruined the story he was telling himself of being Trestatto's hero, the story unfolding before her today.

"Ennio." She let a smile spread over his name. "Do you know why you've been such a stalwart protector of the city?"

He inclined his head, waiting, his gaze boring into hers.

"Because you've worked to ensure it didn't just belong to you but loved you."

"Yes." His smile cut wider. Satisfaction flashed in his eyes.

"Do you know why you've made these people love you? Thousands of them, through the centuries?" She killed her smile. "Because I never will."

As her words hit him, she wriggled halfway free, but then his hold clenched again. Lips against her cheek, he rumbled, "I will have you or I will crush you."

She clawed her fingers through the cut he'd made. He hissed. A guard yanked her back by her arm, and Gia knocked her fist into his face as Ennio broke his hold on her. Another guard grabbed her by the shoulders. She fought wildly now, throwing the guard against the templar cowering to one side of the altar. The pan of dust clanged to the floor, sending an arc of white through the air that set the nearest guards coughing.

Gia stood in the aisle, tensed, facing Ennio. "It's not so easy whether I'm stone or not."

Ennio stalked to the altar. He dropped her dagger and picked up one of the items laid out on the stone. The chisel. He flourished it, glaring at her. "Isn't it? Maybe I'll smash all of them." He watched her, as if ready to drink in her reaction. "All the statues. Lucca told me what the scribe found. Vassilis's little secret. What this can do."

She clenched her hands. "You wouldn't. You need the power they give you."

He let the chisel thunk gently back to the altar. "You're right." He drew up the other pieces on the altar and let them dangle from a finger. Their chains jangled lightly.

Stregna and Alta's icons.

"Those don't belong to you," she seethed.

Ennio drew his head high. His strike had hit true. "When you outlive everyone, possession loses its meaning."

What was he saying? The possibility struck across her gut like a blow, sending bile burning up her throat. Milo couldn't be dead. Ennio had already taken everything from her once. He could not have Milo. She could not be the reason.

She ground out words red hot along their edge. "Where is Milo?"

He grinned wolfishly. "I had to keep him somewhere the screams wouldn't frighten the little wards."

She threw herself at him. The guards caught her and held her back. "I swear I'll destroy you."

"You'd better do it soon. It's not so easy," he mimicked, "once the ceremony's completed. And while I may need to keep the sancts to maintain my power, I don't think I can say the same for some orphan scribe."

She strained against the guards. Her heartbeat thudded.

And something else. Drumbeats.

Ennio's brows drew together.

Gia snarled a smile at him, over the shoulders of the guards barring her way. "I brought my sister to the ceremony just like you asked. Again."

Two of the guards ran to the main entrance. Gia turned to see, through the opening doors, Lena, standing tall out on the steps, the throng surrounding her. Gazing at her. Reaching hands up to her. Clinging to her outstretched arms. Crying, shouting, singing. Kadri and several others stood around her with staffs held sideways, ready to stop anyone emerging from the temple, but allowing adoring faces to press near their returned principessa.

A few of the others beat their drums and launched into the crowd. Lena had finished her speech, and they would help carry word through the people still waiting out in the streets, still coming for the ceremony.

Val turned, sword raised, toward where the doors swung open.

"Half of you with me," Ennio said, and Gia could swear she saw a cloud of fear in his eyes at the sight of her sister. "The rest of you, kill that demon possessing Adalena's form, arrest anyone fighting for her, and take them to the catacombs. Clear the plaza of this disruption and call me once we can recommence the ceremony." His gaze cut to Gia. "I'll be in my sanctum."

"Primo," said a guard, "what of her, should we hold her with the other prisoner in the catacombs?"

Ennio kept his eyes locked on Gia, whose mind raced at what the guard had said. "All the rest of you," he ordered again.

The guards let her go and ran down the aisle, swords drawn.

The little crowd trapped in the sanctuary scrambled away from the doors.

Gia dove for her sword. It scraped over the temple floor with a *shink*. She rose and felt suddenly frozen. Not by any invocation, but a decision.

At one end of the aisle, Lena.

Outlined in the blaze of the bonfire behind her, she raised her weapon as Val fended off the attacking guards with a fury of sword strokes. Gia's blood spurred her to hurry to the battle. She'd won Lena the chance to speak, but she still felt the urge to prove her honor, to show everyone she would always fight for her sister.

At the other, Ennio.

Still flanked by guards. Watching her, he dragged his thumb through the blood dripping down his chest. He swiped it across his tongue. Reminding her he was vulnerable. Tempting her to follow him. To taste the vengeance she'd sought. It called to her, through heartbreaks and centuries.

Ennio's lip curled. One brow flicked up. "This will be exciting." He swept away, out the far end of the sanctuary, guards at his back. He thought he had her trapped, as his principessa or sanct. So certain she would chase after him still—that he'd always have her on his leash.

He really had become a bored child, playing at power, everyone around him mere toys. She'd once thought he was a great man, believed his attention meant she was important, too.

She was still trying to gain it, she realized. With murders and threats instead of dedicated training or favors. Hoping his hate meant she wasn't as wicked as him. He didn't deserve any of it.

Her value was entirely her own. It would live and die by her actions, her choices.

And she chose Milo.

She didn't need to prove herself by killing Ennio or showing herself at her sister's side. She needed to save Milo. She needed him.

Violently. With a vehemence blossoming in her like flames, burning away everything else.

Any thought of telling Milo to stay away from her evaporated. She was more than the person who'd let herself be molded by Ennio. She was more than the shattered pieces. She was someone she hadn't yet been. She could trust her decision. Her hand was sure.

It cut away everything but rescuing Milo—and the knowledge of where he had to be. Ennio and his guard had let it slip. Down in the catacombs, where bodies of dead templars were returned in pomp to Magna's earth, several cells lined one side. A place for praying in penance, where shoddy faith could turn into something as strong and brilliant as a diamond. Buried beyond the reach of hearing.

She whirled, ran, and grabbed ahold of a templar who was standing astonished next to one of the columns along the side of the sanctuary. She slammed him against the granite. "You know who I am? What I've done?" He only gaped at her. "You saw how Ennio left you here with me? Because he doesn't care if you live or die. I've killed templars before you. And I'm taking Milo from this place for good." She ground the heel of her palm into his chest. "So, tell me the first time I ask. Who keeps the key to the catacombs?"

His lips pursed and he shook his head rapidly. "No—"

She yanked him forward and knocked him back again. "Show me where. Now."

The templar ducked his head as he swallowed and rushed out some words. "He's not down there."

Liar.

She dragged him by his robes, out the side of the sanctuary. No other templars moved to help him. She forced him all the way to the entrance above the catacombs, plucked a torch from a sconce, and pushed him before her down the dark stairs. No one would trap her here without sacrificing him as well.

In the dank hall, he ran well ahead of her, cowering away from her sword. She followed through the archways made of gryphon ribs, past the walls lined with long chimera skulls. Sepulchers filled the shadowy corridors. And against one wall, doors to cells were set in stone.

No guard stood watch. She shone the torch at the first cell and pulled upon its door. It opened without any more protest than the whining of its hinges. As did the next. And the next—

In the final cell a form huddled upon a low bed. Gia dropped the torch and grabbed the door's bars. At their rattle, the figure sat with a jerk, his gray hair mussed, his eyes meeting Gia's with a look of terror.

Lucca.

Was he being punished for Milo's escape at the bookshop? Gia had breath only to whisper, "Where is he?"

The storica stared at her like she'd come to finish him off. "I don't know."

Her hands fell to her sides, numb. Ennio was playing with her again. She fled Lucca's stare and abandoned her hostage. Her footsteps rang out as she raced back up into the temple, back down the hallway. She wanted to fight the dozen guards between her and Ennio's defenseless flesh. Tear this place apart stone by stone until she found where he was hiding Milo. But as she emerged from the depths of the temple, screams carried from where the other dozen had gone.

She rushed out to the steps. The attack by the guards had thrown this end of the plaza into a storm of shoving and shouting. Lena was backed against her old pedestal, and Val fought off too many holy guards for Gia to count.

The rest of their group must have scattered to safety, but others strove to protect the principessa. That was where the screaming came from. Trestattans stood between her and more holy guards, grappling, getting knocked to the ground. A guard jammed his hilt into a man's back. A woman curled her arms about her head to stop from being trampled.

Gia launched across the steps. A woman stood, palms out, screaming at a guard. "She's a miracle!" The guard wrenched the woman off-balance by one arm. She struck at his face. He brought his sword up and drove it at her.

Gia reached them just in time to catch the edge of his blade with hers. The guard still had the woman in his grip, and Gia struggled to stop him from crashing both swords down upon her. She shoved her body in front of the woman. Finally, the woman twisted free. The guard directed all his force at Gia now. His sword sliced against her arm.

She yelled at the hot pain and fought him off with all the fury she wanted to fire at every guard concealing Milo from her somewhere, at Ennio, at herself. She reached Lena's side just as another commotion erupted on the far end of the plaza.

"Thank Alta you're all right." Lena's honey eyes trained on Gia, sparking with concern. "Your arm."

Too many other things to worry about. Milo. A unit of militia soldiers entering the plaza—marching toward them. Their thunderous footsteps sent an entire flank of the bonfire crumbling and falling into a heap of ash.

Val threw off two holy guards at once and backed up, shoulder to shoulder with Lena. "Those are my friends," she said grimly. "I will fight them all for you. But we're going to get these people protecting you killed. We need to disappear."

"It wasn't enough." Lena looked despairingly at the multitude of people clumped watchfully about the plaza and packed into the street. People believed her. Just not as many as they needed. "He'll tell everyone whatever he wants and carry on with the ceremony."

Val clasped her free hand to Lena's. "Please let me take you someplace safe."

Lena looked at Gia's injured arm again and nodded.

"No," Gia protested, even as Val and Lena pulled her away. They dove down the steps, into the crowd. She hugged her arm to herself. "We can't leave—we can't leave him!" She didn't know if she was screaming more for the chance to destroy Ennio or save Milo. Her heart collapsed like those ashes with the realization—both were impossible now.

CHAPTER TWENTY-FOUR

TRUTH HAS SHARP TEETH

Magna's earth is as slow-moving as the goddess's heart. Her invocations endure. Alta carves new ways or soothes the old, and her granted favors connect long labors to a rush of grace. Stregna's blessings alight from her empyrean. Her answers to our prayers are the sudden flash of reflected light, known at times only by their afterimage.
—The Book of Invocations

Milo

He was trapped in a room he couldn't get out of. Monsters prowled outside.

They'd come back a few times but left him for longer. Left him to sprawl on the bed, bloodying its thick wool and stuffing.

They even left him with the chains locking his hands in front of him so he could eat some of the food fallen on the floor and drink some of the water the holy guard brought—always the holy guard. Milo never saw any of the militia normally on duty at this station. Ennio wasn't worried about Milo escaping. He was ensuring the story wouldn't escape—that the truth would not run through his city's streets and ravage the lies that lived there.

When the guards had left, after asking only the same one question, he'd wanted to yell his own after them. Was Val truly abandoned at the gate like she'd been told? Was Senna? Babies too young for the older wards to tend were given to families in the city. How many of them were taken?

Milo didn't want to draw Ennio's attention to the wards, though. Didn't want Ennio deciding to use them as leverage for the information he wanted. Milo could only pray for their safety until Gia and the others struck at the Ceremony of Dust. His bloody fingers tapped that hope into his bare breastbone. He had nothing left to offer but his silence.

He'd lost track of days, of nights. He'd recited verse in his head to kill the hours, to take him away from the filth and the pain that stalked him, that had him in its giant maw, worrying him between its teeth. He couldn't compose anything to pass the time better—the pain slipped inside too sharply for him to concentrate that well. He would've liked to make new verses about Gia, lines to tie him back to the one moment he'd been brave enough to stand for what he truly wanted—to dedicate his faith and action to someone deserving. Lines that might unite him to her for a moment more—never to conjure her here; all he wanted for her was to be free.

Could she ever fully escape Ennio, though? Either his invocation had already retaken her, or it would any day now. Milo frowned into the blanket where he rested, waiting for the latest wave of agony delivered by the guards to recede, eddies of pain lapping at him. His panic over Gia's time running out never ebbed. Ennio's words returned to lash him—this had happened before. The templar had always stomped down any threat that rose up to his rule and his goddess.

Except Ennio had failed once—when Milo escaped the monsters driven to his home in the fields. Escaped out through a high window—

One that he could not reach alone at that age, it occurred to him. Jarred loose by Ennio's taunting him about the attack, a lost memory rushed back to Milo. His parents' hands reaching for him. Tossing a chain over his head and lifting him.

A chain that wasn't the burden of unfaithful parents, but a shield and a charge. Something to be carried to a safety only he would reach. Something he could use to call upon a goddess whose name they had whispered to him, taught him secretly outside the city.

His parents had protected him how they could, and then passed him to Stregna's safekeeping.

"How did you get away?" Gia had asked under the stars.

He didn't remember. The next thing he knew, he was safe at the city gate. Now, it was clear that Stregna must have delivered him to the shelter of the sancts. To Gia. He'd thought waking her was the first time he'd ever used the icon, but in his moment of deadly need, hearing a child's desperate plea, the Unseen Goddess must have borne him to safety.

There had always been someone listening to his prayers.

Maybe if he had more time, he might have figured out how to be Stregna's templar after all.

He hung onto the thought as the rattle of the lock and whine of the hinge skittered over his skin. No—it was too soon for them to be back. His stomach churned. The sweat still coating his skin seemed to sharpen its chill.

A shuffling step. A scrape. A sharp intake of air. "I'm so sorry, my boy."

Milo lifted his head slightly. Storica Lucca. Milo shoved himself upright, hands together. His head swam, and he could only watch as the storica let himself gingerly into the chair not sticky with blood, with the help of a short wooden staff. Milo fell back onto his elbow.

Lucca leaned forward. He spoke with urgency. "Ennio has sent me with a final chance for you. He thinks you'll listen to me, and I hope you will."

Milo's voice was a mere rasp. "You brought the guards."

Lucca's pale eyes blinked. "I was trying to help you."

"You set them after me." His own mentor doubted him. His peculiarities. Where this once would have plowed shame through him, anger sprang up now. "After my friends. Ennio could have killed Gia."

"That girl has killed people. She hurt Renz." Lucca considered where his hand gripped his staff. "And me."

"Because you led Ennio straight to us. She's only trying to protect people." He hated how much that sounded like Ennio. Deep in his gut, he clung to the belief that it was different. Gia was willing to risk her own safety to protect everyone Ennio threatened.

"Is that what she was doing when she caused the violence at the Ceremony of Dust today?"

Hope flared painfully in Milo's chest. "Did they stop it?"

"No," Lucca said with a dubious huff. "The holy guard cleared the piazza of the instigators, and the ceremony is going on now."

Then Gia had a day at best before Ennio's prayer swept her back into stone forever. Milo would never see her again. His dying hope burned through his heart like acid.

Lucca drew a small leather folio from his robes. "Primo Sanct—"

"His name is Ennio. Only Ennio." Speaking that one small truth seemed important.

Lucca opened the folio and held it out to Milo, blank pages and charcoal pencil tucked inside. "He's furious about the interruption at the ceremony. He's demanding that you write a confession that can be read at the closing rites this evening. That you invoked a foreign godpower to create the disruption at the temple. Caused strange visions."

Write Ennio a page of lies instead the holy truth of an omelia. "You think I'm a heretic? Or do you want me to become one?"

"It doesn't matter—"

"The truth matters," Milo said. "Will you tell the city? Write it down in the archive?"

"No," Lucca said, leaning forward, hand on staff. His gray brows arced over pleading eyes. "Not if he will spare you. He won't let you come back to the temple or remain in Trestatto. But you could go to another city. You could live."

Escape. Safety from the monsters running him to ground. Stregna had only saved him by bringing him inside Ennio's domain, had only freed Gia to torment her for one brief moon's spell. Milo could let Stregna's name be buried again, swept under more falsehoods and years. Lucca was willing to help write the lies into history for him.

How many times had the truth been churned under? With the blood and bones of those trying to bring it to blossom feeding the soil? His parents. Milo wondered about the unhappy Vassilis. Was he frustrated with the invocation he couldn't find the right design or wording for, or with his head templar, who demanded it in the first place? Had he resisted how he could—had he worked the chisel into the invocation on purpose so there would be some way of destroying its power? Even if it meant completing the sacrifice of those captured, requiring every statue to be smashed?

"Give Ennio your confession, and all this can end."

Milo shook his head, and his vision rippled, his cuts throbbed. "Lies," he muttered. So many lies. A flood of them.

"You must write it."

Ennio would use it to smooth over the story—to calm the city and create a false record of this time in the archives. Soon, everyone would believe it as truth. Ennio's hold over the city would endure. Milo would disappear, one way or another. No one would know what Ennio had done, how fiercely Gia had fought him.

If Milo refused, Ennio would likely prevail, but it might put a crack in his facade of holiness. It might carry the truth forward. It might help the next person who fought to free the city. It might someday help free all the sancts for good.

Gia might be stone before he ever saw the sky or stars again, but Milo would never betray her. He shook his head.

Lucca tucked the folio onto his lap, his grip white over the dark leather. "You must learn how to survive with the choices you have. Obey the temple or be cast out. These are dangerous people you've fallen in with."

"You're the one who landed me here."

"I was trying to save you. I only want to help you." Emotion strained through his thin voice. "Milo, they're going to send you to the quarry tonight if you don't do what they want."

Milo's pulse blinked through his head, through his vision, red and black. He was always destined to be taken by the beasts out there. Better that than letting them claw their way under his skin, into his heart again.

He would not allow the lies of the temple to roost there any longer. He thought of Gia saying the goddesses could be called upon for strength, even without an icon. He made a silent prayer to Stregna to help him endure whatever was coming.

Lucca's staff wobbled as he implored Milo again. "Let me help you. And please, help your friends. Perhaps I've deserved my stay in a catacomb cell, but they're looking for Valentina. She fought the holy guard today. Do the right thing and Primo Sanct will forget all this, say it was demonic visions that confused her. Or else, when they find her—"

"No—" Milo coughed.

But Lucca was wiping a hand over his face as if he couldn't bear to look at Milo any longer. He pushed himself to his feet and was gone. The folio rested closed on the empty chair.

A coughing fit shuddered through Milo. He dropped to the mattress, drawing up his hands to block out this place with all its horrors and temptations.

After a moment, he let his hands fall away. His nails were black, like he'd been inking a book for weeks and never scrubbing them. And his palms—his godlines were shredded, broken, written over by slashes like a palimpsest. Maybe it meant he could choose his fate.

Maybe it meant he had none.

+ ✦ +

Standing in the quarry hours later, Milo felt he'd received his answer.

They'd put balm on his cuts, made him eat and drink, more for the benefit of the militia guards keeping watch from the wall than for his, he was sure. They were too far to hear anything Milo might shout, but near enough to notice if he looked too badly mistreated.

How many times had Milo taken what he'd seen in this city with the best, undeserved, faith?

No others crowded the walkway to watch his execution. Most of Trestatto would be at the closing rites, or already beginning the revels that would run through the final day of the holy month. Assured by Ennio that the culprit had been dealt with.

The holy guards who escorted him here—two men ahold of him, two with torches, and two with sword and spear ready for any serpents that might emerge too soon—said nothing as they unlocked his chains and handed him a knife. The convicted were always afforded the chance to escape. If Magna Mater wanted to bestow mercy, they had every chance to make it out of her quarry—to face the larger beasts of the field, which always caught them.

Ennio's guards crested the slope leading out of the rocky expanse, leaving Milo alone with the thousand shadows squirming like serpents as the torchlight receded.

Mostly, he was relieved. He knew now he wouldn't betray anyone he loved.

But the knife was shaking in his hand.

He could have turned it upon the holy guards before they retreated. They would have ended him fast. Yet beyond the press of monsters in the darkness, Gia could still be waiting. No moon was visible from the quarry, but a desperate faith sparked him to move—to claim a few last moments with her before he lost her forever. Or at least to claim the kind of death he'd always thought his sanct had endured, bravely facing a monster for the city's sake. A bold end.

He scrabbled over the stone. He began imagining it as one of the fantastic stories the younger wards would draw out of him. If he could make it out of the quarry, he could get to clear fields, maybe see the hungry monsters coming before they were on top of him.

The quarry, heavily mined long ago, its stone broken away in hunks, unfolded upward like crumpled parchment. He aimed for the side that wasn't too steep, that let out to the fields. He avoided where the holy guards had kicked the earth hoping to stir up beasts; they would still happily dispatch him if he followed too fast. And he was fast, his only advantage in games and sport growing up in the nido and then in the militia. His fingers ached gripping the rock, but he ignored the sensation. At one point, he held the knife in his teeth to free both hands to climb. He had it back in his hand, though, when the first serpent stirred.

Its legs propelled it from its crevice, serifs on its long, sinuous body. Mouth—teeth—blade—and, possibly the only thing keeping Milo from shouting, from awakening more lurking beasts, Gia's voice yelling in his head that if he could cut her throat, surely he could manage one serpent.

He did, jabbing through its neck—but before it fell limp, its needle teeth dragged across the top of his hand. Milo sucked his own teeth. Serpents had to sink theirs into you fully, clamp their jaws, for their venom to be a worry.

There was decidedly nothing to worry about. Not the final reach of stone he needed to climb, or the fields to traverse in darkness, or the monsters that had been driven near the city.

He was so focused on not worrying, the next serpent was on him before he noticed. Its long tail wrapped around his ankle, making him fall and startle another serpent from the crumble of rock he disturbed. He slashed wildly, catching the first across its open jaws. He struggled to keep his grip—his hands ached; his ruined palms sweated. Another beast followed the second out from under the rock, and another. He couldn't stop. He had to keep stabbing the earth that seemed to be bleeding the beasts before they overwhelmed him.

A pause in the onslaught—but he waited, afraid to move, to draw more of them to the vibrations of his hands and feet. His heavy breath brewed warmly between himself and the rock. He gingerly pushed himself up and waited, then moved carefully around where most of the beasts had emerged, and upward.

He stepped on one more serpent before cresting the quarry's rim. Kicking it away, he shoved himself over the edge. He whirled around in case it followed; whirled again in case anything else lurked at the edge of the fields.

Milo looked to the stars, hoping to orient himself, to recall any nearby shelters, and making sure no flying beast blotted out their sharp light. He'd served overnight watches before, but this was the first time he'd been alone outside the city since a goddess shepherded him to safety.

No fellow militia at his back this time. No icon. No protection of sancts or any invocation.

He took off running.

A path skirted the fields and he followed it, heading away from the city gate and its guards. Taking him farther from Gia—he didn't know how to reach her. His imagination was failing him.

He reached a stretch of olive trees and dove through them. They provided good cover, their branches clawing overhead in the dim, and their rows were open enough for him to see anything coming. He had to keep pushing forward. Soon, he broke out into fields of grain.

The world stretched wide around him, bounded only by darkness. In its vastness, his senses retreated to the most immediate. The crunch of his feet, the rasp of his breath. The blur of the stalks, ghostly against the stars. And the rising dread, as every step delivered him nearer to the inevitable monster he'd face. His bruised hand tightened on the small knife.

He came to an empty field with what looked like cotton blowing toward him. Growing larger and louder. A herd of ventroni, stampeding.

Being chased by something worse.

Their white coats were deadly—one brush against skin would produce a thousand tiny cuts. Milo shot to the right, running to skirt the farthest edges of the flock. But a beat of wings and a fiery cry drove the ventroni into wild, unpredictable patterns. Thundering hooves shook the tilled earth under Milo's feet. A glance back told him he was about to be overrun. He dove to the side. The ventroni barreled past. Milo rolled, holding out the knife in case more followed. But the footsteps were all wrong—it was the loping, half-flight, half-gallop of a chimera hunting the other beasts.

The massive goat-like monster dug in its hooves and snapped wide its wings to slow its chase after the ventroni. It screamed with pleasure at the lone, soft prey it found in their wake. Fire streaming from its long snout lit the field brighter than the stars, burning into Milo's dark-adjusted eyes. He clawed at the earth, scrambling to get to his feet. He made it as far as his knees before the beast was upon him.

He slashed wildly, head ducked, bellowing. He survived the chimera's first pass and was on his feet by the time it rounded. It charged again, snapping its teeth. Milo shifted his stance in the uneven soil. The beast would quickly determine it held the advantage. Last chance to convince it he was too much trouble.

His jab caught against its hide, bristles scraping the back of his hand. He couldn't tell if he'd drawn blood. The knife was sticky from the serpents. Some of his own cuts had reopened.

The chimera wheeled and screeched into the sky. The stars seemed to throb. Milo's heart beat a merciless rhythm, met with the monster's ragged tromp as it came at him for the kill.

And another rumble behind Milo. His spine steeled. He fought to stand. To keep his eyes open against the horror he could see. To meet the beast before him even as the shadow of some unknown monster reaching teeth or claws to rip open his back at any moment towered in his mind.

To achieve a bold death, the only thing left to him now. To show Gia he'd died fighting for her.

One monster at a time.

CHAPTER TWENTY-FIVE

NIGHTMARE

Temples focus godpower, drawing it along paths made familiar by centuries of offerings given and blessings bestowed. And as temples and icons do, certain elements may strengthen the use of godpower, as offerings to appeal to the goddesses and as marks to guide the flow of rendered blessings. A chorus of rainfall may amplify the reach of Alta's gifts. A sigil of templar's blood drives godpower upon his will with the precision and power of an arrow.

—The Book of Invocations

Milo

Milo shouted and struck his knife at the chimera. The furious beat of its bat wings drove a burst of flame just over his head. He ducked low, palm stinging against bloodied soil. The chimera jerked away, screaming. Milo raised the knife, wondering what beast had startled the monster so badly.

And what it was about to do to him.

It passed by, chasing the chimera—pulling a chariot. The chimera's fire licked up the full length of the sword swinging out at it.

"Milo!" Val's shout streamed after her, bright and blazing in his head.

He had to be delirious—dreaming.

She chased the chimera off. It broke away to the side, hooves digging into the soft earth, launching itself out of the reach of Val's blade. She was really here. Milo heaved a breath—sigh of relief and laugh and sob all in one—and let his tired arm drop.

Val pulled hard with her one hand on the reins, steering away from the beast, but the chimera could turn faster than the chariot. It was already racing Val back to Milo and winning.

Milo sprinted for the chariot. Val dropped her sword onto the chariot's floor and extended a hand to him. "Come on!" He grabbed her arm. His feet fought to keep up as the chariot careened.

She swung him up beside her. He ignored the twinge in his shoulder, the soreness of his fingers, to retrieve her sword in exchange for the knife. Val put everything into recovering control and speeding away from the chimera. She'd slowed to grab him, and the beast was close at their back. Milo braced a hip against the chariot's side and struck at the monster just as it lunged for them.

It eased off, only to beat its wings and drive its long, furred body along the side of the chariot. It screamed fire at the horse, who jumbled its gallop a few steps and veered away. Milo swung again and connected, slicing a deep cut across the chimera's haunch.

The beast reeled away. Its sputter of fire died, and it was lost in the darkness. Val straightened out the startled horse's run and steered them around, back toward the city. Milo's hands held the sword loosely, ready to drive away any of the ventroni that passed too near as the herd scattered. Once they'd rounded to the north, Val tugged the reins into one hand again and wrapped her free arm about his shoulders. "Sancts, Milo." She pressed a kiss into his hair.

He didn't even twist away like he normally would, or give her face a shove, but leaned into her hug as the wheels thrummed under them. He needed her to convince him this was real—that he wasn't alone. "How did you know where to find me?" His voice was low, rough with disuse.

"We were trying to get back to Kadri's when we heard. Ennio proclaimed the execution across the city. For the murders and invoking strange gods at the ceremony. The militia was sent to search Kadri's district—"

Milo swore. "Is—" He was still fighting his racing heart and spent breath. He cleared his throat. "Are Gia and Adalena all right?"

"I hid them at the ruins of Stregna's temple." A chuckle vibrated through her. "Though Gia was furious when she got back from the river. Still want me to bring you to her? Or shall I drop you off again with your friend back there? You might be safer."

He shuddered a laugh, even as the need to be with Gia charged him with impatience. "I can't get to her fast enough."

"I told you." Val smirked. "You do love her."

"I do." So much time searching for truth and the right words, and here were the easiest and truest.

Val dropped her arm and took the reins into both hands. Her militia sash ruffled lightly in the night air. She was guiding them around the city, but kept back far enough not to draw attention from the watch on the wall.

"Kadri said she had a friend who could get us back into the city—if he wasn't arrested when the militia swept her neighborhood. Someone who helps people avoid the gates regularly it seems. I saw the sisters safely to the temple ruins, and I came to get you."

"With the chariot you had lying around?"

Her lips twisted. "I was ready to steal it. But we have friends stationed at the stables and eastern gate tonight who'd already heard what really happened at the ceremony. People saw the principessa. They heard her speak."

A flare of faith rose through Milo, kindling warmth within his ribcage. The story of Adalena couldn't be stamped out as easily as Ennio thought. It had caught fire through the city. The truth was still alive. It had saved him.

"To be clear," Val said, "I would have come on foot." She cocked an eyebrow. "I think Gia would have, too, if the moon wasn't going down. What did you say to that girl?"

"I kissed her." The confession slipped out under Val's pointed look. His skin sparked with wonder that he would see her again—with worry that he wouldn't find her before she was lost beyond his reach. The looming new moon swallowed any anxiety about whether Gia felt for him all he did for her, if kissing him back spoke more to her fear of her impending end than anything of deeper feelings. As long as he could be there for her. It would have to be enough.

It would never be enough. He would soon be the boy in love

with a statue like Val had teased. With no hope, and more lost than he'd ever imagined.

"That's—" Val's face broke into a surprised smile. "That's fantastic." Her smile lingered a little too long, became a ghost of itself. "I wish I could—"

Milo squinted, trying to understand through his heartache and exhaustion. "Kiss Gia?"

"No, genius." Val knocked her shoulder into his. "I—" She glanced down at the reins wrapped about her hands, and back up. "Look, when a beautiful girl literally falls into your arms, it's impossible not to be moved."

Milo drew a deep breath. Of course. "You don't think Adalena might feel the same?"

"No, I—" Val's eyes grew wide, and she shook her head a little. "I mean, I can't tell her."

He'd seen Val declare her passion for a milkmaid who'd walked into the city for the first time not five minutes earlier. And while Adalena might be preoccupied planning revolution against the immortal templar hunting them, nothing had ever stopped Val before. Like being in the middle of a chariot race.

"Why not? They only have one day left." He didn't want to accept that, but letting it pass without speaking one's feelings seemed its own kind of defeat too, an affront to truth. "Val, you have to tell her."

"She'd never in a *thousand* days—" Val made a little growl in the back of her throat. "She's the *principessa*."

"And she told us how she doesn't want to be anymore."

"She's still a sanct!" Val raised her shoulders. "Holiest of martyrs, subject of a thousand omelias."

"Not really, they weren't true—"

"They were, though. In a way." She frowned into the night. "She's not perfect, she's better. Braver maybe than anyone I've met."

"With a stick up her ass?"

Val shot him a dark look.

"All right." He wasn't going to push, but the memory of holding Gia flooded his senses. The press of all her softness against him, the swell of her hips, her fingers tangling in his hair as she clung nearer.

It obliterated any doubt. "Sancts are people too. That's the whole point of those stories we were taught. The point of that sacrifice was how valuable their lives were. How they gave up all their days of eating and sitting in the sun. And arguing and feeling lost and feeling loved. And kissing." Val, eyes still on the field before them, nodded. "Except they didn't. Adalena didn't. Her life was stolen. Don't you think she deserves to live it even for one day, and not be treated by everyone like some untouchable half-goddess?"

Val stared ahead a long moment, drinking this in, then swung a wide grin at Milo and said, "I would like to touch her."

He did shove a palm into her face then. "I'm sure you'll come up with something better than that to tell her."

"You'll help me." Val nodded confidently. "You totally owe me."

He gave her another gentle shove, shoulder to shoulder. "I do. Everything."

The night unspooled in moments Milo's exhausted mind could hardly hold onto. Val drew up near the wall and ripped her sash to wind about his palms before they climbed the rope Kadri's friend had set for them. The wall seemed to stretch forever into the dark, into the stars. Milo's palms burned, and the rest of him burned with urgency to get to Stregna's hill. Soon Kadri ushered them inside her home, wrapping Milo in Adalena's cloak to cover his filthy clothes.

He hadn't even realized he'd fallen asleep until Val woke him to cross the city before moonrise, where, under the day's bright sun, he saw the unprotected sancts. As they walked through streets filled with people making frenzied end-of-Sanct's-Month revelries, Milo tapped his fingers with frustration against his thigh.

"Now we could wake any statue, but we don't have the icon to do it." Even if that was the reason the statues were reachable. His mind chased after each possibility like water circling down a drain. Some people hurried through the streets, still eyeing the monsters high in the blue. No monster threatened more dreadfully than the moon, waiting to claw through that sky. Gia's final moon.

Finally, they made it to the gentle slope of the hill on the southeastern side of the city and began the climb past quiet homes through the tangle of long spring grasses.

There were no guards at the ring of sancts near the highest accessible reaches of the hill. Two dozen statues raised their arms higher than the hill lifted them, faces etched with purpose, ecstasy, longing, pain. Milo had read and listened to countless omelias meditating on the meaning of the sancts on this hill, how they must have set aside their devotion to the coward goddess, greeted their imminent death at the hands of monsters with willing sacrifice.

Now, as the sun drenched them, the monsters set at their feet, and the low scrub daubing the crest of the hill, he could only see people who'd witnessed their temple smashed and friends killed, who had nothing left to do but turn to their goddess, pray, and endure.

People he should have freed, if only he'd figured out the truth and spread the word sooner.

Where the roll of hill grew steeper and more jagged, Val nodded to a ridge of granite strewn with vines, erupting in purple springtime blooms, and pushed her way forward. Hidden behind the block of stone, a small entrance allowed them into a cavern where tilted slabs of the old temple held back the wash of earth eroding downhill.

Their bodies blocked most of the sunshine that tried to slip in with them. As they shifted into the surprisingly large space, the light broke between them, casting itself upon the still faces of two figures huddled in the far corner.

His heart halted, then raced. Gia. She crouched beside her sister, balled hands clutched to her chest, but face upturned. As if she'd looked to the entrance of the cavern at the final moment before she became stone.

Relief flooded Milo. He wasn't too late to be here for her. He wanted every last moment of her. His mind scrabbled for any hope, searching for a flaw in the weave to point him in the right direction, like when he made translations, for a pattern to work the broken constellations of tiles into. If he kept at it, he could find some solution.

He knelt before Gia and wrapped his bandaged hands around hers. Willing her to wake. Wishing it could be forever.

Val crouched near and propped an elbow on her knee, her head on a fist. "Moon'll be up soon." She sounded exhausted. Milo wondered if she'd slept at all.

He slumped back onto his heels, and the light fractured.

He blinked, unsure if all of the holy guards' abuse had affected his vision.

Or his hearing—

The slight scuff was the last warning before a spear cracked into his head.

Holy guards. Charging inside. Dragging him back, throwing him against a slab of granite. Kicking into Val's shoulder, knocking her to the ground. Crowding the space—no more swings of spear shafts, just drawn daggers. One was at his throat before he could recover, and swords pointed at where Val twisted and kicked. She brought one guard down before three others swarmed her.

Milo grabbed the arm of the guard on him, pulling the knife away. The spear's heel rammed into his gut. Hands slammed him against the stone, the dagger already back in place, as Val was pinned to the dirt.

Boots on her back. Blades at both their necks. Val spat, blood or grit, then met his gaze. The slightest shift of her head told him to hold.

One more guard emerged through the entry, bearing a torch he handed off to one of the men on Val, and lifted the weapon in his other hand. No spear or dagger, nor sword or bow.

Magna's chisel.

Milo threw himself forward at the flash of its shivering dark metal, mindless of the knife, intent on keeping it away from the girls on the floor just beyond Val.

The guards had him fast, and drew the spear across his chest, to lock him to the stone. The final guard was still walking toward Gia. "No!" Milo shouted. He'd done this—he'd told Lucca about the sancts' vulnerability, he'd lost the chisel, and he must now have led them here. To her.

If wishing could move the moon, his plea would drag it to the sky's summit. *Gia, wake up. You have to wake up, right now. Right now, Gia please wake up, wake up—*

Ennio was going to see his problem destroyed, broken to shards, ground to dust underfoot on his long road of history.

Wood bit into Milo's shoulders and bleeding hands that clutched at it without effect. Vaguely, he was aware of the sting of the dagger at his throat. He could still draw breath enough to cry out as the holy guard raised the chisel high and swung it with full force at Gia's upturned face.

CHAPTER TWENTY-SIX

MAKING OF A MONSTER

A templar who comprehends the peculiar bent and flow of god-power will benefit their invocations, their temple, and their people.
—The Book of Invocations

Gia

Sharp as a chisel, this was no soft working of gentle words through stone. Milo's ragged howl pierced the invocation, but it held fast, and the pain carried on his voice resounded through her stolid dreamtime. Her stone-slogged heart, just flushing with awareness that Milo had come, that he was alive, quaked with the sound. Something was very wrong.

Magna's chisel, though, when it cracked against her stone, didn't affect her at all.

One of Ennio's golden guards stood over her, iron in his hand, frustration on his face. He shook out his arm and swung again, knocking the point against her shoulder, directly at her eye.

Finally, he turned back to his fellow guards. There was talk of Primo Sanct being wrong, and who was going to tell him. Concern that they'd already summoned him, as he'd ordered, wanting to see the statue girls dealt with himself. Consternation that they'd sent one of their guard to bring him before they'd pounced on—

Milo. Breathing hard, shock on his face melting into disbelief. And Val, shoved to the ground until the men dragged her up and pulled her from the cavern. As if they had any right to put their hands on her when she had protected this city faithfully.

Gia's fingers twitched.

The guard who struck her still conversed with his man bearing a torch, his back to her. The ones on Milo were moving him toward the passageway out to the hill. The cavern was almost cleared.

Gia rose, quick as flame.

No time to draw her sword—she had one chance at surprise, one breath before they noticed and reacted. No more whispering to build up a force to take on the ceremony or waiting to hear anything of Milo. This moment required a swift strike. She meant to enjoy it.

She slammed into the guard and wrenched the chisel out of his unwary hand. He recovered and answered with a punch to her shoulder before she could raise it, but she was compelled by a fire burning within her, a fire bound by Ennio's invocation and determined to burn itself out before his prayer stamped it down again for good. She brought the chisel up with all her pent-up rage, knocking back the guard's head. She brought it down on him and made to finish him with a kick.

The wretch with the torch took the chance to toss the flame to the ground and come at her. She threw her weight against him and swung her other leg to kick him into the torch fire.

He rolled away, crying out as she whirled back to the first man.

He'd drawn his dagger.

Her arm was already moving, the churning inside her driving the chisel to block his blade. He grappled with her. He had the advantage—her weapon was mostly blunt. His hand grasped her wrist, fingers crushing all the way around, trying to drag her protective arm out of his way.

All at once, she stopped fighting and let both their hands whip back into his nose. Before he jammed the dagger at her, she dropped the chisel from the hand he controlled to her other.

It would have been so easy to drive it into his throat, exposed from his head snapping back.

She struck out with her elbow instead. He choked and stumbled a step backward. With successive cracks the chisel finally knocked the dagger from his hand, knocked his other arm free of her, knocked him out for good.

Milo was battling with the guards who'd dragged him away, turning a spear against them, trying to bar them from reaching Gia. They broke past him and ran for the guard still rolling about, flame chewing along his gold and purple tunic.

Gia grabbed the fallen dagger and tossed it to Lena, awakened and running for the front of the cave. "Help Val!" Lena slipped past Milo, where he waited with eyes locked on Gia.

She had almost reached him when a hand gripped his shoulder from behind. A blade flashed. Her heart clenched. Before she could cry out, Milo's nostrils flared, and he knocked the dagger away with the spear rod. The guard pulled him over, throwing him out of the cave.

Gia ran after them and erupted from the crevice. A holy guard swung his sword away from Val toward Lena, who threw her dagger past his blade into his throat. The other guard had Milo on the ground. He hacked his sword against the spear Milo was using to block him. Gia drew her sword and threw it against the guard's.

He drove her back. Her strikes came just in time to defend herself. His coursed forward. Her feet shuffled closer to the granite wall. His stalked after. Sun and sweat, skin and metal—no room left, and no time, not even this last day. Her heart raced, flush with panic and anger. No chance to fall into Milo's embrace, only to fall under the sharp bite of the holy guard's sword.

Milo cracked the spear across her attacker's broad back. The guard's next swing was a fraction off, and Gia sprang into the opportunity. She drove his blade down. Milo struck the man again, sending him to the ground.

Gia flipped her sword back and ran to Milo, drawn to him like a needle pulled true. She threw her arms about him, and he dropped the spear to clutch her hard. All the feelings he'd stoked in her at the river rushed up from inside her, unstoppable, unnameable.

Her lips grazed against his neck, near his ear. "A thousand years in stone was nothing to this last week." She leaned back against his arms and told him earnestly, "I wanted to kill so many people. Every one of them standing between us." He only let her go far enough for him to look at her. Half-healed bruises covered his face. His eyes shone, marveling.

He cupped her cheek with one ravaged hand. "I thought he was ending you," he said, his voice filled with wonder clawed through with anguish. He dropped his forehead to hers.

His hand was bandaged. Glancing between the ties of the cloak he wore, she could see where his fingers had scratched raw the skin where his icon used to sit. It took everything Gia had not to pull away and use her sword to finish off the men on the ground. Instead, she lifted the chisel. "Does this look like it can stop me?"

Val ran over. She'd taken a sword off a guard. "How did they find us here?"

Milo frowned. "They must have seen us at the wall and let us pass to follow us back to Gia." He took the chisel from Gia's hand, staring at it. "To use this against her and Adalena. But it didn't work." His eyes lifted to one side. "It doesn't destroy the statues."

Lena was right behind Val. "More are coming." With Ennio. Who was no longer beseeching Gia to join him but seeking to end her. Who was invulnerable again for another year. Her gut knotted. They needed to get out of here, especially before the other guards emerged from the cavern.

Lena asked Val, already striding down the hill, "Where can we go?"

Milo was still lost in thought. Gia grabbed the sword from the nearest fallen guard and pressed it into his bandaged hand, jolting him to move.

As they caught up to the others, the next gentle slope of hill revealed, beyond the clump of statues, a band of holy guards heading for them.

Val slowed. "We're about to be outnumbered again."

What could they do but scatter, and likely get taken one by one? Instinct drove Gia's hand to reach for Milo—she did not want to be separated again.

But he darted ahead. "No. We won't be."

"Milo!" Val called as they ran after him, their shadows rippling over the grass like spilled ink.

He stopped and spun around inside the circle of sancts, arms wide, chisel and sword pointing. "They'll join us."

Val reached him first. "You don't have the icon."

He shook his head. "I didn't understand, but now I do. If it didn't harm Gia, then Vassilis must have meant something else. Something he never told Ennio." He let his sword drop to his side, leaving the chisel raised in the glint of the sun, a pale scrap of the dying moon behind it. "It doesn't break the statues." His eyes gleamed with intensity. "It breaks *the invocation*."

Val's brows rose. Lena's face pinched, assessing. Milo looked to Gia, terrible hope written across his face.

She could already be free. She would never turn back to stone. A thrill whispered over her skin, cutting through her dread. She looked past Milo to where, from among the dozen or so men, a white robe broke into view.

If this was going to work, it had better work fast. "Ennio's coming."

Milo's shoulders tensed as if he was preventing himself from turning around to see. "Good. Let him see us end his lies."

The statue standing nearest was a man, sword on his broad back, hand outreached, appealing, mouth in a forever grimace. Would Magna's chisel truly free him from the curse? Milo didn't deliberate further. A quick rise and fall of his hand, and metal struck stone.

He didn't wait, but struck the statue on his other side, and moved on to the next, and next.

Nothing was happening.

Disappointment rained through Gia. Val and Lena took

stands before the statues. Ready to meet Ennio. Gia tried to pull Milo to join them, but he wouldn't stop. She ran along with him.

"We have to fight." She and Lena were doomed, but they could not stop resisting Ennio. She wanted there to be some concrete solution, some icon or tool to grab to remake this nightmare that refused to end.

It was too late.

The holy guards stopped several paces from Lena and Val, but Ennio advanced to their front. Unafraid. Untouchable.

Eyes on Milo, he listed his head toward the nearest guard. "Well, I'm told he always was a little strange."

Gia flushed hot. How had she ever believed this man was capable of seeing the hidden value in anyone?

Milo slowed then. He let the chisel fall to his side like the sword. His poor wrecked fingers looked ready to let them both slip free. "I got it wrong again," he said quietly. Defeated.

"It doesn't matter," she said, standing close. "We don't have anywhere to run." Ennio had his claws in every corner of Trestatto and had ensured the world outside was no haven. Besides, she wasn't going to cede this ground. This was their city.

Ennio, unhurried, observed them. He was wearing his crown with its blade-edged crescent now the ceremony was complete, and he adjusted something at his neck. Lena and Milo's icons. Gia's pulse battered her from the inside. He was flaunting their powerlessness before him.

He kept his gaze from Gia and spoke again as if continuing a conversation. "It's not surprising you children would misunderstand the ancient writing. Even I've forgotten how to read it, I admit. And Lucca should not have relied on the ward's start of the translation, from what I'm told." He gestured at the guard beside him. "The chisel holds no power over the statues after all." He waved a hand. "Dusty words aren't what's important."

His lip peeled up in pleasure. "I do remember calling you each by name. Taking pieces off the board one by one, until all that remained"—his gaze locked on Lena—"was the principessa."

Gia didn't like him looking at Lena. Reveling in how much she'd lost. She yanked his attention her way. "And me."

Ennio turned toward her. "You disappointed me again. I was sure you would make the right choice this time." At his side, his hand made a fist and kneaded it with his thumb. "You could have ruled with me as the principessa Trestatto and I deserved."

His words sent ice water down her spine. She might have clung to his misplaced trust if Milo hadn't shown her she could be so much more. She said thickly, "Trestatto deserved better than both of us."

Ennio's eyes flashed. "Trestatto loves me."

Lena's laughter rang out, cold and sharp. "The people don't love you. They love the lies you've fed them, the safety you sell them. Some hate you." She shook her head and took a heaving breath. "We've all failed them, but only you have hoarded centuries of opportunity. Someday the city will take it back."

Ennio cocked his head, considering her. "You'll be still and silent one way or another. Even as statues part of the time—safely locked up—you and your sister can give your lives to the bounty of Magna Mater." His words rang out, as if he led a crowd at rites. "Who can say that you both won't be able to serve, like all sancts, as the goddess and I intended for eternity?"

"No." Milo's voice was rough, carved out with horror, but it carried—across the hillside, to Ennio, and through Gia. He knew her imprisonment would be absolute, that Stregna had done all she could against Magna's will. His hands clenched. "No!"

Her blood sang in agreement. Ennio would never lock her up in stone—statue or temple—ever again. She'd only just begun working with the others, helping to make this city a home to all. If Ennio took that away from her, he'd be leaving her with only what he had drilled into her. Only what he had shaped her to be.

A tool for killing monsters.

Milo muttered at her side, furious and despondent. This beautiful boy she'd ruined, the poetry that was going to die forever when Ennio completed his execution. "This is all my fault. I should have known—" He blinked, his long dark lashes glinting in arrows of sunlight. "I led them here. I couldn't get the story right at all. And now—"

Now there was nothing left to do.

She set her jaw. Nothing but kill as many of Ennio's men as she could.

Darkness bled in at the edges of Gia's vision. Milo was too hard on himself, but he *was* wrong about one thing—this was all *her* fault. She was the one who had delivered this monster what he needed to feed off the city. She shifted her feet on the uneven ground, readying for battle. No point now in dreaming of what she could have become. What she might have had. Only one last chance to destroy herself along with as much of Ennio's power as she could.

Ennio clapped his hands together, as if the sound could erase Milo's protest, and turned his sharp gaze to him. "Milo. With whom Gia has placed her loyalty." His mouth pursed, then he lifted his head high, drawing a long breath in. He went back to using his templar voice. Beneficence laced with arrogance. "I was glad to send our ward out of the city, with my guard set to watch for him, knowing the Great Mother would either let him perish in the fields or use him to guide us to this threat. In this, we have been fortunate. Now, Adalena and Gia can be returned to Magna Mater's bosom."

Milo murmured, just to her, "I'm so sorry." She drank in one last look of the sincere intensity in his eyes. His voice caught fire. "You deserved a chance. I'd give anything—"

He wouldn't have to. Her fingers tightened on her hilt. It was her turn to make a sacrifice.

"Sadly, there's no such purpose left to our wards now." Ennio's words were regretful, but as he looked from Val to Milo, a smirk grew on his face. "Except as a sacrifice to ensure no more disruption comes to the system that has kept Trestatto safe for centuries."

"Safe?" Milo's voice cracked out like the snap of a flag. "Who has been safe?" He gestured at Lena. At Val. Walked forward, past them. Farther.

What was he doing? Gia moved alongside him—wanted to grab him back, but none of this mattered, they were trapped in Ennio's game as they had always been. As they advanced across the empty stretch of grass, she looked about and spotted a few battered guards from the cavern making their way down the hill, looking ready for retribution. They were surrounded.

Ennio wasn't worried. The guards nearest him stepped forward, their swords clinking as they drew them, but Ennio didn't flinch or fall back. He was invincible once more. He'd already beaten them.

Milo shouted again to him. "Who's safe? The sancts? The people of the city?"

Just before the guard to the right of Ennio lifted his sword against the boy flinging mere words at his exalted Primo Sanct,

Milo's eyes flashed with something more than sunlight. "It's really only ever been you."

Gia swept forward with her sword to block the guard's before it cleaved Milo in two. Startled, Milo stumbled behind her, but not far enough. They were about to be destroyed. She didn't know if she hoped to be spared seeing him cut down, or that his end was at least quick and fed her fury to bring as many of Ennio's favorites with her into death.

Gia threw everything she had into fending off the holy guard as the others rushed forward. She could hear swords ringing out against each other, Lena and Val thrown into the fight. Everything was flashing blades, singing metal. Milo lifted his sword against a guard that advanced on him, knocking away his attack, but still pressed near Gia catching her opponent's sword against hers. Blade shuddered against blade. Her hands trembled on her hilt. Her heels sank into the grass. Would the guard spare her life to keep her locked in Ennio's invocation forever?

She was done with mercy.

Gia threw the guard back and gave a quick kick, driving him to the ground. Before she could deliver the killing blow, Milo stalked over him, through the cleared path to Ennio.

There was no point in fighting him, she wanted to scream. Milo, reaching a placid Ennio, raised not his arm bearing the sword, but the chisel.

Even less purpose to this. Gia let her frustration burn through her limbs as she struck away the other guard's blade and shoved him back, turning again just in time to see Milo wrench the chisel down against his one-time savior.

Nothing happened. Milo stood before a defiant Ennio, unmoving, tension writ across his back. Ennio, weaponless, backhanded

Milo hard and shoved him away. Milo stumbled to one knee, sword and chisel falling from his hands. He stared, curls stuck with sweat to his brow, dazed, as if this blow had finally undone him. Ennio cast a pitying look upon him, even as a satisfied smile cracked across his face, under that insolent crown—

Gia drew a sharp breath. Even some of the nearer guards stilled.

Milo smiled up at Ennio, bruised and beatific.

A single drop of crimson blood trailed down Ennio's temple, where the blade crown had cut him.

CHAPTER TWENTY-SEVEN

SMOKE AND STONE

The frozen may flow, and the flowing may fly. Transcendence distills the essence of a thing, releasing it to the next state—and unlocks what is held in the heart of living things at the moment of epiphany. Templars must be mindful of the temper of things—rain sought from a raging river may brew a tempest.

—The Book of Invocations

Gia

The battle took a breath. Then everything moved even faster. A few guards realized what had happened and moved back toward Ennio, who seemed confused by everyone gawking until the droplet of blood fell past his eye. He blinked and wiped at his face. Looked at his red hand.

Gia stared. That smear of red across his face lit up everything inside her. All her thoughts, buzzing chaotically a moment before, came home in one stinging truth.

Ennio could die today.

The chisel wasn't meant to be used against the statues at all, but the templar who had invoked them. With that strike, Milo had fully broken the invocation and Ennio's immortality at last.

The knowledge reflected in Ennio's face. It ground down to a sharp diamond spark in his eyes, flashing at Gia, and he reached for Milo. Ennio cursed or prayed or growled—Gia couldn't hear over the roaring in her head. Ennio's bloody hand struck Milo's brow, and Milo convulsed. He cried out, catching himself with one hand, clutching his side.

"To me!" Ennio shouted. His guards, running or fighting past Lena and Val, converged on Ennio, and Milo, and the guard on the ground before him.

And Gia. Rage and terror searing through her.

Her boots shoved deeper into the grass. Her sword swung high.

Milo reached for his fallen sword. Ennio retreated. He half stumbled taking steps down the slope. She had him. After a thousand years, her strike would finally fall true.

Then her hilt slipped from her grip. Her feet failed to find the ground. Had she been struck? Was she falling? She felt no pain.

None at all.

Her sword fell away along with the pain of all the fighting, of seeing Milo hurt, of despair. Metal to earth. There was nowhere for pain to house itself in her—her body was too quick for it. The strike Milo delivered to Magna's templar seemed to ring through her, setting every atom of her spinning and spiraling and speeding.

Milo, staggering to his feet, stared at whatever she was

becoming, his face lit with sublime shock.

This was transcendence. Like Stregna's templars or warriors of old, giving themselves over to battle-fury. Rising to a place of power untethered.

She drifted higher. Saw wider—

The frozen ring of sancts breathing to life, figures freed from stone, long-held cries released with ecstasy, arms relaxing like sighs—or, as the sancts laid eyes on Ennio, reaching for weapons.

Holy guards, stopped in the midst of the woken statues, forced to engage them, in a chaotic melee. A few reaching the templar—his name slipped through Gia's mind like the sword through her fingers, a stone through water. Through air. There was nothing left of her to hold onto that smallness.

Val, face upturned, open-mouthed.

Lena. Lit up like an actual torch, a blaze of beauty, long and sharp, cutting her way into the sky.

Was Gia a holy flame? She was not Gia, she was released from Gia, from all the pain and shame and fear. All the ties and tides between her and others were gone. She was unbound by body or blood. She was something else.

Something wild and terrible.

She ripped through the air, away from the tumult and shouts.

One cry trailed after her. "Gia!"

That name tried to capture her, but she didn't want to return to the past that bled through it, to put back on the guilt that weighed it down. Another call was claiming her, pulling her to annihilate herself absolutely into the presence of the Unseen Goddess—or in a final outburst of violence.

"No, no—" That voice still reached her, an arrow piercing the sky.

Like the sky, she perceived all about her; everywhere, everything. The tall girl—Val—sweeping her sword against a guard's, turning her face back up and crying out. "Adalena!"

And Lena became Lena again, shimmered back into herself—a little.

Val was drawn back into the battle, which several more statues had joined, but Milo lurched forward and echoed her. He pressed on with more words scattered into the sky. "Adalena! Come back!" He cast his gaze about at the sancts taking up the fight. "Your people!" he called up to Lena. "You want to protect your people! The sancts are waking, and they need you, to explain everything that's happening. And all the people of the city! You're the only one who can lead them now. Or the city will be broken forever."

With each stream of words, it was as if a tide rocked the shimmer of Lena nearer and nearer—to those calling for her on the ground, and into herself.

Val spun away from a guard to see if Milo's words worked.

Lena plucked herself from the air, stretched her toes back to the grass, and reached her hands out to grab hold of the first thing to reach her—Val's arm. Her fingers clung to Val as if reassuring herself she had fingers to grab with—that she would not ascend again. Milo, seeing Lena's choice, returned with a fury to crying out to a girl who was already gone.

What was once a girl watched on, wondering at all their anguish. It felt so easy now to let herself be pulled away, to fall slowly upward toward the goddess's sublime embrace.

Val locked her own free hand onto Lena's arm. "Why is this happening? Didn't Milo break the invocation?"

Lena shook her head. "We were already free of stone—

the chisel must be part of the invocation, sending those it was laid upon into the next state of being."

"What is that?"

"Stregna's domain." She stared up at what was Gia, eyes aching. "Epiphany."

Lena didn't see the guard coming at her back. If she had remained transcended, she would have. She would be untouchable by any blade.

Val shoved Lena to one side and broke toward the attacker. She pinned the guard's sword to the ground and barreled her shoulder into him.

They both fell over in a tumble of limbs and swords. Lena staggered, too.

The hillside quaked.

The part of the sky that Gia had become looked for the source.

The bleeding templar was crouching in the grass, protective guards surrounding him. His one palm shoved into the earth, fingers splayed across the green blades. His other hand held the chisel. He struck it again to the ground. His will, twined with released godpower, rumbled through the hill. Sancts stumbled, fighters were thrown apart. A rift carved itself across the slope, cutting under a still-shouting Milo's feet. His eyes flared wide as he plummeted.

Lena raced his way, where he'd landed on hands and knees in churned up earth. "It's Ennio!" she shouted. "Now we're enough to overpower him." With an iron edge to her voice, she ordered, "Get my sister back!" Then she ran for where Val charged, sword high, for the guards and templar.

Milo grabbed his sword from where it had fallen and got to his feet. Cloak snapping behind him, he ran under where she was only a shimmer in the sky, calling out, calling home. "You have to come back, Gia! You're the strongest person I know, I know you can do it. Get down here and finish this fight."

He didn't stop shouting, even when the last few guards came running down the hill from the cavern or fighting sancts and surged toward him. A shadow chased after them, growing larger like a widening mouth.

A gryphon dove from Trestatto's sky, all the way to its blessed hillside. Its lynx paws clawed through the earth and bounded up again to catch a holy guard and wrest him in its sharp beak. Another guard, wide-eyed, fell upon the creature, fighting to free the first man. The gryphon's wings slashed out, writing blood through the air.

The remaining guards rushed again for Ennio. The first took a swipe at Milo, who knocked his sword away. Even as he grunted with exertion, even as another gryphon circled the hill watchfully, Milo never ceased his plea to the girl becoming sky, barely took his eyes from her transcendence. A guard shoved Milo hard as he passed. Milo staggered back, closer to the schism in the earth. Still spilling out words.

But she was not her sister and would not be bidden. Becoming herself again would mean plunging back through the hardest instincts of her heart. She wouldn't.

Stregna had caught her up in a moment of despair, turning from all her slain hopes to pursue death—perhaps the goddess would not even have her, would cast her back down.

No. It would be better to lose herself to battle-fury. Let her wrath consume her at last.

There was absolution in destruction, too.

The second gryphon snapped its beak and sent a cry

resounding against the hillside, the threat of monstrous power setting the world trembling.

Yet not as fearsome as she.

Flush with potential, every piece of herself unlocked, awash in the flood of violence released from her heart—she seared across the sky, reached out, and grazed her power against the gryphon.

She obliterated the beast. The sky exploded as the monster's form ripped apart, its energy shredding through the air. Milo's scream for her was lost in its annihilation. The other gryphon vaulted back up into the blue, bearing its meal away.

She could do anything now. She was thought and power alone. Before her fire burned out, she could run through existence, faster and faster until all the small people and cities and continents and worlds blurred away into something too soft to catch at her. To hurt.

Except—

The boy. Shouting with all his breath, reaching for her with words. They rippled over her, passed through her. Why did he keep calling that name, with such longing? Why would he want that mess of anger and guilt back? Thinking of them snarled a part of her into those emotions, and the boy's words caught on them, drawing her attention further. Stoking irritation within her.

He always wanted to understand the sancts and stars, everything she could see easily from here, everything she was flowing through, that was flowing through her. She could show it all to him now—even if it tore him apart.

She burned through the air, pulled herself just a little back into the body that was Gia. He wanted her to put that body back on, the one she was reduced to for so many years in stone. She could let that all go, rise easy as incense, exult herself beyond the stars, beyond the reach of corrupt men, of monsters' claws—of herself. Such lightness.

She swept before the boy, whose outstretched hand snapped back at the brush of her blurred form. She could sense his pain. So sharp. Her hair lifted about her face. Her voice was the rush of wind extinguishing a thousand candles. "You would hold me? I'm in the hand of Stregna now. Only a breath escaping as soon as it is drawn. Merely the final flash of sun over an unreachable horizon." She pressed nearer, forcing him back against the broken earth.

His eyes shone, but he blinked away the tears and let her fire burn into his eyes. "I would free you. I was trying—" He braced a hand to his side. "Please, believe me. Gia, you can finally be fully yourself. Live the life he stole."

She could feel that life, at the far edges of her vastness. It tasted of dust and blood. "I am free. I can be anything now. I can sense it. Rapture or rage. Let Stregna's holiness burn away every unworthy part of me. Or flatten this little city, bend it to the earth it barely scratches the sky from. I could become vengeance." Then this place, these people, would stop calling her back with memories of the horror she was.

She flared brighter. The air about them rushed faster—a squall that would tear him apart, but only bear her away.

The boy grimaced but spoke through bared teeth. "You're more than that." He heaved a breath. "You're more than a sanct. More than your rage. Someone this city needs. Someone I need." His speech was like lightning, a bolt of truth fissuring into her infinity. It sparked a memory of how she fit perfectly in his arms, the faith in herself he stoked, and she pulsed with who she was.

"Someone you still need to be." His words washed over everything, turning dust to starlight. Blood to rich wine. She tasted it all, bright and sharp as anise on her tongue. His eyes, brown and blazing, towed her nearer. "Someone I know is not going to finish herself off like Ennio really wanted."

His words sharpened her like a blade. "I wouldn't give him the satisfaction." She felt her mouth snarl into a smile.

Milo shuddered with an inhalation, and Gia pressed a hand to his chest. Wondered at her hand—at everything she almost gave up. It was her turn to shudder. "Milo, I—"

He stroked his free hand down the curve of her shoulder. "Let's show him whose city this is." His voice was shallow, spent.

Magna's solid assurance beneath Gia thrummed through the soles of her feet. She was herself again, and they had a fighting chance now. "You did it. Ended the invocation." He nodded, gripping her shoulder harder. "Are you all right?"

The world tore itself apart.

The uneven crack of earth beside them rained pebbles and grit as the hill shook beneath their feet. Masses of soil and stone tore themselves away from the ground. They rose, forming into echoes of the beasts of the wild, gryphons and serpents and chimeras, like the clay and jeweled beasts set about the city turned giant.

Ennio never had much imagination.

Gia and Milo held on to each other as the ground tossed them like an ill-trained horse. Milo rasped in her ear, "The invocation binding Magna's godpower—"

"It's freed now." From beyond the cleft of earth, a human figure went flying over their heads. Gia's heart—clenched back inside herself again, desperate to save her city and all the sancts—thundered like the footfalls of the earthen beasts chasing this way.

She was about to yell to Milo that his no-killing rule was finished, when the fracture in the hill gave out, and all of them—Gia, Milo, beasts, Trestatto's blessed ground—fell into a chasm waiting below.

CHAPTER TWENTY-EIGHT

THE BLADE CROWN

Through invocation a goddess may be called to rend or restore a piece of the earth. Godpower may strike to sever or as a hand to reach out to hold safe. This may be used to preserve the structures of cities or the lives of their citizens or their treasures of knowledge—to make the storehouse of the unseen less ephemeral.

—The Book of Invocations

Gia

Gia's hands tore at the air. The earth caught her, a heap cradling her landing. As she rolled over in the soil, Gia realized this wasn't any underground recess, but the buried temple of Stregna. Several times the size of the cavern that Val had found, this had been the main sanctuary. A dais stood at one end, surrounded by carvings that swept up the high walls. Half the stone rooftop lay shattered upon the granite floor. Earth rose steeply in a slope to the top of the ruined hillside.

Several others on the hill slid down with the rending of the earth. Sancts and guards tumbled together in the sunlight cutting through swirls of dust. Lena scrambled from her knees near to the foot of where the earth spilled over the temple stone.

Ennio stood halfway up the slope.

Monsters emerged from the dirt.

Lena called out for her people to pull those buried from the cascade of earth. She rushed to one nearby and shoved soil away with both hands. Disturbed worms and insects wriggled and scattered.

Gia regained her feet, but before she could make a move, a limb of clay and stone whooshed through the air, catching her across the chest. She was back on the ground, gasping for breath.

Tits, these beasts were strong.

Milo thrust the sword he'd somehow hung onto into the monster—a misshapen gryphon—and dislodged some of its bulk. Ennio had less stone to work with here than when he'd pull his beasts from the quarry, but even if Milo and Gia and the others could tear the monsters apart, Ennio would only make more.

She dragged herself up again and stumbled to Milo's side. The gryphon swiped out, but she was ready. She dove under its arm and clawed at the hole Milo had started. The beast reared up, wings of shattered stone reaching wide, pulling her feet from the floor. Milo shouted and slashed at its haunch. When it crashed back to the ground, it crouched low as if to crush Gia. She tucked her feet, rolled back, and kicked its jaw.

Its head went flying, smashed into a galaxy of dirt across the temple tile-stones. Gods, she was glad to have a body again.

She and Milo punched and hacked at the rest of the monster.

As it toppled, she swept her gaze across the temple. Lena had most of the sancts fighting the other beasts and the guards left on their feet. As soon as one beast was torn apart, Ennio pulled another into existence. Serpents of roots and rock twined around people's ankles, holding them back. The sancts broke through the pebbles and earth only for them to reform around their legs and drag them further into the temple. Gia saw a few others up on the hilltop fighting invoked beasts, two-headed wolves and chimeras snapping their jaws, keeping the sancts there at bay. A gryphon from the sky pounced upon them. Ennio stood clear from danger, a few guards orbiting him, furiously directing Trestatto's earth against his own people.

Across the sanctuary, Val had dragged an entire chimera off a sanct it was clobbering—but now the beast backed her into one of the temple walls, crushing her against its frieze. Her arms bulged as she ripped clods of the monster away, her face a strained grimace.

Gia scrubbed her grimy hands over each other, burying the mud deeper into her godlines. Her throat burned. It was too much like the day Ennio had first trapped them, and like the sancts she'd seen on her first journey down into the city—fighting beasts dotted with jewels, their faces indelible marks of the true horror they'd felt in the final moments Ennio granted them. Chaos and pain rooted in the choices she had made.

She turned to Milo, who was looking dazed. He half-leaned on his sword as if unsure of what problem to tackle next.

Gia knew. "We have to stop this." She clapped her hand to the sword's pommel. "I need to kill Ennio."

His eyes flashed, focused again. He pulled the sword away. "I'll do it."

If he thought she was making a murderer of him, after everything he'd been through for her, he had as much dirt in his head as that gryphon did. She yanked at the hilt. "I have plenty of blood on my hands already, you aren't—"

He dragged the sword back. "That's why you shouldn't have to do this."

Hands swooped in from his side and gripped the sword. Lena tugged it away from him. "I'll kill him."

Gia protested, "I'm the one who caused this."

Lena shook her head once. "I should have protected you from him long ago." Milo let his bandaged hands fall away.

"All the people of Trestatto are going to need you," Gia argued, "and I still need to make this up to you."

Lena pulled the dagger from her belt and flipped its handle to Gia. "So help me."

Gia took the blade. Milo gave her arm a squeeze and ran to help Val. Lena hefted the sword and raced for the jagged slope of earth, Gia beside her.

Under their feet, the pieces of temple roof skittered. They rose. They threw both girls back. Ennio was blocking them. Gia scrabbled as she slid down the stone and jammed her elbow against its edge to haul herself past. Lena launched herself forward, over the shards that spiked up at her like thorns.

Blood dripped down Ennio's face from across his brow as he stooped. He struck the chisel again to the churned-up earth, and the last shards of broken roof swept together with mounds of fallen soil to form something unlike any monster that ever stalked the Orabellian wilds.

Lena halted. Gia hastened to her side.

The creature loomed over them, stouter than the most

ancient pine in Trestatto's groves, its limbs twisting masses of earth made shaggy with broken roots and sharp with the blades of temple roof.

All the other monsters stilled. All of Ennio's power flowed into this one. Most sancts' struggles waned, though others still battled guards. And Val was trapped by the frozen chimera, feet kicking, fighting for breath. Milo endeavored to free her.

Ennio swiped a hand across his eyes, and blood dripping down his mouth painted the smile that grew there. "You can't win this," he told Lena and Gia from between two of his last guards. "You're too soft. That's why I had to take the city from you. You failed to stand against our enemies." He beat his bloody hand against his chest. The neck of his robe was stained red, where the last two icons lay. "Only I am strong enough to protect my city."

Lena's back was straight as her sword. "Even water can carve through stone given enough time." She rolled her shoulders and shifted into a fighting stance. "This city was never yours."

She launched herself at the monster.

It punched out. Lena was quick, sidestepping its too-long forearm slamming into the ground. She harried the beast, her sword ringing out against its stony thorns. Again it lunged for her; again her sword beat it away. Gia stomped forward and drew its attention, dragging the dagger down its leg. Roots snapped. The beast swung at her. Gia ducked, but it knocked her on her back with a blow bearing the force of three gryphons. She struggled to fill her lungs.

While Gia distracted the creature, Lena made her move. She sank low, her lithe spine bowing to the ground, and sprang up through the monster's wide-set legs.

Gia gasped for air as her sister rushed up the slope, outpacing the beast's swing as it whirled around after her. Lena met Ennio's guards, the battle a froth of blades lit by the sun angling into the temple, too quick for Gia's eyes. Breathing again, Gia rolled to her knees and threw herself away from where the monster's limb smacked the earth. She clambered over the dirt, only to press herself low again as a living, breathing gryphon swooped down into the chasm.

The guards standing before Ennio dove from the span of its wings as they cut wide through the temple. The gryphon landed near the stone monster pinning Val against the wall. Milo spun, half hanging on the arm of the beast he struggled to pull back from Val. He threw an arm up blocking her from the gryphon, whose haunches rippled, taut with power.

Ennio's creature was the only one untroubled by the gryphon. It crashed a foot almost on top of Gia. She sprang away, desperate to distract it. If Gia failed, Lena would pay. The beast pummeled the bottom of the slope, and Gia dodged and darted, barely ahead of its clod fists with their spiky knuckles.

A final guard barreled out from behind Ennio at Lena. He had the advantage of higher ground, but Lena rushed into his attack, her sword like liquid in her hands redirecting the power of his blows. She whipped her blade around his, driving it down, pulling him past her. Without looking back, she kicked behind her and sent him into the dirt.

With no one between him and Lena, Ennio pulled all his power back into himself. His towering monster slowed and toppled over. Gia clutched her arms about her head as it fell, nearly atop her. It slammed into the ground, crushing Ennio's own guards trying to return to his side.

Gia bounded over the fallen beast. The monsters would keep

coming, earth or bone, and only stopping Ennio would give any of them a chance to survive.

He drew himself upright with the dropped sword of some guard or sanct in one hand, the chisel in the other.

Lena angled her sword at him. Any strike against Magna's templar must be fast and true. If he could invoke his goddess again at will, he could break Lena's bones inside her or direct her own blade against her. That was, once he marked her with his blood—and he was bleeding everywhere.

Their swords crashed together. Lena fended off Ennio's forceful blows with a piercing, cold fury. He answered with a surge of wrath. A goddess's power drove his blade to a holy violence. It battered Lena's.

Gia launched herself into the fight. Heedless of either sword, of any threat of invocation, she jabbed the dagger at Ennio. She forced him to hold her off, to sidestep, to shuffle his feet over the uneven ground. His eyes—distracted, wild—blazed at her.

He'd called her his one regret. She'd make sure of it.

Ennio shouted prayers. Blood coursed from his shredded brow and godpower poured through his bones and blade. He threw Lena back and turned toward Gia, letting out a snarl of menace. Scarlet overran his cheekbones. He would not forfeit the crown he'd wrought.

His sword sliced Gia's knuckles. She gritted her teeth. Her feet stumbled backward.

Ennio wiped the scarlet from his eyes and reached for her, his bloody lips finishing an invocation of destruction.

Lena thrust herself between them. Ennio pitched his attack back to her.

He was once the mightiest warrior for Trestatto, but centuries had passed since he had any cause to fight for his life. Like he said—after so long, even his memory failed.

All of Lena's winding, fluid moves crystallized into a single sharp blow, driving her sword straight through Ennio's center.

He fell against Lena, who let go of her sword as its hilt wrenched from her hand. His eyes flared wide, disbelieving. He gasped a breath. Fresh blood bubbled from between his lips. Lena, mouth closed, nostrils flaring, wrapped an arm about his shoulders and settled him upon the uneven earth. The iron crown tumbled from his head.

Every monster crumbled to the ground.

Sourness churned in Gia's belly, but she turned from Ennio and ran down the slope for Milo and Val. Milo and a woken sanct, both holding swords, stood over the limp, bleeding gryphon. A slash cut across Milo's cheek like a stroke of red ink. Val fell back to the temple floor, palms braced to thighs, breathing hard, but alive.

Milo dropped the sword to clutch Gia's hand, and relief passed through her, like a rush of wings—not of gryphons or strix, but some softer fledgling.

One or two of the guards rose to their feet, sluggish as if the shock of seeing Ennio bleeding out was still hitting them like a great wave, but the sancts were on them at once. One guard gazed up at the sanct standing over him and gestured a prayer, touching his fingers to his forehead.

Lena untangled the icons from Ennio's neck. Cradling his head, she stripped them from him. She let him fall back again, and stood.

A man—the first sanct that Milo struck trying to wake—stood over a guard staring up the slope at Ennio's body. "Do we dispatch them, Your Eminence?"

"No," Gia interrupted. An imprint of Ennio's blood remained on Lena's tunic, the sharp line of the blade crown angled across her shoulder. "Sorry, Lena. But no. No more vengeance." If Lena wanted her to help with her duties to the city, Gia was starting with this. She looked to Milo and squeezed his hand back. "It's time for all of Trestatto to come together."

Milo drew a ragged breath and smiled, pleased, and wan under all his bruises.

His teeth were traced with blood.

He collapsed.

She didn't understand, as he fell to the temple floor, scattered over with soil like dark stars—and soaked with blood. "Milo?" She crouched beside him, pulled back the dark cloak. Oh, gods, his tunic was stained nearly as dark, slick, and sticky. The gryphon, or the guards, or—

Milo's eyes, ringed with pain, searched her face, as if some answer to what was happening to him lay there. She ran her hand up under the ruined tunic and found the rip in his flesh, on his side. Milo grimaced. Her stomach heaved. His ribs jutted from the wound. Snapped and stabbing through him from inside.

Ennio had done this—striking Milo with his bloodied hand and his freed godpower. Ennio was reaching out yet, taking Milo away from her. Fracturing her world apart again. Cracking her heart in two.

This wasn't something she could solve with a sword. Her helplessness loomed before her, a terrifying abyss.

"Lena!" Her voice broke into a sharp wail. Alta often granted her sister the power of small healings. Lena had her icon. She could help. Val vaulted over the crumbling chimera, and Lena hurried down the slope, slipping the copper icon over her head.

Kneeling at Milo's other side, Lena placed an open hand on his wound and muttered an old familiar prayer. Behind her, Val twisted her hands together. Gia's fingers carved furrows in the soil as they flexed, as she watched and waited. Forget fixing the city or making a better world. All she cared about was mending this one small part of it.

Lena broke off with a hiss. She met Gia's eyes with a terrible tenderness. "It's too much."

No. The word beat like a drum with every lashing of her blood as Lena stood and grasped Val's arm, holding up the other girl who shook, staring at her dying friend. No. Val cried Milo's name and tears streaked down her cheeks.

No.

If Alta couldn't save Milo, Gia knew a way her sister goddess could. She leaped up, ran past shocked sancts and guards, from one figure laid out in this temple to another. She grabbed the crown from where it had fallen near Ennio. He was dead, and now a new templar could use the blade to invoke Magna. Gia could lay the original invocation for turning beasts to stone on Milo. She could heal him.

She raced down the slope to Milo's side, her heart in a panic that his soul might already be gone in those few moments—flying beyond the grasp of her fingers, beyond a canopy of branches barring anyone's following, beyond clouds that blotted out the stars.

She knelt again by his side. She put on the blade crown.

Milo's eyes found her with relief, then sharpened. "No." His lips had gone dry, barely moving.

A cry broke from her chest. She heaved a breath and asked, "Please. Please let me." She grabbed his hand, stroked the curls plastered to his brow over his temple. Her hands trembled. "I can save you. I know the old invocation. You'll wake and be healed. You'll be safe."

"You'll be gone." The bleakness in his voice nearly broke her. His eyes told a softer story. "I don't want to wake up in a world without you."

She pleaded. "I can't live in a world without any possibility of you." He was her hope for a better world. A better self. Her unsteady hand traced over her forehead, like a prayer. She was bleeding from the crown, trails of blood falling in place of the tears she was holding back, burning her eyes.

She reached for his brow. His hand snapped up, fingers encircling her wrist. She waited, a storm inside her. If he said no again, it would shatter her.

He must have seen this in her face. Finally, he gentled his grip. Ran his hand along her forearm. Comforting. Guiding.

She daubed the mark upon his brow. Uttered the invocation, willing her voice not to waver as she dragged the words up from centuries ago, from her throat near choking on tears.

"We'll keep you safe," she promised when it was done. No one would forget the story of the last sanct in Trestatto.

He nodded and leaned his cheek against her hand. "I love you."

At this, she couldn't speak. Her tears threatened to overthrow her, and she didn't want to send him away like that. She pressed her gentlest kiss to his battered hand. Oh gods, this was like dying, but which of them was dying? Milo would be still as death for the rest of her life, lost to her. He'd only awaken to a time when she'd have been dead for years. It was almost worse than laying his body in the ground. The bright life they should share was being broken, sliced apart, shattered across a century.

His breath grew labored, shallower. His eyes flared with understanding. She squeezed his hand harder. She wanted to keep him. She had to let him go.

He drew in a shuddering breath, and barely expelled it before he had to draw another. He fought to hold it, holding on to now, holding on to her. Yet he couldn't shelter them forever, and his last breath was spent on a final, aching, "Gia."

In its wake, the temple was quiet—Val wept, onlookers murmured—as Milo's skin went white and unyielding. His dark hair paled. His fingers went cold in her hand.

She felt like two Gias—one a shell of herself, a husk, about to catch fire and obliterate itself and everything around it. And a smaller Gia, huddled far away from that hurt the first held back, a clenched fist holding on to her love like a beating heart.

She wanted to rage. Tear the whole city down this time; make blood flow because his stilled. But she couldn't. She had to build it back into something worthy of Milo, for him to wake in.

Without her.

The sob she'd buried deep in her chest cracked her open, broke free. In the violence of her tears, her hand fell away from the statue that was Milo. His fingers still reached for her.

"Can't you undo it?" Val asked, hollow-voiced. "Use the crown again, and—bring him back!"

Gia answered as much for herself, to kill her hope that she'd ever see Milo again, as for Val. "The invocation is unbreakable," she pronounced in a wrung-out voice. Even to the templar who laid it. She turned to Val, who still clutched her sister. "I wish I knew another, anything else, but I don't." If she'd studied here more faithfully, instead of running to Magna's temple at every chance—the thought cleaved through her.

Tears swelled in her eyes. The sunlight sifted down through the temple, crawling nearer to where Milo lay. She blinked away the tears, letting them wash freely over her cheeks, and noticed something dangling from the fingers of Lena's free hand. "His icon." She pulled it into her own, and Lena let her. "He doesn't like to be without it."

Gia placed it upon Milo's chest, where it belonged.

CHAPTER TWENTY-NINE

THE LAST SANCT

The flow of the Sisters' godpowers is as the turning seasons, each fitting in its time of grief or growth, all joined into one unending cycle.

—The Book of Invocations

Gia

They broke the blade crown.

Gia tried to enlist Val, who insisted Dario be the one to work on the holy relic, to ensure only the circlet was removed and no damage came to Magna's icon.

Now, the blade rested in a sheath at Gia's belt as she stood upon the city wall beside her sister. The morning sun baked the stone and painted the surrounding fields a soft gold. They'd spent an hour reviewing the fortifications the militia had put in place to ward off monsters, now that the great invocation was broken. Archers and spear-bearers bristled along the wall. Lena spoke with the new general she'd selected with the advice of Val—who stood on her other side, red sash blown taut across her chest by the early summer breeze.

Lena said she could feel safe only with Val—who'd protected her while the city was against her—as her personal royal guard. This was Val's new duty with the militia, which Lena planned to keep separate from Magna's temple, as she intended to divide her own roles as templar of Alta and principessa. She still insisted that once the city and the nearest fields were secure, she would invite emissaries from other Orabellian city-states and the empires to the north and east to collaborate on making their lands safer for everyone, but also that she'd establish a council, chosen by the people of the city, and ultimately leave ruling to them. As Lena finished with the general and they started down the steps together, Gia wondered what it must be like to be granted so much power that you wanted to give any of it up.

She supposed, since she had rashly made herself Magna's head templar, she might find out.

This hadn't gone over well with many of the templars. Gia couldn't blame them, though Lena had declared all of Gia's actions sanctioned as part of the war Ennio had started. Gia couldn't bring back the men she'd killed, only give them proper funerals rather than hiding their deaths as Ennio had and apologize to the ones she'd hurt. That had also been received with mixed results. Guards handpicked by Val waited for her at the bottom of the stairs, a sign of the still-tenuous shift in power.

When Lena and the other sancts had descended Stregna's hill, gathering their friends who had helped them at the Ceremony of Dust, many others joined them in the streets as they made their way across the city. The story they had seeded that awful day on the temple steps had spread, and when people saw Lena walking through the streets, healing any woken sancts in need, the belief in it rushed across Trestatto less like wildfire than a rising, relentless tide over waiting fields.

Ennio's militia leaders made a few noises of resistance, but their command didn't hold over all the people who refused to fight against Principessa Adalena. When they'd reached Magna's temple, a number of the templars were ecstatic to see the missing sanct safe and revived.

Under Lena's direction, the militia had driven away most of the monsters Ennio had stirred toward the city. Extra sentry patrols were dispatched to protect farther farmland and towns. People were still frightened, seeing gryphons land inside the city, serpents sneak into the streets. Gia hoped Magna's temple might teach citizens to protect themselves from the occasional beasts who made it past the walls. Maybe open its coffers to pay for daggers and bows and arrows for anyone who trained with them. And to forge bells for an updated alarm system through every district. Her temple would help them see how they could all take care of each other.

Today the gates stood open. Lena sidled beside Gia. "We're going to check in with Kadri next. Want to come?" Besides the new general, Lena had instituted new orders at the gates, and put Kadri and her cousin in charge of monitoring them. Lena now included Gia in overseeing all aspects of governing the city. It was nice to spend so much time with her sister, and Gia needed every chance to learn if she was going to survive the politics of remaking Magna's temple. For now, she'd put Templar Daniela in charge of the everyday management of things.

Today, Gia had somewhere else to be. She shook her head. "I have to get to Stregna's temple."

"Gia," Val said, drawing something from her belt bag. "Things have been busy, with—" She gestured up the wall. "Everything. Some of the militia just found this, cleaning out the station nearest the gate. They brought it to me." The smallest smile Gia had ever seen Val give whispered over her face. "I'm sure he would have wanted you to have it." She handed Gia a folded piece of parchment.

Gia realized what she held, its creased corners sharp like a star, a ripped edge like a flame. She fought to swallow. "Thank you."

She needed to stop at Magna's temple. She needed a chance to read Milo's words in private.

+ ✦ +

Her guards waited outside the archive.

Gia settled against the wall under the carving where she knew Milo had spent hours studying. She tucked her knees to her chest and unfolded the parchment.

A poem.

The writing was shakier than the precise script she'd seen among his things at the temple. Storica Lucca had carefully collected Milo's work and left it on his desk in his empty cell. The storica was helping Gia go through all the surviving invocations here, carved on tablets or the temple walls, to see what ways she might learn to call upon Magna. Together, they might even succeed in remaking some of those prayers that had been lost since her time, crumbled to dust. The old man, full of regret, poured every effort into creating some hope for the future, even beginning to teach Gia to read modern Orabellian writing. And if Gia was getting a second chance, she was bound to extend that to everyone emerging from under Ennio's rule.

Rusty streaks marred the page and cut across her heart. But even as she labored to decipher the script, they could not obscure how Milo's writing spoke to her.

About her.

While locked up by Ennio, Milo declared this was his only confession to make. He anguished that Gia would succumb to statue form forever before he could see her again. His lines told how he wanted to return to her, to let no wall of stone divide them, no ocean of time stand between them. How he wrote these lines not to invoke her there with him, never to imprison her again, but for him to be freed to pass where he might fold her hand in his again.

Gia read the words until their lines embroidered themselves upon the dim when she closed her eyes and let her head rest back against the wall. She could almost imagine him here among the patient books.

She didn't need the poem as a reminder of Milo. She still caught herself seeking out his reaction to things people said, looking for a glimpse of his intense gaze under his dark curls, before it all crashed over her again. She ached at the memory of his hands on her, his mouth delivering kisses as sweet as prayers. Nearly every day she wished she could ask him something. There was so much he could be helping with. While Stregna's woken templars would do their best, none of them could use the icon. It remained Milo's. He would have led the temple well—making it again a place of study for any Trestattans who wished to learn, with historical archives, as Lena hoped. They were all working to restore things that had been lost, to address issues that had arisen. The world was getting better, but it held a hole in the shape of Milo. Sometimes, Gia felt as if she teetered at the edge of it.

She was doing what she could.

She spent the rest of the day up at Stregna's temple, using her icon to shift earth and uncover the remains of other buried chambers branching off the great sanctuary so it might be rebuilt. Lena had been helping her learn invocation, but their goddesses, while sisters, had their own temperaments, and Lena always focused on learning how best to call upon Alta, for healing or bringing rains to crops or the other ways Alta blessed her people. Gia was still slow and couldn't do much at once, not without risking hurting any of the templars or other Trestattans who came to help. She had not dared trying to move Milo's statue from where it lay near the sanctuary's beautiful carved wall—nor let others try, as the path up from the floor was uneven and soft-churned earth. She hadn't even attempted using the chisel. Over dinner at Magna's temple, Julia, the ward, had eagerly told Gia to use it and make the stone beasts dig out the temples, but this was difficult, careful work. Like making things right always was, it was turning out.

So much work still to be done—most of all by Gia—figuring

out how to face the evil of the past, manage it, and move forward, knowing mistakes were bound to be made again. They needed to rout the worst of Ennio's circle from the temple, and injustice from the city. But Gia was itching to make up for her own deeds. Lena's declaration absolving her wasn't enough. Gia had already paid for the rebuilding of the bridge she'd burned down and for the shop owners and their families to be fed and housed with the coin and treasure Ennio had amassed at his temple. But it wasn't really Gia's money or fine lamps or tapestries, and it felt good to get her hands dirty with work she could do herself.

An afternoon of clearing several rooms of earth at Stregna's temple gave her some small pride. And then, beyond the stretch of wall they had seen jutting from the hill, they found another chamber, the marble fallen in on itself to create a protected space. It was much smaller than the cavern Val had shown them, where they'd hidden after the Ceremony of Dust—where Milo had returned to Gia when she'd emerged from stone for the final time.

Tucked against the angled marble, a remnant of the time before her long stone journey waited in the buried room.

The templars helped reach it, dusted it off, and marveled at how it had endured, thanks to an invocation laid upon it. Eventually, it was passed to Gia. She held its deep blue leather cover and read—easily, in the familiar script of her time—its gilt title.

The Book of Invocations.

How Milo would have delighted. She sat on the hillside and flipped carefully through its wide pages. The sun dipped low, and shadows swelled toward her. As she considered returning to Magna's temple, where she and Lena and Val were staying, a line snagged her attention.

"Any breath bearing true faith will stir Lady Epiphany to extend her grace." So different from the challenge of calling upon Magna. She read on, soaking up the words she had never studied. Instructions for invoking. For templars to work together. *"Templars must remember their goddesses' power flows together, as sisters share bone and blood and breath."*

Gia pulled Milo's poem from where she'd tucked it into her breast band, above her heart. She unfolded it and spread it flat upon the book, one page over the other. Considering.

The ink of the book showed through the thin parchment like a whisper. Gia's fingers splayed across the verse as if they could draw up the hope she was too fearful to feel herself, even as an idea dawned in her mind like the sunrise come early.

She went to her sister for help.

Watching everyone stream through the halls from dinner, Gia told no one else her hope, a small boat on an ocean of doubt. She couldn't stand the idea of pitying looks, or worse, the disappointed faces of Val or the wards if she failed. She braced for Lena, at the desk in her room, to sigh and explain why it wouldn't work, that Gia would know this if she'd properly studied the book she'd hauled home.

But Lena listened, brows drawn pensively, and told Gia she would be glad to try.

She insisted she needed at least a small assembly to invoke Alta best, people who cared for Milo. So Gia let her gather Val and Lucca and Julia. Val even carried Acci against her chest as they made their way across the city. The cat had found them again at Magna's temple months ago, and skulked about the place, sleeping in different rooms, as if still looking for Milo.

Their little procession climbed down into the sanctuary as the sun sank away and shadows spilled over the hill. The guards she and Lena had set to keep watch near Milo were used to her visits by now, and always gave her space as she took up their vigil. Tonight, one asked if he might join the group's communal prayer for Milo. Gia nodded, and they made a circle around his statue.

Gia stepped forward and knelt beside Milo's still form, as pale as the moon she waited for, hugging the book and poem pressed inside to her chest. Lena stood near, reassuring hand on her shoulder, and began invoking Alta's blessing. The others echoed Lena's call for reconciliation, for communion, for grace. Gia let their words wash over her, the chasm where Ennio had died feeling like the belly of some colossal monster, until a blade of moonlight at last cut down into it.

It lit up Milo's words, when Gia opened the book before her. His words, marked with his templar blood—a beacon to godpower. Just as Ennio had focused Magna's with the blood he'd touched to Milo's brow, when he worked destruction through his body, this could direct Stregna's, sent through the burnished silver icon resting upon Milo's unmoving chest.

Milo's words, calling to be returned to Gia. To pass through the stone keeping him from her. To be freed.

If she gave breath to them. If she could somehow convince Magna and Atla and Stregna to work together, to answer three templars' prayers at once. Fear rose through her again. To kill it, she pricked her finger upon the iron blade at her belt and pressed the blood to Milo's firm brow. She rooted herself in the strength of her unbound goddess. With full faith in Milo's words, with fierce trust in the people around her, with true belief in her potential to mend what had been broken, she began to read.

CHAPTER THIRTY

LADY EPIPHANY

"Nothing is ever truly lost—only changed."
—From Stregna's Hymn, The Book of Invocations

Milo

He hadn't wanted to go, didn't want to again be sent on to safety by someone he loved—someone he'd lose. Yet, he couldn't deny Gia, not when she was desperate to save a life rather than end one—his life, his heart reminded him with a bittersweet pang. His soul clung to that last moment with her like a tide dredged from the shore, ready to rush back if only the current would allow.

Suddenly, through the stone that had crashed over him, Milo could sense every part and the whole of the temple dedicated to the goddess his parents had tried to teach him in secret, who he had found again through Gia. Every atom in its walls drifting sedately through millennia, as slow as his own stone form. The moonlight slipping nearer to where he lay seeming to swirl, as if the temple wasn't ruined but hosting elaborate rites with every censer burning.

Gia, beside him. Her beautiful face no longer streaked in tears and blood but limned in starlight filtering down through the hole Ennio had torn in the earth. Her speeding heart, flush with a longing he was anguished to answer.

Her sister, and more heartbeats circling them, calling him home. Val and Julia, Lucca and Jason; the taste of honey suddenly on their tongues, electricity lifting the hair along their arms, as the three summoned goddesses visited their power upon them.

Magna's force—no iron but malleable gold—yielding to Alta's appeal, welcoming a bolt straight from Stregna, not to him, but through him, brimming every part of him with holy unity.

Milo's desperation transmuted to hope as it found reception in the goddess's hearing. He wondered if he would be as Gia was, half man and half stone, drowning every day. The air infused with godpower laughed. Not warmly, but nothing cold. The shiver of a zephyr through a forest of leaves bearing the knowledge: as the three states flowed into each other as a greater whole, the sister-gods' power was stronger when worked together, and he would be restored to himself fully.

Gia's realization that the goddesses' blessings woven into one were succeeding in waking him tasted sharp and sweet. Like the breath Stregna bestowed upon him. Like the cry Gia loosed when his hand took hers, warm in the reaching silvery light. Like the kiss with which she claimed his mouth, that ignited his blood, that drew them both into an urgent embrace, that he would've gladly kept unbroken for longer than any centuries of stone.

EPILOGUE

Gia

Neither one of them wanted to be alone.

On the walk back to Magna's temple, with their friends around them and Acci winding between their ankles, their hands wouldn't give each other up. Not until they reached the nido, and Milo disappeared under an avalanche of hugs. Even the youngest wards insisted they weren't too tired to join the celebration that broke out in the dining hall.

Julia wiped away the tears she'd been crying since the invocation took effect, telling the story to the smaller children. Jason kept clapping Milo on the back, and while Lucca looked uncertain, at the edge of the gathering, Gia told Milo how the storica's lessons had allowed her to read the poem that freed him, and Milo gave him a solemn nod of gratitude—before Val caught him up in her tenth bone-crushing hug of the night.

After hours of talk and cheer and food, Milo looked a little ragged from all the noise and attention. As everyone drifted to their chambers, Templar Daniela sent someone to freshen up the bedding in Milo's cell, and his hand again found Gia's. The other scratched along his jaw.

Gia could see a tracery of scars over his palm. His passage through the stone had faded the half-healed cuts Ennio's men had written there to thin lines, the pale script telling a story of how much Milo had done for her. The deep wound made by his broken ribs had vanished.

Now, his eyes were tensed, their gaze distracted.

He didn't need to lie alone anywhere after the past several weeks. "You need a shave," she told him. She scrunched her nose. "I'm surprised the wards recognized you, honestly." Milo squinted at her, and she skimmed her knuckles up his stubble to his cheekbone. "Surprised they didn't shriek that a gryphon had gotten into the temple."

A smile crept over his face. He finally seemed to find the energy to pull his thoughts into words. "I'll visit the barber tomorrow."

She gave his hand a tug, all teasing washed from her voice. "I'll take care of you."

He let her lead him with backward steps to the room she'd taken as her own, their gazes strung between them like the silk cords festooning the colonnades during Carnival. Glimmering and wound together in one.

She backed against her door. As her free hand worked it open, a heady look brewed in Milo's eyes. Steps sounded around the corner, and she towed him into the chamber to the chair that she pulled away from her desk and its lamp. She had water left in her bowl and jug, and a clean cloth on the little table in the corner. Her dagger she kept sharp.

While he sat, she unstoppered a small bottle of oil and tipped it over her fingers. She caressed his jaw and swept it over his stubble. Her fingertips traced around his mouth as it pulled into a smile and chased her thumb with a kiss.

She brushed a curl from his face, tucking it behind his ear, and cupped her hand to the nape of his neck. He leaned into her hold. She drew her dagger and brought it to his throat.

She'd done this once before, but now her only need was him. The only threat between them the growing possibility that this would end with Milo half-shaved and well-kissed.

He angled his jaw up at her. Let her drag the blade against his skin. It carried smoothly over his jawline and cheek. She paused to wipe the dagger on the cloth.

His dark eyes drank her in, like they wanted to soak up all the light of her. Like when she'd first seen him from her pedestal. Except the pang of longing on his face was something else now. Something more of wonder.

At some point, his hands had found her hips. He hooked his thumbs into her belt and let his fingers dig into the fabric of her tunic. Gia breathed deeply through her nose to keep her knife hand steady. She needed a better angle. She eased into his lap, and now his fingers splayed across her back to steady her.

She guided the blade over the planes of his face. The face she'd watched in vigils too many nights, its stone a century between them. She let the painful memory slip away in the flaring of the lamp. The scritch of the blade.

Milo pulled a face so she could shave his upper lip and she let out a huff of laughter. He kissed her hand again when it passed before his mouth, and her breath hitched. But when he leaned in nearer to her face, she pulled back.

She held the dagger up between them. "Not finished."

His voice rasped as rough as his last unshaven cheek. "Gia."

He traced a hand up her spine.

She passed the dagger's edge over the dark stubble, then let her lips bless his smooth skin.

His hands found her hips again. Tugged her nearer. The iron clattered to the stone floor.

Their words carried back and forth between them on a shared breath.

"I wish I could have been here for you. All this time."

"You were." Their lips grazed each other. "You always were." They sealed their breath together. Kissed slow and sweet like the hint of oil between them. He dragged his mouth across the corner of hers, wrote more kisses there and upon her jaw and down her throat.

At the desk in her chamber, Gia flipped through the carefully-sewn pages of the dictionary Milo had made her. He had been tutoring the other woken sancts in the current writing system, but at Gia's insistence that she needed to study harder to aid her work at Magna's temple, he'd made her the collection of translations. Today, he left a parchment of phrases for her to practice deciphering.

When she finished the first, she snorted, sending Acci, curled at her feet, to slink away to a patch of sunlight cutting across the tiles. By the time Milo appeared at her door, ushered in by a guard who closed the door behind him, she was blushing. She stood and waved the list at him to distract from her warm cheeks. "Did you give this list to every one of us?"

He grinned and huffed a laugh. "No." His eyes flared. "Please don't show that to your sister."

"But she wants to learn, what if she needs to know how to read *bosom*—" He grabbed for the parchment, which she swept out of his reach.

He responded with a tug on one of the curls that had escaped her braid this morning. "We're supposed to join everyone on the piazza."

Gia turned her head to kiss his knuckles there. "And I suppose being late for Lena's big day would make me a real monster."

"Mmm, I've spent enough time with real monsters." He pressed his lips to her forehead. "I prefer you to chimeras and serpents. Much better kisser." She laughed so loud he winced, but it turned to a smile.

They headed down the halls of the temple, guards and Acci trailing. Gia smiled again, to herself, as they passed Milo's cell, an excellent plan for later taking form in her head. Not every knock at Milo's door after dark needed to be a ward asking for a story to tame a nightmare.

Out on the great plaza, a crowd gathered. Lena was easy to spot, surrounded by adoring Trestattans and accompanied by Val. People carried boughs cut from the temple's sacred grove, ready to take them up another hill and re-sanctify Alta's temple, which so far was only a scattering of flagstones where people could stand for outdoor assemblies. The city was eager to see its principessa lead rites, though, and she eager to teach them about the goddess Alta.

As Gia and Milo reached the others, a woman lifted a flower crown out to Lena.

"Ha," Gia said to her sister after the woman moved on to

smudge her branch in the bonfire built in front of the plaza. "Milo and I are new templars, too, and no one's bringing us flowers."

"Well," Lena said, with a sharp little grin, "I am their long lost principessa returned to them."

"By us!" Gia protested and flicked one of the primroses on Lena's crown, making petals scatter.

Lena bit her lip and pulled one of the blooms from the crown. "Of course," she told Gia. She turned pointedly away from her and reached up to tuck the flower behind Val's ear. Her smile turned more solemn. "I would never forget anyone who saved me."

Val brushed her fingers over the petals, gazing back at Lena, her full lips parted, her large dark eyes blinking. Still in awe of her favorite sanct, after all these months.

At least that was what Gia thought, until Milo groaned, "By the Sisters, just kiss her." Gia was pretty sure he was talking to his friend. But it was Lena who went up on her toes to press her lips to Val's, in a prim little kiss—until Val wrapped her arms around Lena and lifted her right off the cobblestones, kissing her back.

Whoops went up from the crowd as Gia asked Milo, "You knew?" Val, beaming, gently set Lena down. Her sister looked almost as dazed as Gia felt, pink blushing over her cheeks pulling into a smile.

"You saw them together the whole time I was a statue, and you didn't?" He tugged at Gia's hand, so she let him lead her away to claim and prepare their branches, Milo laughing over the crackling bonfire. He nodded hello across the flames to Renz, who was up and walking again at last. Gia stared into the fire, awkwardness burning in her belly. She'd made her apology, and Renz's family seemed so ready to be in the good graces of the principessa, it was accepted. Gia forced her eyes up in time to see Renz nod back, either grateful to Milo for saving his life, or cowed by the shined-up icon hanging from his neck. At least he was polite. Gia may have been a templar now, working to make Magna's temple into a refuge for people who needed it like herself, but she wasn't above delivering a threatening look when called for.

Things sat more heavily between Milo and Lucca, who had not come today. Milo only spoke in passing with his old mentor. He said he needed more time to trust Lucca again—to be sure of his trust in himself. She was glad Milo had kept busy with sancts asking for lessons and wards for tales of everything that had happened. He stuck to the simpler monsters of the quarry in his stories for them. And he prayed—she had overheard him murmuring words to Stregna as easily as he did bits of his verses to Gia. She liked to picture him sharing that sure, uplifting faith with others someday, once Stregna's temple was rebuilt.

Gia inhaled deeply, breathing in the cleansing smoke of the pine branch she chose.

When they rejoined Lena and Val, Senna had found the principessa in her crown of flowers and was telling her how she wanted to be confirmed as templar to Alta's temple.

"It may be rebuilt just in time for you to live there when you are," Lena said with a wry look at Gia. Lena took the girl's hand. "But you can start learning about Alta today." She began sharing how rites at her temple were held—always with passing of wine and sharing of bread—and she led Senna and the rest of the gathering out onto the Via Sanctus.

Gia watched Lena, so at ease in a crush of people flowing about her—nodding hello, listening, looking over Senna's head to

Val, who said something Gia couldn't make out that made Lena's placid face break into unchecked laughter.

As they made their way through the city, more Trestattans joined the procession, bringing fresh baked seed cakes and crescents of honey-covered dough to share among the celebrants. Woken sancts were among them, accompanied by the families that had taken them in. Places were being found for all as the city remade itself. People sang as they bore their boughs, the smoldering aroma of cedar and lilac branches mixing with the sweetness of the song.

Here and there, people stared from windows or the sides of roads, dubious looks upon their faces. It was a tumultuous time, and some were clinging to their beliefs of Primo Sanct. Gia turned away from the dark windows and dark looks and linked hands with Milo, who was humming along with the song carrying down from the front of the procession. Who knew what story would be told of this time centuries from now.

They headed up the forested hill, and the way grew steeper. Val swung Senna, still trailing Lena, up onto her back, to carry her the rest of the way to the temple they were rebuilding. Gia held tighter to Milo's hand, thinking of the last time she'd walked this hill, descending alone and confused and angry, and how different it was now, with him, with everyone here. Milo worked his hand against hers, palm to palm. Their fingers interlaced as they made their way over the hillside, among the greenery of pine and ash and birch, under their branches tracing patterns in the sky like the constant paths of stars.

THE END

ACKNOWLEDGEMENTS

Some stories feel as if they take a thousand years to write, and all stories need the faith and care of many to become what they're meant to be. I'm fortunate to have a multitude of wonderful people to thank for their help bringing Milo and Gia's story to bookshelves.

The greatest of thanks to my brilliant editor Tamara Grasty, for seeing the heart of Milo and Gia and helping to sculpt their book into the best version of itself. And to my fantastic agent Lee O'Brien, for joining me on this journey and believing in my writing. I am so grateful for our partnership and all your tireless work.

A huge thank you to Page Street YA and each person who helped to polish this book, give it the cover of my dreams, and bring it to the world, including Emma Hardy, Rosie G. Stewart, Monique Vieu, Lauren Knowles, Cas Jones, Krystle Green, Lauren Cepero, Elena Van Horn, and Lizzy Mason.

Immense gratitude to my friends and Pitch Wars mentors, Alechia Dow and Sheena Boekweg, who opened the first door for this story and have never flagged in their support as they've taught me so much and cheered me along. And to every volunteer with the Pitch Wars mentorship program, particularly its founder, Brenda Drake, and the many mentors who offered critiques and encouragement for this book and others over the years, including Tobie Easton and Kristen Ciccarelli. All the love to my classmates, especially Loretta Chefchaouni, S.A. Simon, Samantha Elden, Kyla Zhao, Rosalie M. Lin, M.K. Hardy, Miranda Sun, Kara Allen, Amber Chen, Ky Jackson, Sara Codair, and Erin Fulmer for the help and moral support as this book found its home.

Thank you also to my first writing family, the spectacular AMM Round 3, and the entire AMMfam. Special thanks to the beautiful Emma Theriault, my first mentor, and to Jamie Elisabeth Funk, Alex Higgins, Alexandria Sturtz, Susan Lee, Graci Kim, Bridgette Johnson, Julie Abe, Roan, Erika Cruz, Jessica Kim, Linnea García, and Jenna Voris.

Sincere thanks to Beth Phelan and everyone with #DVpit, and Despina Karras and #PitchDis, all doing such important work championing stories for every reader.

Thank you to Rosiee Thor, Renée Reynolds, Anna Rae Mercier, and Seabrooke Leckie, for reading early pages and all your guidance. To Sierra Elmore, my very first critique partner and forever badass. To Jules Arbeaux, for believing in Milo and Gia when my faith was waning. To Sarah Germer, fellow writer of gremlin girls, for always bringing the chaos to my DMs, for sending me disinfectant during the pandemic when it was harder to find than a literary agent, and for being an amazing critique partner. E grazie mille alla mia amica Miriam Cortinovis.

Heartfelt thanks to Erin Grammar, for all the Saturday mornings huddled over laptops and steaming cups and the one blessed power outlet. To Courtney Kae, supportive friend extraordinaire, for always screaming with me through every long wait and wild twist. You are sunshine in a world of grumpy, and I'm so grateful for you. To Jenny Howe, the best drafting buddy, the strongest model of persistence, and one of the smartest, kindest people I know. This book simply would not exist without your belief in me and my words.

Boundless gratitude to Heidi Christopher for fiercely loving

Gia from the first moment she walked down that hill and for being the glitter glue holding everything together so often; and to Kate Havas for always standing up for Milo, for inspiring me to keep growing as a writer, and for the brilliant suggestion to add a certain shaving scene. I can never thank you enough for being there through all the sprints and chats and rejections and break-throughs. Any success I've found belongs as much to you both, and I am endlessly thankful to call you friends.

To my teachers, whom I hope know what a powerful force they are and forever will be, and to my students, who always inspire me just as much. To all librarians fighting to get books to the readers who need them, and specific thanks to those who made a welcoming space for this writer and her two little bookworms.

To you the readers, for sharing this story. If you see yourself in it, know that I believe you are, undeniably, the hero of your own story.

Finally, thank you to my family. To my mother, Leslie Kuss, for always encouraging her daydreaming daughter and reading so many fledgling drafts. To my father, Cameron Kuss, for teaching me to be a rabble-rouser and to love a good murder mystery. To my big sister Melissa, who is in fact a goddess, and my little brother Trevor, who I'd never let the monsters get. To my children Sophia and Nate, for showing me the way back into make-believe, for letting me ramble through plot snarls, and for always rooting for more cats and murders. Your creativity and intelligence and heart could inspire a thousand odes. And to David, my best friend, truest partner, and absolute saint of a man, who has supported me in every way. You're an answered prayer and the reason I believe in love stories.

AUTHOR BIO

Leanne Schwartz has spent about half her life at either the library or the local theater, where she has played Lady Macbeth, Lady Capulet, Clytemnestra, and Hera—perhaps one reason she writes such vengeful, murderous girls. When she's not teaching English and poetry, she can be found baking pizzelle, directing scenes for the student Shakespeare festival, and singing along to showtunes. She lives in California with her family.